THE
MORMON
CANDIDATE

A NOVEL

AVRAHAM AZRIELI

Author Photograph by Richard Dalcin.

Printed in the United States by CreateSpace, Charleston, SC (Paperback Edition, 2012)

Disclaimer: This is a work of fiction and is not meant to be construed as real.

ISBN: 147519451X
ISBN-13: 147519451X
Library of Congress Number: 2012907013
CreateSpace, North Charleston, South Carolina

ALSO BY AVRAHAM AZRIELI

Fiction:

The Masada Complex – A Novel
The Jerusalem Inception – A Novel
The Jerusalem Assassin – A Novel
Christmas for Joshua – A Novel

Non-Fiction:

Your Lawyer on a Short Leash
One Step Ahead – A Mother of Seven Escaping Hitler

AUTHOR'S WEBSITE:

www.AzrieliBooks.com

A NOTE TO THE READER

As in every novel, the characters, incidents, and dialogues are products of the author's imagination. Other than historic events and figures, any resemblance to actual events or persons, living or dead, is entirely coincidental, and statements of fact or opinion should be treated as fictional. However, as far as the factual background against which the story is told, every effort has been made to remain true to reality.

More specifically, while the political process of US presidential elections is familiar territory for most readers, the Church of Jesus Christ of Latter-day Saints (also known as the "Mormon Church," "Mormonism," or "LDS") is a mystery to most outsiders.

Therefore, especially with respect to the Mormon Church, including its theology, inner workings, and religious practices, this book is based on extensive research. The quotations from Mormon scriptures and materials are correct, and the descriptions of rituals, customs, and hierarchical structure are based on authentic documentary sources.

For readers interested in further exploration, a bibliography of primary research sources is offered at the end of this novel.

How convenient it would be to many …
who, whenever their origin was involved in obscurity,
modestly announce themselves descended from a god.

– Washington Irving, *Knickerbocker's History of New York*

PART I:

The Victim

CHAPTER 1

The roar of engines bounced off the storefronts as hundreds of motorcycles rolled down Main Street in a slow-motion stampede. Most were Harley Davidsons, ranging from barebones Sportsters to specked-out Road Kings, mixed in with Japanese-made cruisers that were chromed up to resemble the Harleys. As far as he could tell, Ben Teller was the only one riding a BMW—a dual-purpose R1200GS in black and yellow that stuck out like a giant wasp.

He kept a steady pace, occasionally waving at the spectators along the sidewalks. Oversized American flags fluttered from light posts, and loudspeakers played the Marine Corps cadence. Ben sang inside his helmet, "*From the halls of Montezuma, to the shores of Tripoli, we fight our country's battles...*"

Lined up on the front steps of the Thurmont Public Library, elderly veterans in wool caps and decorated chests saluted the passing motorcycles. Many of the riders responded by touching their helmets in quick salutes.

At the exit from town, two fire engines were positioned on opposite sides of the road, their lights rolling, sirens blaring, and ladders extended overhead with a banner tied across:

Marine Corps Veterans' Annual Ride

The houses gradually spread out, fronted by manicured lawns and political signs. The Democratic and Republican parties, more than ever polarized by issues small and big, were fighting bitterly over every elected office in the country—school boards, state and federal legislators, and the biggest prize of all—the White House. With the elections only weeks away, voters' passions ran high, evidenced by trampled signs and hostile graffiti.

The road cut across a valley of corn fields, bare and colorless with the early winter, and swept left toward the hills. The riders began to form a single column.

Ben slowed down to let a another bike in. The passenger pillion was occupied by a boy, perhaps eight or nine, holding on to his father. Ben gave him a thumbs up, and the kid grinned ear-to-ear under his three-quarters Captain America helmet.

Higher into the hills, the turns became tighter, the trees thicker along the road. The riders gave each other more room.

Ben's mind entered that special zone of riding, a combination of mental abandonment and total focus. His hands operated the levers on the handlebar, his feet pressed and tugged on the gear and brake pedals, his torso shifted left and right to force the massive BMW to lean into each corner. It was like a dance rhythm on a fast beat—a rush of action, then a slowdown, a deep bow into a turn, and a sudden acceleration out of the turn with an eager roar from the exhaust, up another stretch of road, then an encore—tap the brakes, downshift, tilt into a graceful curve, and roll back the throttle to straighten up and accelerate. The sensation was simultaneously intense and tranquil, a feeling of both isolation and camaraderie. He was confident in his skill yet aware of the fragility of the balance between joy and catastrophe.

An angry snarl tore Ben out of his reverie. Headlights appeared in his side-view mirror. A second or two later, the full blast of an exhaust hit him as a Harley flew by, barely a foot from his elbow. It was painted stars and stripes, including the full fairing, backrest box, saddlebags, and even the eggshell helmet. The rider's leather jacket wore the emblem of the Marine Corps, and Stephen Cochran crooned "*Going down the back roads*" at full volume from the speakers.

Passing the cruiser with the kid and four more motorcycles, the Harley cut back in just in time to take a tight left curve. Riding a big hog like this required top skills, and as the rider leaned sharply into the turn, the chrome pipes scraped the blacktop, shooting off a spray of sparks.

By the time Ben followed the others through the turn, the stars-and-stripes Harley was way ahead, back in the left lane, blowing by a bunch of other bikes, its engine howling angrily.

Moments later, the road flattened out, passed by a modest church, and crossed a meadow whose green had turned dull and pale with the season. A few cows grazed behind a fence, and a lone farmhouse sat next to a muddy pond. The side of a wooden barn served as a makeshift billboard for a mural artist, who depicted the incumbent US president smoking a cigarette, grinning crookedly under a red beret marked with the Communist hammer-and-sickle symbol. A moment later, Ben caught a quick glimpse of the other side of the barn, where Joe Morgan, the GOP challenger for the White House, appeared in a checkered red-and-blue shirt, his smile pearly and his hair coifed, holding a book with a white cover.

The string of motorcycles disappeared into the next range of hills, and Ben downshifted in preparation for the tight twists ahead.

A challenging mountain road, with other vehicles to consider, demanded full concentration. The bike became part of him, or maybe it was the other way around. As they emerged from a tight turn, Ben twisted the throttle, and the GS leaped forward with the power of one hundred horses at the rear wheel. The rapid acceleration sent a rush of adrenaline through his veins and an involuntary grin to his face.

Farther up the hill, he came around another turn and began to speed up when he was startled by the sight of brake lights coming on one after the other in front of him.

Ben pressed hard on the foot pedal, which operated the rear calipers only. It was an old habit from the days of his small Yamaha, a precaution against locking the front wheel and entering an irreversible slide, which was unlikely on this ABS-equipped bike. Sure enough, the telling grind of rapid brake clasps indicated that the electronic system was preventing a slippage while the bike decelerated harshly.

But the ability to stop on a dime came with no assurance that those who followed close on his heels could do the same. A second later, he heard from behind the sound of rubber grating on the asphalt.

The sharp decrease in speed matched the hard pushback of the handlebar on his arms. Momentarily paralyzed by the certainty of impending disaster, Ben's mind flashed visions of last winter's deadly pileup on I-95, especially a photo he had snapped of a bloody hand sticking out from a wrecked Honda. The photo had won him a three-figure fee from *NewZonLine.com* and a second-place Lifelike News Photography Award from the Maryland Association of Freelance Journalists. All this went through his head as he forced his foot off the brake pedal and maneuvered onto the gravel shoulder, passing the others on the right, his ears filled with the sounds of rubber squealing, followed by banging, metal scraping, and cursing.

Meanwhile, the GS went off the paved asphalt, lurched sideways, descended into the drainage ditch, and leaped over the opposite bank toward a cluster of young trees. Ben rose to stand up on the pegs, which separated his own weight from the bike's center of gravity, and defied every natural instinct by twisting the throttle and sending power to the rear wheel while focusing his gaze back at the road, where he wanted to return. The massive motorcycle responded by straightening up and obeying Ben's leftward tilt enough to avoid the woods. The momentum helped the tires keep traction while plowing the dirt and weeds on the way back to the gravel shoulder.

He didn't stop, though, but kept going at low speed, standing on the pegs to maintain control as he passed by everyone else and reached all the way to the top of the hill, where he finally stopped, set down the kickstand, and killed the engine.

Pulling his Canon Rebel from the backpack, Ben snapped a bunch of photos of this rare traffic jam, hundreds of motorcycles on a mountainous road.

The cause, he found out, was a tragic accident at the highest point, where the road twisted left to begin its descent on the other side of the hill. A sign directed at a dirt parking area on the right:

Camp David Scenic Overlook

A group of bikers stood at the edge. Ben joined them.

Panoramic views of Pennsylvania, West Virginia, and Maryland surrounded the overlook. Closer in, nestled among the trees five or six miles away, a few red roofs indicated the location of the presidential retreat at Camp David.

But no one was looking at the views because, down below, at the bottom of the steep, rocky precipice, rested a stars-and-stripes Harley, smoke rising from its motor. The rider was sprawled on a boulder near the bike, his helmet askew yet still strapped on.

A couple of riders ran to a trailhead at the far end of the overlook while someone phoned the police.

Ben gazed through the viewfinder, zooming in on the rider's face.

The man's eyes were open and his lips moved.

Ben took a rapid series of photos.

Suddenly the man's mouth opened wide and his chest heaved as if trying to rise. But the brief effort was cut short, his body slumped, as if deflated, and his head fell sideways.

Stepping aside, Ben used a USB cable and an adaptor to save the photos to his iPhone. With the last photo opened in an editing application, he blurred the rider's face, saved it again, and attached it to a text message to Ray Burr, the editor at *NewZonLine. com*, who was paying him $1,000 per month for being first to be offered anything Ben reported:

> *Ray, do you want this for $250? (You have 60 seconds.) Follow-up updates at the usual $50 apiece. Here's the text for the news flash:*

> *Ben Teller reporting live: It's 1:28 PM at the Camp David Scenic Overlook near Thurmond, MD. A participant in the annual*

Marine Corps Veterans' Annual Ride lost control of his Harley Davidson and fell over a steep hillside. Other riders are climbing down to perform CPR. This is breaking news. Watch for updates.

Back at the edge of the overlook, Ben watched the men reach the body below. They pulled him off the boulder to a flat clearing and removed the riding jacket, revealing a khaki, military-style undershirt. One of them began pressing the chest while the other did mouth to mouth. Ben snapped more photos.

His iPhone pinged.

There was a reply text from Ray: *I accept. But where's the face?*

Ben typed quickly. *Where's your heart?*

The answer was typical Ray: *My heart is in driving online traffic to NewZonLine.com. This is hot stuff. I'll give you an extra $250 for the face.*

After a brief hesitation, Ben replied: *The guy's still warm. His family doesn't know. How about one hour?*

Ray's retort was: *How about one dollar?*

It was painful to let go of the extra $250, but publicizing victims' faces, while not illegal, was beyond his boundaries. Ben groaned and typed: *You're a vulture. Watch for updates.*

CHAPTER 2

First on the scene was a Ford sedan with dark windows and a few antennas—an unmarked police cruiser that was as easy to spot as if it had a bar of rolling lights on the roof. It arrived from the opposite direction, where the road wasn't blocked. The driver, a state trooper in uniform, stepped to the edge of the overlook and glanced over the side. Ben did the same. Down below, one of the men looked up from the body and shook his head.

The trooper returned to his car and used the radio to report. Ben trailed him and caught the last few words: "…lost control. Not surprising. We had reports of drinking at the launch site."

"Excuse me," Ben said, "I was there. Didn't see any drinking."

The trooper put away the radio. "Thank you, sir."

Ben made a point of gazing at his nametag. *O. Porter – Inspector.* "I thought you'd want to know."

"I'll put it in the report." The trooper got into his Ford and shut the door.

By now the area was crowded with bikers who had left their stranded machines and walked up the hill to find out what had happened. A few congregated around a heavyset woman with bleached hair and pink boots. "He was flying," she said. "We were leading the ride, but he passed us real fast, like a bat out of hell."

Ben elbowed his way closer.

"Must have lost it on the turn," someone said.

"There was another bike," she said, "a little one, right?"

"Yup." Her partner was a burly man with a bushy beard and a beer belly that filled a tight red t-shirt with crosshairs over the words *Battle for the soul of America!* "Some piece of shit sport bike," he added. "One of them Italian lawnmowers."

Ben asked, "Ducati?"

"That's it." He spat on the ground by his woman's boots. "Her son got one of those. Always in the shop."

"He's your son too," she said.

Everyone laughed.

Ben asked, "What color was it?"

"White." She pointed downhill in the direction they had come from. "Came out of nowhere, like a ghost. Must've freaked out the Harley speeder, made him lose control."

"That's bull," another rider said. "That idiot was an accident waiting to happen, the way he was going."

There was a round of approving grunts from the riders.

"Whatever." She made a rolling motion with her hands toward the overlook. "Poor bastard."

Sirens sounded in the distance. A few minutes later, an ambulance arrived, followed by a fire engine and several police cruisers. The officers sent everyone back to their bikes and set up a perimeter with red flares.

Ben sent off a news update to Ray, reporting that the injured veteran was presumed dead, and attached photos of the emergency vehicles and the covered body at the bottom of the precipice.

He stepped aside and stood by the GS to watch the ride get back underway. The roar of engines shook the air. After a while, among the column of slow-moving bikes, he recognized the boy in the Captain America helmet, who wasn't smiling anymore. Neither was his father, whose motorcycle seemed to have suffered nasty scrapes and a broken signal light. He veered toward Ben and stopped.

The father reached to shake Ben's hand. "Thanks!"

Ben shook his hand. "What for?"

"For getting out of the way. I expected you to slam into us like the mother of rear-enders."

"No sweat."

His eyes scanned Ben's motorcycle. "A twelve-hundred GS, right?"

"Yes."

"Sweet."

"Thanks." Ben looked at the boy. "Hey, pal. How're you holding up?"

"We fell," he said in a thin voice, struggling not to cry.

"Captain America doesn't get scared easy, true?"

The boy nodded and sniffled.

Ben reached into the pouch mounted atop his gas tank, fished out a replica of a Marine Humvee, and handed it to him. "Here, that's for you."

The boy took it and tried the wheels on an open hand. The inner springs made the wheels spin back, generating sounds of popping gunfire. "Cool!"

"Appreciate it," the father said. "You a Marine?"

"My dad was," Ben said. "He sent it to me from Kuwait, back when I was a kid."

The father's eyes widened. He reached to take the Humvee from his son. "We can't accept this—"

"Don't worry about it," Ben said. "It's no longer age appropriate for me."

"Thank you, mister," the boy said.

"Ride safely, buddy."

They rejoined the moving line of motorcycles, and the boy raised his new toy in a farewell greeting. He was smiling again.

Ben watched Inspector Porter make his way down and start a search of the crash site. At one point, he glanced up and saw Ben snap a photo.

A moment later, a uniformed officer approached, signaling him to move aside.

Ben walked off to the end of the ledge and over a pile of rocks that were held together with concrete to prevent mudslides. From there, he resumed his observation, snapping an occasional photo.

Porter glanced upward every once in a while but failed to see
Ben among the bushes far to the side. He kept turning over rocks
and pushing aside shrubs around the crashed stars-and-stripes
Harley as if searching for something specific. Turning to the
victim, he removed the man's wallet and watch. He went through
every pocket, ending with the boots, which he pulled off and felt
inside with his hand before slipping each one back onto the dead
feet. He even turned the body over and ran his hands on the back,
buttocks, and thighs the way an officer would search a detained
criminal. His efforts were rewarded with an item stashed under
the victim's belt behind his back. It was a perfect place to hide a
gun, but Porter pulled out a square object that looked like a piece
of cardboard, about the size of a DVD case, which he examined
closely before putting it in the pocket of his jacket just as Ben took
a photo.

When Porter was done, the body was strapped to a stretcher.
A group of firefighters and police officers used a fair amount of
muscle work to bring the body up. They set it on the ground near
the ambulance.

An EMT pulled on latex gloves and removed the wool blanket,
except for the face, which he left covered. Ben snapped a few
photos discreetly and stepped closer.

There was little blood, but when the EMT lifted the khaki
undershirt, the victim's chest had an unnatural color, as if the skin
had been painted in livid purple on the inside. He was lean, with a
muscular chest and a flat stomach, over six feet, about forty years
old. The black boots could have been army surplus, but it was hard
to tell.

The EMT checked for a pulse in the small of the neck, listened
with a stethoscope over the chest and ribs, glanced at his wrist
watch, and scribbled on a writing board. Ben looked over his
shoulder. *Patient's Name: Zachariah Hinckley.*

Pulling the undershirt back over the victim's chest, the EMT
tried to tuck it in as much as possible.

Ben leaned closer and peered at the undershirt. Above each
nipple was an insignia, about the size of a pinky. The one over
the left breast was V-shaped and the one over the right breast was

a reversed L. A third insignia marked the navel with a horizontal line that seemed almost like a silkworm embedded in the garment.

The EMT replaced the wool blanket over the body and turned to beckon one of the officers to help him load it. Ben got his camera ready, bent over, pulled the blanket off, and photographed the undershirt.

"What are you doing?" Porter was still panting heavily from the climb up. "This is a restricted area!"

Ben raised the camera and snapped another photo of the stretcher. "Freedom of the press. Ever heard of it?"

Porter covered the body and gestured at the EMT to take it away. "Interfering with the scene of an accident is a crime."

"Who's interfering?" Ben looked around.

"Hand over your camera!"

Taking a step back, Ben said, "Do you know Fran DeLacourt in Hate Crimes? I have her on speed dial."

Already on the move to grab the camera, Porter paused, his hand outstretched in midair. Lt. Francine DeLacourt was the type of a woman men didn't mess with, and Porter's reaction revealed that he not only knew her, but wasn't an exception to the rule.

"Say hello to her from Ben Teller, will you?"

After a hard glare, Porter turned and went to his Ford.

Ben returned to his motorcycle and used the iPhone to send all the photos to himself by e-mail, followed by an update to Ray:

> *Ben Teller reporting live: It's 2:39 PM at the Camp David Scenic Overlook near Thurmond, MD. The annual Marine Corps Veterans' Ride has resumed following a tragic interruption earlier when Z.H, a male participant, age estimated at 45, lost control of his Harley and crashed over a cliff. CPR efforts were unsuccessful, and he was confirmed dead at the scene.*

He attached photos of the stretcher, covered in a blanket, first at the bottom of the hill, then being carried up, examined by the medic, and loaded into the ambulance. He didn't send the photos of the symbols on the undershirt. There was a story here, and he wanted to investigate further before tipping his hand to Ray.

Before putting away the iPhone, he checked the *NewZonLine.com* homepage. His first report was midway down the list of Top-Ten news pieces, with his name as the source. He clicked on it, and his own photo came up—a headshot that Keera had taken on the balcony at their townhome last year, shortly after he started freelancing for Ray. It clearly wasn't a professional portrait—his longish hair was still damp from the shower, his eyes seemed even darker against his pale face, and his cheeks were smooth shaven, which happened at most once a month. Basically he looked like a kid who wasn't too happy about having his picture taken.

Ben rode the twisty road downhill in complete solitude. Ten minutes later, he pulled into a Shell gas station at the intersection. The attendant, a bearded man wearing a turban, looked up from a pocket-sized religious book. "Hello," he said in a singsong accent. "Many motorcycles today."

"Yes," Ben said. "It's the annual Marine Corps ride."

"Very nice." He collected Ben's money and turned on the pump.

Outside, while filling up, Ben noticed the security cameras mounted high under the flat roof sheltering the pumps. One of them covered the exit from the gas station, presumably to catch the license plates of any wrongdoers.

Picking up the receipt inside, Ben peeked over the counter. A TV monitor showed the feed from the cameras, rotating among the four. One view was of a man with longish black hair standing at the cashier, and it took Ben a second to realize it was him. He rubbed the week-old fuzz on his cheek, and the man on the TV did the same. Then the view switched to the camera pointed at the exit. It had a wide enough scope to capture a section of the road coming down from the Camp David Scenic Overlook, just before the stop sign at the intersection.

Ben asked, "Do you record the feed from the security cameras?"

The attendant nodded.

Ben handed him a $20 bill. "I'm a freelance journalist for *NewZonLine.com*. Can I look at it?"

"You have ID?"

Ben handed over his press card.

He showed him to an office. The system was old, combining a VCR and a bulky TV. He handed the remote control to Ben and returned to the counter.

The TV screen was divided into squares, each showing the feed from an individual camera. Ben turned off the recording and rewound the tape while peering at the square that showed the exit and the section of the road.

The camera had captured several cars, vans, and a Coke truck exiting the gas station and turning onto the main road. Finally he saw a dark sedan pass by. He stopped and rewound the tape. Playing forward, Ben watched carefully.

The Ford sedan crossed the screen from right to left in front of the exit, heading in the direction of the overlook. The recording quality was poor, typical for a slow cycle of twenty-four hours with the same tape being recorded over and over. But the driver was visible though the window with enough clarity to resemble Porter.

For the next few minutes, with the system replaying at regular speed, several more vehicles appeared on the screen, leaving the station. Then, very briefly, something passed from right to left.

Ben played it again. Now that he was expecting it, he could see a motorcycle at a speed much higher than anyone would expect to see on the approach to a stop sign at an intersection. The rider must have reached the intersection without stopping and taken the turn quickly.

Watching it a third time, he paused every second or two, until he had the image on the screen. He snapped a few photos of the hazy image with his Canon. It would take some effort to improve the image, but the essentials were there—a white Ducati and a rider dressed in white leathers and a white helmet.

As the woman back at the accident site had said, it looked like a ghost.

CHAPTER 3

The confirmation of the white Ducati's existence changed everything. Furthermore, it had come downhill immediately after the accident, yet no other bike had passed through for nearly an hour afterwards. These facts eliminated any remaining doubts in Ben's mind. There was a story here!

He rode back uphill.

Red flares still lined the road to block off the overlook area, leaving a single lane. He continued down the other side. Slowing down to a crawl, he scanned the road for clues. The hundreds of stranded riders had left surprisingly little trash—a few snack wrappings, cigarette butts, and a Ravens baseball cap. The only evidence that the road had served as a parking lot for over two hours was plenty of oil spots, a typical byproduct of aging Harleys even when well maintained.

But what Ben really sought was evidence to support the proposition that the white Ducati had waited here earlier.

A plausible scenario was forming in Ben's mind: A guy with a Ducati, who's too cheap to pay the modest entry fee to participate in the Marine Corps Veterans' Annual Ride, instead skips the starting point near I-70 and waits somewhere along the route to join the ride midway. When the roar of engines approaches from downhill, he starts up the Ducati and gets going. But rather than a slow-moving hoard of slogging bikes, bunched together in the camaraderie of veterans, an out-of-control, stars-and-stripes hog races around a blind curve. Zachariah Hinckley, totally unprepared for the Ducati's sudden appearance on the road, weaves to avoid a collision, struggles to regain control just as the road reaches the top of the hill and turns sharply. Failing to make the turn, he flies over the edge of the Camp David Scenic Overlook. The Ducati rider, not realizing the severity of the accident, keeps going, secure in the knowledge that other riders will help the embarrassed patriot get back in the saddle. Or maybe he does see Zachariah's calamitous spectacle but is too scared to stop, adding himself to a long tradition of hit-and-run instigators of roadway accidents.

It was a plausible scenario, but for it to be true, the Ducati rider must have been waiting for the rally to catch up. Where had he waited?

Ben kept going, his eyes shifting left and right, scanning both sides of the road. The stranded riders had left too many tire tracks on the gravel shoulders, making it impossible to see any evidence of a single Ducati that might, or might not, have waited here earlier.

Half a mile down the road, Ben gave up, twisted the throttle, and accelerated away.

But a moment later a trailhead flew by, barely registering in his peripheral vision.

He hit the brakes, slowed down, and made a U-turn. Back a short distance uphill, he stopped on the side of the road and dismounted the GS.

It was an unmarked fire trail. Judging by the weeds, it was getting little use, which made it easier for Ben to notice the fresh tire marks.

Out of habit, he used his camera to scan the ground, taking photos as he proceeded.

A single track went in from the main road. He walked beside it to avoid disturbing the evidence. It stopped after ten feet or so, the weeds growing evenly across the trail.

He noticed a depression where the motorcycle's kickstand had rested on the ground. Because a kickstand was always on the left side, Ben realized that the rider had backed in off the main road and had waited here, ready to ride out easily.

Up close, the imprint left by the kickstand—about the size of a toddler's foot—was uneven. Ben's own bike, like most others, had a small plate welded to the bottom of the kickstand, and it usually left a flat depression in the ground. This one was mostly flat, but with a wiggly line along the middle, which must have been sharp as it had sliced the weed stems and pushed down on the ground with the weight of the bike. He traced the line. It was about the length of a finger, but its shape resembled his favorite road sign—*Sharp Turns Ahead.* He figured it could be a welding line, or perhaps the plate at the bottom of the kickstand was cracked, which would be unlikely with steel but possible if the Ducati manufacturer had cut costs by using plastic plates.

After snapping a few photos of the odd kickstand depression, he retreated toward the road slowly while searching around for additional clues. A light-colored speck in the bushes attracted his attention. He reached in and picked it out. It was a cigarette butt. Up close, the brand was unfamiliar to him: *Prince.* The tiny logo was some kind of a royal crest with the word *Denmark.*

Was this a trace left by the Ducati rider? There was no way to know. He chucked it.

The tire track itself provided little information because the dirt was packed and the flattened weeds had not acquired the form of the exact tire thread. Back near the road, the dirt was dug in where the Ducati's rear wheel must have spun freely before connecting with the blacktop.

Ben returned to the site of the accident. An oversized tow truck equipped with a massive hitch and a crane had backed up to the edge of the overlook. Long chains dangled down to the stars-and-stripes Harley at the bottom. A few police officers were watching the process, but the unmarked Ford was gone. Ben parked the GS, removed his helmet and jacket, and took photos of the Harley slowly rising through the air.

The truck driver maneuvered the crane to position the motorcycle on the flatbed, unhooked the chains, and began to tie down his sad-looking cargo. The police officers, meanwhile, put out the flares and cleared the road.

Ben approached the truck and snapped a few photos up close. The Harley was equipped with large stereo speakers front and back. A built-in Sony music system in the center of the dashboard had a docking bay for an iPod or another type of a player. But the bay was vacant, and as Ben walked back to his motorcycle, he recalled Stephen Cochran blaring from the Harley when it had sped by him earlier.

He noticed the blinking light on his iPhone and found three missed calls from Keera. His girlfriend, in the midst of her fourth year in medical school, didn't have time to follow the news. But she must have overheard the TV at the nurses' station or in a patient's room, reporting the fatal accident at the veterans' ride.

Before Ben had a chance to call Keera back, his iPhone rang and her photo popped up on the screen, her teeth glistening white against her dark-chocolate skin.

He answered, "Hey, Beautiful."

"Are you okay?"

"Sure. And you?"

"I got worried. What happened?"

"One of the guys was going too fast, lost control on a turn. Did you see my reports on *NewZonLine?*"

"I saw the photo. It's awful!"

"Could have been worse," Ben said. "Ray wanted me to un-blur the face."

"I'm not surprised. She's a pimp."

"What does it make me?"

Keera sighed. "A cute guy with potential."

"Where are you?"

"Still at the hospital. Just finished rounding in the ICU with Professor Lichtenwalt. These patients are so complicated—everything's going wrong at the same time, all systems crashing, and he's totally calm." She imitated him. "We'll adjust oxygen to X, change med Y to Z, and watch for A, B, and C."

"Sounds simple. Child's play."

"He's such a god. I'll never be able to handle—"

"You will. There's still residency and fellowship and—"

"Board exams."

"Which you'll ace. Listen, every cocky professor was once an anxious student like you."

"Sorry, coach." Keera laughed. "Must've left my self-confidence in the locker room. Where are you?"

"Still at the site. Poking around a little."

"Why? Is something wrong?"

"I don't know. Probably nothing. See you later, okay?"

The last police car drove off, and Ben was finally alone. He strapped on his camera bag and made his way downhill. His riding boots were the wrong footwear for the rocky, steep path, and he slipped a few times.

The large boulder where Zachariah Hinckley had landed bore no physical scars. Ben gave it a thorough search, just in case. He noticed moisture in one area and bent down to sniff it.

Urine.

Scanning the boulder, Ben didn't find anything else to indicate that a man had died here only a short time earlier.

It wasn't hard to locate the spot where the Harley had hit the ground. It was a shallow gulch where soft soil had accumulated. The dirt was imprinted with depressions left by the handlebar, foot pegs, and saddlebag. Dark blotches showed where engine oil and brake fluid had soaked in. Red and blue paint had scraped onto small rocks, and a few pieces of broken plastic dotted the area.

Ben used rocks to mark a square of about ten steps across. He went down on all fours and began his search. Moving methodically from one end to the other, back and forth, he peered at the ground. Wherever he saw any manmade debris, he checked it carefully and put it away outside the search area. He passed dirt through his fingers, feeling for anything that could have come from the accident.

After an hour-long search, with half the area covered, he had collected a handful of plastic shards, three bolts, and part of the Harley Davidson insignia.

A wet area, about the size of an open book, smelled of gasoline. Next to it was a flattened bush with tiny red berries, which caused Ben to almost miss the sand-colored item, mostly covered in dirt. At first he thought it was a dry leaf or a piece of wood, but when he touched it with his finger, it felt too hard and smooth to be a product of nature.

He cleared off the dirt, uncovering a rectangular piece of plastic. Digging it up with his finger, Ben found himself holding an iPod Touch, colloquially called iTouch. It was identical to an iPhone but without the phone function. This one was encased in a protective shell of the same color as Zachariah Hinckley's military-style undershirt.

Blowing on it, Ben delicately cleaned the screen and the sides, where tiny buttons were encased in small grains of dirt.

The iTouch was off, but otherwise seemed undamaged.

He glanced up toward the road. No one was watching.

With a finger pressing down on the power button, Ben held his breath.

For a moment, nothing happened. Then, an iTunes logo appeared, followed by Stephen Cochran's song, which had been playing just before the crash.

Back uphill at the scenic overlook, the sun was already halfway down to the horizon. Ben put on his helmet and jacket, mounted his motorcycle, and took off just as the familiar gray Ford arrived, its tires screeching.

As they passed opposite each other, Ben caught a glimpse of Porter's face in the driver's window. Had he realized the victim's iTouch was missing and rushed back to look for it?

Whatever it was, Ben had no intention of waiting to find out. He accelerated downhill, grinning at the thought of the fastidious Porter hiking down the hillside once more and digging around for an iTouch that was already secure in Ben's camera bag. The inspector didn't seem like someone who enjoyed being one with nature.

CHAPTER 4

On the second floor of the townhouse, Keera felt the rattle of the garage door rising in its tracks. She wrapped herself in a towel, went downstairs to the kitchen, and opened the connecting door.

Ben rode into the garage and turned off the engine. He was clad in a black-and-yellow riding suit, with a matching helmet and gloves, and black boots that could have come right out of a World War II film, except that they were made of Kevlar—or so Ben claimed.

She waited at the door, leaning against the frame, watching his methodical disrobing. First the helmet came off, setting free his dark hair, which framed his face. His eyes were dark too, and serious, but with a naughty glint that often kept her on the verge of laughter. The riding suit came off, revealing a t-shirt with the iconic image of James Dean and the words: *Cars Suck!* Under his boxer shorts, his legs, which rarely saw the sun, looked like long sticks of chalk.

He bowed.

She clapped. "You should be on stage. They'll tip you like crazy."

He took her in his arms. "It's not good for couples to compete."

"Different clientele." She kissed him on the lips. "Mine are going to laugh at your puny white ass."

His hands descended, feeling her through the towel. "I see your point."

"Not now." She pulled away. "No time."

Inside, he dropped his camera bag on the kitchen table, unzipped it, and pulled out the Canon. "You have to see these photos. I couldn't ask for a luckier break—the guy literally died on camera for me."

Keera gave him an angry look.

"What?"

"You feel lucky the guy died in front of you, and I would have killed myself to keep him alive had he made it to the hospital. We're some match..."

"It's my job. I don't want people to die, but catching disasters on camera is how I make money."

"Blood money."

"Doctors also live off people's suffering. Would anyone go to the doctor if they weren't afraid of dying?"

"Afraid of dying in front of your camera!"

"I provide an essential social service."

"For voyeurs and necrophiles."

"You have a dirty mind. Don't you think that regular folks who see my gruesome photos become more careful on the roads? Or you'd rather have them end up in your hospital?"

"Aren't we clever?" She started on the few dishes in the sink. "Think of his wife, or girlfriend, getting a call from the police. Sorry to tell you, but your guy fell off his bike and died. Check out the Internet for his last photo. Have a nice day."

Ben chuckled.

"It's not funny. I don't want to get a call like that, you know? I don't want to!"

"Accidents can happen to car drivers too. Or to elevator passengers. Remember that woman in Tyson's Corner? Got her head stuck—"

"I'm serious!" She shut off the water and used a towel to dry the dishes in rapid motions. "Why do you have to ride a motorcycle, with all these cars and trucks speeding by, all these idiots texting or yakking on the phone or doing their makeup? And anyway, that BMW beast costs as much as a new Toyota Camry!"

"I'm not a Camry kind of guy." Hugging her from behind, Ben snuggled his nose in her wet hair. "And you're not a Camry kind of a girlfriend."

"Then buy a Porsche."

"I like my bike. It gets me where I need to be no matter what traffic is like."

"It'll look funny with a baby seat strapped on."

Ben stepped back, almost falling over. "Are you…?"

"What if?"

He faced her, peering at her face for a clue.

"Why does it scare you so much? Is it the responsibility? The… what do you call it? *Commit—*"

"I'm not afraid of commitment," he said. "I'm committed to you."

She held up her hands, turning them around. "Do you see a ring?"

"You're not pregnant," he concluded, sinking into a chair. "Wow, you really got me."

"Chicken."

"I don't see myself as a dad, that's all."

"I wonder why. How're you going to change if you're avoiding—"

"Please, I'm not in the mood for a therapy session." He turned on the camera and showed her the LCD screen in the back. "Look at these. He's saying something."

"It's too small. I can't see." Keera walked to the stairs. "I need to get dressed and ready."

"You look totally ready to me." He followed her. "Wait up."

"Why?" She stopped halfway up the stairs, looking down at him. "You want to make a baby?"

When Keera came back downstairs, Ben was standing in front of the TV in the living room. He had connected the Canon so that the photos appeared on the large screen and was scanning through them like a fast slide show. "This is good stuff," he said. "But something stinks—"

"I'm late," she said. "Let's go."

He turned to her. "Mama Mia!"

She posed with a hand on her hip, her coal-black, curly mane cascading over half her face, down to her chest. The red dress wrapped her from chest to knees without shoulder straps or buttons or anything else to disturb the smoothness of the cloth clinging to her feminine contours.

Ben raised the Canon and snapped a few photos.

"Don't you have enough of those?"

It was true. He never tired of photographing Keera, something she found either flattering or annoying, depending on her mood and the state of their relationship. She had teased him that his compulsive photo taking was due to his subconscious expectation of her walking out on him one day, leaving him with only digital images and deep regrets.

Keera put on hot water to boil. "What's bothering you?"

He pulled up the first series of photos he had taken from the overlook. "You see the guy lying there. He's trying to say something."

"How do you know? Maybe he's just moaning in pain."

Ben focused on the man's face, which filled the TV screen. "Look at his lips! He's speaking, pronouncing something with a great effort."

She watched.

"What's he saying?" Ben paused the slideshow. "At first the lips are closed. What letters do that?" He counted on his fingers. "B, F, M, P, V, or W."

"He could be praying."

Ben ran the photos quickly forward. "He only said one word before—"

"Oh, Jesus!" Keera turned away as the man in the photo twisted and slumped, never to move again. "I don't want to see this!"

"Don't you see people dying in the hospital?"

"It's not the same!"

"Look again. Here. He's saying something." Ben played it slowly. "It's a message. Or a name. Could be that he knew the guy on the Ducati and was trying to name him. What do you think?"

"His wife," Keera said. "I think he's saying the name of his wife, the person he loves most."

"How do you know he's married?"

"You can tell when a guy is married. He's groomed, well-dressed, clean. I mean, look at him. He's like…together."

"I'm not married and I'm like…together. Am I not?"

"No." Keera combed his hair with her hand, clearing his face, tacking it behind his ears. With the back of her hand she felt his cheek. "How long since you've shaved?"

"Okay. He's married." Ben flipped through the photos quickly. They were taken in quarter-second intervals, which turned the rapid slideshow into a virtual video clip. "The guy knows he's dying. The last thing he can say should be an important message."

"You're really clueless," Keera said. "I'll bet you it's the wife's name."

Ben ran through the photos back and forth. "His lips close twice, so the word has two of the letters B, F, M, P, V, or W."

"Barbara," Keera said. "Or…Mirabelle."

"Pamela," Ben said.

"Could be something more exotic: Villanova?"

"That's a university, not a girl's name."

"Wilhelmina?"

"Come on," Ben said. "Even if he's married, the guy rides a Harley. He can't be with a Wilhelmina. It doesn't jive. How about Barbie?"

"You wish." Keera thought for a moment. "Could also be two names, like Mary-Beth."

Peering at the Canon's feed on the TV screen, Ben was unconvinced. "Look at his face. I can't believe he made that kind of effort to stay alive another minute just to say someone's name."

"Don't you believe in true love?" Keera dropped a tea bag in a cup and filled it with hot water. "Wouldn't you call my name—"

"Wait a minute!" Ben grabbed his iPhone and got on the Internet. "I can Google him. *Zachariah Hinckley Maryland.*" He typed the search and waited a minute. "I'll be damned. Here they are, in Silver Springs. Zachariah and Palmyra Hinckley."

"See? Pal...my...ra." Keera pointed at the man's lips in the slideshow on the TV. "P, then M."

"Maybe."

Ben drove Keera's twelve-year-old Mustang while she used the vanity mirror to put the finishing touches on her makeup. "Your mom called," she said. "We had a nice chat."

"Yeah? What about?"

"About you. What else?"

He downshifted and went faster. "And?"

Keera flipped back the visor and sat back, wrapping the winter coat tightly around herself. She grabbed the door handle as he took a turn without slowing down, tires screeching, and sped up on the straightaway. She tried to whistle a tune, not very successfully, and it deteriorated into laughter.

"You blinked first," he said, lifting his foot off the accelerator. "You're dying to tell me."

"Nothing to tell," Keera said innocently. "Girl talk. You know."

"Come on, out with it!"

"She's concerned about you. That's all."

"And you happen to agree with her." Ben took another turn and stopped in front of the club. "Let's see. First, he's still riding that stupid motorcycle. Second, he's still pursuing that foolish freelancer gig. Third, he's still not—"

"—eating enough," Keera ended the sentence. She leaned across toward him, threaded a hand under his jacket and shirt and rubbed his belly while imitating his mother's voice. "He's a skinny weed! Make him eat!"

"I'll eat you any time." He took Keera's face in his hands and kissed her. "Any time."

"How about tomorrow night?" She stepped out of the car. "At your mom's place. She's making chicken soup with those golf balls."

"Matzo balls."

"Yes, those." Keera raised her coat collar. "Bye."

He watched her trot to the door in her high heels and long legs. Wisteria's Secret was an upscale version of an unsavory nightclub. Its location, on Wisteria Avenue, gave it its name, a clever play on the famous lingerie catalogue company. Ben waved at the bouncer and drove off. At the end of the dark street, he turned the corner and sped up the road toward the circular neon sign of Starbucks.

CHAPTER 5

The usual faces were there, pecking at their laptops while the baristas joked around about something. Ben didn't have to ask, and the cashier yelled, "Skinny chai latte, hot, for Ben," and collected the money while exchanging pleasantries.

The table in the back was his favorite, providing a full view of the place while ensuring privacy. Ben set aside Zachariah's iTouch and untied the plastic bag that held the debris he had collected at the accident site.

There were perhaps twenty items. He examined each one and passed it from one pile to the other. The bolts could have come from anything, but even if they came from the Harley, it meant nothing. A shard of hard plastic had most of a white star against blue and red. A metal brace with two little holes could have fallen off the engine. A hose clamp, made of rubber, looked as if it had torn away from its position. A zipper tab, bent badly, had the tiny letters *US* stamped into it. And a chrome cap from a gas tank. He set it aside, but then picked it up again and held it up. The top part was an original Harley Davidson piece, but the bottom part—the threads that would screw into the fill-in hole in the gas tank—seemed disproportionately large.

He took paper napkins, grabbled each end, and tried to detach the cap from the threads part. It took some wriggling, but they started to turn in opposite directions until the threads section separated from the chrome cap, which had its own original threads stamped in. It appeared that the original cap had been made for a smaller tank opening and was fitted with a larger threads part to fit a larger opening.

He set aside the two pieces.

Taking a sip of chai, Ben turned on the iTouch. No password was required. He checked the e-mail folder. It was empty. Same with text messages. Past sites visited on the Internet had a list of addresses, all of them for the *Washington Post* news website. He clicked on one of the links and an article appeared.

> *Presidential Candidate Joe Morgan to Speak at Watergate Hotel:*
> *In an appearance jokingly dubbed 'I'm not a crook!' GOP presidential candidate Joe Morgan will deliver a speech tonight at the Watergate Hotel, where burglars paid by the Nixon reelection campaign once broke into the headquarters of the Democratic National Committee.*
> *Morgan is expected to sprinkle a few potent jokes meant to emphasize the stark differences between the dirty politics of four decades ago and his own campaign to 'Restore America's Soul.'*
> *The fundraiser, at $10,000 per attendee, comes with a seven-course meal and a video presentation of the candidate's achievements as a single-term Maryland governor and a successful businessman. A Mormon bishop and a rabbi will say a joint prayer in line of the first-ever Mormon presidential candidate's declaration that he'll govern the country "on behalf of all faiths."*
> *With the elections only weeks away and his lead in the polls widening every day, the campaign's aggressive fundraising reflects GOP confidence that victory is at hand – provided there's enough cash to continue dominating the airways with anti-incumbent commercials while making sure that nothing happens between now and November to disrupt Morgan's confident march to Pennsylvania Avenue.*

Checking a few of the other articles Zachariah Hinckley had read on his iTouch, Ben found that they all dealt with the presidential elections, particularly with the GOP candidate and his rising prospects of winning the White House.

Moving on to the iTunes memory, he found a bunch of songs, mostly eighties and a few military marches.

He put the iTouch down on the table, disappointed. It was an older model, which explained why Zachariah Hinckley used it as a music player on his Harley. He must have carried a phone as well, which Porter probably had removed after the accident. But he had used the iTouch to surf the Internet for articles about Joe Morgan. It was odd, but unlikely to be related to the accident or the elusive Ducati.

Using his iPhone, Ben called Fran at her Maryland State Police office.

Her voice mail came on. "You've reached Lieutenant DeLacourt at the Hate Crimes Unit. If this is an emergency, dial nine-one-one. Otherwise, leave a short message."

"Hey. It's Ben Teller. I found an iTouch near the accident site at the Marine Veterans' Ride today. I'll stop by tomorrow to drop it off."

After Ben finished his chai and read some of the newspapers left by other customers, a question occurred to him: If there was nothing to Zachariah's iTouch but a music collection and a paltry Internet surfing history, why had Porter rushed back for another search? And why had Porter conducted such a detailed search to begin with?

Having reported from many other accident sites, Ben knew how police operated. In a multi-vehicle collision, investigators focused on recreating conditions to figure out the trajectories and examine mechanical components for failures that could have contributed to the accident. It was obvious the police did not give any credence to the rumor of a white Ducati and treated this as a single-vehicle accident due to driver error.

But with respect to victims' belongings, the efforts to collect and inventory items was not related to accident investigation but was done to ensure safe delivery to bereaved family members. Police teams were trained to engage in this process with a methodical and well-practiced empathy, but with hardly any sense of urgency.

Back at the overlook, the uniformed officers had done all that, following routine procedures even at the less common occurrence of a vehicle falling off the road and down the hillside. But Porter's behavior had been odd, even if his job included investigating road accidents. Ben planned to ask Fran about it.

His attention was drawn back to the iTouch. If there was anything hidden on it, he wanted to find out before handing it over to Fran.

Like its iPhone sibling, the iTouch home screen was filled with icons. He started to check each of the fifty or so applications, just in case.

Most were junk, things that came with the device or were added for free, such as games involving military battles, warships, submarines, fighter jets, and even face-to-face combat with nothing but spears and short swords. There was a CIA vs. FBI game, a Putin look-alike in a judo outfit, and KGB minions on a mission to control the world against an American president who resembled G.W. Bush, as well as a game featuring James Bond, played by a young Sean Connery, who used a water gun against baldheaded masterminds. Another icon brought up a Johnny English game involving a karate duel against violent female ninjas. A sailing ship icon led to a game featuring a knightly woman who wielded a yellow sword against pirates and a giant sea creature with tentacles.

Ben looked closely. The sword in the woman's hand was actually a pencil, complete with #2 designation, a sharpened lead tip, and an orange eraser at the top that blinked like a tiny turn-signal. He touched the blinking eraser, and a new screen opened, showing a photo of a soldier. It took Ben a second to recognize Zachariah Hinckley—much younger, with buzzed hair and a deep tan. At the bottom of the screen, a line appeared: *We're the United States Marines. What's our motto?*

Ben touched the screen, and a keypad appeared. He typed: *Semper Fidelis*

A banner flashed across the top: *Welcome to my journal!*

CHAPTER 6

Z.H. Journal Entry # 1:

You are reading this journal because I'm no longer alive. My death, most likely, was caused by the events recorded here. This journal, therefore, is intended to ensure that my death wasn't for nothing.

What you'll read here might cast doubts as to the purity of my faith or the goodness of my heart, but the truth is that my actions have not been motivated by vanity or rebellion, but by my devotion to the three things I love more than anything else:

My church, the True Church.

My country, the United States of America.

My children, who deserve to know the truth about their father's life.

For things to make sense, I have to start with a bit of history: My name is Zachariah Hinckley. I had a blessed upbringing in most respects. Both my father and my mother, who now rule their own heavenly world in the Celestial Kingdom of God, traced their ancestral lines back to the early restoration of the true gospel in the Church of Jesus Christ of Latter-day Saints.

Having been blessed by the prophet Joseph Smith himself, our family survived the persecution of Saints in New York, Ohio, Missouri, and Illinois, the building of God's kingdom in Nauvoo and the exile from there on to the long march to the Salt Lake, and the Gentiles' wars against our people. My ancestors' unwavering faith in the face of mockery, violence, and bereavement had lain

the ground for the building of New Zion with Brother Brigham
Young. Their faith still burns in me.

In our small town of New Hebron, an hour west of Salt Lake
City, my father led our family righteously, with my mother as his
helper. Being the youngest of eight, I was the apple of everyone's
eye.

There's nothing better than a Mormon childhood. I was
surrounded by love, friendship, and happiness. I excelled in
school and loved the afternoons and weekends at our ward—the
New Hebron Ward of the Church of Jesus Christ of Latter-day
Saints—which my great-great-grandfather had established back
during the time of the pioneers. At the ward, we studied the *Book of
Mormon* and learned how the lost tribes of Israel came to America,
how Christ ministered to them and how He came again in 1820,
together with God the Father, to Palmyra in upstate New York to
tell Joseph Smith to restore the True Church after 1,700 years of
abomination and falsehood.

On Sundays, everyone came together at the ward to bless
newborn babies and remember those who departed to eternal
life. Everyone shared their testimonies—declarations of faith in
the True Church—as well as emotional stories of miracles and
personal revelations. On Mondays, we had Family Home Nights,
gathering around the dining table to enjoy my mother's cooking,
study the scriptures together, and give testimony of our love for
each other, for the blessing of a family sealed together for eternity,
here and in the afterlife.

Like all good Mormon boys, my life progressed through the
wonderful milestones set by our prophets and apostles, whose
commands came from God. You could say that I learned the
blessing of obedience at the same time that I learned how to walk,
talk, write, and eat with my own knife and fork. And until recently,
my obedience to our church authorities had been total in every
respect.

At the age of eight, my baptizing celebration drew relatives
from all over Utah, Iowa, Idaho, Wyoming, California, Nevada,
and Arizona. At ten, I spoke in front of the whole ward about how
the sin of pride was hard for me to avoid because of my father's

prominence, having just been called to serve as Stake President—a volunteer clergy in charge of all church affairs for the region.

My father was a stern man, but I still remember how he trembled with joy when I, his youngest, advanced to the Aaronic Priesthood at age 12. My mother was more expressive. Her tears flowed freely when I first fulfilled my duty as Deacon to pass the sacramental bread and the water to the congregation. She even sobbed at my Eagle Scout ceremony, and my framed certificate soon hung over her kitchen sink so she could look at it all the time.

At 14, I advanced to Teacher, and at 16, to Priest, which entitled me to recite the prayers over the sacramental bread and water and fill in for the adult priesthood holders in conducting meetings and even in baptizing converts. And, finally, like all worthy Mormon males, I advanced to the Melchizedek Priesthood and experienced the secret Temple ordinances, rituals, and oaths, which endowed me with all the powers and authority of God. There are few occasions in life more dramatic than the first participation in the rituals—so special and secret that we had to pantomime the punishment for revealing them to Gentiles by pretending to slit our throats and slice our stomachs in pretend disembowelment.

As a holder of my own Temple Recommend Card—the laminated admission card to the Temple and the most sacred rituals of the Church of Jesus Christ of Latter-day Saints—I was a true Saint.

Living in Utah, where a Temple is never too far, I regularly served as a proxy in baptizing dead souls. The process had two parts that were performed at different times by different proxies. The first part required stamina to endure 30 or 40 immersions in the baptismal bath while the dead people's names were read from a list. Taking the Temple ordinance rituals for the dead was easier, but also a slower process that took a lot of time. But serving as a proxy for the dead gave us, male teenagers who were selected for this honor, a sense of great importance.

After that, it was only a matter of time until our bishop certified me as worthy, and the letter came from Salt Lake City to call on me to serve as a Missionary.

My imminent departure was a cause of mixed feelings for my parents, as I was the last child still living at their home. I had spent the previous two summers working in my uncle's CPA office, entering endless lines of numbers into a slow and capricious computer database at $3 per hour, to save up enough money to pay my expenses during my Mission. I was about to earn the most prized feather in a Mormon man's cap—the honor of saving Gentiles from a life of apostasy and ignorance of the True Church, and later, an afterlife of hell.

Behind my typical 18-year-old's bravado was a good deal of nervousness about going away for 2 years, most likely to a foreign country. According to church policy, the place of service is revealed to each missionary only a few weeks beforehand.

I was right to be nervous! My assignment was New York City!

It could have been Somalia, as far as I was concerned, because from our small town in Utah, the urban jungle was more intimidating than a real one.

Several intense weeks at the Missionary Training Center in Provo taught me the art of "tracking" – approaching Gentiles with intriguing questions to make them curious about the Mormon faith. We practiced greetings and light-hearted opening lines to be used on Christians, who could always be enticed to hear 'another testimony of Christ.' We acted out situations that commonly occurred as prospects agreed to hear more. We used videotaping to record and watch ourselves declare our solemn, hearty personal testimony that the LDS principles were true, with the goal of reaching such level of emotional sincerity that our prospects were moved emotionally. We practiced praying and singing catchy hymns, and we learned how to read the gospel with prospects while sharing deeply personal experiences of salvation and miracles. The key was to create a moving experience so that the prospect felt the Holy Ghost as a sort of "warmth of kinship" in their bosom. That feeling would turn a Gentile into an "Investigator" who's willing to learn more.

Our trainers practiced with us repeatedly, as if we were in acting school. We learned how to challenge a Gentile ever so subtly: Are you ready to set a date for baptizing into the True Church? That was the goal. Later on, a baptized convert would be committed to the Gospel and would work hard to feel the truth, to become more righteous and worthy of the priesthood or, in the case of women, of serving her priesthood-holding husband.

The Church's multiple Missionary Training Centers prepared tens of thousands of us to go out with fervent dedication to every country in the world, except those that banned missionary work, such as China and the Islamic countries.

I reached New York City in my black suit and tie, carrying 2 suitcases with everything I needed for the next 2 years. I knew there would be no vacations, no family visits, and no phone calls home other than Christmas and Mother's Day.

But my expectations of feeling repulsed and dismayed by the Sin City never materialized. Rather, it was the most exciting time of my life. I loved the daily cycle of proselytizing to men and women of all colors and ethnicities, to people who spoke Spanish, Italian, Portuguese, French, or English with an Irish accent so thick it sounded like a foreign language.

Missionary training was a work-in-progress. Every night in the walk-up apartment, prayers and intense discussions went on about how best to approach a prospect. Tracking only had a chance to work when we emphasized the similarity of our LDS faith to mainstream Christianity while avoiding the differences. At first we only shared the common belief in the divinity of Christ so that converts opened their hearts. Their salvation required initial ignorance. It was for their own good. Those who agreed to be baptized needed time to become part of a ward and grow attached to our warm community and wholesome way of life. The more detailed teachings were left for later. In time, they would discover how the True Church was alone among the falsehood of the other so-called Christian churches, as Jesus Christ and God the Father had told Joseph Smith in the First Vision.

Frequent visits from local LDS leaders and missionary officials helped us survive emotionally under the constant barrage of rejection and ridicule. Successes were few and far between, most people unwilling to hear our pitch for Jesus Christ and His restored church. But among those polite enough to listen in whatever language they understood (we had translators on standby), the most challenging were the Yiddish speakers. Not many of them were left in the Bronx by 1988, but enough of them humored us with curiosity and a glass of water while making us realize how staunchly Jews clung to a religion many of them weren't even practicing on a regular basis.

I returned home to Utah greatly matured. My faith had solidified by the challenges and by the successes—I had baptized eleven converts, a good average for which I was commended. But the biggest change in me was an awareness that New Hebron and the rest of Utah felt like a small town. I had seen the real America, experienced its greatness and diversity, and wanted to go back out there and make a difference. I decided to study computer science and join IBM or another large corporation that offered opportunities to rise to leadership positions. You'd think I was naive, and perhaps I was. But even now, with all that has happened since, some of my boyish enthusiasm still persists, mixed with a sadness for unfulfilled dreams.

Our bishop called me in for a meeting. He explained that the divine mission of our True Church to eventually lead the United States depended on sending young men like me into every branch of the government, where our personal excellence would bolster the Mormon image and extend the reach of our True Gospel. The reports from the mission director in New York had suggested that my dedication, deference to authority, and resilience would make me an excellent military man. The bishop therefore instructed me to pray and fast so that God would reveal to me which part of the armed forces I should join.

Naturally, I obeyed.

After a week of praying and skipping meals, an explicit and unambiguous revelation came. God told me what my next mission would be. I was going to enlist in the United States Marine Corps.

CHAPTER 7

Ben's phone rang, tearing him out of Zachariah's story. It was Fran. "That's quick," he said. "You check messages on a Sunday night?"

"I get an e-mail alert whenever a message is left."

"Government efficiency. Impressive. Where are you?"

"At home, watching Lilly cook dinner. You're on speaker, by the way."

"Hi, Lilly," he said. "What's cooking?"

"Ethiopian red lentil stew. I'm making it with lamb this time. You want to join us?"

"I'll take a rain check."

"He's too busy," Fran said, "playing accident investigator. What's up with that?"

Ben looked at Zachariah's iTouch. "It's a long story."

"Give me the short version."

"Biker was speeding, flew off the road, crashed, and died. I stuck around to take photos of the cleanup, went down to look around at the crash site, and found an iTouch half-buried in the ground. Being a good citizen, I'm going to bring it to my friend at the state police so she can pass it on to the family."

"But your nose is itching, smelling a story, right?"

In the background, he heard Lilly say, "Ben found another conspiracy?"

"That's unfair," he said.

Fran was laughing. "We're worried about you. It's not the toll road again, is it?"

"I was right about that," Ben said. A year earlier he had spent months pursuing a rumor that the body of a missing Washington lobbyist was buried by his unhappy client in the foundations of a toll road overpass in Montgomery County. "The contractor was dirty."

"But the lobbyist was alive!"

Fran was correct. The lobbyist had run off to St. Thomas, fearing for his life, and resurfaced only after his client was arrested for overcharging the federal government.

"So tell me," Fran said, "what is it now? Harley Davidson is orchestrating an insidious cover-up to hide the fact that the victim was actually testing its concept flying motorcycle?"

"That's bad," Lilly yelled from the kitchen. "I'm calling Keera!"

"She's calling Keera," Fran said. "It's for your own good."

"No problem," Ben said. "Have your queen call my queen."

"I heard that!" Lilly's voice sounded closer. "You're in trouble, boy!"

"Laugh all you want," he said. "Even paranoids are sometimes right. I'll see you tomorrow, okay?"

"Stop by after ten," Fran said. "I have a team briefing first thing in the morning. But you can still join us tonight for…what was it, sweetie?"

"Ethiopian lamb stew," Lilly said.

"It's tempting," Ben said, "but I'm in the middle of reading something good."

CHAPTER 8

Z.H. Journal Entry # 2:

Boot camp at Parris Island required very little adjustment for me after serving two years as a Missionary, almost a decade of Boy Scouting, and a lifetime of happy obedience to church authorities. The simple diet, physical exercise, and pride in excellence were also ingrained in me. It was as if I exchanged my Missionary's uniform of a dark suit and black tie for the soldier's uniform of fatigues and dog tags, the authority of our bishop for the clout of our drill sergeant, and the ascetic life of long days filled with pavement pounding and upbeat proselytizing for the military routine of dawn-to-night drilling, spit and shine, and weapons training.

It was that last element—the process of integrating weapons into the fabric of our minds and bodies—that later popped up as an unexpected hurdle for me. Guns had been part of my life—for hunting and for protection during camping trips in bear country, so at first I totally embraced the military's drive to forge a unity of man and his firearm. I had somehow suppressed the fact that all this effort had a single goal: To kill people.

In retrospect, I realize that my troubles started on the first day of basic training, at the moment I signed for my new M16 without realizing how my faith and my new best friend contradicted each other. While this conflict continued to simmer all the way to one fateful day on the beach, it was compounded by my mates, whose adjustment to military life was slower than mine. They accused me of arrogance, but I dismissed it as a passing manifestation of stress and physical pain because arrogance was a character trait no one had ever accused me of before, certainly not back in Utah or on the Mission, where all my friends had been fellow members of the Melchizedek Priesthood, Saints, destined to eternal afterlife of ruling our own worlds as gods.

Crisis came on a day that started as an exciting stepping stone in my development as a US Marine—the first full-fledged practice attack on a fortified target. I was selected to lead one of the two forces. Prior to our nighttime departure, back in camp, I rehearsed with my troops fake attacks on our bunkhouse. They made snide remarks about loss of precious sleep time, but went along in true Marine spirit.

It started at midnight with 25 miles of a fast-paced hike through sand dunes and chest-high water in full gear, guns held above heads. We assembled for a two-pronged beachhead attack as bullets flew over our heads toward the early sun, which peeked over the ocean behind us. A group of visiting Marine officers, who flew in from their respective units for the occasion, prepared to observe us and grade our performance.

The target was very realistic, an out-of-use bunker with a maze of tunnels, perched above a small bay near Fripp Island that had once been identified as a potential Nazi landing site. It had since served as a perpetual fake enemy base for training drills.

I led my force from the southeast, while another force came in from the northeast. To prevent cross fire, we were to shoot only with the rising sun at our backs, an easy-enough rule to follow in theory, but much more difficult in the reality of an adrenaline-filled attack.

The battle got underway, me in the lead, shouting orders and pointing here and there. I found myself inside the bunker, running down the open-top tunnels, shooting short bursts of bullets ahead to drive away imaginary defenders. The noise and gun smoke were overwhelming, and sand flew off the walls, clinging to my goggles, still wet from the seaside approach. The visiting officers shadowed us overhead, running along the tunnels. They were in full gear, including vests and helmets, not an unreasonable precaution considering the proximity to live rounds.

I was going fast, having memorized the layout beforehand, heading to the rear of the compound where a flag had been posted in the radio room. It was us or the other force, and the winners would get to ride buses back to the base and enjoy extra hours of sleep while the losers hiked all the way back, loaded with their gear. I was determined to win it for my team.

But when I turned a corner, a very realistic mannequin popped up in front of me, clothed in military fatigues and checkered headdress, and I froze. I wanted to shoot it, I really did, but my trigger finger refused to budge. The soldier behind me, not expecting this sudden halt, bumped into me, and we both fell. As I hit the ground, my weapon accidentally discharged. The bullet singed my cheek and lodged in the dirt wall next to us, kicking off a spray of sand.

One of the instructors overhead blew a whistle and yelled, "Medic!"

My second-in-command took over leading the troops, and I was dragged back through the bunker tunnels to the staging area on the beach, where a field surgeon smeared iodine on my face and used me as a teaching prop for the medical trainees. They removed my uniform, and that's when someone said, "What's with the sissy underwear?"

CHAPTER 9

Sissy underwear? Ben put aside Zachariah's iTouch and pulled the Canon out of the camera bag. He browsed through the photos he had taken earlier until he reached the body on the stretcher.

There were three close-up photos of the dead man's undershirt, focusing on the odd markings over his nipples and navel. The khaki color could definitely pass for military-issued underwear, but the markings were not of a military unit.

Ben used his own iPhone to find out more. Google search results for *Mormon underwear* solved part of the mystery. It appeared that members of the LDS church—"Saints," as they called themselves—were required to wear a particular type of blessed undergarments. The symbols were identical to what he had seen on Zachariah's undershirt at the Camp David Scenic Overlook. Their particular designs had originated from symbols of the Freemasons, an earlier affiliation of the Mormon prophet, Joseph Smith.

One of the Google results led to a video clip of an interview with the CEO of Marriott Hotels, who told the interviewer how his sacred undergarments had protected him from burns in a boating accident. Ben expected the interviewer to ask Mr. Marriott whether he was aware that any item of clothing worn flush against the skin would delay contact between fire and the skin, which was the reason toddlers' pajamas are skintight. But the interviewer seemed too stunned by hearing one of America's most prominent businessmen express belief in the magical powers of his underwear.

One piece of the puzzle, though, remained missing. The Google articles described the undergarments as white, which was the dominant color at all the Mormon temples, because in the eternal afterlife the gods and angels wore white too. But Zachariah's undergarments were military khaki. Was there a special dispensation for Mormons in uniform? Ben returned to the journal, hoping to find the answer there.

CHAPTER 10

Z.H. Journal Entry # 3:

The paralysis that had prevented me from shooting the mannequin was at first shocking. Somehow the intense training of boot camp had failed to prepare me for the act of actually aiming, pulling the trigger, and shooting to kill a person. In every other respect, I was more physically and mentally resilient and obedient than any other guy in my outfit. But killing stood against everything I had ever been taught. The realistic-looking mannequin forced me to face this barrier and almost killed me by setting the stage for the exposure of my sacred undergarments.

"What's with the sissy underwear?"

I still cringe at the memory of that question. Up until that day, I had not worn the sacred undergarments in boot camp, relying on the special dispensation for physical exercise, severe sweating, and soiling involved in basic training. As a result, my bunk mates had not seen the undergarments. I had actually prepared a little speech for the day when we would first dress up in our parade uniform, which would be the first time I would wear the undergarments. But the previous night, about to depart for the drill and the first use of live ammunition in a mock attack, I hastily put them on as an extra measure of security.

My mother had ordered this set for me after hearing that the church was allowing a color variation—khaki-green instead of white—for military service. It was identical to the military-issued underwear everyone else was wearing, other than the sacred symbols, which no one noticed as we got ready in the dark.

Considering how the accidental discharge could have killed me, wearing the sacred garments had been the right decision. But the exposure turned into a circus that exceeded even my high threshold.

When the drill concluded with the opposite force winning, everyone congregated at the launch area, where a hot breakfast awaited the wet and exhausted soldiers. The officers went to a command tent set up higher on the dunes.

When my buddies came over to check on me, I was lying exposed in the triage area with bandages over my pretend wounds and an IV line stuck in my arm. They were disappointed over losing the battle and the prospect of hiking back to base while the other team got extra sleep time. Word of my trigger-freeze had already spread, and now the 'sissy underwear' became a major attraction.

I tried to explain, but my prepared speech turned into gibberish, and they started joking about bullets ricocheting off my holy underwear and multiple wives waiting to serve me in Utah. Someone dragged several terrorist mannequins out of the bunker, lined them up on the ground next to me, stripped them, and used a marker to draw breasts and pubic hair, followed by a made-up version of a Mormon marriage ceremony.

I was too numb to defend myself, barely managing to grin stupidly as if all this was very funny, while inside I was dying.

One of the guys pretended to hear God's voice, telling him to dig around for a gold-plated porn video, which a sex-obsessed angel named Moron had buried on the beach. Everybody started digging around, laughing hysterically, and I rolled on my side, reached for my M16, and opened my mouth to wrap it around the end of the barrel and take the bullet I had failed to shoot at the mannequin.

Suddenly someone yelled, "Attention!"

The word had the effect of a bucket of cold water, not only on me, suddenly realizing what I was about to do, but also for the others, who lined up and stood in attention.

An officer was marching toward us from the command tent. He wasn't especially large or muscled, but despite his medium height and rather skinny build, the way he carried himself was nothing short of powerful. His face was shaded by the visor of his cap, his eyes hidden behind mirrored sunglasses, and his shoulders bore a captain's insignia.

Everyone saluted. I managed to get up and raise my hand to my forehead.

He returned the salute. "What's going on here?"

No one answered.

A wave broke nearby, emphasizing the silence that replaced the yelling and hooting.

He reached me and removed his sunglasses. His eyes were dark and penetrating. He gestured at the IV line and the bag that had fallen to the ground next to me. "Do you want air bubbles running up your bloodstream?"

I picked it up and yelled, "Sir! No, sir!"

"That's right."

My eyes were drawn to his chest, where a small pin glistened. I've never seen a real one before, but I knew what it was: *Medal of Honor!*

He looked around, saw the painted mannequins lined up on the ground by the stretcher. "What's this?"

One of the guys said, "Mormon wives, sir!"

There was a round of laughter, quickly dying.

Another wave crashed.

The captain measured me up and down, taking in the markings on my undershirt and the bottom piece that looked like long johns that were cut short below the knees. I expected him to laugh or turn around and leave us to the drill sergeant's wrath. But instead this officer, who was as remote and as important as any God, began to unbutton his field uniform shirt.

One button after another came loose, until the bottom one was open, and he grasped the lapels and pulled his shirt open, all the way, its front coming out from his pants' waistline.

Under the captain's shirt, lit by the rays of the morning sun, was a piece of cloth resembling a large bib, cut square just above his pants. It was worn over his khaki undershirt, made of the same material but bearing horizontal stripes along the bottom front. He pulled it free, and we saw strings, or threads, dangling from each corner.

"This is a tzitzit," the captain said loud enough for everyone to hear. "It's a small Jewish prayer shawl, worn under the shirt. You can look it up in the Bible, both in Deuteronomy and in Numbers. Any questions?"

There were none.

"We are Marines!" He held up the corners of his tzitzit while walking up and down the line. "We don't care about your skin color or your faith. We only care about serving honorably in the defense of the United States of America and the principles for which it stands! Understood?"

Everyone yelled, "Sir! Yes, sir!"

The captain buttoned up his shirt, tucked it in, and walked away, unaware that he had saved my life.

From that day on, I wore the sacred undergarments all the time, and no one ever uttered another Mormon joke in my presence.

CHAPTER 11

Keera was done early. A CNN debate between the presidential candidates had kept many of the Sunday night regulars at home, and the club manager decided to shut down at ten thirty p.m. rather than continue to pay for heating and for idle staff that consumed drinks on the house. The last few customers were cordially asked to leave, and the music stopped.

Stepping out, Keera shuddered at the sudden cold. Her coat ended at the knees, which was fine for a car ride but not for standing outside in the cold night. But Ben didn't know of the early closing. For a moment, she hesitated. Should she return inside and call Ben? He was probably working, and Starbucks was around the corner, a three-minute walk, maybe less if she hurried.

With practiced caution, Keera glanced up and down the pavement to make sure no one was loitering. It would not be the first time that an enamored drunkard misinterpreted her suggestive dancing as a personal, desirous invitation or otherwise felt entitled to a more tangible reward for his paltry tipping. That was the reason Ben insisted on picking her up every night, but she saw no one tonight and liked the prospect of surprising him at Starbucks.

She crossed the two-lane street and headed to the next corner, her ears attuned to any sounds of danger. It was quiet.

Engine noise broke the silence.

Keera glanced over her shoulder and saw a single headlight, stationary, past the club and all the way at the other end of the street.

The *Wisteria's Secret* neon sign turned off, and the street fell into darkness, except for the headlight.

The engine revved up, but the headlight still didn't move.

Keera stopped walking. She could run back to the club, which was halfway between her and the motorcycle, but it could easily take off and get there before her. As if confirming her fear, the biker revved even higher, the engine practically screaming.

It occurred to her that it might be Ben, making a foolish joke to get back at her for urging him to give up his motorcycle for a car. Instead of working at his usual Starbucks hangout, he must have driven her Mustang back home and gotten his motorcycle.

"Ben? Is that you?" She headed back in his direction, her suspicion confirmed by the light color of the motorcycle, which in the dark seemed yellow.

He stopped revving the engine, which declined to a steady clatter.

Keera stepped off the curb. "This is really stupid, you know?"

The headlight started moving toward her while she was crossing the street. It advanced slowly, weaving from one side of the street to the other, playfully snaking its way toward her.

Keera stopped. The engine sounded different from Ben's BMW, which was quieter and smoother.

And as the bike accelerated toward her, it became apparent that it was smaller as well.

"Shit!" Tearing off her high-heeled shoes, Keera ran away, making a beeline to the sidewalk.

In seconds, the motorcycle was right behind her. Not bothering to turn, she tossed her shoes backward in the general direction of her pursuer.

CHAPTER 12

Z.H. Journal Entry # 4:

With Ronald Reagan handing the White House keys to George H.W. Bush, the Soviet Union began to dismantle, and the Cold War, which had dominated our training and constant readiness, was over. Almost overnight, the world was at peace and my service seemed destined to pass in relative tranquility.

During the three months of communications training at Fort Mead near Baltimore, I attended services at a Silver Spring Ward. The local bishop, Maynard Higdon, a lawyer in the US Attorney General's Office, took me under his wing. He was knowledgeable in our scriptures and history, and we had long discussions about Prophet Joseph Smith's accomplishments in raising a military force to defend our Mormon brothers and sisters in the early days of the True Church. The Nauvoo Militia, for example, at one time had numbered 4,500 soldiers while the US Army barely reached 8,000. Bishop Higdon helped me understand that it was my religious duty to excel as a Marine and be prepared to kill the enemy, whoever he was. Also during that time, Bishop Higdon allowed me to date his daughter, Palmyra, who was 17 and gorgeous.

We married on a humid summer day in a solemn ceremony at the Washington DC Mormon Temple. A day later, Saddam Hussein invaded Kuwait. Soon President Bush declared an ultimatum, and we shipped to the Middle East aboard the aircraft carrier USS Dwight D. Eisenhower. For a Marine, getting into real action was the goal, and I was no exception, especially as I was eager to prove myself capable of shooting the enemy.

Jump forward eight months, and I was an old hand at combat, crusty and confident as any of my mates. Victory was sweet, but I missed Palmyra, who was heavily pregnant with our first child. During my rare calls from Kuwait on a field telephone, I could hear the underlying pain in her voice despite her upbeat tone. It was comforting to know that she was surrounded by her large family while I was on the other side of the world, serving our nation. In her letters she described how everyone was praying for my safe return.

The thought that I might die in battle had occurred to me, but as the Iraqi army was mostly back behind the border, shamed and defeated, we were engaged in relatively safe cleanup operations in Kuwait. The liberated country was practically in ruins, and armed gangs roamed the broken highways and bombed-out cities.

On a hot day on February 28, 1991, everyone gathered around the TV set outside the command tent to watch President Bush declare a cease-fire and congratulate us—the armed forces of the United States and 33 other nations—on our success in liberating Kuwait.

The end of combat operations meant that most Marine Corps units would leave Kuwait soon. There were rounds of high-fives and jokes about lusty girlfriends waiting stateside. For me it was the answer to private prayers for a chance to make it home in time for the baby's arrival.

After a short briefing, a group of us was sent on a routine task— escorting a Red Cross team to a small village nearby, where a local doctor claimed to have diagnosed a breakout of cholera. Turned out to be a lie, intended to lure us into a trap, but we didn't realize it until it was too late.

Our destination was a local health clinic. Only eight of us went on this supposedly peaceful errand. We travelled in a small convoy, with the Red Cross truck between two Humvees.

The clinic was a one-story building marked with a spray-painted red crescent. It was located on a dead-end street, blocked by a roundabout in front of a school. We stopped at the curb by the clinic. On the opposite side of the street was a gas station, which at the moment was being supplied—or so we assumed—by a fuel truck. The driver was busy with pipes and spigots, and we didn't pay much attention to him. What did attract our attention was the sight of many women in head-to-toe black burkahs, sitting on the doorstep at the entrance and on all the windowsills, practically blocking every opening that faced the street. A few held infants in their laps.

This odd reception must have seemed normal to the Red Cross team. They proceeded to get out of their truck and unload the medical supplies.

Our commander, a young second lieutenant from Nebraska, took their cue and ordered us out of the armored Humvees.

We were going to set up defense positions on the street, but as soon as we were out in the open, the shooting started—not a few random shots, but a barrage of bullets that rained on our vehicles and hit the road around us. I still remember the initial shock of seeing all those fiery barrels sticking out from the windows of the health clinic over the shoulders of the cloaked women, who remained seated, except that now their hands were pressed to their ears.

CHAPTER 13

Keera ran into Starbucks barefoot and turned to look out through the glass door. The motorcycle was gone, the street outside dark and quiet. She waited, expecting it to reappear, but it didn't, and Ben was suddenly beside her, holding her, talking to her. Everyone else—baristas and customers alike, circled her with worried faces. Catching her breath, Keera told them what had happened.

Despite urging from the concerned baristas, she refused to let them call the police. "He didn't touch me," Keera insisted. "Some ass, showing off, that's all. And I'm almost sure I got him with my shoes."

After a cup of hot chamomile, they got into the Mustang and drove back to the club. Ben found her shoes on the street. One of them had a broken heel, which was nowhere to be found.

Back behind the wheel, he said, "We should call the hospitals in the area, check if a biker came in with a stiletto stuck in his chest."

"I hope it's in his eye," Keera said. "He was waiting there, engine running, and I thought it was you. I was going to kill you!"

"I know you too well to try something that stupid." He glanced over his shoulder and pulled into the road. "And speaking of stupid, this job isn't for you. I want you to quit."

Keera buttoned up her coat. "And how am I going to pay for med school? And my half of our expenses?"

"We'll figure it out."

She was quiet for a moment. "We?"

"I'm making good money."

"Sometimes you do, sometimes you don't." Keera fiddled with the radio controls, trying to clear up the static noise. "Besides, I like my job."

"You call that a job?" Stopping at a red light, Ben turned to her. "Dancing in your underwear in front of horny men?"

"A few women too. Good tippers."

"I'm happy for you."

The light turned to green, and he threw the clutch, making the Mustang squeal off the mark, racing through the next light as it turned yellow, and making 70 mph on the on-ramp to I-95. The convertible top rattled in the wind.

She reached across and rested her hand on his knee.

Ben merged into the late-night traffic on the highway and slowed down to match the going pace. "Was it a BMW like mine?"

"The jerk at the club?" Keera shrugged. "Couldn't tell in the dark. All motorcycles look the same to me."

"Did you get a closer look when he passed you?"

"Barely. He went too fast. But I think it was white, not yellow. Same with the guy's riding suit and helmet. He flew by like a—"

"Ghost?"

"Exactly! How did you know?"

He hesitated. "A good guess."

At home, Keera went upstairs to change and Ben turned on CNN, which was showing snippets from the presidential candidates' debate earlier. A quick post-debate poll showed Joe Morgan six points ahead of the incumbent Democrat. A proven record as a successful business leader gave Morgan advantage over the president's muddled economic record during his first term in the White House, and his frequent references to his deep faith resonated with church-going voters troubled by the secularist worldview of the liberal president. Noting the polarized electorate, the moderator asked whether this election, like the previous one, would come down to voters' participation rather than preferences among those eligible to vote.

A writer for the *Wall Street Journal*, who often participated in CNN political shows, predicted that even Christian Evangelists would come out to vote for Joe Morgan despite their ambivalence about his Mormon faith. "Listen carefully to his subtle message about Christian interdenominational brotherhood!"

A clip from the debate showed Morgan responding to a question about the Middle East. "Our spiritual roots," Morgan said, "reach all the way to that troubled region of the world. Like all Americans, I'm enraged by Islamic fundamentalists' attacks on our fellow Christians." He pressed a hand to his heart. "When a Muslim Brotherhood mob burns down a church in Egypt, I feel as if my own church was torched. When Hezbollah fanatics detonate a bomb during Easter mass in Lebanon, I feel as if my own Easter was blasted. When Palestinian terrorists shoot at Christmas pilgrims in Bethlehem, I feel as if my own family's Christmas was fired upon. Every attack on our Christian brothers and sisters makes me feel as if our Savior Jesus Christ is under attack. As president of the United States, I will end the current administration's failed policies of appeasement and dishonor."

"He's smooth," Keera said from the staircase. "All those Catholic, Protestant, and Lutheran brothers and sisters now know that Joe Morgan is a fellow believer in Jesus Christ."

"It's not so simple," Ben said. "Mormon beliefs are quite different."

She cuddled next to him on the sofa. "How do you know?"

He held up Zachariah's iTouch. "The veteran who died today was a Mormon. I've been reading his journal."

"What?" Keera sat up straight. "You can't do that! It's private!"

"Dead people have no privacy. His organs are probably floating in pickle jars at the pathologist's office right now."

"That's disgusting!"

Ben laughed. "Don't be so sanctimonious. I know what you guys do in medical school to those poor cadavers."

"That's totally different!" She picked up the green-cased iTouch. "You're not going to publish it, are you?"

He shook his head.

"Then why are you reading it?"

"He wrote it to ensure that his story is known in case he dies."

"Then give it to his family. It's none of your business!"

"It might be." Ben took Zachariah's iTouch from her hand. "It might very well be my business."

"Internet voyeurism business? More traffic for Ray?"

"Fancy words, but her fees pay my bills—"

"You're too talented to have to stoop like this, make a buck on the back of this poor dead schmuck. That's not business. That's...I don't know. *Greed!*"

Ben held up the iTouch. "This is important for me. Way, way, way more important than money, okay?"

There was something in his voice that made Keera pause and peer closely at him. "What's going on?"

"I'm not sure yet." He got up from the sofa. "I need to read the rest of it."

CHAPTER 14

Z.H. Journal Entry # 5:

Being under fire wasn't new to me after fighting Iraqi forces throughout Kuwait. Conditioned by training, my mind tuned out the noise and fear, and I began to follow the set routine: Seek cover! Check self and others for injuries! Return fire!

Without thinking, I dragged the injured lieutenant with me behind one of the Humvees. Seven of us made it to this temporary shelter. The eighth was dead on the street, together with the five bodies of the Red Cross members.

I checked for injuries. There was a bullet in my thigh, another had passed through my left arm, which was still functional, and a third had put a hole in my right boot, clear through my foot.

But I felt no pain.

The others were all injured as well, and the Humvee shook as hundreds of bullets continued to hit it on the side facing the clinic.

It was time to return fire. I dropped down and rolled on the ground to the front of the Humvee, next to its oversize tire, and peeked out until I had the first window of the clinic in my gun sights. But all I had to aim at were black-clad women sitting shoulder-to-shoulder, shielding our attackers, whose guns protruded through the windows between the women's heads.

I tried to shoot, but couldn't. My old demon—the mental block against killing—returned to paralyze me. I tried harder, but my eyes were drawn to a girl, maybe two years old, who rolled off her mother's lap. Her face turned toward me, twisted with screaming I could not hear.

Beside me, one of my buddies yelled something. I glanced and saw him claw at his neck, his hands red with blood. We were running out of time!

With my gun aimed at the women, I ordered myself: Shoot! Shoot! Shoot!

The Arab women looked at me through the slits in their burkes.

It was useless. There was no way I could make myself shoot at these women.

Giving up on forcing my finger to press the trigger, I rolled back behind the Humvee. None of my buddies could do much more than keep their heads down, bite their lips, and attempt to tie tourniquets. Three seemed unconscious. I had to do something.

Reaching the radio inside the vehicle involved maneuvering my body to remain as low as possible, and that's when the pain really hit me. It was a shocking sensation, to be torn like this with overwhelming hurt, like a deafening voice that reached every corner of my brain, ordering me to lie down, curl up, and cry.

And I did cry, loud and bitterly while I grabbed the radio and dropped down to the ground, the spiral cord extending to its max.

Regaining a measure of self-control, I started calling for help. I kept repeating the name of the village and our unit number, but my voice didn't even reach my own ears in the middle of this firestorm, let alone hear if anyone responded.

I kept at it until I realized that the radio had died.

Sitting with my back to the Humvee, I aimed my gun upward and pressed the trigger, emptying the magazine so that the enemy would think we were shooting back. It was then that I noticed that the fuel-truck driver at the gas station across the street was busy with some kind of a contraption under the rear of the tanker. My first instinct was to yell at him to seek shelter before he got hit by a bullet, but then I realized what he was doing.

Explosives!

I felt cold fear. It was one thing to get shot. Either you die immediately or get fixed up by surgeons. But to be burnt alive meant torture, often months of slow, horrible death, or a life of deformity and pain that was worse than dying.

The driver was done with his preparations and sprinted away from the tanker.

I prepared to launch myself in a mad dash across the street to defuse the explosives. My chances were slim—the area was exposed to the gunmen in the health clinic who, I now realized, were careful not to hit the tanker. How long did we have before it went off?

The sound of helicopter rotors penetrated through the racket. Someone had heard me!

It appeared over the school at the dead end. The Seahawk was a common navy chopper that could do reconnaissance and transportation pretty well, but its weapons weren't the best choice for urban combat. The pilot must have been in the area and heard my radio transmission.

A single gun began blasting from above, and the fire from the health clinic declined.

I rolled back to my position by the front tire and saw that the chopper was spraying the clinic with great accuracy, the rounds poking an almost straight line of holes just above the windows. Not a single Arab woman was hurt, but they all jumped out and lay on the ground in front of the building, and the gunmen were no longer shooting.

The Seahawk hovered above us, releasing an occasional burst of bullets toward the clinic, while we scrambled to get into the Humvee, the three unconscious Marines thrown in unceremoniously. We had to get out of here before the tanker exploded!

Our driver had been hit in the head. The helmet had saved his life, but he lay groaning in the back, pressing a rag to the wound. No one else seemed in better shape than me, so I climbed behind the wheel and lifted my immobile left leg over the door sill.

The engine was off. I tried to restart it, but nothing happened. I tried again.

And then the explosives went off under the rear of the tanker.

The blast threw up a small fireball, but it failed to rupture the tanker. Flames engulfed the rear section. The driver must have left a fuel line running, and I could feel the heat on my face.

"Get rolling, soldier!" The order came through a loudspeaker from the helicopter above. The voice was commanding but even, not anxious. He repeated, "Get rolling now!"

There was nothing I wanted to do more than obey the order, but the starter revolved freely, the engine not catching.

"It's dead," I yelled. "Can't get it going!"

As if he heard me, the voice from the chopper said, "Try the other vehicle. Tanker's about to blow."

Moving myself over to the other Humvee wasn't easy, but I made it, only to find that its cabin was totally destroyed, the dashboard and steering wheel in pieces. Someone must have left the armored door open on the side of the clinic, allowing them to shoot up the inside.

Back outside, I looked up at the chopper and passed a hand under my throat. To my right, the fire under the tanker raged audibly, as if exerting itself to melt through the steel tank and ignite its content. There was no doubt that the ensuing inferno would turn us into living torches.

Throwing open the Humvee's doors, I yelled, "We've got to walk out of here. Right now! Let's roll!"

There was no response. My buddies were either unconscious or incapable of moving.

Behind me, the Seahawk descended.

I gesticulated frantically. "Get away!"

"Take cover," said the calm voice on the loudspeaker.

Hovering low over the front of the tanker, the chopper's door opened, and boots appeared. Right above the truck's driver cabin, the pilot maneuvered even lower, and a slim-built man in Marine uniform jumped to the cabin's roof. He looked toward me, our gazes met, and I recognized the dark-eyed captain from last year's beachfront drill, who had shown us his Jewish tzitzit.

My automatic reaction was to salute him.

He nodded and slipped into the cabin of the tanker through an open window.

A few seconds later, the tanker jerked and began to move forward, at first slowly, then gaining speed as it roared out of the gas station and up the street, the rear end trailing flames. I followed the truck with my eyes, expecting to see the captain jump out, but the tanker suddenly exploded. Hot air blasted my face, followed by a thick cloud of bitter smoke.

CHAPTER 15

Ben dropped Zachariah's iTouch on the desk. He got up, ran out of the study, and pulled open the glass doors to the balcony. Leaning against the doorframe, he gulped in the cold air, inhaling as deep as he could.

In a second-floor window of a townhouse across the way, the blue glare of a TV was a lonely sign of life. Otherwise the street was quiet, the air still.

But in his mind, there was no peace. The fiery images from Zachariah's journal replayed—the last salute to the Marine captain, the gasoline tanker blowing up, the dark smoke taking over everything.

Back inside, he opened the *contacts* folder on his iPhone, searched for *mother*, and clicked on her e-mail address—vetwidow@google.com. He typed a short message:

> *Hi Mom,*
> *I heard you're making soup. Just what I need!*
> *We'll be at your place around 6 p.m. or so.*
> *Love,*
> *Ben*

CHAPTER 16

Z.H. Journal Entry # 6:

Writing about it now, two decades later, the events of February 28, 1991, are still fresh in my mind. The skeletal remains of the gasoline tanker were still burning when an infantry company evacuated us after setting up a perimeter to keep off the Arab insurgents, who tried to come back at us with renewed vigor after the tanker failed to incinerate us.

I woke up three days later in a field hospital. Army surgeons had removed three bullets from my body, screwed together various bones, and put my shattered right foot in a steel contraption. I asked about the captain who had saved us, and a nurse told me that nothing was left of him—not even his dog tags. She had heard that he was awarded a second Medal of Honor in recognition of his bravery.

After a few weeks at a US military hospital in Germany, I arrived at the Bethesda Naval Hospital, where Palmyra was waiting with our newborn son, Paul. I began a long process of surgical procedures, rehab, physical therapy, and endless sessions with a kind navy psychologist.

Meanwhile Palmyra took care of Paul and, after I started coming home for weekends, became pregnant again.

Through it all, not only did Palmyra's immediate family help us, but all the members of the Silver Spring Ward stepped forward to support us in every respect. Brothers and sisters we barely knew began to bring over home-cooked meals, provide transportation and childcare, and pay our bills. They took Palmyra and Paul on trips to the museums in DC and on vacations to Florida. And they set up a hospital rotation. After every one of my numerous surgeries, I found a ward member sitting by my bed, smiling at me, squeezing my arm with affectionate encouragement. Even my mental ups and downs at the hospital did not scare them, or the hellish months of forcing my legs to carry my weight again, or when nightmares left me trembling from horror and in a cold sweat. It was during those awful months of physical pain and mental agony that I truly understood why we, the Mormons, call each other brother and sister.

A year later I was honorably discharged from the service and moved back into our small apartment. Our second child, Martha, arrived without a hitch, and I started taking computer science classes at the University of Maryland in College Park. I was finally back to normal life, enjoying my wife and adorable children. My pain level was manageable, I worked out to regain strength, and my mind grew calmer. Having earned top grades in my first term, I registered for a full load as a regular student, aiming to graduate in less than three years.

Meanwhile, like all men in the Mormon Church, I resumed my priesthood duties, taking part in ward activities, such as teaching, officiating at children's baptisms, and ministering to families in distress.

Once a week, I volunteered at the Washington DC Mormon Temple, serving as a proxy in receiving endowments for the dead—the second part of the sacred process of baptizing into the church. The first part—the immersion in the great baptismal bath—was usually assigned to young men who had enough stamina to submerge repeatedly as proxy for the dead, whose names were called by the officiating Saint. The lists were prepared by church investigators—experts who roamed the world to find and extract identities of deceased persons who had been deprived of knowledge of the True Church during their mortal lives on Earth. At that time, in the early nineties, the Lord rewarded our efforts with discoveries of hundreds of thousands of Holocaust victims' names in neglected records. It gave me a wonderful feeling to help save those poor souls through baptisms and ordinances so that they could accept the Gospel of Jesus Christ of Latter-day Saints in the afterlife and win admission to the Celestial Kingdom of God.

Studying full-time at the university was especially rewarding. It gave me structure, which I had gotten used to in the Marines and, before that, during my New York mission. I enjoyed the mental and intellectual focus, which substituted for the distressing memories that continued to haunt me. It also helped to be surrounded by young men and women who had not experienced war, who had not felt the stunning punch of a nearby explosion or smelled the nauseating stench of rotting human flesh.

But during a family dinner at my in-laws, Palmyra's dad took me aside and suggested that I drop out of school and take a full-time job. He had already taken the liberty of asking a colleague at the US Attorney General's Office to contact a Saint who held a high position at the US Department of Veterans Affairs, where a job had opened in the records division that "involved computers."

Because my father-in-law presented this as merely an opportunity for me to consider, I declined for the simple reason that studying computer science had been my aspiration even before enlisting in the Marine Corps, and now that the government was paying my tuition, there was every reason for me to stay the course.

When I told Palmyra about the conversation and my decision to stay in school, she surprised me by urging me to reconsider. A well-paying job with full benefits was a good idea in her opinion, while she took care of our home and kids. "You're smart," she said, "you can figure out computers by yourself."

I spent a whole evening explaining to her my desire to earn a college degree, not only for the knowledge and the pleasures of learning and discovering, but also for the credibility and status that a degree would confer. I went to sleep assuming the issue was laid to rest.

A couple of weeks later, the wife of our new bishop invited Palmyra, me, and our two kids to dinner at their home.

Bishop Morgan, who had taken over the volunteer bishop position from my father-in-law (who in turn rose to State President of our region), lived near us in Silver Spring. He was selected for the lay leadership by the church authorities after proving himself as a devout Saint and a successful businessman. As part of his responsibilities, the bishop met with each family in his ward a few times each year to take stock of our spiritual and communal lives and verify that we tithe to the church ten percent of our earnings, as required. We assumed this was the purpose of the dinner invitation.

The house was unlike anything we'd seen before—a massive redbrick residence, surrounded by lush grounds and tall trees. With Christmas approaching, the long driveway was lined with candle-like lights.

Joseph Morgan was a charming man, about forty-five, with a blond wife and six beautiful children. I knew he was a business executive in a large investment bank, but had no idea he was so wealthy.

We began dinner with a prayer of thanks, which the bishop concluded: "We are especially grateful that Brother Zachariah has recovered from his wounds and has resumed civilian life with grace and success. We pray that his life continues to be blessed with great joy in his celestial marriage, his children, and his work for the True Church, as he continues to progress spiritually in the priesthood toward exaltation."

After dinner, the women cleaned up, and he invited me into the library. A glass-fronted wall of shelves held precious volumes, a collection of classic books that the bishop's grandfather had started to accumulate a century ago. Bishop Morgan pointed out a section that included first editions of all of Joseph Smith's works, autographed by the prophet himself with personal dedications to family members and close supporters.

We sat in oversized leather chairs before an unlit fireplace, sipped hot cider, and discussed the recent election of Bill Clinton, the young governor of Arkansas, as president. Bishop Morgan spoke with indignation about the Democratic Party's audacity in pitting the pot-smoking, draft-dodging, serial womanizing Clinton against the incumbent president. We both agreed that the American public had lost its moral compass, electing Clinton in lieu of the more experienced Bush—a former CIA director and vice president, whose first term had included throwing the Iraqis out of Kuwait after forming an unprecedented international coalition. "I am confident," Bishop Morgan declared, "that Bill Clinton's presidency will prove to be the absolute worst presidency in American history!"

From this dire prediction about Clinton's future, Bishop Morgan switched to discussing my future. "The Church needs you," he said, "to take the job at Veterans Affairs."

His words felt like a body blow. A bishop has the final word on all the affairs of the ward and its members, including family and private matters. He determines who deserves to hold a Temple Recommend Card enabling entry and participation in the sacred rituals, appoints all the ward clergy and leadership staff, arbitrates marital and family disputes, and disciplines those who sin against the Church or fellow Saints in words, deeds, or disobedience. In other words, he speaks for the Church and, therefore, he speaks for God.

How could I say no to God?

Bishop Morgan suggested that fasting and prayer would help me embrace the calling to serve. He must have seen the pain on my face, because he took my hands, and we sang together the hymn "Sacrifice brings forth the blessings of Heaven."

CHAPTER 17

"Unbelievable!" Ben put aside Zachariah's iTouch and turned on the laptop. He went to Joe Morgan's campaign website:

www.JoeMorgan4President.org.

The homepage banner said: *Restore America's soul!* The rest of the page was taken by a photo of Morgan in jeans and a flannel shirt, standing at a podium on a makeshift stage, surrounded by haystacks and American flags. The left side of the photo captured part of his audience—men, women, and children waving flags and signs that said: *We Believe!*

Ben clicked on the button for *Candidate's Bio.*

All major milestones in Morgan's life were listed: Born in Illinois, son of successful industrialist, Eagle Scout, two-year mission for the LDS Church, college and MBA at Harvard, and, as Zachariah's journal described, a wealthy businessman in the early nineties who eventually turned to politics, serving one term as governor of Maryland and now the GOP presidential candidate. There was no mention of leadership positions in the Mormon Church.

At the bottom was a photo of Morgan's home in Silver Spring—a redbrick mansion that fit Zachariah's description.

A list of links to his major speeches included the one titled: "*My faith is a private matter.*" Ben clicked on the link and a small YouTube window opened.

Speaking at the Ronald Reagan Presidential Library, Joe Morgan declared: "Article Six of the United States Constitution says, and I'm quoting: '...*but no religious test shall be required as a qualification to any office or public trust under the Unites States.*' Let me say to all those who wish to pry into the private spiritual life that my family and I deeply cherish: There's no curtain to peek behind, no dark secrets to uncover, and no unusual customs to leer at. You would do better to direct your energy at seeking your own spiritual joy. And to my fellow citizens, my fellow Christians, and my fellow Republicans, I say this: All you need to know is that my faith will continue to inspire me to serve my country to the best of my ability. And when you elect me as president of the United States, I will serve as leader of all Americans without preference or favoritism to any particular race, ethnicity, or creed!"

Ben pulled up Wikipedia and searched for Governor Joseph Morgan, finding a more detailed biography. He clicked on the heading *Mormon Church Lay-Leadership Positions* and there it was, the confirmation to Zachariah Hinckley's story:

> *1991-1995: Lay Bishop, LDS's Silver Spring Ward in Maryland*
> *1995-1997: Lay Stake President for all LDS wards in the State of Maryland*

These were important clergy positions, but Ben didn't remember hearing any discussions of them during the presidential campaign or even during the primaries last year. Joe Morgan had obviously been considered by the Mormon Church leaders to be worthy and faithful enough to serve in influential positions in the church hierarchy, yet his record of ecclesiastical prominence was curiously absent from the political discourse.

Ben went back to Zachariah's iTouch, but the low battery warning was on. He used the charger from his own iPhone to juice it up a bit, which gave him an idea. Using a USB cable and a few minutes of tinkering with the application, he managed to copy it to his own iPhone. He touched the sailing ship icon, the knightly woman appeared, waving a sword-like pencil at pirates and cutting off the sea creature's tentacles. Ben pressed the pencil's orange eraser, Zachariah's face popped up and asked for the motto, and Ben typed *Semper Fidelis*. The banner appeared: *Welcome to my journal!* Opening the file, he verified that all of it was successfully copied.

He disconnected Zachariah's iTouch and put it aside. Now he could read the journal on his own device.

CHAPTER 18

Z.H. Journal Entry # 7:

My first three years at the US Department of Veterans Affairs were spent transferring paper archives to electronic files. Together with a dozen other employees, I sat in a cubicle all day, every day (except for lunches, cookie breaks, and frequent leg-stretching walks up and down the drab hallways) and keyed in veterans' information from a stack of paper files into the computerized database.

Like most government equipment, by the time it was installed the new system was a decade behind the private sector. Reading *PC Magazine* made me feel like Moses, looking over at the digital promised land but forbidden to enter it. Also, I was having a hard time sleeping, a condition that required medication, especially with three little kids and a pregnant wife who constantly shared the frustrations of her days.

In early 1995, I was promoted to manager, which gave me short-lived hope of making a small difference. I spent three months writing a detailed report that listed the shortcomings in the way the department handled electronic data and outlined improvements. My boss, the section supervisor, duly sent my recommendations up the chain of command, where they disappeared into a bureaucratic black hole.

One day, out of the blue, Bishop Morgan invited me for lunch at his office on the top floor of the Nibberworth Investment Bank in Rockville. Before we bit into our sandwiches, we spent a few minutes studying the scriptures. The bishop spoke about an important element of our faith—the salvation of the dead. He explained the words of Paul in I Corinthians: *Else what shall they do which are baptized for the dead, if the dead rise not at all? Why are they then baptized for the dead?* No other church but ours follows Paul's prescription for the ritual of offering salvation to the dead, as Joseph Smith had taught.

Historically, Brother Morgan explained, it had started with Saints who performed posthumous baptism rituals for their parents and grandparents who had passed on before the restoration of Christ's True Church by the Prophet Joseph Smith. But like all virtuous customs, it had expanded through additional revelations to include all souls of dead Gentiles, whose identities were continuously collected through extensive investigations globally called *extractions*, which the Church pursued no matter what the expense was in time and money.

Bishop Morgan described his recent visit to the magnificent genealogical center at the Church headquarters in Utah, where huge underground archives contain hundreds of millions of names and family lines going back centuries, which had been extracted from various records all over the world for posthumous baptizing.

Joe Morgan was an eloquent man, and I was grateful for the knowledge and warmth he shared so generously. I had no idea that this was more than a gesture of religious and emotional support from my bishop, as busy as he was with both his professional and ecclesiastical responsibilities. When I was leaving, he invited me to come with my family to dinner at his house the following week.

CHAPTER 19

Ben went back to the living room and turned on the TV. His camera was still connected to it. He got the slideshow function going again and ran it backward through the photos from the Camp David Scenic Overlook. When it reached the victim lying at the bottom looking up, Ben zoomed in on the face.

Zachariah Hinckley seemed to be looking straight at the camera. His lips pronounced one word before his body twitched in a final, fatal spasm.

Keera had thought the word was "Palmyra," but now Ben suspected it was a different word. A message.

He zoomed in even further, and the lips filled the screen. The photos changed slowly, and Ben said it out loud with the lips: "Pal…my…rah." It was possible, but the lip movements didn't fit perfectly. He rewound and tried again, this time saying: "Post… hue…mous." He did it twice more, and it fit perfectly.

Sitting on the sofa, he shook his head. "That's what you're saying," he told the dead man on the screen. "*Posthumous!*"

The discovery told Ben that Zachariah Hinckley's death had something to do with the posthumous baptisms described in the journal. But those events had occurred sixteen or seventeen years earlier inside the cloistered world of the LDS Church, making an investigation very challenging.

CHAPTER 20

Z.H. Journal Entry # 8:

After dinner, Bishop Morgan's teenage daughters took charge of our kids, whisking them to the lower floor, where a large room had been set up as a miniature Disneyworld. Palmyra joined Emma Morgan in the kitchen, and Bishop Morgan took me to his study for the customary hot cider.

"Let me show you something special." He opened one of the glass doors, reached up to a high shelf, and pulled out an old leather-bound book. He showed me the spine:

Book of Mormon
First Edition
New York
1830

This was the original work, the divine word of God, which had launched the Church of Jesus Christ of Latter-day Saints by Joseph Smith, the Prophet, Seer, and Revelator. All my life, from early childhood, I have studied the more modern editions of the *Book of Mormon*, together with the Bible, the *Doctrine and Covenants*, and the *Pearl of Great Price*—our "Standard Works" of holy scriptures. But this was the very first edition!

"The Prophet inscribed it to my great-great-grandfather," Bishop Morgan said. "I rarely take it out, but I wanted to share it with you." He opened the book on the title page, which carried a handwritten dedication:

To George Robert Morgan,
Blessings unto thee from the Angel Moroni.
Joseph Smith Jr. 1830.

Clearly enjoying my utmost awe, he opened the book on a page marked by a silk string and showed me something even more incredible. "This side note," he said, "is also in the Prophet's own handwriting."

Prophet Joseph Smith's words and revelations were studied by all Mormon men. Part of being a Saint was the practice of our Prophet's famous revelation about baptizing the dead. His words on this subject, quoted in the Doctrine and Covenants, were recited often. I was awed by seeing these very words scribbled by his own hand on the blank half-page above a chapter beginning in the first edition of the *Book of Mormon.*

I presume the doctrine of "baptism for the dead" has ere this reached your ears, and may have raised some inquiries in your minds respecting the same. I cannot in this letter give you all the information you may desire on the subject; but aside from knowledge independent of the Bible, I would say that it was certainly practiced by the ancient churches; and Saint Paul endeavors to prove the doctrine of the resurrection from the same, and says, "Else what shall they do which are baptized for the dead, if the dead rise not at all? Why are they then baptized for the dead?"

In the margins of the opposite page, beside the printed text, were strange markings in ink, clearly made by hand. I pointed. "What are these?"

"Reformed Egyptian," Bishop Morgan said in a voice touched by tremor. "Same as the translated holy texts!"

I nodded. He was referring to the translation by the Prophet of the *Book of Mormon* from the ancient gold plates given to him by the Angel Moroni in upstate New York in 1827, and the ancient

Egyptian papyri that a traveler had brought in 1835 to Kirtland, Ohio, where the Saints had moved after their exile from New York. Our prophet, Joseph Smith, was also a Seer, capable of translating foreign languages. He translated the papyri, finding them to contain the personal journals of the ancient Hebrew patriarchs Abraham and Moses. Those translations, together with other revelations, became known as the *Book of Abraham* and the *Book of Moses*, as part of our gospel in the collective scripture titled *Pearl of Great Price*.

"These Egyptian letters," Bishop Morgan said, "were added by the Prophet's own hand!"

Peering at these markings, I trembled.

"I compared it to the Prophet's other notations." The bishop gestured vaguely at the glass-covered shelves of old books. "It's authentic."

After returning the precious volume of the *Book of Mormon* to the high shelf and closing the glass door, Bishop Morgan shared with me that he had recently experienced a personal revelation: God was concerned that we have neglected to save a special class of souls—the bravest souls of our nation, the men whose courage in battle revealed their souls to be of the highest selflessness and idealism, men who had shown through their valorous sacrifices a great superiority to common men and thereby proved that they had progressed to a higher level of righteousness, almost as high as us, Latter-day Saints, even though they were uninformed of the True Church during their mortal lives on Earth.

According to Bishop Morgan, his personal revelation had been blessed by the First Presidency of the LDS Church in Utah, after the Quorum of Twelve had discussed and confirmed its authenticity. He decided to call on me to assist in this sacred project.

The first round of baptizing would be for winners of the US Medal of Honor. He explained that the medal was first created in 1862 by the US Senate and signed into law by President Lincoln during the Civil War for servicemen who "most distinguish themselves by their gallantry and other seamanlike qualities." In 1917, other medals had been introduced, making the Medal of Honor the highest honor and even more indicative of true battlefield courage in the face of hostile enemy action.

The instructions I received from Bishop Morgan were simple. Search the computer records at the Department of Veterans Affairs and extract a list of the servicemen who had been awarded the Medal of Honor since 1917, together with their correct birth names, birth dates, and names of immediate relatives.

Particularly important was the information about their wives. If a hero's wife was also dead, her soul should be offered salvation through posthumous baptizing as well. That way, they could be sealed in a celestial marriage in the afterlife and spend eternity together as godly parents in perpetual procreation in their own earth-like star. The few living honorees, as well as dead honorees' wives who were still alive, could not be baptized by proxy. Instead, they would be visited by LDS missionaries and given the opportunity to convert by choice—without being told about the secret baptizing of their dead comrades or husbands, of course, until after they had converted and could be trusted to keep Church secrets from the Gentiles.

I was to create an electronic file for all the data, save it on a floppy disk, and deliver it to Bishop Morgan personally. I was not to discuss this endeavor with any other person. The list of heroes and their wives would then be divided into several groups and assigned to various Mormon wards for posthumous baptizing ceremonies and temple endowments.

But while several wards would be called to conduct the posthumous baptizing rituals for all those heroes, our task would be special. As the recipient of this revelation, Bishop Morgan was given the special honor of officiating for the most courageous of all—the servicemen who had been awarded the Medal of Honor more than once. He instructed me to create a separate list of their names in preparation for a special ceremony scheduled for the following week, on Veterans Day, at the Washington DC Temple, where he would personally serve each of those exceptional heroes as a proxy in the baptismal bath.

I was excited and honored by the opportunity to bring salvation to the most highly decorated American soldiers and give them the opportunity to rise to the Celestial Kingdom of God.

The Monday after the meeting with Bishop Morgan, I went to work with renewed optimism, finally knowing why God had directed me to this otherwise uninspiring job at the Department of Veterans Affairs.

The actual process of extraction was not straightforward. By now, all veteran files had been converted into electronic data that could be searched by several parameters. However, medals and citations were not a searchable parameter. I came up with a plan to search through pension records because Medal of Honor recipients received a higher pension, as did their surviving spouses. I separated the list by noting the handful of honorees who were still alive and therefore not eligible for posthumous baptizing, but could be approached by LDS missionaries, as well as the few surviving wives of dead honorees.

In the privacy of my cubicle, I labored on this tedious process of cross-searching Medal of Honor recipients, dates of death, and wives' names and status. When a match popped up, I pulled up the personal file on my screen and saved it to the floppy disk. The pension records went back only to the beginning of World War II, but I assumed all previous honorees and their wives were all dead. My regular work wasn't very demanding, and I kept working on the Medal of Honor list on and off for the rest of the week. But on Thursday, a familiar date appeared in my search: *February 28, 1991.*

I knew this date!

I sat back and shut my eyes against the sudden inferno of memories—the hail of bullets from behind the Arab women, the Red Cross team sprawled on the road in bloodied white coats, my own body perforated and bleeding, the chopper appearing over the school like a guardian angel.

I attempted to chase off the storm of memories, but failed. I could see the dark-eyed captain giving me a quick salute before he slipped in behind the wheel. I saw the fuel tanker, its rear on fire as it roared away, up the street, far enough to blow up without incinerating us. I imagined the captain burning inside the driver's cabin and wondered: Had he felt the explosion, or was he knocked unconscious before realizing that it was his time to die? Had he seen his uniform ignite into flames, or had he died not knowing that he had saved our lives? Had the blast blinded him, or had he seen for himself that his sacred Jewish undergarment had failed to protect him?

CHAPTER 21

"What the hell! Ben!" Keera hurried down the stairs and started pulling aside curtains and opening windows. "Are you crazy?"

The sudden yelling tore Ben off the small screen, and he stood up, watching Keera go around the living room and kitchen area until she was done opening all the windows. He was still standing there, disoriented, when she came over to him, tore the cigarette from his hand, and went to the sink where she dropped the burning stub in the drain hole and ran the waste disposal unit long enough to liquefy a whole watermelon.

"I'm going to kill you!" She waved her hands in the air as if spreading the smoke would help. "How can you do this to me?"

He shuddered in the sudden cold. "I didn't mean it, didn't notice I was—"

"Didn't notice lighting up a cigarette? Inside our home? After all your promises?"

He shook his head.

She pulled the throw-blanket off the sofa and wrapped herself. "Did you notice buying this Marlboro?"

"I've had it since—"

"Since you promised to quit?"

"I did quit."

"Okay, Mr. Reporter. Let's review the facts."

"It wasn't a conscious thing. I was reading and—"

"A burning cigarette appeared between your fingers?" Keera pantomimed drawing from a joint. "Have you switched to writing fiction?"

Ben dropped back into the easy chair while she went to the powder room and came out with a can of flowery aerosol, which she started to spray around.

"It's going to smell like a bathroom here."

"Better than a nightclub." She looked at her watch. "It's one thirty in the morning!"

"I said I'm sorry. I've kept what's left of the last pack in my camera bag since I quit. Never touched it in all those months."

She sat next to him. "You really didn't notice lighting up?"

"I swear." He took her hand. "Why would I do it here, knowing how you hate it? I'm not suicidal."

"Good point." She looked at the iPhone in his hand. "Still reading? What's going on?"

He sighed. "I'm not sure yet."

"Tell me."

"Tomorrow. Go to sleep." He grabbed the Marlboro pack from the coffee table and tossed it in the garbage. "There. It's over. Promise."

They held each other.

Keera slipped her hands under his shirt.

He pulled them out and led her to the stairs. "Don't you have to be in the hospital at some ungodly hour tomorrow morning?"

She purred, making him laugh.

CHAPTER 22

Z.H. Journal Entry # 9:

On Thursday, the evening before Veterans Day, I drove to Bishop Morgan's home and gave him a floppy disk containing the two lists. One list had over a thousand names, but the second list was much shorter, containing the names of the heroes who had won more than one Medal of Honor. He asked if the two lists in total included all the names of Medal of Honor recipients since 1917, and I nodded. He held my hand between his hands and recited a lengthy blessing for my good health and joy in my growing family, as well as success in my government job, my service to the church, and my relationship with God.

I went home feeling terrible despite the Bishop's blessings, which I had earned through deceit, born of my need to cover up my even worse sin—failing to do what he had told me to do, which was like disobeying God.

Our youngest, Maxine, was colicky, the others were suffering a winter cold, and Palmyra was too tired and irate to hear about my agonizing turmoil over the sins of lying and disobedience I had knowingly committed.

That night, sleep came only after I took an extra pill. But sometime during the night, I awoke to find Palmyra shaking my shoulder. She said that I had been yelling incoherently. Paul and Gilead appeared in our bedroom door in their pajamas, their eyes wide. I apologized, explaining that I must have been dreaming about the war. We calmed them down, gave them each a dose of bubblegum Motrin, and put them back to sleep.

Having drenched myself with sweat, I took a shower and returned to bed.

Palmyra was nursing Maxine in the rocking chair. She asked me what was wrong.

I told her that I had disobeyed the bishop's instructions and had lied to him about it.

She was as loving and as understanding as any good Mormon wife would be, but also clear in her desire that I confess to Bishop Morgan, repent, and obtain absolution.

In the morning, as I was eating breakfast with the children, Palmyra asked when I would be calling Bishop Morgan. My response, that I wasn't going to confess, shocked her. She pulled me away from the kitchen table and whispered urgently, "You must talk to Bishop Morgan! Disobedience is a terrible sin!" I explained that it would be a bigger sin to betray the Marine captain who had saved my life not once, but twice. Whatever level of afterlife his soul was occupying, I knew he surely would not accept the Mormon Gospel, and therefore his posthumous baptism would be a needless insult to his memory and his soul. I didn't think God wanted me to do it.

Palmyra wasn't convinced. "God wants you to obey Bishop Morgan!" She wiped away tears. "That's the truth!"

A couple of hours later, while I was already at the Department of Veterans Affairs, busy on a crossword puzzle at my desk, a hand-delivered envelope arrived from Nibberworth Investment Bank. Inside was the floppy disk I had given to Bishop Morgan the previous night. He had scribbled a note on the disk in his familiar, tidy handwriting:

> *Brother Zachariah,*
> *God sympathizes with your righteous dilemma and good intentions.*
> *However, your heart knows this: Lies + Disobedience = Sin.*
> *The list must include ALL Medal of Honor recipients.*
> *Joseph S. Morgan, IV*

My body started trembling. Exposure as a fallen Saint who had disobeyed and lied to his bishop was an offense that could lead to punishment, or even a trial and excommunication, resulting in loss of my family and all my friends, not to mention my eternal salvation.

On top of it, I realized the only way for Bishop Morgan to find out was from Palmyra. Her betrayal stunned me. Our marriage had been sealed in the Temple, and like all Mormon wives, her personal salvation depended on serving her husband with complete loyalty and devotion. Only I could bring her into the Celestial Kingdom in the afterlife.

One of my coworkers heard me groan and came into my cubicle to find me trembling. I told her it was a food allergy and ran off to the bathroom, where I indeed lost my breakfast in one of the stalls.

Back at my desk, I realized there was no one I could call to share what had just happened. Not only did it involve a secret assignment from the Church, but copying veterans' personal information and passing it to outsiders was a federal crime. Even my elderly parents, who perhaps could be trusted to keep my secret and offer kind advice, were now living with one of my sisters in Utah and had too much riding on the divine prospects of what would happen at the approaching end of their mortal lives. They would be horrified at my failure and would tell me to repent and obey Bishop Morgan.

And worst of all, I could not consult with Palmyra. The one person in the world whose loyalty to me had been certain, whose love had been total, and whose support had been unquestioning, was suddenly unavailable. How could my wife disclose to Bishop Morgan what I had shared with her in the confidence of our marriage?

The answer was simple: My wife felt it was her duty to me. How could she stand by and let me destroy my spiritual future, lose the right to progress to exaltation and eternal godhood? How could she let me destroy her chance of salvation and afterlife glory, which depended on me through our sealing in a celestial marriage? By informing Bishop Morgan, Palmyra was saving me—and herself— from a spiritual catastrophe and eternal damnation.

Was she wrong?

I couldn't answer.

Was I right to disobey and lie to the Bishop to protect the Marine captain—a dead Gentile!—from posthumous baptism?

I couldn't answer that either. What did I know about the dark-eyed captain? Not even his name! Perhaps I was wrong about the strength of his Jewish faith, perhaps his soul would delight at the chance of accepting the True Church, achieving salvation, and progressing to the Celestial Kingdom of God?

CHAPTER 23

In Ben's mind, Zachariah's talk of a floppy disk triggered a memory. He set down the iPhone and went back to look at the photos stored in the Canon's memory. There were a few dozen snapshots he had taken of Porter's meticulous search of the accident site, but the one Ben was looking for had been taken very quickly. The object Porter had found stashed in the back, under the dead victim's belt, was about the size of a DVD case, thin and square. Ben had managed to snap a photo just as Porter was slipping the object into the pocket of his jacket. By zooming in on it, Ben could see something that resembled a floppy disk.

Shifting the focus to Porter's face, his expression was inscrutable. Had he known of this floppy disk? Had he been conducting such a thorough search in order to find it? Or was he just collecting evidence? And if so, why put it in his pocket and not with the victim's other belongings?

Ben realized the ramifications of the story. The old floppy disk, which contained the Medal of Honor recipients' personal information and had Joe Morgan's handwritten note on it, would prove that the presidential candidate had directed the copying of confidential data from government computers for secret LDS baptizing rituals of dead heroes. If this came out, it would outrage not only veterans and their families, but many other voters.

The events at the Marine Corps ride now made sense. Zachariah had been in possession of evidence that could derail Joe Morgan's presidential campaign. The mysterious white Ducati had waited to confront him, or to cause the crash. Inspector Porter, conveniently nearby, had searched the body and removed the incriminating floppy disk.

It was a plausible theory, but Ben hoped that Zachariah had taken precautions against losing the floppy disk. The answer, Ben hoped, would be in the journal.

CHAPTER 24

Z.H. Journal Entry # 10:

The ceremony at our magnificent Washington DC Temple took place in the afternoon of Veterans Day. Only the necessary few Saints were allowed to attend and witness. My job was to load the floppy disk into the computer and make sure that each name was displayed and called by the temple worker in charge of the ritual.

Bishop Morgan climbed into the baptismal bath, a huge container made of white marble and resting on twelve giant oxen, also white, which symbolized the twelve tribes of Israel.

The temple worker, standing in the water next to the bishop, watched the auxiliary computer screen set up next to the baptismal bath. When I clicked on the first name, it appeared before the temple worker, who recited the prayer and declared, "For and on behalf of Lieutenant Darrin Farley, as a proxy and stand in, you are now being baptized to the church of Jesus Christ of Latter-day Saints." He then pushed Bishop Morgan backward, immersing him completely in the water, and pulled him back up.

Only then, seeing the glowing joy on Bishop Morgan's face, did I realize how this whole thing amounted to much more than providing a spiritual rite for dead heroes. With each successive hero's name and dunking, Bishop Morgan's expression became more elated until he was echoing the temple worker's declarations at the top of his voice and falling back into the water for the repeated immersion with a joy that seemed to heat up the lukewarm water in the baptismal bath. I watched him while my fingers hit the keys, going down the list. I wondered whether Joe Morgan somehow felt that he was uniting with their souls, infusing himself with their virtues, and acquiring their courage.

There were nineteen men who received the Medal of Honor twice, and I heard their names one by one as the temple worker declared each one.

Dread came over me as the dates on the left side of my screen approached 1991. I had avoided looking at the captain's name when I had copied and pasted his information from the VA pension records to the list on the floppy disk. His wife was still alive, so I had no need to deal with her information. And now, as the blinking curser reached that line, I averted my eyes, clicked on it, and quickly covered my ears to block out the temple worker's voice as he declared the captain's name, followed by Bishop Morgan's cheerful repetition before his face disappeared underwater.

Bishop Morgan was helped out of the water and down the few steps to the floor. Standing there in his dripping temple undergarments, he turned to face the twelve oxen. His athletic body straightened up, and he saluted. This was not part of the ceremony, and everyone watched him in silence. After a long moment, Bishop Morgan turned and left.

No one paid attention to me, sitting at the computer, deflated and guilty. And what I did next, while instinctive and without a second thought, in time turned out to be a lot more fateful than anyone could have imagined. I ejected the floppy disk, which contained the lists of heroes and was etched with Bishop Morgan's handwritten note, and took it.

I spent the afternoon driving around aimlessly, too confused and angry to go home. As twilight descended on the suburbs of Washington, I passed by a motorcycle shop – Ironman Cycles of Gaithersburg. A ramp out front propped up a Harley Davidson painted in the colors of the American flag. I got out of my car and went over to look at it up close. A cardboard sign on the seat said: *Reserved for a Veteran!*

There were many flags raised that day all around the nation's capital, but for some reason, that stars-and-stripes Harley Davidson made me all choked up. I stood in attention and saluted. Then I went in and bought it.

CHAPTER 25

There was another journal entry, but Ben needed a break. He felt that the purchase of a Harley Davidson was a turning point in the story. Zachariah Hinckley had been transformed by the heroes' posthumous baptizing ceremony, not just from a car driver to a motorcycle rider, but from a devout LDS family man, a good son, husband, and father, to a man possessed by an urge to get away from where he had been until then—physically, mentally, maybe even spiritually.

Ben made sure that the journal was safely saved on his iPhone. Sitting back in his chair, the adrenaline rush slowly subsiding, he was overwhelmed by a craving for a smoke. For a moment he considered fishing the remains of his cigarettes out of the trash. Instead, he stepped back out to the balcony. A few deep breaths and stretching his arms sideways, as if he were nailed to a cross, somehow staunched the urge. He went back inside and locked the glass doors.

After leaving a note for Keera on the inside of the front door, where she wouldn't miss it in the morning, he went upstairs, undressed, and slipped into bed, scooting close to Keera until his body spooned hers and his face rested on the pillow by her nape. She stirred but didn't wake up, her breathing slow and peaceful.

Gradually his own breathing calmed to match hers, the tension in his muscles loosened, and the rapid slideshow in his mind went from Zachariah Hinckley's life and death to something less defined, flashes of sights, of trees and farmhouses, viewed through the framed face shield of his motorcycle helmet.

PART II:

The Ghost

CHAPTER 26

Keera woke up at six. She slipped out of Ben's embrace and stood beside the bed for a moment, watching him sleep. His hair covered most of his face, and he snored lightly. She pulled the blanket off his shoulder and kissed the tattoo—a football helmet protecting a bottle of Bud Light.

A half hour later, she was downstairs, dressed and ready for her twenty-five-minute commute. The coffeemaker had started automatically, and she poured herself a cup, adding a few drops of milk for color.

About to leave, Keera found a yellow Post-it note stuck to the inside of the front door. Written in Ben's familiar cursive, it said:

> *To: Hopelessly romantic*
> *From: Cynic w/ potential*
> *Message: Zachariah didn't say, "Palmyra!"*

Keera laughed. She was intrigued. If not his wife's name, what was Zachariah's last word? Did he provide an answer in the personal journal that Ben was reading?

She took a fresh Post-it note and scribbled:

> *To: Cynic w. potential*
> *From: Hopelessly romantic*
> *Message: Did he say, "Nosy reporter! Buzz out of my private journal!"?*

It was cold in the garage, especially when the door rolled up and a puff of outside air ruffled the pile of newspaper in the recycle bin. The Mustang took a couple of tries to start, and Keera revved up while setting the radio to NPR. She glanced in the mirror and backed out of the garage, hitting something that made a lot of noise.

"What was that?" She stopped the car and got out.

Behind the Mustang, she found a portable basketball hoop on its side. She recognized it as belonging to the neighbors at the other end of the six-unit townhome building. It was odd. Who would roll a basketball hoop all the way over here and leave it by the garage door?

Checking her car, Keera found a small dent in the rear bumper, not very noticeable beside all the other dents and scrapes she had accumulated over the years.

There was no sound of anyone waking up, especially not Ben, who could sleep through a thunderstorm. None of the neighbors were out, and Keera had no time to spare. She dragged the fallen basketball hoop out of the way and got back in her car.

Ben found the yellow Post-it note stuck to the coffeemaker and laughed. He drank his coffee while watching the news. Starting with CNN, he switched at every commercial break to another channel—NBC, CBS, FOX, and back to CNN.

Every development in the economy, international affairs, and even sports, circled back to the coming elections: Will it help Joe Morgan win the White House, becoming the first Mormon president?

In a segment about elections paraphernalia, the FOX News anchor showed a photo of a bumper sticker that said: *President Joe Mormon!*

"We asked the Morgan campaign," said the anchor, "about the twisting of the candidate's last name to send such a sectarian message, a jab of prejudice masquerading as humor. A spokesman for the candidate replied that Governor Morgan feels that the only test of faith for a presidential candidate should be whether he believes in American exceptionalism."

CHAPTER 27

Z.H. Journal Entry # 11:

My VA therapists always reminded me that the best cure was the human ability to forget. It was the most important capability we possessed, they explained, the mental mechanism that files away painful memories. In the two decades since my injury, I've become very good at tucking away the year of blood and gore in Kuwait, the year of multiple surgeries and physical therapy at Bethesda Naval Hospital, and the years of trying to fit my deformed self into a square life of a husband, a father, and a breadwinner in a government job that was becoming less meaningful every year.

My faith helped me make peace with life. As a Latter-day Saint, I was taught that my mortal existence was temporary. To earn my place in the most exalted Celestial Kingdom, I must serve righteously as a Saint, as a man of the priesthood, and as the head of my growing family. We've always participated in all the ward's activities, and Palmyra has served as a leader in the Relief Society— the LDS women's organization dedicated to supporting the all-male priesthood through charitable work for needy Mormons and Gentiles.

Our children made us proud as they stood up to speak at testimony time, especially Gilead, who at three years old brought tears to everyone's eyes when he recited for the first time the foundational testimony of the LDS church with a few cute variations: "I know...I know...that Jesus...he told our Prophet...

Mister Smith...to be good...because we...we are the only...only only only...true church...because we are saints."

Shortly after the Medal of Honor baptizing ceremony, Bishop Morgan was called to serve as Stake President and passed the ward's bishop mantle to a friendly CPA named Canaan Linder, whose wife Nora had grown up with Palmyra. We became close friends, and Brother Linder called on me to serve as leader of the church's Boy Scout troop, which over the succeeding years gave me the opportunity to spend time with my boys and officiate at each one's Eagle Scout Award ceremony. As the years passed, I rarely thought of the heroes' posthumous baptizing.

Meanwhile, Joe Morgan's prestige grew within the church's national leadership. As the CEO of an investment bank listed on the stock exchange, his income was a matter of public record and of many Saints' admiration, as ours was a faith that encouraged material success. But his financial and ecclesiastical prominence did not diminish his friendliness. We still saw him, Emma, and their growing children at ward meetings and attended his occasional religious lectures. But even those contacts declined when he made a surprising decision to quit an immensely successful business career in favor of political office.

Joe Morgan's run for governor as a Republican in the mostly Democratic state of Maryland was a long shot, but he won on a businesslike platform against a Democratic incumbent with a closet full of skeletons. Four years later, however, the Democrats nominated a strong candidate and Morgan declined to run for a second term in Maryland. Instead, he decided to seek the GOP nomination for president of the United States. He lost the primaries to a senator, who in turn lost the general elections to the Democratic candidate.

Over the years, my peaceful existence gave the illusion of a secure existence, both present and future, for me, Palmyra, and our children. In addition to Paul, Gilead, and Maxine, we had Anderson in 1997, Lynne in 1999, Michael in 2000, Martha in 2002, and Deborah in 2004. My beautiful children filled my life with light, which fought a continuous match against the recurring dark moods that preyed on my mind. Nothing could totally cure the chronic aches of my physical injuries and the mental pain of battlefield trauma, but advancements in prescription drugs for physical pain and mental distress helped maintain the illusion of normalcy, and my Harley Davidson took me into the hills of western Maryland whenever I needed to get away.

There was no reason for me to doubt that my righteous obedience entitled me to what every Saint expects after old age and natural death: Palmyra and I would continue our eternal marriage in the next phase of existence, immortal in the heavenly Celestial Kingdom, procreating as a god-father and a god-mother for eternity, while I no longer had to spend five days a week at the Department of Veterans Affairs.

But then, last year, Joe Morgan announced his intention to seek the GOP nomination again, and my life took an unexpected turn for the worse.

At first I dismissed his second run as a symbolic act, another futile challenge to GOP conservative voters to get over their prejudice and give a Mormon candidate a chance to win the primaries.

But despite my doubts, and in defiance of all the TV talking heads' predictions, Joe Morgan used his impressive record as a business leader to establish himself as a credible hope for pulling the country out of its prolonged recession. It also helped that our leaders in Salt Lake City had invested many millions over the past couple of years in wonderful "*I am a Mormon*" TV commercials that featured wholesome brothers and sisters in their regular, all-American jobs, homes, and sports activities, to show that we are just like everybody else and not some odd cultists, as our detractors have always claimed.

It had been a nail-biting experience for all of us to watch Joe Morgan as he slugged through the mudslinging of the primaries, fought last-minute challenges at the convention, and emerged as a winner, capturing the GOP nomination for the presidency.

We watched his acceptance speech on a large-screen TV set up in the ward house, and when the Republican Convention in Florida erupted into cheers and balloons, here in Silver Spring everyone jumped with joy. There were hugs and prayers all around as if it wasn't just Joe Morgan being chosen to lead, but our True Church was finally becoming mainstream. This legitimacy, for us Saints, was not a goal in and of itself, but a giant step toward the ultimate goal set by Prophet Joseph Smith—who himself had run for US president—to win recognition by all Christians that ours was the only True Church.

While everyone was celebrating, a force of terrible distress gripped me. I slipped away and walked home, leaving our car for Palmyra and the kids.

The floppy disk had spent all these years in the drawer of my nightstand. I slipped it into the inside pocket of my riding jacket.

It was chilly, but I took my stars-and-stripes Harley Davidson out of the garage and rode it to a solitary park near the Potomac River. Too distraught, I neglected to lower the kickstand, and the motorcycle fell over. When I picked it up, the left side was muddied, soiling the American flag.

I walked into the woods and stood there among tree trunks, chirpy birds, and tiny raindrops. Tremors passed through me, fear that a great wrong was about to happen because of my failure. It wasn't the baptizing of the dead. I had no doubts about our duty to try and save all souls, here and in the afterlife. My distress had been triggered by Morgan's presidential candidacy.

But why?

I recalled the expression of elation on Morgan's face as he stood in the baptismal bath all those years back. He was ecstatic. He seemed to believe that the ritual imbibed him with special powers, that it prepared him for a divine destiny. And now, with Morgan becoming the GOP presidential nominee, I realized how being baptized in proxy for the most courageous men in American history had fueled his conviction that he was destined to reach the top—to become the commander in chief. This misguided certainty, which had radiated from his wet face back then, had been the engine of his ambition ever since. And it was my fault, for I had stolen the veterans' names for him.

I fell to my knees and cried for God to guide me.

And then I heard the voice, the same voice I had heard so many years earlier, blessing my enlistment in the Marine Corps. Now it was telling me that Brother Morgan must announce proudly his faith in the restored True Church and reveal his service as proxy in baptizing the fallen heroes who had won the Medal of Honor multiple times.

Perhaps I should have realized, based on my past experience, what dire consequences might result from obeying a revelation, but what choice did I have?

I returned to the Harley and took off for Florida. I stopped near Richmond, Virginia, to refuel and check Morgan's campaign Internet site. He was on his way to Jacksonville, Florida, for his first event as the GOP nominee, demonstrating the importance of the Sunshine State in the battle for the White House. I called Palmyra to let her know that I would be away for some time and hung up before she could ask anything. Ducking behind the windshield, I sped south on I-95 while light rain began to fall.

CHAPTER 28

Ben put down the iPhone. The mention of the dropped Harley Davidson had bothered him, and now he realized why: The mysterious imprint left by the kickstand of the white Ducati near the Camp David Scenic Overlook.

In his closet-sized study was a wall of shelves. He pulled out the *Album of Modern European Motorcycles*.

His own bike, a 2011 R1200GS, was featured at the front of the BMW chapter, which came first, followed by Moto Guzzi, Triumph, and Ducati. He browsed the Ducati models. Only the Monster 848 was photographed in white, and it was impossible to tell whether it was a standard color or a custom paint chosen by the photographer.

The large photo was taken from the side, but a few smaller photos were taken from all angles. With a magnifying glass, Ben peered at a photo taken from the rear. In the lower-left section, ahead of the rear wheel, the bottom plate of the kickstand stuck out slightly. He turned on his camera and flipped through the photo archive to find the images of the depression left by the kickstand on the dirt-and-weeds path near the overlook. Beside the winding line along the middle, the depression mark seemed larger and the shape was oval, not round like the standard plate.

Shelving the album, Ben decided that the kickstand plate on the white Ducati must have been an aftermarket slip-on, a common and sensible accessory that many bikers added in order to enlarge the footing of their kickstands for better support on poor surfaces.

The bottom shelf was lined with editions of *BMW MOA Magazine*, as well as *Rider* and *Cycle World*. The last one was the most promising.

He pulled a copy and looked through the advertisements, noting the vendors' names.

Using his iPhone, Ben searched each of the vendors' inventory of Ducati accessories for kickstand plates. The fourth website he visited offered a whole selection for on-road and off-road motorcycles. Most curiously, some of them had patterns on the bottom "for added traction."

A moment later, he was gazing at a kickstand plate that, photographed from the bottom, showed a welded-on realistic-looking snake.

With the Canon's back screen next to the iPhone, comparing the two images, he couldn't tell whether the same snake had been pressed into the ground, leaving a print in the weeds on the path near the Camp David Scenic Overlook. But it looked similar.

Satisfied with this bit of detective work, Ben replaced the magazine. He wondered whether the Ducati rider had chosen the snake pattern for a purpose, as a symbol of affiliation of some kind, or as a meaningless decorative touch.

CHAPTER 29

I rode south toward Florida. At a gas station halfway down I checked the news and found out that Morgan would be heading back to Maryland after a fundraising breakfast at the Ritz Carlton in Jacksonville. I still had over five hundred miles ahead of me, which meant I would likely miss him. Heading back north on I-95, somewhere in North Carolina, I left the highway and found a public campground. There was no attendant at this time of night, and I curled on the ground next to the Harley and slept until morning.

It was late afternoon when I reached the northern VA outskirts of metropolitan DC, just in time for rush hour. Barely able to keep the bike upright through endless stop-and-go traffic, I finally made it to Silver Spring as the sun was setting.

There was a big crowd at the Morgan home, judging by the number of cars outside. A black Chevy Suburban blocked the driveway. Two men sat inside. One of them came out as I approached and raised his hand. He said something I couldn't hear—eighteen hours with the Harley engine's drone in my ears had left me practically deaf.

He waited as I dismounted the bike and struggled with stiff hands to pull out my wallet. I showed him my driver's license and my Temple Recommend Card—the laminated card that identified me as a Mormon in good standing who was eligible to participate in Temple rituals.

"Ch…church business." I could barely speak after all those hours on the bike.

He took my identification cards, stepped aside, and spoke to his wrist. After a moment, he handed them back and waved me through.

My legs ached as I paced up the long driveway and approached the gate, which was part of a wrought iron fence, well-concealed with ivy, that surrounded the house. The gate was unlocked remotely. I pushed it and went through.

The front door was opened by an aide.

Clean shaven and wearing a white button-down shirt with sleeves folded to his elbows, Joe Morgan left a room full of advisors to greet me. He smiled warmly, glancing up and down at my riding apparel. "Brother Zachariah, what can I do for you?"

"Con…gra…tu…lations!" I cleared my throat. "Sorry, I'm—"

"Dear Lord!" He gripped my hands. "You're frozen!"

I nodded.

He took me to the kitchen, sat me near the stove, and poured a mug of hot cider.

Emma Morgan must have called Palmyra, who arrived moments later. Morgan didn't leave my side, even as his advisors kept popping their heads into the kitchen with growing frequency.

Somewhat recovered, I asked to speak with him in private, and we went to his library. It hadn't changed much in the years since I had last been there, back when he was the lay bishop of our Silver Spring Ward. The only change I noticed was on a section of the wall between two windows, which was now covered by portraits of men in uniform. On closer examination, I saw that each one had a small brass plate on the bottom of the frame with a name. It took me a moment to realize these were the names on the list I had given him a decade and a half earlier. These were the heroes who had been awarded the Medal of Honor by the president of the United States more than once, the heroes Morgan had served as proxy for in their posthumous baptisms into the Church of Jesus Christ of Latter-day Saints.

He stood next to me, smiling brightly. "Nice, isn't it?"

I looked away from the portrait of the dark-eyed Marine captain. "A great achievement—winning the nomination."

"Thank you."

With a gesture at the portraits, I asked, "Do you think they helped you?"

He smiled. "I needed all the help I could get. Still do. Winning against a sitting president is very hard."

"And the heroes have given you courage? It must be hard, with all the nasty attacks and ugly TV commercials."

"Of course." He glanced at the photos. "You know, any man who thinks himself capable of serving competently as president of the United States is either a fool or a madman. What irrational arrogance would it take to think you have the strength to command the largest armed forces in human history? Or that you possess the wisdom required to know when to turn the nuclear keys and unleash hell on earth?"

His sincerity calmed me down. Perhaps my task wouldn't be so hard.

"But someone has to do it, and it is an act of courage." He touched one of the photos—an Air Force pilot in World War One. "They helped me overcome my doubts and seek the White House despite my human weaknesses."

"That's…humble."

Morgan chuckled. "Remember what the *Book of Mormon* says in *Ether*, twelve? *'I give unto men weakness that they may be humble; and my grace is sufficient for all men that humble themselves before me; for if they humble themselves before me, and have faith in me, then will I make weak things become strong unto them.'* Do you understand?"

I nodded.

"The real challenge begins now. The fate of the country will be determined in November. But we have faith that God is on our side, don't we, Brother Zachariah?"

"I had a revelation about it."

"Really? What is it?"

"Also from *Ether*, an earlier verse, in chapter four: *'For the Lord saith unto me: They shall not go forth unto the Gentiles until the day that they shall repent of their iniquity and become clean before the Lord.'* God wants you to give testimony to the Gentile voters."

Morgan looked at me politely, waiting for an explanation.

I gestured at the heroes' portraits. "About them. You must confess before the elections."

To my surprise, he didn't seem upset at all. In fact, he laughed.

Fearing that my words were not getting through to him, I spoke more slowly and deliberately. "Tell the American people about the posthumous baptizing of the Medal of Honor winners. You must give testimony to the Gentiles, whose votes you are seeking. *Thus saith the Lord!*"

He squeezed my shoulder. "I don't know what you're talking about."

Could he have forgotten? But here were their faces, looking back at us from his library wall.

"I'm talking about them." I pointed. "Tell the voters how you ordered me to extract these heroes' names and copy their personal files from the database of the Department of Veterans Affairs. Tell the voters how you immersed in the sacred water for these heroes, how you were baptized in proxy for and on behalf of each of these heroes, how you saved these heroes' souls by giving them the True Gospel in the afterlife. And also, tell the voters what it meant for your own soul."

"I have no idea…what you mean."

The slight hesitation was like a hairline crack in his smiling mask, a glimpse of the truth, which made my self-doubts disappear, now replaced by incredulity: How could he lie so blatantly to another Saint?

"Brother Morgan!" I pulled the floppy disk from my inside pocket and held it out for him to see his own handwriting on it, demanding that I add the last name to the list. "Remember now?"

His cheerful expression disappeared. He leaned forward and looked closely.

"Well?"

He straightened up and looked away.

"God wants you to come clean to the Gentiles. God spoke to me. It was a revelation."

"Who are you to receive such a revelation? Have you forgotten the sin of presumption and arrogance?"

"I am a man of the priesthood, a Latter-day Saint, and therefore have the power of God's revelation." Again I quoted from memory. "It says in *Doctrine and Covenants*, sixty-eight, four: '*And whatsoever they shall speak when moved upon by the Holy Ghost shall be scripture, shall be the will of the Lord, shall be the mind of the Lord, shall be the word of the Lord, shall be the voice of the Lord, and the power of God unto salvation.*' Do you question the right of every Saint—including me!—to receive the Lord's revelations?"

"You had a false revelation," Morgan said. He reached up to the high shelf, opened the glass door that protected his collection of old books, and pulled out the leather-bound first edition of the *Book of Mormon*. "Let me read to you what the prophet said about false revelations—"

"You should fast and pray," I said, repeating the advice he had given me in times of distress. "Fast and pray, and God will tell you as well."

He put the book down on a side table. "You're crossing a line of secrecy that must not be crossed by a good Saint."

"This should not be a secret." I raised the floppy disk. "Your own handwriting. Do you want me to hand it over to CNN?"

He didn't answer.

"You must give testimony to the Gentiles. *Thus saith the Lord!*"

"Any fact that doesn't promote the True Church is a lie."

"The truth cannot be a lie, and hiding the truth cannot be a virtue. Gentiles are God's children too. They'll respect you for confessing."

"You're naive! We've been at war with the Gentiles since they exiled the Prophet Joseph Smith from New York, Ohio, in Missouri, Illinois—until they finally lynched him and chased us all the way to Utah! And they still await the opportunity to pounce on us again! But in a matter of weeks, as I become president-elect of the United States, it will be the realization of Joseph Smith's prophecy that the Saints shall rule over America!"

"God told me clearly that you must—"

"Why would God want to destroy our True Church's chance for a divine victory over the Gentiles?"

"The truth must be told." I shook the floppy disk before him. "*Thus saith the Lord!*"

"Let me look at it again." Morgan reached for the disk.

Stepping backward, I held it to my chest. It was understandable that he would want to possess the only hard evidence of his involvement in assembling the list. I had to keep it out of his hands, or else Satan would make him defy God's will.

"Brother Zachariah!" Joe Morgan held out his hand. "Give it to me now! In the name of the Prophet, as your apostle and church authority, I order you!"

"Tell the truth to the Gentiles," I repeated. "*Thus saith the Lord!*"

"Stop saying it!"

"*Thus saith the Lord!*"

Recognizing my determination, Morgan turned and left the library—to call for reinforcements, I assumed. His only alternative to confession was to take the incriminating floppy disk from me, by force if necessary, and destroy it so that no physical evidence remained to support my story. I had to hide it somewhere safe, a place that he and his people would never think of looking.

Palmyra arrived home shortly after me. They must have told her that I had slipped out via the library window, but she dared not say a word. I showered, ate a meal with my children, and went to bed. As far as I was concerned, I had delivered God's command to Joe Morgan, and he had to comply.

For the first time in years, I slept peacefully, secure in the knowledge that I had finally put things right. And if, by the time you read this journal, Joe Morgan has not complied with my Medal of Honor revelation, please do whatever you can to force him to confess publicly of his deeds. I believe his confession is essential for my salvation—the key to my entry into the Celestial Kingdom.

CHAPTER 30

Ben moved his thumb over the screen, trying to bring the text forward, but there was nothing more. The journal ended there, on the day after the GOP Convention. But what had happened in the weeks between the convention and Zachariah's death on Sunday? Morgan had not confessed to any posthumous conversions of US war heroes. He had not spoken of any details of his Mormon faith, for that matter. Had he managed to locate the floppy disk that Zachariah had hidden—or was it the item Porter had pulled from Zachariah's body? Had Morgan somehow succeeded in silencing Zachariah to cease his demands for a public confession, or was Zachariah killed in order to silence him?

Ben picked up the iTouch and searched for additional journal entries. There were none. Whatever events had led to the violent end of his life, Zachariah had left untold. It was now up to Ben to uncover the facts and find out whether Joe Morgan was involved. He hesitated. The harassment of Keera outside the club last night seemed to have been a meaningless prank by one of the customers. But what if it had been the Ducati from the overlook?

Dismissing the idea as preposterous, Ben began packing up his gear for the day ahead. The story had become irresistible.

CHAPTER 31

It was too early to go to Fran's office, so Ben rode first to Ironman Cycles in Gaithersburg. He had been there before to buy accessories, but today he went straight to the service entrance and asked for the Harley Davidson technician.

The lanky, gray-haired man was wiping his greasy hands on a blue paper towel as he glanced at Ben's GS. "A BMW? How about switching to a real motorcycle?"

"My girlfriend already owns a vibrator."

"Ouch!" The technician made as if he was cowering. "That hurt!"

They laughed, and Ben asked, "You heard about the accident at the vets' ride?"

"Tragic," the technician said. "Always happens to the nicest guy."

"You know him?"

"He was a customer with a very special bike. We took care of him. Good guy. Real good. What a shame. Are you a friend of his?"

"Not really. I'm a reporter, and having witnessed the tragedy, I thought it would be worthwhile to write a piece in his honor."

"Oh, yeah?"

"I'm looking to speak with someone who rode with him regularly, learn more about him, what he was like, and so on. Any idea?"

"Let me ask."

Ben waited.

The technician came back a moment later. "My manager says you should talk to Rex. They rode together."

"Do you have a last name or a phone number?"

He shrugged. "Can't give it to you. Privacy, you know?"

"Can you tell me anything about Rex?"

"He works at Best Buy in Gaithersburg. But don't tell him I said so."

"Understood. Is he riding a real motorcycle?"

The technician laughed. "Dyna Super Glide, full dress, black with solid chrome wheels, lots of electronics."

Ben rode around Best Buy to the rear. The employee parking was almost empty, only a used Kia and a small pickup truck. He realized the store wasn't open yet and waited. A while later, more employees arrived. Finally a motorcycle showed up—not a Harley, but a skinny motocross with a tall seat and a symbolic headlight. The rider, a teenager carrying a Mac backpack, waved at Ben and yelled, "Nice ride, man!"

"Thanks. I'm waiting for Rex."

The kid changed direction and came over. "They texted me to come in to cover for him. He called in sick or something."

"Really?"

"Lame. Probably gone fishing." He caressed the yellow gas tank of the GS. "Smooth baby. Didn't know Rex rode with Beemer guys."

There was no easy way to answer this implied question without lying, so Ben just said, "Do you?"

"Are you kidding?" He pointed at his motocross. "This piece of crap won't keep up with real bikes. See ya!" He headed for the service door at the back of the store.

"Hey," Ben said, "what's Rex's sweet spot?"

"North Point."

The sky was heavy with clouds. It was going to rain, and the temperature was dropping. Ben plugged North Point into the GPS, slipped the helmet back on, and rode off.

CHAPTER 32

It was drizzling at North Point, which reached into the flat expanse of the Chesapeake Bay east of Baltimore like a thumb that had been flattened by a roller. Ben rode through the main part of the state park, which was completely deserted. A second area, northward on the park's shore, had a parking lot and a jetty reaching into the bay. There was no Harley in sight, only a beige Chevy pickup truck. Ben rode toward it, making a round detour. It was an older model, but in spit-and-shine condition, with new tires, dark windows, and a few antennas on the roof. A single sticker on the rear bumper showed a Harley Davidson logo with the word *Freedom!* Ben parked next to it, got off the bike, and replaced his helmet with a Ravens cap.

A lone fisherman stood way out on the jetty, his rod in a holder, his hands in his pockets. He heard Ben's boots on the wooden planks, glanced at him, and turned back to face the dark water. But he must have been listening carefully to the steps because, when Ben got within a few steps of his back, he suddenly swiveled, launched himself at Ben, and shoved him against the railing while pointing a long, serrated knife at his neck.

Ben grabbed the hand with the knife. "Hey!"

"You following me?"

"I'm...sightseeing!"

"Don't lie!" He pressed the tip of the knife to the skin.

"Are you nuts?"

"Talk, or I'll spill your juice and feed you to the fish!"

"I'm a reporter."

"And I'm a ballerina!"

"It's about your friend, Zachariah Hinckley. I need to talk to you, okay?"

Rex didn't let go. His bearded face was up close, and his breath smelled of garlic. "How did you find me?"

"Ironman Cycles, then Best Buy. A kid on a motocross told me you come here to fish." Ben lowered his hands. "I want to talk, that's all."

"Why?"

"I was at the ride yesterday. Zachariah passed us, speeding like crazy as if someone was chasing him."

"You're lying." There was less confidence in Rex's voice, but his grip remained tight, holding Ben's upper body out over the railing and the dark water.

"He was in trouble with his church, right? The Mormons?"

"Shut up!" Rex sheathed the knife, still holding on to Ben, swiveled him around, and patted him from head to toe.

"I'm not packing anything," Ben said. "Will you answer a couple of questions?"

Rex stepped back and looked around. He pulled his fishing rod from the holder and started rolling back his line.

"What are you afraid of?"

With the fishing rod in one hand and the bucket in the other, Rex jogged toward land.

Ben stayed with him. "He was your friend. Don't you care about the truth?"

"I care about staying out of other people's business."

"Your dead buddy isn't your business?"

They reached the Chevy pickup, and Rex dropped his stuff into the bed.

"Talk to me. You'll feel better."

Rex got in the driver's side and unlocked the passenger door. "Two minutes. That's it!"

"Okay." Ben sat down and shut the door. "Nice truck."

Rex turned on the engine. The vertical part of the dashboard, which normally would hold the radio and climate controls, instead had a flat piece of gray steel that covered the whole area from the glove compartment to the steering wheel. He pressed his thumb to a fittingly small pad, and after a few peeps, the steel plate clicked open and slid aside, revealing a touch-screen filled with icons. It was held in place by a solid-looking steel frame. He pressed an icon for an application, and a series of bars appeared, rising and falling like a music synchronizer. On the side was a small image of the truck with a line going through it repeatedly like a scanner. A red light began to blink in the spot representing the passenger seat.

"Fancy," Ben said. "Best Buy sells this stuff?"

"Are you recording?"

"No." Ben pulled out his iPhone. "This is the only electronic device I'm carrying and it's not recording right now."

"It's traceable. Turn it off."

Ben complied. "Traceable by whom?"

A few more applications came up, and loud music—opera, of all things.

"Great sound system."

Rex scanned the area through the windows and side mirrors. "You may not mention my name to anyone, or I'll—"

"Fish food. Got it."

"I knew Zachariah from his mission years in New York. My family hosted him for occasional dinners, gave him some leads on prospects for tracking, stuff like that. I was a couple of years younger, so we weren't close, didn't keep in touch or anything. But I ran into him one day at Ironman Cycles, so we caught up on life, family, bikes, technology, the military."

"You served too?"

"Long time ago." Rex rubbed a service ring on his index finger. "We started riding together on Saturdays, maybe once a month, nothing too formal. Neither of us rode on Sundays, so it worked out good, became a regular thing."

"Yesterday was a Sunday."

"It's a first. Zachariah never missed Sunday services with his family."

"And you?"

"I work on Sundays. It's our biggest day, lots of customers come in."

"Are you also a Mormon?"

"I'm a Jack Mormon. Do you know the phrase?"

"Someone who cheats on the rules?"

For the first time, Rex smiled. "Let's say that I like my coffee too much. An occasional smoke too."

"And Zachariah? Did he keep the rules?"

"Never saw him drink coffee, tea, or alcohol, if that's what you mean. I'd offer him a cigarette every time I lit up myself, but he wouldn't try it. Women batted their eyes at him all the time too, but he wouldn't even flirt. Drove me nuts, being single myself, you know?"

"Did he ever express doubts about his faith?"

"Look, we weren't close. Rode together some Saturdays, took breaks, had a meal on the road, nice conversations, that's all. I could tell he was under pressure. Family, eight kids, volunteering, but he kept it together. Very organized. Serious."

"In what way?"

"Bike always clean, riding boots shining, gas tank topped off." Rex fumbled with the touch screen. "He insisted on fueling up every sixty miles, like a clock. God forbid he had less than half a tank of gas."

"That's odd."

"You had to know the guy. He remained a Marine, you know?"

Ben nodded.

"Are you a veteran?"

"Football injury." Ben rubbed his shoulder. "Not fit for service."

Rex turned and measured him up and down. "You're too skinny for a football player."

"I'm intense," Ben said. "If Zachariah was such a straight arrow, what happened to him? Why did he ride on Sunday, speed up recklessly, get himself killed? It doesn't fit the description you've just given me."

"He wasn't doing well the last few weeks."

"In what way?"

"He was in some trouble."

"With whom?"

Rex shifted uncomfortably. "With the Church."

"What trouble?"

"I don't know. A disagreement."

"Really?" Ben kept an even tone as if he knew nothing. "About what?"

"He had something they wanted. They talked to his wife, put him on trial, suspended his religious status—"

"In what way?"

"He lost the right to enter the Temple. He was very upset about it. Also during Sunday services at the local ward, he had to stay in the back, not included in anything. Can you imagine? The guy has all these kids, they go to services together, and Dad has to sit in the corner like he's wet his pants."

"Sad."

Rex craned his neck, scanning the area. "Look, I don't know much more—"

"You know enough to be scared. Why?"

"They broke into his house, messed it up. Same with his car. Even his office at Veterans Affairs."

"Did he call the police?"

"File a complaint against other saints?" Rex laughed. "Disputes are resolved by local bishops or someone higher, like the stake president or an official back in Salt Lake City. Mormons don't trust the Gentile authorities."

"Still, if it was so bad, he should have sought help. The police could—"

"Even if he did, there are people inside who would make sure the interests of the Church are protected."

"Really?"

"It's a century-old strategy, ever since the US Army marched on Utah and forced the great compromise on Brigham Young— renounce polygamy and give up the dream of an independent New Zion. The LDS Church learned its lesson."

"What lesson?"

"Like the cliché—*If you can't beat them, join them.* Look around you! Mormons control huge corporations, banks, the media, even Congress."

"That's the same ugly stuff bigots say about Jews."

"Jews are nothing compared to us. Jews have no central authority, no hierarchical structure, no single strategy they must follow. Jews are individual entrepreneurs. Jews go after personal goals, their own ideas and opinions. Latter-day Saints can't do that. We're told to obey our bishop. The Mormon Church is like an army with a clear chain of command and an army of loyal soldiers. Where do you think Harry Reid and Orrin Hatch get their marching orders? Or the thousands of Mormons in key positions in the FBI, CIA, and every other branch of the government? And the White House is next!"

"How's Zachariah connected to this?" Ben watched Rex's reaction. "Was he disobedient?"

"No," Rex said. "The guy was a good Mormon. Totally."

"So why was he in trouble?"

"I don't know. Really. He never told me."

"Do you think they killed him?"

Rex held both hands up. "I didn't say that!"

"But you suspect—"

"You draw your own conclusions." He reached across and opened Ben's door. "If I were you, I'd drop the whole thing."

Ben stepped out. "What about his bike?"

"What about it?"

"You said that they broke into his house, his car, his office. But you didn't mention his bike."

"It was sitting in his garage. They pushed it over, but that's it." Rex engaged the reverse. "Good-bye!"

"One more thing. Did he ever mention a suspicious Ducati?"

For the first time, Rex's expression showed fear. He reached over, grabbed the handle, and slammed the door shut. A moment later, he was gone.

Back on his bike, Ben lingered for a moment in the empty parking lot. The rain was falling steadily now, and he looked out to the Chesapeake Bay, which merged into a gray mist of water and rain, hiding the opposite shoreline.

CHAPTER 33

Fran's office at the Maryland State Police headquarters looked out over the parking lot. Ben glanced through the window at his GS, which had attracted a few state troopers. One of them pointed at the air-cooled boxer engine and explained something to the others.

"There's nothing here about a floppy disk," Fran said, looking up from her computer screen. "They would have put it into the accident report."

"Does it say anything about the search?"

She scanned the report again. "It's all basic, routine. Here's the list of personal belongings retrieved from the body: wallet with cash, credit cards, driver's license, an ID card from the Department of Veterans Affairs, keys, sunglasses, a tube of sunscreen, and a mobile phone—basic AT&T phone service with no data, e-mails, or web surfing capacity. That's all they found on him."

"I'm telling you," Ben insisted, "that Inspector Porter pulled something from the back of the victim's pants that looked like a floppy disk."

Her finger hit a few keys on the office phone.

A male voice answered. "Community Liaison Section. Inspector Porter speaking. How may I help you, Lieutenant DeLacourt?"

"Can you come over to Hate Crimes? I have a visitor from the press who'd like a word with you."

"Sure."

When Fran hung up, Ben said, "Who said I wanted a word with that creep?"

She grinned. "Aren't you a type-A investigative reporter?"

"Don't tell him about the journal or about my meeting with Rex."

"Why not?"

"He might be involved."

"Inspector Porter? Don't be ridiculous!"

"How well do you know him?"

Fran sat back, exhaling. "He's new to Maryland, but he's got an impressive law enforcement résumé, from what I hear. Came highly recommended."

"Humor me."

She rubbed her cropped hair. "Fine. But I won't lie if he asks me, and neither should you."

Inspector Porter arrived with a friendly smile. "Mr. Teller, isn't it?"

"You remember my name." Ben shook his hand. "I'm impressed."

"This is for you, Inspector." Fran handed him the iTouch. "Teller poked around the accident site after you left and found this. You can add it to the inventory."

"Thank you," Porter said. "Did you turn it on?"

"Yes," Ben said. "Interesting music selection, if you like country. Or silly games. The battery is drained so you'll need to charge it first."

"Appreciate your dropping it off." Porter turned to leave.

"Quick question," Fran said. "Ben is following up on the accident. He was asking about an object that he saw you remove from the body."

"He's right." Porter smiled. "It's in my office. I'll be right back."

As soon as he left, Ben said, "Why did you tell him? Now he'll—"

"He's a state trooper. He won't risk his job to steal from a corpse."

"How do you know?"

"Don't be paranoid."

Porter reappeared with a brown envelope. He shook it over Fran's desk, and a DVD case fell out. It was black, with the movie title in red: *The Apprenticeship of Debbie Cravey.*

"Enticing," Ben said. "Have you watched it?"

"No one has watched it." Porter pointed to the sealed plastic wrapping. "I added it manually to the inventory in the paper file, but kept it out of the electronic records."

"Why?"

"As the ranking trooper on the scene, I had to make a decision. The deceased had a wedding ring on and looked like he could be a father." Porter rested his hand on the DVD. "Next thing, a nosey reporter would find out and put it up on the Internet. The family is suffering enough, don't you agree?"

"Isn't it part of the evidence in the case?"

Porter shrugged. "What case? It was an accident."

"It's standard procedure," Fran said, preempting Ben's next question. "We're sensitive to families' feelings, especially when there's no suspicion of a crime."

"None." Porter slipped the DVD case back into the envelope. "The traffic investigator measured the tire marks, calculated trajectories, and so on. It was a straightforward situation of lost control. No doubt about it."

"Really?" Ben met his eyes. "No doubt?"

"Recklessness, that's all. Typical for bikers, wouldn't you say?"

"In what way?"

"Taking unnecessary risks." He smiled again. "How about you, Mr. Teller? Do you take unnecessary risks?"

"Define 'necessary.'"

"That's enough," Fran said. "Thank you, Inspector."

"You're welcome." Porter turned to leave.

"Wait," Ben said. "One more thing."

"Yes?"

"How come you showed up so quickly after the crash?"

"My job is to liaise with the community, to be the face of the state police with civic organizations, churches, etc. That includes attending public events, making sure everything goes smoothly."

"Especially with reckless bikers?"

Porter took a deep breath, filling his chest, which made him look as if he stood at attention. "I take special interest in events involving my fellow veterans." He turned on his heels and left the office.

"What branch?"

"Excuse me?" His departure interrupted for the second time, Porter's veneer cracked. "Are you talking to me?"

"Your service," Ben said. "What branch of the armed forces?"

After a pause, he blurted, "US Army Police."

Only when the sound of Porter's steps died down the hallway did Fran burst out laughing. "You're such a jerk!"

"He's lying."

"Unlikely."

"Is he a Mormon?"

Fran dropped into her chair. "I don't know. There are hundreds of people working in this building. A few of them are Mormon, I assume. Some are Muslims, some are Jews, and some are dykes like me. Don't ask, don't tell, you know?"

"I ask and tell for a living."

"And I fight hate crimes for a living. I also give seminars about tolerance. Okay?"

"Point taken," Ben said. "And thanks for not telling him about the journal."

"What journal?"

"Exactly. Can I get a close look at that DVD?"

"You want to see Debbie in action?"

"Do you?"

"Ha!"

Ben laughed. "I just want to see if I can trace it to a store. They might remember Porter buying it."

"Here we go again."

"There's no way Zachariah Hinckley watched porn."

"He was a guy, wasn't he?"

"I'm a guy and I don't watch porn."

"Because you have Keera, who could beat you up if she wanted—which might not be a bad idea, actually."

"I agree. But what about this case? It could be explosive."

"Not really. Who cares if Joe Morgan got into a bath in his underwear and acted out being baptized for dead guys?"

"He's running for president!"

"And other candidates go to their churches and participate in their unique rituals, which might seem weird to outsiders. Wasn't George Washington a Freemason? And Nixon a Quaker?"

"Do you want another Nixon?"

"I don't see Morgan going bananas. It's not his style."

"Being well-groomed and earnest doesn't mean he's not harboring ugly secrets. Don't they teach in police academy that con artists are the most charming, upstanding, trust-inspiring people?"

Fran laughed. "They teach that about politicians too."

"Morgan's beyond the pale."

"Why? Everyone's entitled to a few religious illusions."

"Baptizing the nation's heroes after stealing their personal info from government computers?"

"There's no proof of that."

"How about probable cause? Aren't you supposed to investigate reasonable suspicions of a possible crime?"

"I run the Hate Crimes Section. Not the Hate-mongering Section."

"Wow!" Ben watched her for a moment. "Are you afraid?"

"I'm not afraid, but I'm not suicidal either, professionally speaking. Any investigation of candidate Joe Morgan would become national news instantly. Starting something like this requires a really solid basis. I would have to go to the top for approval before doing anything, or I'd get fired on the spot."

"Why don't you?"

"Go to the commissioner with what? With your suspicions? The journal on the iTouch, which might be complete fiction, the grumbling of a disgruntled and confused man who can't even ride his motorcycle safely?"

"And what if it's true? What if Morgan did do what Zachariah said?"

"What if? The statute of limitations has run out several times already, so we couldn't prosecute Morgan even if it's true. And according to the journal, Zachariah stole the data, not Morgan."

"Morgan only stole souls."

"*Wooooo!*" Fran made like she was scared. "The souls are angry! They're coming after Morgan!"

"It's not a joke."

"Isn't it? Do you believe sloshing around in water while chanting incantations and yelling names actually does anything to souls of dead people?"

"Of course not."

"Then nothing happened. It's meaningless."

Ben approached the window and looked out. No one stood by his motorcycle now, and the rain had resumed. "Don't you care about poor Zachariah, getting railroaded by Morgan and his saints?"

"It's a free country. He could have quit the Mormon Church."

"And lose his wife and kids?"

"You're exaggerating."

Ben leaned on her desk. "We're not talking about the Protestant Church here, or the Lutheran, or even Catholic, where an unhappy customer can leave and go worship Christ in another church down the street. Mormons live all-inclusive denominational lives. Their spiritual past, present, and future depends on serving the LDS Church in good standing. Their livelihood depends on fellow Mormons. Their children's daily activities are run by Mormon volunteers. Their underwear is holy, their diet is righteous, their family relationships are celestial, and their social circle is joyously Mormon. Every aspect of their lives is totally intertwined with other Mormons and is strictly governed by the LDS Church, its rules, and its authority. How could Zachariah Hinckley leave? The journal shows how he was trying to remain a good Mormon and do the right thing at the same time!"

"By enforcing a supposed revelation from God?"

"Mormons believe in revelations," Ben said. "A revelation for a Mormon is like an order from the police commissioner for you."

"No commissioner would order an officer to pressure Joe Morgan to make a confession that could derail his run for president."

"But it's the truth! Don't we have a moral obligation to finish what Zachariah started?"

"Why should voters be told about rituals Morgan might have conducted as part of his religious duties many years ago?" Fran waved her hand in dismissal. "Your biker dude was having a midlife crisis, manifested as a religious spat with his former bishop. Maybe he was jealous of Morgan?"

"Jealous?"

"Of Morgan's wealth, of his rise to the top, of his running for president while Zachariah remained a lowly government employee. Maybe the divine revelation was inspired by envy, and Morgan was right to blow him off, which left Zachariah depressed, causing him to ride his Harley off the cliff."

"It's a theory," Ben said, "that doesn't fly when you factor in the Ducati."

"It doesn't exist."

"And if I find it?"

"You won't. It's a ghost. And this whole baptizing stuff will never become big news and make you lots of money."

"It's not about money."

"Fame. Whatever. I'm telling you that his journal is not enough evidence to go on the air, and even if it does come out, people will see it as political smear and religious bigotry."

"I can defend my integrity. I'm an independent freelancer, and Ray will vouch for it. My job is to bring out the truth so people know about it."

"It doesn't matter. Joe Morgan has neutralized the whole Mormonism factor. People already know he's a 'Saint.' They accept his different way of worship, including the Mormon baptizing of the dead. It's a curiosity, an oddity, that's all. Voters want to know that Morgan can be an effective president—run the country, deal with Congress, fix the economy, defend America—these are the real issues voters want to know about, not his personal religious practices. Nobody cares."

"Well," Ben said, "I care."

In his office, Porter plugged Zachariah Hinckley's iTouch into a wall outlet using a universal USB cable and adaptor. He let it charge for a few minutes, turned it on, and waited for it to boot up. When it did, he unplugged it and slipped it into a glass of water. The screen twitched and several applications opened rapidly before it died.

Through the window he saw the reporter walk across to his black-and-yellow motorcycle. He put on a matching yellow riding jacket, helmet and gloves, and mounted the bike. Porter was ready with his binoculars as he rode off, and jotted down the license plate number. Signing into the Motor Vehicle Department database, it took less than a minute to obtain the address.

Using a non-police pager, he copied Ben Teller's address and sent it as a text message. The reply came seconds later:

> *Already traced him yesterday after news/photos came out.*
> *Lives w. a negro dancer/med student. Vulnerable.*

Porter smiled. It was a pleasure to work with a professional. He typed a reply:

> *U R efficient.*
> *Make him go away.*

CHAPTER 34

Ben didn't expect Palmyra Hinckley to answer the house phone herself so soon after her husband's death, but he hoped someone else would answer. Instead, there was a recorded message in a man's voice: "God's blessing upon you. This is the Hinckley residence. If you are calling about funeral arrangements, please check again later. If you wish to offer your prayers, please join us at the Silver Spring Ward today at noon. Thank you."

It was 1:10 p.m., and Ben had stopped at a Subway for a quick sandwich, which he almost finished. Dumping the rest in the trash, he got back on the GS and headed down to Rockville, taking Rt. 29 South to the new Intercounty Connector toll road—a luxury he allowed himself only due to the brief window of time he had to catch Palmyra in a prayerful and, hopefully, talkative mood.

Having seen the incredibly elaborate spires of the imposing Mormon Temple near the beltway, he assumed the local ward would congregate in a smaller version of the temple. Instead, he found himself walking up a few steps to a one-story building that could have passed for a modest office or a warehouse. There was no cross outside, only a sign that said:

The Church of JESUS CHRIST of Latter-day Saints
Silver Spring Ward

The letters for *JESUS CHRIST* were much bigger and bolder, standing out from the rest of the sign. It reminded Ben of Zachariah's description of the techniques taught at the Mormon missionary training camp about how to approach Christian prospects with a mild pitch that the *Book of Mormon* was merely another testimony of Christ.

He pushed the door and entered. The foyer was empty, and he went through another set of doors into a meeting room. It was full despite the midday hour. The men all wore short hair and formal suits, probably on lunch break from their government or business jobs. The women, however, wore colorful dresses with longish sleeves. They were mostly blond or redheaded, their hair long and pulled back in a wholesome style.

Ben walked to the back of the room, taking a seat next to an elderly couple. The man reached over and offered his hand, which Ben shook. The wife smiled and nodded in approval when Ben slipped off his yellow riding jacket and tried to tidy his hair, which was long and unruly, unlike every other man in the room. And he could do nothing about his few days of not shaving.

Up front, a teenage boy stood at a lectern and, regaining his focus, returned to reading loudly from a book. He was speaking English, but the syntax was biblical.

At two p.m. sharp, a bespectacled man stood and went to the podium. The boy stopped reading, glanced at the man, who pointed at his wristwatch, and leaned closer to the microphone to give his testimony of faith, as Ben remembered reading in Zachariah's journal: "I know that Joseph Smith is a true prophet, that the *Book of Mormon* is true, that the Church is true, and that the Gospel is true."

The men departed quickly, and the ladies lined up to hug and kiss a woman and her children, including the boy who had read from the podium.

When the room finally emptied, Ben approached. "My condolences," he said.

As upset as she was, her eyes red and puffy, Palmyra was still an attractive woman. She looked her age, and the wide hips told of having delivered the eight children who now circled her protectively. They were between six and nineteen years old, boys and girls who resembled their parents' light coloring and long limbs.

"My name is Ben Teller. I was riding with your husband yesterday."

Palmyra glanced at the yellow riding jacket he was holding. "Satan made him buy that bike. I knew it would ruin him."

One of the girls, twelve or so, began crying. An older sister hugged her.

"The bike didn't kill him," Ben said.

Palmyra looked at him, waiting.

"Do you know why he went riding yesterday?"

"What do you mean?"

"He never rode on Sundays. Why did he go yesterday?"

She looked at her kids. "My husband was…a good father…but he had problems."

"With Joe Morgan?"

She inhaled sharply. "Who are you?"

"I'm a friend of Zachariah. Maybe his only friend."

"I've never heard of you."

"I have!" It was the oldest son, by his looks. "You're the guy who reported from the accident. I saw it on the Internet!"

"Excuse me!" The bespectacled man returned to the meeting room and approached with a raised finger pointing up, either as a warning or an indication toward the heavens. "What is going on here?"

"This man is bothering Mom," the older boy said.

"Sir!" The man inserted himself between Ben and Palmyra. "I am Bishop Canaan Linder!"

"It's an honor, Bishop." Ben bowed. "I was offering my condolences to Zachariah's family. Is that forbidden?"

"This is a sacred place of prayer and love!"

"Tough love?"

"Come, dear." The bishop held Palmyra's arm. "Nora brought the car around."

Ben dropped a business card into her purse. "Your husband was a brave man. He deserves the truth to come out. Call me."

The bishop led Palmyra and her children outside, where a blue Suburban was waiting by the steps, a woman at the wheel. The Hinckley clan piled in, and they were gone.

"Bishop Linder," Ben said, "can I ask you a couple of questions?"

"I'm sorry." He locked the front doors of the ward house. "I have to get back to my office."

"You're a CPA, correct?"

He hurried to his car—a white Honda Accord that was parked in a tight spot between the wall of the meeting house and the next building.

"It must be very hard," Ben said. "Tax advice and spiritual advice require very different skills."

The bishop fumbled with his keys. "Who told you about me?"

"Zachariah said you were a good friend. How did you feel about his trial?"

"Dear Lord!"

"Losing temple privileges is very painful, isn't it?"

"I must go!" He found the key fob and unlocked the car. "I have a client waiting!"

"It's a heavy punishment for a father," Ben said. "Humiliating, don't you think?"

Bishop Linder got in, slammed the door, and locked it. But rather than drive off, he took out a phone and made a call.

Ben waved at him through the front windshield and went to his motorcycle. He pulled out his iPhone and texted Ray:

Accident yesterday developing; potential big story.
Need 2 talk 2 U. In person. ASAP.

Ray's instant reply: *Meet face-2-face? R U going low tech on me?*

Ben typed a reply: *Cut the bull. Can U meet? Or I go elsewhere.*

That got her attention: *9 a.m. 2moro @ our global HQ*

Ben laughed. The global headquarters of *NewZonLine.com* was Ray's basement in the rural part of Montgomery County, and she was the only employee. Not bad for a news site that attracted several million visitors every day.

A new e-mail popped on his iPhone. His mother was replying to his message from last night. She didn't write anything, only put in a smiley face. It made him laugh.

Next he called Keera. She was probably busy with a patient as his call immediately went to her voice mail.

He left a message. "It's me. I'm running around, getting somewhere, I think. I'll tell you later. My mom's expecting us at six. Can you make it home by five thirty? I'd rather drive together. Love you."

The rain stopped and the sun appeared between the clouds. Ben took his time getting into his jacket, helmet, and gloves. The GS was parked perpendicular to the sidewalk, which required backing up into the street, always a strain on his legs with such a tall bike. As he was about to ride off, a car appeared and blocked his way. It had an oversized *We Believe!* bumper sticker in the GOP colors and a smaller one that said: *Joe Morgan 4 America's Soul!*

The four young men were clean cut and neatly dressed. They looked like high school kids, maybe early college. He recognized at least two of them from the ward.

Ben switched off the engine, lifted the helmet's face shield, but stayed on the bike.

One of them stepped forward. "We're here to ask you to leave Sister Hinckley alone."

"Did she send you?"

He pointed at the ward house. "Sir! This is a sacred place of—"

"Of prayer and love. Yes, I know. Your CPA bishop has already advised me."

They looked at each other.

"Can you tell me about Joseph Smith?"

"He was a true prophet of God," one of them said.

The leader hushed him with a hand and addressed Ben. "Sir, we're asking you politely. Please leave the Hinckley family alone. They are grieving!"

"Are you a missionary?"

He nodded.

"Doing your mission in Rockville, Maryland, must be a real treat, compared to Iraq or Afghanistan, right?"

"Sir, we're not looking for trouble. Please stop disturbing—"

"I heard you. Anything else?"

He shook his head.

"Then move out of my way." Ben turned on the engine.

"Sir!" He held up his finger, resembling Bishop Linder. "I'd like an answer. Are you going to leave them alone?"

Ben gripped the accelerator and revved the engine.

"I demand an answer!"

"Look." Ben pointed at the guy's neck. "Your holy underwear is showing."

His young face became red. He signaled the others and they turned to leave, but suddenly he turned and kicked the front wheel of the motorcycle. It was a strong enough kick to cause the GS to tip sideways. Ben struggled to keep it up, but all he managed to do was slow the fall as the bike dropped on its side.

Ben expected the four missionaries to jump into their car and escape, but they didn't. Instead, they circled the GS, trying to figure out how to lift it up. Ben pointed at the rear rack and grabbed the handlebar himself.

When the GS was back up, Ben put down the kickstand and looked for damage. There was none.

The one who had kicked the bike held both hands up. "Please forgive me. I didn't mean to cause harm."

"Go away before I cause you harm." Ben got back on the GS and rode off.

CHAPTER 35

"What's this, Mom?" Ben had just entered his mother's small apartment and was helping Keera out of her coat when he saw the unlit candles, wine bottle, and braided challah bread on the dinner table. "Why are we celebrating the Sabbath in the middle of the week?"

"Do you ever come here on a Friday night?" His mother kissed him and Keera.

"You know we can't," Ben said. "Keera works Friday nights."

"I'm sorry, Mrs. Teller," Keera said.

"Don't be silly, sweetheart." She held Keera's hands and looked her up and down—mostly up as Keera was a foot taller. "You look wonderful! But it wouldn't be the end of the world if you put on a few pounds, yes?"

Ben sighed, but Keera laughed and said, "I'll try."

They sat at the table.

Mrs. Teller lit the candles with matches, and Keera chanted the Hebrew blessing in her traditional *Falash Mura* tune, unique to the Jews of Ethiopia.

The two of them covered their eyes, and Keera repeated after her the Hebrew words. Ben then recited the blessing over the wine and bread.

"Wonderful," Mrs. Teller said. "I made matzo ball soup from scratch, with chicken legs, just the way you love it."

"This is a message," Ben explained to Keera, gesturing at the candles, bread, and wine. "She's signaling that you're the chosen one, and here's how you do a Jewish dinner on Friday night, even if it's Monday."

His mother carried the soup bowls on a tray. "Is it a sin to encourage my only son, who's dating a gorgeous med school student, to marry her before someone else—with more brains in his head!—steals her from you?"

Keera pretended to concentrate on the soup, but eventually she met Ben's eyes and they burst out laughing.

Ben wiped his lips and chin with a napkin. "Sorry, Mom."

"What's so funny?" She slurped a spoonful of hot soup. "Life is not only about fun and games. Nothing wrong with taking responsibility for the people you love."

"It's a code," Ben said. "She wants grandkids."

"Is that also a sin? God forbid that my son should grow up a little, find a real job, and support you so you don't have to work on Friday nights."

"Mom!"

"He works pretty hard," Keera said.

"Taking pictures?" Mrs. Teller collected the bowls. "I read an article in *Modern Women* magazine by a very famous psychology professor about how some people prefer photographs to actual life. They prefer to be observers rather than participants. Isn't it interesting?"

"Fascinating." Ben pulled his camera from the bag and snapped a few photos of his mother and Keera.

"You see?" Mrs. Teller went to the kitchen. "What did I tell you?"

Keera laughed. "Was he better as a boy?"

Speaking from the kitchen, Mrs. Teller said, "He wasn't easy, I can tell you that. Especially in the years after...well, growing up without a father...he kept testing me. Every other day there was a note from a teacher about a schoolyard scuffle or a call from another mother about one of Ben's pranks."

He rolled his eyes.

"And I had to work to supplement the little allowance we received from the navy. I always worked in bookstores so that I could bring Ben with me. Even before he knew how to read, he'd sit on the floor and look through one book after another, searching for pictures. I think that's when he fell in love with photography."

Keera helped her bring the serving dishes to the table. "And now, as an adult, is he more like his father?"

"Oh, that's a tough one." Mrs. Teller considered the question. "They're different. My husband, of blessed memory, was more matured. He had to be, with all the responsibility for the men under his command."

"It must have been hard, even before you lost him." Keera hesitated. "I mean, caring for a child while your husband was so far away."

"But there was pride." Mrs. Teller took a deep breath. "I was so proud of him! It's different for young people today. You assume that all politicians lie, that all wars are wrong, that it's all about money. You're cynical, and maybe you're right. Wars make some businessmen very rich. But we were raised by the greatest generation, the men and women who fought the Nazis. We were raised to serve our country. We believed Bush and Powell and Schwarzkopf when they said that Saddam must be kicked out of Kuwait, that it was a matter of liberty and international law."

"And now?"

"Now?" She gestured vaguely. "Who knows? Did my husband die for freedom or for Exxon and Shell and their rich CEOs?"

"You don't really believe that," Ben said. "The first Gulf War was a just war. No despot would ever again invade another country after they saw what happened to Saddam in Kuwait in ninety-one."

Mrs. Teller caressed his cheek. "Just like your father, an idealist, trying to save the world, yes?"

"That's right, Mom. Every day."

"Eat, children," she said, "before the food gets cold."

Ben forked a piece of meat and put it on Keera's plate. "Eat! Eat! There are children starving in Ethiopia!"

PART III:

The Editor

CHAPTER 36

Ray ran NewZonLine.com from her late grandparents' farm in northwest Montgomery County. A row of birch trees blocked the view from the country road, but up close there were visible signs that this was more than just another rural property. Three satellite dishes sat on the roof of the main house, which was covered with solar panels. An industrial-sized diesel-operated generator sat on a concrete pad next to an shed, where Ray's pair of customized vans were parked. A video camera followed Ben as he walked up the steps to the front porch. The lock on the door clicked open and he entered small foyer. Only when the door behind him clicked locked, a second door unlocked, allowing him inside. There were two elevators. Ben skipped both of them and took the steps down to the basement.

Ray's obsession with redundancy manifested again in the multiple plasma screens that covered the basement walls. Ray was sitting at a bank of keyboards, her back to a line of computer servers that hummed and emitted heat.

"Good morning," Ben said.

"Here's the man!" She beckoned him to a seat and pointed at a monitor. "Look at this rating chart. You're still hot, baby."

The chart tracked the total visitor traffic on the NewZonLine. com website and rated each story based on the number of hits by visitors who stayed on the story for more than eight seconds, which was the minimum time it took for an Internet-savvy person to absorb a headline, a photo, and the essence of one paragraph of text. Ben's last news flash from the Camp David Scenic Overlook was at the second spot, right behind a report about an alleged shooting at the president's reelection campaign office in Waterloo, Texas.

"It's yesterday's news," Ben said.

"It's the dead body." She manipulated a mouse to bring the news piece onto another screen. "They love it. Do you?"

Ben stared at the photo. It was the one showing Zachariah Hinckley just before his death, lying on the ground at the bottom of the precipice, looking up at Ben. But his face was no longer blurred as in the photo Ben had sent to Ray yesterday. Rather, Zachariah's face was clear and easily identifiable. "Take it down," Ben said. "It's not the photo I sold you."

"Same one," Ray said. "And, not to be too lawyerly, but our standard agreement says that we can edit and alter the material we buy from you to improve its accessibility to readers. And this," she pointed at the chart, "proves my point. People are dying to see someone else dying—it's a magnet!"

"Where did you get his face?"

"My genius programmer unscrambled it."

"The Romanian?"

"She's in Latvia, actually." Ray laughed. "Talk about globalization. I've never spoken to her, but she's a wiz with images and as cheap as a wild goat."

"How did she do it?"

"Something about the original algorithm staying with the file. You can ask her." Ray scribbled an e-mail address on a piece of paper. "But be warned—she'll ask you to sponsor her for a green card."

Ben glanced at the piece of paper and dropped it on the desk. "I don't care about the software. It's the principle."

Ray maneuvered her electric wheelchair to another keyboard and pulled up a spreadsheet on one of the screens. "Here's your account. I threw in another two-fifty. It's only fair."

"I don't want the money." He pointed at the photo. "This man served in the Marine Corps and was injured so you can sit here safely and play God."

"Are you turning Republican on me?"

"I'm an Independent. And you better take down the photo, or we're done doing business."

"I thought we're just starting. What's with all the secrecy?"

Ben sat down and told her about Zachariah's journal, the meeting with Rex, and what happened at the Silver Spring Ward with Palmyra, the bishop, and the young missionaries.

Ray listened intently, glancing at the screens every few seconds, but not interrupting. When Ben was done, she leaned back in her chair. "It's interesting, but where's the story? You don't have evidence of anything."

"I have the journal."

"A bunch of text on your own iPhone? Who said you didn't write it yourself?"

"I can find evidence."

"The vanishing Ducati? The floppy disk that never was?"

"They're both traceable," Ben said. "But I can't do it on spec. It'll take money. I need to set up surveillance on Porter, Bishop Linder, Palmyra, maybe pay off someone inside the LDS Church to steal copies of their computer data. There must be a record of Morgan being baptized as proxy for these heroes."

"Pay off someone on the inside? What are you smoking? Those Mormons are more straight-laced than my grandma."

"Give me some credit. There's meat to this story, and I can dig it out of the freezer."

"And then what? Even if you have proof that Joe Mormon was baptized on behalf of a bunch of Medal of Honor winners, then what?"

"The guy's running for president!"

"So? He's a religious man, and that's what they practice. Nobody wants to know the details. There's no juice in a story about some Mormons in a bath, chanting prayers. It's not interesting, and frankly, there's something endearing about it. I mean, they're trying to save the lost souls of American heroes. Even if you don't believe in it, you can see the good intentions behind it."

"What about stealing the data from the Department of Veterans Affairs?"

"Zachariah Hinckley stole it fifteen years ago. Now he's dead. Case closed."

"Not if I manage to retrieve that floppy disk from Porter with Morgan's own handwriting on it."

"In your dreams. If it ever existed, which is questionable, it's been destroyed already."

"And what about Zachariah's death? This thing could explode into a full-fledged murder investigation!"

"What murder? You're speculating." Ray turned the wheelchair halfway to face another computer, which had just beeped. "Hey, look at this baby!"

An incoming e-mail brought a photo of a three-car accident in Olney. Two of the drivers were hitting each other. With a few key strokes, Ray bought the photo and published it under the tagline: *Fender-bender turns into bloody fistfight.* Within seconds, the piece rose into the *Top-50* news list.

Another ping signaled a new e-mail.

"I have to return to work," Ray said. "The people are hungry."

"For the next pound of flesh?"

"Violence sells."

"Obviously," Ben said. "Will you help me? I'll give you exclusive on the story."

"Not interested." She was already working on her keyboard.

"Do you want me to start doing business with the competition?"

"Nobody will front you money for this ghost hunt."

"Don't be so sure."

"Forget the Mormons." Ray turned to face him. "I'm saying this as your friend, not just as your publisher. Nothing good will come from it. Chasing Morgan for his church work smacks of religious persecution. A witch hunt. It's un-American."

"It's my job."

"You're doing well selling accident photos. Or, better yet, find me a juicy murder-suicide. That would be worth a pile of cash!"

Ben got up to leave. "Is it political? Do you support Joe Morgan? Is that it?"

Ray laughed. "Get me photos of Joe Mormon screwing an altar boy behind his wife's back, and I'll publish it in a second. But this baptizing stuff isn't sexy. It won't excite readers."

"That's the only criteria?"

"Ride safely, buddy. And say hello to your better half."

"You do the same." Ben gestured at the Latvian's e-mail.

"I'm waiting for Keera's brother."

"She's an only child."

"Still poling at Wisteria's Secret?"

"Until the spring," Ben said, halfway up the stairs. "She's graduating in May, starting residency at Johns Hopkins."

"Better marry her before she becomes a doctor and realizes you're an inadequate match."

"Ha!" Ben walked up the stairs.

"You could become her househusband." Ray's voice came from the intercom by the front door. "Show her you can cook, clean, wash, change the kids' diapers. It's pretty acceptable these days."

"Thanks for the advice."

"Don't mention it."

Outside Ray's house, next to the driveway, a stream ran down a shallow crevice. The banks were lined with frost where the sun couldn't reach. Ben watched the dark water running. It was still early, and he zipped up his riding jacket to keep warm. The conversation had not gone the way he had hoped, and Ray's decisive rejection to the story was unsettling.

The iPhone vibrated. A text message from an undisclosed number. He opened it.

Mr. Teller, Please meet me today at the site of the accident. I can be there at noon. No photos or recordings please. God's blessings. Palmyra Hinckley.

It was half past ten a.m. and Ben realized he could easily make it to the Camp David Scenic Overlook on time. He typed a one-word reply: *Confirmed.*

CHAPTER 37

Ben rode down Main Street in Thurmont. Being the only motorcycle in sight, it was a very different experience compared to riding with hundreds of others on Sunday. A few flags still hung from poles, but the barriers and cheering crowd were gone, and everything else was back to normal—with the exception of election signs and stickers all over town.

He made the turn onto the winding road. Posted speed limit was 45 mph. A second sign warned against littering—$250 fine!—and a third warned of deer crossing the road.

Riding through the hills, now completely alone, he began to relax. The road did not connect to another town, and the weekend traffic of sightseers was gone. It allowed him to go faster, take the turns with a deeper leaning, and accelerate with full throttle. It made him smile.

A light-blue Chevy Suburban was parked at the Camp David Scenic Overlook. As Ben was dismounting his bike, Palmyra Hinckley emerged from the Suburban, accompanied by an elderly man in a long winter coat and silver-rimmed glasses.

"Hi." She had been crying, but her posture wasn't bent under the sorrow. She shook Ben's hand firmly. "Let me introduce Dr. Neibauer. He's been a great help to us."

Ben shook the man's hand as well. "Family physician?"

"I'm a psychiatrist," Dr. Neibauer said. "Zachariah was my patient."

Palmyra walked to the edge and looked down. Dr. Neibauer put his arm on her shoulder. Ben waited.

After a few minutes, Palmyra said, "I wanted to see…where Zachariah died."

"That rock," Ben pointed, "over there, that's where he was lying when—"

"When you took his photo?" She said it with bitterness. "Do you think God approves of such disgrace?"

Dr. Neibauer patted her arm.

"It's wrong! A dying man deserves respect! And privacy!"

Ben pulled out his iPhone, found the first e-mail he had sent Ray from the accident site, and opened the photo attachment. "This is the photo I sent to my editor. You can see that I blurred Zachariah's face."

Palmyra looked at it. "So…how?"

"Technology," Ben said. "They removed the blurring and published it." He pulled up the Internet, found NewZonLine. com, and scrolled down the news headlines to the accident report. "I told my editor this morning to take down the photo, or I'll never do business with her again."

"Thank you. Please forgive me for accusing you unjustly. I've never imagined being in such a situation. A scandal. We're good people." She wiped tears. "How could all this happen to us?"

"Perhaps," Dr. Neibauer said, "it would be helpful for you to hear Mr. Teller describe the events of Sunday."

She nodded.

Ben told them about the festive atmosphere at the launching area, passing through Thurmont with the annual Marine Corps Veterans' Ride, the column of motorcycles on the winding hilly roads, the stars-and-stripes Harley passing everyone at high speed, the crash site, and the state police investigation, which concluded that the accident was the result of reckless driving. "But I don't believe it," he said. "Your husband was in trouble, wasn't he?"

"It's personal," she said. "Please respect our privacy and not publish anything untoward. I believe that the good Lord will reward your consideration."

Ben nodded. The sound of a passing car drew his attention—a beige pickup truck with dark windows that drove by quickly, disappearing around the curve.

"My husband was a sick man," she said. "He came back from Kuwait almost twenty years ago completely broken—in body and in spirit. The navy did what they could, with God's help, and Zachariah was back on his feet. Our community helped us build a life together. A good life. We worked hard, raised children, and did our best to honor the Lord and earn the right for exaltation in the afterlife. Have you read the *Book of Mormon*, dear?"

"Not yet." Ben almost laughed, but held it in.

"You should," she said. "It will change your life. And your afterlife too."

"I'll give it a try, now that I hear how helpful it can be. Did Zachariah feel the same?"

"Oh, yes!" Her face brightened up. "We studied it together every Monday evening—we call it Family Home Night, when everyone stays home to study the holy scriptures and sing hymns. It's the most wonderful custom of our faith. Do you have a family?"

"Only my mother. And my girlfriend. We live together."

"Without marriage?" Palmyra swallowed hard. "This is not what the Lord expects of his children."

Dr. Neibauer cleared his throat. "We were discussing Zachariah."

"Yes, I'm sorry." She took a deep breath. "I was just saying how we loved the *Book of Mormon* so much, especially Zachariah. My husband can...could...recite whole paragraphs from memory. And he could sing beautifully also, which the children loved."

Ben nodded sympathetically. "But he became sick again."

Palmyra was taken aback. "Sick?"

"Mentally," Dr. Neibauer said. "Post-traumatic stress disorder. It wasn't his fault, you understand? The trauma of the war, in particular the attack that killed his friends and badly wounded him in ninety-one, left him with irreparable brain damage."

"He had brain injury?"

"There were no bullets or shrapnel lodged in his head. But our brains are much more sensitive than our legs or even internal organs. New research shows that nearby explosions, the severe pounding of high pressure, causes tiny injuries inside the brain matter which cannot be detected in medical tests or magnetic resonance scans, but that leave permanent injuries nevertheless, resulting in long-term mental disease and emotional instability. That's what happened to Zachariah."

"I understand you," Ben said. "You're saying that Zachariah was crazy, correct?"

Dr. Neibauer took off his glasses. "The word 'crazy' is not a medical term. He was mentally ill, yes."

"But he functioned well for years. What triggered his recent illness?"

"He was never completely fine," Palmyra said. "He always had issues. Difficulties."

"Such as?"

"Typical symptoms," Dr. Neibauer answered for her. "Nightmares, mood swings, lack of interest in his work."

"That's right," she said. "Life for him was, in a way, harder than for others. I used to blame myself, and he always told me not to, that it was his problem." Her voice cracked. "He had such a good heart!"

"Mental illness," Dr. Neibauer said, "is not a static condition. Patients go through ups and downs, like the economy. As a psychiatrist, I work very hard to maintain the patients' balance through therapy and medication. Do you understand?"

"Yes," Ben said. "But with Zachariah, you failed?"

"Not exactly." He put his glasses back on. "Zachariah was a veteran. His healthcare was provided by the Veterans Administration system."

"You don't work for the VA?"

He glanced at Palmyra before answering. "I'm in private practice. My involvement with Zachariah was as a friend of the family."

"You worship together?"

Dr. Neibauer nodded. "Our church encourages brotherly assistance to fellow saints in times of need. We stand together before God, you understand?"

"Were you called in because of his dispute with Joe Morgan?"

Dr. Neibauer removed his glasses again. "What do you mean?"

"You know what I mean. Let's say that Zachariah told me everything from his point of view. I'm here to hear yours."

He pointed at Ben with the glasses. "Young man, let me explain something. Mental illness often masquerades itself behind a facade of normalcy, coherence, even eloquence. But as a journalist, you should be able to distinguish facts from fantasies."

"Mrs. Hinckley," Ben turned to Palmyra, "did your husband suffer from hallucinations?"

She looked at the psychiatrist, her lips trembling.

"Hallucinating," Dr. Neibauer said, "is usually drug induced. Zachariah was a saint. He didn't even touch alcohol, let along drugs. His behavioral issues were rooted in chemical imbalance due to PTSD. He was a very ill man."

"So he invented the whole thing?"

"Insane people rationalize their behavior to justify aggression and unreasonable demands. But often what you hear is nothing but grandiosity and paranoia. Zachariah Hinckley was a very sick man, I assure you."

"Wasn't he too sick to stand trial before church officials?"

Palmyra groaned, turned, and walked toward the Suburban.

Shaking his head, Dr. Neibauer said, "These are confidential church matters. Who told you about—"

"I'd like to know your professional opinion," Ben said. "Wasn't Zachariah too sick to stand trial?"

"It wasn't a real trial!" The psychiatrist struggled to control his rising voice. "It was a curative effort! An attempt to confront him with reality! Shake him up!"

"Was it your idea?"

"Yes! I recommended it! Brother Zachariah needed to face the consequences of his belligerence!"

"Belligerence? Or illness?"

"Both! That's why forcing a patient to suffer for his actions—"

"Shock therapy?"

"Exactly!" The psychiatrist rubbed his hands. "By making him experience the social degradation, familial humiliation, and ecumenical castigation, for a faithful saint like Brother Zachariah, it would be a most effective form of mental conditioning."

"What's that?"

"The creation of a mental association between bad behavior and painful consequences."

"Like mice with cheese and electric shock?"

"That's the concept. Yes."

"Did you succeed? Did punishing Zachariah cause him to form a mental association between pain and pressuring Joe Morgan?"

The psychiatrist peered at Ben as if trying to diagnose his mental illness.

"Really, I'd like to know. Was the shock therapy successful?"

"Obviously not." Dr. Neibauer waved his glasses at the overlook and the precipice below them. "In my line of work, a patient's suicide means total failure. It's our worst professional hazard."

"Do you feel guilty?"

The psychiatrist looked at Palmyra, who stood by the open door of the Suburban, wiping her eyes with a tissue. "Our faith provides great comfort. We know that after this mortal life, there is a wonderful future for us with our heavenly father, where we will unite with our family and live forever in His blessed presence."

They joined Palmyra. She used another tissue to blow her nose and dropped it in a small plastic bin that sat on the floor between the front seats, overflowing with trash. Ben glimpsed the interior of the car, which was tidy yet aged.

"Thank you for meeting with us," Palmyra said. "Please respect my husband's right to rest in peace."

"Respecting his wishes," Ben said, "should come first, if we want him to have peace. Don't you agree?"

"I'd like to pray for him now." Palmyra walked toward the edge.

"One last thing," Ben said.

She turned. "Yes?"

"You didn't tell me what triggered the last crisis." Ben smiled to dull the edge of his prying while shifting so that he stood between her and Dr. Neibauer.

"He was angry with me," Palmyra said.

"Why?" Ben stepped closer to her.

"I went through his stuff to find what he was talking about."

"The floppy disk?"

She nodded. "An old-fashioned thing. About this size." She formed a square with her two fingers and thumbs.

"Was anything written on the label"

"Maybe. I'm not sure."

"What was on the disk itself, the memory?"

"I'm not good with computers."

"Go on," Ben said, continuously shifting to block the psychiatrist's access to Palmyra, who clearly didn't want to lie.

"I tried it in the computer, but it didn't work."

This was shocking news, but Ben kept his voice even. "You found a floppy disk, put it into disk drive, but the data didn't open on the screen?"

"And it froze the computer, so I had to tell him." Tears flowed down Palmyra's face. "He was very upset. We argued, and he stormed out. The whole house shook from the engine of his cursed motorcycle. I hated that thing! It's evil!"

"Now, now, calm down." Dr. Neibauer got around Ben and gripped Palmyra's arm. "Let us pray now."

"Where is it?" Ben followed them back toward the edge of the overlook. "Can you give me that floppy disk?"

"I cut it to pieces," she said. "Tiny little pieces. Flushed them all down the toilet. Good riddance!"

Ben watched the psychiatrist and the widow stand at the edge and pray, their eyes on the rocks below, where her husband had died. Was she lying about the floppy disk? She seemed to be telling the truth. But what if Porter had pulled a floppy disk from Zachariah's body on Sunday, and not a porn DVD as he had claimed? Why had Zachariah kept two floppy disks?

There was no point in asking her more questions. Dr. Neibauer was intent on ending the session. Ben turned back and noticed that the Suburban door was still open. He went over, leaned through the open door, and turned over the trash bin on the passenger seat. He fingered through the litter—moist tissues, candy wrappings, used eyeliner, cotton pads, crumpled mail envelopes, supermarket coupons, a broken pencil, and a clump of light-colored hair. He glanced over his shoulder. Palmyra was still praying, but the psychiatrist was looking at the view, perhaps trying to pinpoint the roofs of the rustic buildings of the presidential retreat at Camp David.

Stuffing everything back in the trash can as quickly as he could, Ben felt a sharp edge scrape against his fingers. It was a laminated card, cut in half. He rummaged through the pile again and found the second half, but before he could examine it, Dr. Neibauer's voice startled him.

"Mr. Teller! What are you doing?"

Ben shoved the pieces in his pocket, stuffed everything back in the bin, and turned to see the psychiatrist walking toward him. "Looks new," Ben said. "Incredible condition for such an old vehicle!"

Dr. Neibauer reached him and glanced into the Suburban before shutting the door. "We believe in raising large families, which requires large cars, but necessitates frugality. You understand?"

"I do," Ben said. "What I don't understand is how a good family man like Zachariah Hinckley could be driven to this." He pointed at the overlook, where Palmyra was still standing in prayer. "And don't try to sell me the PTSD or microscopic brain injuries, because I'm not buying."

The psychiatrist pursed his lips. "Pathological obsession, Mr. Teller, could be a manifestation of mental illness. In some cases, it could be fatal."

"Same with pathological lying, Doctor."

CHAPTER 38

Ben watched them drive off. He understood the message Dr. Neibauer came to deliver, but it only fueled his determination to uncover the truth. He took the pieces of the laminated card from his pocket and held the two together. It had Zachariah's name and photo on it and the signatures of Bishop Linder and another man whose title was *Stake President.* A quick Internet search on his iPhone led Ben to an image of a similar Temple Recommend Card.

Reading more about it on a Mormon website, he learned that this was basically an admission card to a Mormon temple that was issued by the LDS Church only to members in good standing, certified by their ward's lay bishop and the regional president on an annual basis. While all members and Gentile guests were welcome for services in any local ward, the temples of the Mormon Church were only accessible to saints holding a Temple Recommend Card.

Those qualified saints entered the temples not for regular prayers, which took place in the local Mormon wards, but to participate in elaborate rituals and ceremonies, including marriages, sealing of families together for eternity, baptizing, endowments for the dead, and other secret procedures called "Ordinances" involving washing and anointing of various body parts and a reenactment of the multiple levels of the afterlife heavenly world.

The Temple Recommend Card and the participation in temple rituals were honors bestowed only to saints who continuously observed the Mormon rules, participated in ward activities, obeyed the church authorities, and sent 10 percent of their income to the LDS headquarters in Salt Lake City. The loss of a Temple Recommend could be the result of punishment, such as "Disfellowshipment," which was like suspension for a period of time with attached conditions for reinstatement, or "Excommunication," which was a permanent removal from the LDS Church and often resulted in total banishment by all relatives and friends who remained in the church.

Ben assumed that the Temple Recommend Card had been cut in half due to Zachariah's trial and punishment by the LDS authorities. Holding the pieces in his hand, Ben went to the edge of the overlook and looked down to where Zachariah died. Had this been an act of desperation, an escape from unbearable pain? Had Zachariah Hinckley killed himself after the rest of his world had collapsed? Dr. Neibauer had pushed too hard to convince Ben of this theory, which had the opposite effect, convincing Ben that it wasn't the truth.

Looking again at the Internet article on his iPhone, Ben clicked on a highlighted term: *baptizing the dead.* It linked to an article about an ongoing dispute regarding the Mormon Church's efforts to identify and baptize Jewish victims of the Holocaust. The article mentioned a DC lawyer named Larry Ginsburg, who had represented Jewish organizations in the dispute. A click on his name linked Ben to his biographical page on the law firm's website.

Ben called the phone number.

A secretary answered, but indicated that Mr. Ginsburg was on a conference call and could not be interrupted. She took Ben's name and phone number.

As he turned to head back to his motorcycle, something caught Ben's attention. About halfway down the cliff, over to the side, a leafless bush had a piece of paper stuck in it. There was lettering on it in black and red, but it was too far to read. At first he thought it was part of a cigarette pack, tossed away by a careless visitor, but it didn't resemble any of the brand designs.

Aiming the Canon, he zoomed in on the paper. He could read the word "Radio," but the way the paper was entangled with the shrubbery made it impossible to identify further information. Ben hesitated. He could try climbing straight down the cliff, but it would probably be easier to climb from the bottom up. Strapping the camera bag to his back, he headed for the footpath that went around the cliff all the way to the bottom.

Indeed, it was easier to climb up the cliff—as long as he didn't look down. It wasn't a straight-up rock, but rather a very steep patchwork of granite boulders, loose soil, and shrubbery that was bare from the early winter cold. He found footholds and small crevices for his fingers, carefully making his way on a zigzag trajectory upward.

His iPhone rang.

Leaning forward, his cheek pressed to a chilly rock, Ben managed to pull it from his pocket and look at the screen. It was Keera.

He answered, putting it on speaker. "Can't talk right now. You okay?"

"I'm fine," she said. "Where are you?"

"Long story." He felt his right foot slipping off its hold. "I'll call you later."

"Is this about the Mormons? Please tell me it's not!"

His foot slipped off. He grabbed the phone between his teeth and managed to grip a rock ledge before falling off.

"Ben? Are you there?"

He tried to speak, but the sounds were mere growling.

"What's going on?"

Unable to find solid footing by feeling with the toe of his shoe, he pulled up with his hands, now both feet in the air, and lifted himself over a boulder, turning at the same time so that his bottom rested on the shallow rock shelf. He was panting hard, which must have sounded terrible on the phone.

"Ben! What're you doing?"

Finally he could take the phone out of his mouth. "Don't worry. I'm not having sex."

That made her laugh. "The thought never occurred to me, despite all that huffing and puffing."

"I'm searching the accident site again."

"Anything new?"

"It's still kind of up in the air." He glanced upward at his target. "Nothing to worry about. I'll see you at home. We'll have Mom's leftovers."

The rest of the way was as treacherous, but he took his time and made sure he had solid footing before reaching into the bush and pulling out the piece of paper—or rather, a piece of thin cardboard from a Radio Shack package that had originally been bigger than a pack of cigarettes, but not by much. The brand was 3M.

High Density Floppy Disks
5-Pack – 1.2 MB – 5.25"
Made in Mesa, AZ. 1994.

Immediately questions flooded his mind. Had this piece of packaging fallen off Zachariah's Harley as it fell over? Ben glanced up toward the overlook, maybe three stories above him, and imagined the stars-and-stripes Harley Davidson tumbling through the air, separating from Zachariah, and the impact as the bike and its rider hit the ground hard, an instant of devastating destruction for both. Had this piece of cardboard been in Zachariah's pocket? Or somewhere on the Harley? How had it separated and flown up into the shrubbery on the cliff?

He felt the cardboard, examining its condition. It was a bit wet, but not destroyed as it would have been after weeks or months outside, exposed to the elements. Two days was feasible, only slight discoloring and dampness, enough to wipe any fingerprints and clear away any threads of cloth or hair. No lab test would prove that the floppy disk packaging came from Zachariah, but what was the likelihood that someone else had tossed this over the side in the past few days? No one had used floppy disks in years, at least since the late nineties. Statistically, there was little doubt that this Radio Shack package of floppy disks had come from Zachariah.

Had it flown off the bike or the body after the accident? Ben remembered a slight breeze on Sunday. Or had Zachariah taken it out before the accident and thrown it away just as it happened? Or immediately afterward, as he lay dying at the bottom?

Ben folded the thin cardboard and put it in his pocket. Were there five floppy disks out there? That would explain how Porter had found one, and Palmyra found another. If neither of those two floppy disks was the real one, then three more were out there, hidden by Zachariah, and only one of them carried the data and Joe Morgan's incriminating handwritten note.

Looking down at the spot where Zachariah had taken his last breath, Ben quickly shut his eyes against the onslaught of dizziness. The dead Marine veteran had either been a meticulous planner or a troublemaker in the grips of a nervous breakdown. Whatever the case may be, Ben couldn't stop this investigation, which was turning into a treasure hunt.

He was holding on to rocks and shrubbery halfway up a cliff. It was time to move on, and the only way was up. He tightened the shoulder straps of the camera bag and resumed climbing.

The climb proceeded well, which gave him a growing sense of confidence. It also helped that the angle moderated by a few degrees, a minor difference to the eye, but a tangible advantage for a climber hanging on by his hands and the tips of his riding boots.

The edge at the top was enforced with concrete, forming a long beam across, which prevented erosion of the overlook's edge. The concrete beam stuck outward a bit, and Ben had to plan the last bit of climbing so that he reached a point where there was enough support for his boots in order to allow his hands a good grip on the outer lip of the concrete beam.

It worked well, and he was able to reach up with one hand, then the other. Testing that he could hold his weight, he started to pull up, his feet dangling in the air.

And just as his head cleared the concrete beam, he saw the toe of a white boot fly at him, kicking him square in the forehead.

CHAPTER 39

Getting kicked in the head, even with both feet on solid ground and a football helmet on, would be dangerous, but a boot to the head over a hillside seven or eight stories high was surely fatal. That was the quick realization that flashed through Ben's consciousness. As the impact threw him backward, he caught a glimpse of a white figure at the edge of the overlook above.

The rest of his body followed his head, rolling over backward. He began to slide down the precipice, head first, back to the rocks, when the camera bag hit a protruding rock, broke the downward motion for a second, and twisted him around.

Facing the hillside again, Ben tried to grab a hold of the rocks or shrubbery, but he slid down again and dropped through a straight-down section, hitting another rock ledge, this time with his knees. He grasped a bush growing out of a crack. Its roots tore out under Ben's weight, but it gave him a brief reprieve, enough for his vision to focus and grab another bush, which also tore out. He slid down some more, shoved his fingers into a chink, felt his hand lose skin, but held on until the toe of his boot found a nook.

Finally he was stationary, his body pressed against the face of the rocks. The pain in his head was dull, his breathing shallow and rapid, and his mind only now beginning to digest that he had just been the subject of an assassination attempt.

Craning his head, careful not to lose his balance, Ben tried to see if his attacker was still up there. But the cliff was uneven, and the spot where his fall had been interrupted was slightly in, hidden from view by anyone standing at the edge of the overlook above.

He had to make a decision. The method of the attack—a kick in the forehead—was intended to make it look like an accident. It was unlikely that the attacker would try to shoot him from above. But risking another climb up was out of the question. He might not be so lucky a second time.

After a few minutes of waiting, he started moving sideways like a crab. He had about a third of a football field to reach a more moderate incline, where the vegetation was thicker. Once there, he picked up speed, reaching the footpath without further incident. From there, he ran uphill. It had been about six minutes since the attack, but if the Ghost had assumed that Ben was dead, he might have taken his time searching the GS before leaving, unwittingly giving Ben a chance to snap a photo, hopefully getting a clear shot of the Ducati license plate.

At the last hairpin turn up the path, Ben heard the telltale sound of an engine from above. His ear was attuned to motorcycle sounds, and this motor sputtered at low RPM, rising to a high pitch as the rider revved it up.

Ducati!

He pulled out the camera, keeping up the pace, and got it ready.

The motorcycle engine sound pitched high. It was accelerating!

As he cleared the path, camera held upfront, finger on the shutter, a white Ducati was making a sharp turn out of the parking area and onto the road, speeding off with its engine practically screaming. Ben held down his finger and snapped a series of photos, but he already knew that none of them would show the license plate due to the angle.

Instead of slowing down, Ben kept running, making it to the GS just as the Ducati's sound faded downhill.

The top box on the rear rack had been pried open and searched. His helmet was on the ground next to the front wheel, but Ben didn't stop to worry about it. He never left anything worth stealing in the box, other than the helmet. He slipped it on, shoved the camera in his backpack, dug his keys out of his pocket, and started the GS while mounting it. A few seconds later, he was accelerating across the parking lot.

About ten miles of mountainous road separated the Camp David Scenic Overlook from the two-lane road that connected Thurmont with I-70. The Ducati was lighter and more agile than the top-heavy BMW GS, enabling it to run downhill through the twists and turns at a higher speed. Once the Ducati reached the intersection, there would be no way to know which way it went.

Ben operated the bike with well-practiced motions despite a pounding headache. He was still panting from the extreme physical effort, and his arms and legs hurt as he shifted gears and executed deep turns at high speed.

On the plus side, the Ghost likely assumed that Ben was dead at the bottom of the hill, which meant that only one of them was aware that this was a race.

A couple of minutes into his mad dash downhill, Ben noticed the blinking red light on the instrument cluster. It was the ABS indicator, positioned prominently because the GS was one of only few motorcycles that allowed the rider to disable the ABS for off-road excursions. This was done by pressing a designated button, but then the indicator light would be solid, not blinking. A blinking light indicated a problem.

A tight turn was coming up, and he downshifted, putting the ABS indicator out of his mind. Right now he had to catch the Ghost. He focused his diminished mental and physical capacities on the mechanics of steering the GS through the curves and the fast straightaway sections in-between at maximum speeds.

A sign popped up by the roadside, indicating that an intersection was coming up in one mile.

As far as he could remember, the next sharp turn was the last, followed by a flat stretch of road that ran parallel to a stream that was gushing with runoff from recent rains. He was finally recovering from the trauma at the overlook, his reflexes sharpening as he executed each step, keeping the speed high on the approach to the turn.

Downshift.

Lean into the curve.

Start to accelerate halfway through.

Let the GS straighten up from the turn.

Hug the edge of the road.

Complete turn.

Rush forward.

The rear light of the Ducati appeared far ahead, near the intersection. Ben could see the white back of the riding jacket as the Ghost leaned forward on the low-hanging handlebar.

Yes!

Ben rolled the throttle all the way, pushing the GS to its limit, the RPM reaching redline before he up-shifted. Bowing forward over the gas tank, he tucked his head behind the small windshield, the instruments under his chin showing his speed approaching 60, 70, 80 mph, the ABS indicator blinking, the wind screaming.

There were two of them, babies, following an adult deer out of the woods, crossing the road for the water.

Ben let go of the throttle. For a brief moment he expected them to sprint across and be gone from his path. But the sound of the GS must have startled them, and they froze.

Squeezing the brake lever on the handlebar, he felt the front wheel lock and begin to slip.

Of course!

The blinking light!

The ABS malfunction!

Once the front wheel lost traction, it was too late to recover. All that was left for Ben to do was avoid a head-on collision with the deer.

He kicked down the foot brake to lock the rear wheel and, using his body as a counterweight, manipulated the heavy bike to enter a sideway slide while coming down on the left. Leading with the wheels, Ben and the GS came down together, slid sideways, and clipped the grown deer at the legs, sending it up and over.

The slide down the road was almost surreal in its smoothness until something—a pothole or a crack in the asphalt—tore Ben from the GS. He began to tumble over and over. The world became a spinning slideshow, and there was nothing he could do to stop it.

He wanted it to be over, but also feared getting smashed by the motorcycle, which was moving in the same direction.

He finally came to rest on the shoulder of the road and immediately popped up and looked around, expecting to see the GS hurtling toward him. But the bike was on its side farther back, its movement halted by the foot pegs and other protruding parts that, most likely, were now either bent or broken.

"Shit!" His voice sounded very loud inside the helmet. "Shit! Shit! Shit!"

His hands flexed without pain. His legs bent and straightened. His arms too. He wriggled his toes inside the boots.

Everything worked.

But everything hurt too.

He dropped flat on his back, lifted the helmet's face shield, and breathed deeply to fight off a tide of nausea.

Feeling better, he sat up and took stock of his body. Nothing seemed to be broken, and the pains were of the bruising variety, not of torn muscles or ligaments, both of which he had experienced at one point or another. His riding boots were scraped badly, the soles torn off, attached only near the toes. His BMW riding pants and jacket were scraped at the joints— knees, elbows, shoulders—and the underlying armor peeked out in some places. Removing the helmet, he found a dent the size of an egg.

The iPhone survived in the inside breast-pocket of his jacket, protected by the chest padding that lined the jacket. He considered calling for help but decided to try getting out of there without alerting anyone to the fact that he was stuck on a side road, alone and defenseless. The attempt on his life, right after meeting the two Mormons, had changed everything. It had not been a coincidence that Zachariah's widow had asked to meet at the Camp David Scenic Overlook—an isolated spot that was ideal for an "accident." Was Porter involved in setting it up? Were there other rogue troopers at the state police? The last thing he wanted to do was give them a second chance.

Limping back to the bike, Ben noticed that the engine was still on and turned the key to shut it off.

Farther back, up the road, the two fawns stood by the doe, most likely their mother, who was lying motionless on the road. They smelled her face, but still she didn't move.

His camera bag was near the bike, the shoulder straps torn. He unzipped it and pulled out the Canon. It appeared undamaged, thanks to the heavy padding in the bag. He turned it on and snapped a few photos of the two fawns. The camera worked fine.

Feeling inside the bag, he found the roll of duct tape, the fix-it-all every adventurous motorcyclist never travelled without. He used it to tape the soles of his boots and parts of the jacket and pants.

The effort of lifting up the GS came with a lot of grunting, and when it was upright, he taped up the broken signal lights and cracked windshield. The gearing lever was bent inward, and he pulled it back out. The left side of the handlebar had formed a right angle over the gas tank. Planting a boot against the front of the engine, he muscled it back to semi-straight. The clutch lever seemed to work fine.

The top case was missing from the rear rack. He couldn't see it on the road, where lines of scratches in the black asphalt and pieces of plastic told of the GS's long slide. Scanning the area, he noticed it on the opposite side, farther than where he had ended up. It must have been torn off the rack and had flown over him in the direction they were moving. He retrieved it and secured it to the rear rack with long strips of tape.

The fawns scattered as he approached. The doe, a full-size white-tail deer, was still alive, its eyes following him. The legs were broken, the belly was bleeding from a long tear, and the mouth was open, the lips trembling.

Was it in pain?

Most likely.

He had to do something, but killing it wasn't possible. He couldn't kill a living thing.

The sound of running water gave him an idea. He took off his riding jacket, lay it flat next to the doe's back, and rolled her over onto it. Grasping the sleeves, he dragged it off the road, across the gravel shoulder, down a short embankment, and into the shallow stream. He maneuvered around so that the injured deer was lying in the cold water, yet its head was out, resting on the grass.

Ben knelt and petted the head.

A few minutes later, the water reduced its body temperature enough to render the injured doe unconscious.

It was over.

When Ben finally pulled into the garage, wet and cold on his mangled GS, Keera's Mustang was already there. As he was getting off the bike, she appeared, saw him, and covered her mouth. That was the extent of her reaction. Keera had a sharp tongue and knew how to use it to inflict real damage when circumstances warranted it. But she was all love when it really mattered.

She helped him take off the wet jacket, riding pants, and taped-up boots, and supported him up the stairs and into the bathroom, where he sat on the ledge of the bath while she filled it and made him swallow a couple of pills. The rest was a fog of hot water, dull aches, and Keera gently scrubbing him with a sponge. The last thing he remembered was falling asleep in her arms under the bedcovers.

PART IV:

The Lawyer

CHAPTER 40

Ben woke up and felt warm lips on his forehead. In that brief transition from sleep to waking, he thought they were the doe's lips, trembling as it descended into oblivion. But when he opened his eyes, there was Keera, all dressed up, emitting her morning aroma—a mix of shampoo, perfume, and toothpaste.

"Hi, baby." She smiled. "How're you feeling?"

He tried to stretch, and the pain made him stop immediately. He groaned.

"I thought so." She held out two pills. "These will take the edge off and help with any inflammation. Take a hot shower and do some stretching, but carefully."

"I love you," he said, but she was already running downstairs.

Everything hurt, but not to the point of paralysis. Ben skipped the hot shower and the stretching, instead slipping into a sweat suit and medicating himself with a tall cup of steaming coffee.

On the TV, news analysis of recent opinion polls showed Joe Morgan running an average of 6 percent ahead of the incumbent president. A report showed the GOP candidate at a campaign stop on a factory floor in Pennsylvania. He was standing on a wooden shipping crate, propped up by a forklift.

"The current administration," Morgan declared, "has no faith in American exceptionalism! This country is ready to reject the socialist ideology of government bailouts, handouts, and takeovers that destroy the true spirit of competition and keep good people out of work and out of hope! As your future president, I pledge that restoring faith in American manufacturing will be my number one mission! I believe that you and I can do it together!"

The crowd of workers applauded him, and the camera returned to a smiling news anchor.

In his study, Ben saw the plastic bag of debris from Zachariah's Harley Davidson and felt lucky to be alive. He picked up the cap of the gas tank, unscrewed the two bases, and examined each one. He remembered what Rex had said about Zachariah's insistence on filling up every sixty miles, a habit Rex attributed to perfectionism. But was there a different reason? Had Zachariah modified the gas tank? Could the real floppy disk be hidden on the Harley?

Browsing the photos on the Canon, he found the tow truck with the remains of the stars-and-stripes Harley Davidson on its bed. There was a telephone number stenciled on the door of the truck. He dialed it.

A woman answered.

"Hi," Ben said. "I'm calling to find out where you guys took my friend's motorcycle after an accident on Sunday. It happened at the Camp David Scenic Overlook. Last name Hinckley."

"Spell it, honey."

He did.

"Let's see," she said. "A 'ninety-five Harley?"

"That's it."

"It says here that it was taken to the police yard."

"The one in Pikesville."

"Correct." Her fingers hit some keys. "Wait. There's a second entry. Yesterday. The police were done with it, so they called us to pick it up and take it to a shop."

"Which one?"

"Ironman Cycles in Gaithersburg."

Before riding to Gaithersburg, Ben stopped at Bob's BMW Motorcycles in Jessup. The service manager came outside with a writing board and balked at the sight. "Ouch! What happened to you?"

"Hit a deer."

"Looks pretty bad."

"The deer looks worse." Ben beckoned him over and showed him the indicator for the ABS, which was blinking. "It malfunctioned, and the front wheel locked up on me."

He knelt by the GS and poked around near the engine. "There," he said. "I see it."

"What?"

"Wire's detached from the ABS module." He drew a screwdriver from his breast pocket and fiddled with it. "The bracket's still tight. Looks like someone pulled out the wire. Whoever did it knows what he's doing. Did you cheat on your wife or something?"

"I'm not married." Ben watched him reattach it. "Maybe it got caught on a branch while I was off-roading."

"Unlikely, but you never know." He stood and turned the ignition off and on. "Should work fine now."

"Thanks." Ben pointed to the left side of the GS, which was scraped badly. "Please go over everything else, make sure it's safe to ride. I'll bring it back next week to fix the damage."

"What insurance company do you have?"

"Progressive."

"Let's verify it's mechanically sound. Give me thirty minutes or so." The service manager pushed the GS into the shop and maneuvered it onto a lift.

"I'll be in the showroom," Ben said.

Lined up across the showroom were over twenty new BMW motorcycles, ranging from a light off-road model to a luxury touring bike. The walls were covered with shelves of parts and accessories. In the rear was Bob's museum of classic motorcycles and racing paraphernalia, which Ben never tired of ogling. But today's visit was all business. He needed new gear to replace what had been ruined by the crash.

One of the guys came over to the apparel section and helped him pick out new boots, pants, jacket, and a Schuberth helmet. He paid with a credit card, cringing at the amount. But it was better to buy new protective gear than to fix broken bones and torn muscles.

He changed into the new riding outfit, discarded the taped-up boots and torn suit, and went back to the service area to watch through the glass wall as his wounded GS was being tended to.

The rear part of the building at Ironman Cycles, behind the service area, was a cavernous warehouse filled with new and used motorcycles of various makes—Harley Davidson, Yamaha, Kawasaki, Ducati, and BMW. Some were still in shipping crates, others assembled and ready for the showroom up front. Price tags dangled from used bikes, whose owners must have traded them in for a new ride.

The far-back corner was reserved for wrecks. A makeshift cardboard sign showed a sad face, the mouth curved down, the eyes dripping with tears. About ten wrecked motorcycles, some standing, some too badly damaged to remain upright, lying on the ground like maimed horses.

Zachariah's stars-and-stripes Harley Davidson was no longer the proud motorcycle it had been prior to flying off the Camp David Scenic Overlook. It was a heap of twisted metal. Two plastic bins held the many parts that had been broken off in the crash or were removed by the police during its search. The seats had been sliced open, the inner padding strung out. The side bags were open, the leather cut in long lines. Even the tires were cut, their internal lining exposed.

But Ben had come here to look at one thing.

The filling hole on the gas tank was missing its cap. The odor of gasoline was still strong. Ben tried to fit in the cap he had found at the accident site. The oversized thread matched the size of the hole, but the tank had been deformed by the impact, and he could not screw on the cap. A close examination of the thread confirmed his suspicion that Zachariah had modified the tank to enlarge the hole.

Ben tried to insert his hand through the opening, but the sharp edges cut into his skin. The next bike over was a sporty Yamaha with a smashed front end. It was equipped with a chain drive, which was properly greased. Ben rubbed his hand against it until it was smeared with dark grease. Trying Zachariah's gas tank again, with a bit of force he managed to slip his hand into it.

Watching his hand disappear into the hole, Ben cringed, expecting to feel a snake bite or mouse nibble, but there was nothing inside but a puddle of liquid at the bottom of the tank. Turning his hand, he felt up the inside of the tank all around. There was nothing other than a thin layer of goo from fifteen years of sealed containment. He felt the sharp edges inside the bent-up metal tank, which until days ago had been a perfect, teardrop-shaped gas tank in a shining American flag pattern.

Voices came from the other end of the warehouse.

Pulling his hand out, Ben shook it to get rid of the drops of gasoline.

The voices were getting closer.

Glancing at Zachariah's Harley for the last time, Ben saw no other place where a floppy disk could have been hidden safely and not been discovered by Porter's thorough search.

Walking away, his shoulder rubbed against the cardboard sign with the sad face, and he paused. Zachariah Hinckley had not been the kind of a man to modify a well-designed cap without a good reason.

Halfway down the warehouse, two salesmen were busy with a shipping crate. One of them noticed Ben, who smiled and said, "Just looking around."

Without waiting for a response, he made like he was examining one of the motorcycles. When the two salesmen refocused on what they were doing, he headed back to Zachariah's Harley. Shoving his hand back into the gas tank, he pressed downward through the puddle of gasoline and the layer of goo. The bottom felt soft.

Sliding his hand farther in, he managed to get his fingers to the edge of what felt like a loose floor inside the tank. Digging under it blindly, he forced the flat piece to rise until it stood up inside the tank. Feeling under it, Ben touched plastic-type material that was wet and gooey. He worked to separate it from the real bottom of the gas tank, digging his nails through years' worth of accumulation.

Finally loose inside the tank, it felt like a small package, padded with multiple layers, the outer of which was disintegrating.

"Hey there!" One of the salesmen approached. "Can I help you?"

"I'm good." Struggling to maintain a grip on the small package, he bent it while pulling his hand out through the hole. He half-turned to hide his hand and the item he had just pulled out of Zachariah's gas tank. "What a tragedy—such a beautiful machine! What happened to this Harley?"

"Heard it was fatal," the salesman said. "Are you in the market for a Harley? Winter is the best time to buy a bike, you know."

"I was thinking about it." Slipping his soiled hand and the gooey package into the pocket of his new jacket, Ben grinned. "My girlfriend's busting my balls to buy a car, not a second bike."

"Uh oh!" The salesman laughed. "Time for a new girlfriend!"

When Ben arrived at Ray's place, the vehicle gate swung open, the steel door unlocked, and the wooden front door opened for him as if by magic. He went downstairs to the basement, where all the plasma screens on the wall showed the same photo: Candidate Joe Morgan in a set of white Mormon undergarments.

"You like?" Ray waved her arms grandly. "I'm thinking of adopting it as our corporate screen saver."

"Very attractive," Ben said. "Did the Latvian do it for you?"

"For free? Are you kidding? I found it on Google Image—could be authentic, you know? Snapped through Morgan's bedroom window or a hotel room."

"Photoshop." Ben pointed at the neck. "See the line here? It's a headshot of Morgan combined with a stock photo of a Mormon man in sacred undergarments."

"Too bad." Ray reset the monitors. "How's the witch hunt going?"

"Ha."

"You look like hell," she said. "Are you back to playing football?"

"How did you guess?"

She pointed at his forehead. "What's this?"

"New makeup I'm trying."

One of the monitors showed the view from the surveillance camera outside, focusing on the black-and-yellow GS upfront. "And your beast looks like road kill. What's going on?"

Ben told her what had happened yesterday at the overlook—the meeting with Palmyra and the psychiatrist, the empty floppy disk pack on the cliff side, the kick that almost sent him plummeting to his death, and the abortive chase.

"Gee," Ray said, "if you were James Bond, the series would be over after the first installment."

"Thanks for your sympathy and support."

"Did you get any photos?"

"Of the Ducati?" Ben shook his head. "A useless side-view, out of focus. He was real fast. But I might have something else. It's from the dead guy's Harley. Haven't opened it yet."

Pulling the flat package from his pocket, he walked over to an ancient laundry basin, which Ray now used to stock up on dirty dishes. He rinsed some of the goo off the package, exposing soft, gray material that had already dissolved into tatters. He removed the outer layer, exposing another, then another, seven or eight layers in all.

Inside was a floppy disk—a black plastic disk resembling a small turntable record, encased in a flexible plastic sleeve. The Radio Shack paper sticker on the sleeve had deteriorated, flaking off when Ben touched it. He couldn't see any handwriting on it, but it might have disappeared over time.

"Five-and-a-quarter inch." Ray held it between a finger and a thumb. "Late eighties, early nineties. Big institutions and government agencies used it well into the nineties. The smaller diskettes with the hard plastic shells came next. Remember those?"

"Vaguely. What can we do with it?"

"Upload it!" Ray drove her power wheelchair around the line of computer servers.

Ben followed her. "You have a floppy drive?"

"I can handle punch cards too." She turned on the lights over a wooden counter piled with electronic odds and ends. "Please, step into my office."

He watched her boot up an old desktop computer and slip the floppy disk into a drive. The machine made grinding sounds. On the screen, an icon appeared. Ray clicked twice, and the document opened.

User ID: Zachiboy
Password: DCMTDBS
File: BFD111995

"Wait a minute," Ben said. "There must be more. Look for another file—lists of names, personal information, service records."

Ray clicked back to the directory. "This is the only file on this floppy."

"Can't be. Maybe it's encrypted?"

Trying two other methods of searching for data, Ray shook her head. "There's nothing else. Sorry." She reopened the document. "He's giving us a user name and password—the keys to open a file. But where is that file?"

"Another floppy disk?" Ben groaned. "That would be number four."

"Four?"

"The first disk I saw was the one Porter removed from the body. He showed me a porn DVD the next day, but I bet he switched them, though what he had found was a decoy. The second one was found by Palmyra Hinckley at home. She tried to open it, but the computer froze. She destroyed it. Probably another decoy. Now we have the third." Ben snapped a photo of the screen and glanced at the rear of the Canon to make sure it was legible. "This is a clue to the location of the fourth floppy disk."

"Good luck." Ray ejected the floppy disk. "This dead guy is screwing with you. And for what? The Mormons' baptism for the dead? It's old news." Tossing the disk into a garbage can, Ray rolled back to her desk. "Stop wasting your time."

"Then why did they send the Ghost after him? And after me?"

"I don't know. It may be unrelated—his accident and your kick in the head. There're some very upset dudes out there from your previous investigations."

Ben looked at her. "Come on!"

"Okay," she said. "Even if the Mormons are trying to intimidate you to make you drop the investigation, I think they're overreacting. Even if you managed to find that floppy disk with Morgan's hand scribbling, this story will die in forty-eight hours."

"How do you know?"

"I've released thousands of news items and watched them rise and fall on the charts of Internet hits. This one isn't going to catch fire. Every religion has its quirky rituals. Americans are tolerant, especially with something that's been known a long time like the Mormon posthumous baptisms. Old news, no news."

"And the cover-up? The Ducati attacks? Isn't that hot news?"

"Only if they manage to kill you." Ray laughed. "If that happens, make sure to send me a photo of you gasping for your last whiff of air."

"I'll put it on my to-do list." He headed upstairs.

"Make sure it's a good photo," she yelled. "Don't blur your face!"

CHAPTER 41

They shook hands, and the lawyer beckoned Ben to a sitting area. The corner office was larger than the average living room. The floor-to-ceiling glass walls overlooked Capitol Hill on one side and the White House on the other.

A secretary brought in fresh coffee and sugar cubes—white and brown.

Lawrence Ginsburg was an elegant man in his seventies. He wore a blue buttoned-down shirt, a red-striped tie, and matching suspenders. He poured a cup for Ben. "Sugar?"

"Thanks." Ben popped a white cube into his mouth and broke it up with his teeth, sucking on it.

"Isn't it getting too cold to ride?"

"I use a heated jacket." Ben showed him the loose wire and connector. "Why did you agree to meet with me?"

Ginsburg chuckled. "Not because I expected you to pay my usual fee."

"Which is?"

"Eight hundred dollars per hour for local matters. Ten thousand a day plus expenses when I'm travelling."

"Do clients actually pay that kind of money?"

"Willingly." He poured himself coffee in a mug that bore the firm's name in gold letters: Shulger Roberts & Ginsburg. "Have you considered law school?"

"Not for me." Ben sipped from his cup. It was good coffee.

"Why not?"

"I'm too honest."

Ginsberg laughed.

"No offense."

"None taken. Many of my colleagues fit the stereotype."

"But not you?"

"I was cut from a different cloth."

"Tell me," Ben said.

"The mail room," the lawyer said. "Right here in this building. That's where I started, making seventy-five cents per hour. The firm was called Shulger & Roberts back then. I worked here through college and law school. Other than the time I clerked for Justice Brennan, I've been here my whole adult life—a very fortunate life."

"A busy life too. Your name shows up in every major legal battle before the Supreme Court."

"That's how I learned to respect the media."

"You looked me up?"

"We have to, ethically. Whenever I get a call, my secretary does a conflict check of the person's name to make sure none of the other three hundred lawyers here represents you or someone suing you."

"I'm not involved in any legal matter."

"Not anymore." The lawyer glanced at his notes. "We found one case from about a decade ago. *Ben Teller vs. Maryland High School Football League, et al.* Verdict for defendants. Must have hurt to lose the case."

"My shoulder hurt, and my pride—being carried out on a stretcher in the middle of the state championship game. The case, however, was painless."

"Sports lawsuits are hard to win."

"I wouldn't sue. My insurance company sued on my behalf to recover medical expenses."

"A subrogation suit." He glanced at the notes again. "You majored in English at College Park, earned a master's in political science from Johns Hopkins, did an internship at the *Baltimore Sun*, declined a job at the paper, now in your fourth year as a freelance journalist-photographer with a nose for corruption scandals and car wrecks."

"But you still decided to see me."

"I figured you're onto one of my corporate clients."

"Fair enough," Ben said. "But actually, I'm here about one of your pro bono clients—the Gathering of Holocaust Survivors."

"A wonderful organization." Ginsburg put down his cup. "What do you want to know?"

"I'm researching the proxy baptisms issue."

The lawyer's face hardened. "Oh."

"Weren't you the lead counsel in negotiating a settlement agreement with the Mormons?"

"A settlement? Three settlement agreements. And three hundred thousand broken commitments. Dealing with the Saints is like trying to shake hands with a fish!"

"That's harsh."

"Let me show you something." He turned to the door. "Barbara!"

A moment later, his secretary appeared in the door with a writing pad. "Yes, Mr. Ginsburg?"

"Please bring in the timeline from the Gathering vs. LDS file."

When she left, he gestured around the vast office. "You see all this? Fancy, isn't it?"

Ben nodded.

"My parents didn't get to watch me grow up, become a man, start a family, build a law firm. Do you know why?" Ginsburg pointed at a photo on the wall of a formally dressed young couple with two kids—a toddler girl and a baby boy. "They couldn't get out of Germany. The US State Department didn't want Jewish immigrants, so my parents were stuck in Hitler's hell. But my mother's older sister was living in Baltimore and managed to obtain visas through an adoption agency. My parents put us on a train to Holland, where we boarded a ship to England, another one to Newfoundland, and then to Baltimore. My sister was two, I was less than a year old. Can you comprehend what it took for my parents, who had already lost everything under the Nazi Nuremberg Laws, to give up their last precious possessions? To let go of my sister and me? To send their cute and helpless babies across the Atlantic with total strangers?"

Ben shook his head.

"The bravest people in that whole terrible war were parents like mine, giving up their children to save them. To save us." He blew his nose. "They died in Auschwitz and we grew up with my aunt and uncle in a tiny apartment above their shoe store on Charles Street. I always felt my parents' presence, though. They were watching me from above, still do, expecting me to work hard and bring honor to their memory, to the memory of my aunt and uncle, may they rest in peace. They expect me to be good to my sister, to my wife and children, to my colleagues and my clients."

The secretary returned, carrying an easel. She set it up with a large poster, which had a list of dates down the left side with corresponding entries for each one.

"For me, this case started in ninety-three." Ginsburg pointed to the top entry. "I had served voluntarily for many years as counsel for an organization called the Gathering of Holocaust Survivors. During one board meeting, someone mentioned rumors about Mormon baptisms of dead Jews. I thought it was a joke, but asked a former classmate, who had moved to Salt Lake City, to search the archives. He found my parents on the list of converts to the Church of Jesus Christ of Latter-day Saints."

"Your parents?"

"Yes! My father and mother, whom the Germans murdered for being Jews, were baptized by Mormon strangers! Can you think of a worse injustice?"

"No."

He pointed to the next item on the list. "We sent investigators to Utah and discovered it was a widespread operation, directed from the top, of baptizing Holocaust victims. Lists of names, which Mormons obtained from Nazi records of death camps, were processed at the LDS headquarters in Salt Lake City and assigned in batches of names to Mormon wards, where saints were put to work as proxies in baptismal baths and temple rituals for the dead. It was hard to believe that thousands of otherwise upstanding Americans would engage in such a secret, ghoulish enterprise!"

"It's odd."

"I thought our investigators were exaggerating. But when we approached the Mormon leadership with this information, they didn't deny it. On the contrary, they claimed it was the most charitable act imaginable—saving souls! We held a series of meetings to explain to them that forced baptisms represent pure evil for Jewish people, that our whole history is filled with horrible suffering inflicted on us for our faith, that for seventeen centuries, Christian popes, bishops, kings, and crusaders had tortured, burned, and killed an incalculable number of Jewish victims for our refusal to convert, for our denial of Christ as a true messiah."

"That must have upset them," Ben said.

"Not really. They were sympathetic and expressed a genuine desire to prevent any harm to the relationship between Mormons and Jews. They accepted our conditions, and we entered into a detailed settlement agreement in ninety-five. They promised to stop all posthumous baptisms of Jews, other than the deceased family members of current members of the LDS Church. They also agreed to remove all the names of Holocaust victims who had already been baptized posthumously and delete all records of those baptisms."

"Sounds like a good solution."

"We were satisfied, but our relief was premature." Ginsberg pointed to the remaining list of dates. "Researchers kept finding Jewish names—many thousands of names, and not only pre-ninety-five, but new baptisms. The Mormons even baptized Yitzhak Rabin a year after his assassination! Can you imagine? I called the lawyer representing the LDS Church and asked him which of Rabin's relatives was the Mormon who was eligible to submit the late prime minister's name for baptism. After repeated inquiries, he called me back with an apology. But then we found out that all other Israeli prime ministers from Ben Gurion onward, including Golda Meir, had been baptized, together with Israel's presidents, starting with Weitzman. The Mormons baptized the founder of the Zionist movement, Theodor Herzl, and many other famous Jews, on top of thousands of Jews from lists they continued to collect from all over the world."

"What did they say to that?"

"Again, the Mormons were apologetic and conciliatory. We entered another settlement agreement in two thousand and one. But they continue to do it, and we continue to protest."

"Why do you keep going?"

Ginsburg pointed at the photo. "For my parents, I shall not rest. I owe it to them to protect Jewish victims from such abuse."

"Where is the abuse if you don't believe in the validity of the ritual?"

"You miss the point. This is not some esoteric religious ceremony the Mormons engage in for their own spiritual fulfillment. Rather, the massive effort to baptize millions of dead people is a calculated marketing tool for the living—long term!"

Ben laughed. "Baptizing the dead as a marketing device? It's ridiculous."

"It's brilliant, that's what it is. Imagine this scenario: A hundred years from now, a young Mormon missionary meets my great-granddaughter and tells her about Joseph Smith and his golden tablets and the Celestial Kingdom. She rolls her eyes. He pulls out his iPad, version fifty-seven, which will probably have built-in holograms, and shows her that her ancestors—my parents!—were Mormons, together with other famous converts such as Rabbi Herzog, Chagall, and Irving Berlin. How's that for a marketing pitch to Jewish prospects?"

"Pretty strong," Ben said, "but my understanding is that Mormons believe that the posthumous baptism is only an offer, an invitation to souls in the afterlife world to join the Mormon faith, accept Joseph Smith's gospel, and win eternal salvation."

"True," Ginsburg said. "That's what the nice guys in Salt Lake City told us—it's only an invitation, an act of charity for the dead who couldn't embrace Smith's message during their lives, but the souls can refuse, and then nothing happens, right?"

"That's my understanding."

"Then why are the dead listed the same way as regular saints?"

"They are?"

"Listen, what the Mormons do is bigger than anyone realizes. They're collecting records of dead people's names from every country in the world—Catholics, Lutherans, Baptists, Russian Orthodox, Armenians, Muslims, Hindus, as wells as war victims, natural disaster lists, and royal tombs, not to forget Adolf Hitler, Charlie Chaplin, Joseph Stalin, Mother Teresa, and every pope, rabbi, imam, and ayatollah—all of whom they've baptized by proxy into the Church of Jesus Christ of Latter-day Saints. But the rituals aren't merely invitations to join. That's just not true, because LDS Church membership rolls include all the names, over a million Jewish Holocaust victims and tens of millions of others, who are listed as Latter-day Saints. There's no notation that they never actually accepted the Mormon faith, no distinction between real baptisms of living, willing converts and posthumous baptisms done by proxy for dead people. A hundred years from now, who will remember that my parents, or Albert Einstein, never in their lifetime accepted the Mormon faith? Who will be able to step in and defend my parents—Jewish martyrs!—from being used as marketing props for Mormon missionaries?"

"I can see why you're dedicated," Ben said, "but what's the value of reaching more agreements with the Mormons? They're obviously shameless liars."

"Not at all. Mormons do not lie. It's a sin!"

"Now I'm really confused."

"Welcome to the club." Ginsburg sighed. "Let me tell you something that has taken me many years to understand. Mormons are ethical, wholesome, upstanding people. They never lie. They always tell the truth. However, their definition of the truth is different than that of the rest of us."

"You've lost me."

"What is truth to you?"

"Facts. Reality."

"Same for me. But for the followers of Joseph Smith, the truth is limited to faith-promoting facts." Ginsburg pointed at the easel. "Mormons would never lie to grieving Holocaust survivors. Rather, they share with us their faith-promoting version of the truth."

"How can there be more than one version of the truth?"

"Because under LDS Church doctrine, only faith-promoting facts are classified as true. That's the only truth to them. Conversely, facts that put the LDS Church in a negative light, facts that deviate from the official version of history, and facts that create doubts about the Mormon faith in any way, are not faith-promoting facts and are therefore untrue. And the blanks left by such facts are filled by Mormons with invented faith-promoting information, which become the truth no matter what actually happened."

"You're kidding, right?"

"It goes to the root of their young religion. I won't bore you with details, but the fundamental story of the *Book of Mormon*—that Native Americans are the descendants of the lost tribes of Israel, who came to North America in biblical times and built two competing civilizations that engaged in extensive warfare—this story was proven to be fiction through archeology, genetic testing, and the Native Americans' own oral history and ancient customs, all of which bear no trace of Israelite roots. It's complete fiction. That's why the basic requirement of being a Mormon is the ability to deny historic facts and ignore current science."

"It's not very different than other faiths," Ben said. "There's not a shred of archeological evidence for the hundreds of thousands of Hebrews who supposedly built the Egyptian pyramids, crossed the Red Sea, and spent forty years in the Sinai Desert."

"True, but the Mormon story is less than two centuries old, harder to excuse contradictions by the passage of time. Consequently they engage in heavy-handed suppression from the top." Ginsburg pulled a volume from a shelf. *No Man Knows My History – The Life of Joseph Smith*, by Fawn Brodie. "This author," he said, "who also wrote an excellent biography of Thomas Jefferson, was a devout Mormon. She taught at Brigham Young University and spent years researching original documents, including Smith's own writings and journals, his wife's papers, and family members' letters, court records, early LDS Church records, saints' personal letters and journals, and newspapers of the era. The resulting biography was probably the most meticulously researched work ever produced about the founder of Mormonism. Every fact was grounded in original, authenticated documents, every description and statement checked and rechecked to make sure it was factually correct."

"And?"

"Fawn Brodie was put on trial by her Mormon Church. Her book, her facts, were not faith-promoting and therefore, by definition, untrue. Her descriptions of Joseph Smith's treasure-digging trickery, his con artist enterprises, his criminal conviction for fraud, the evolution of his stories about encounters with angels, Jesus, and God, the multiple versions he told about how he had found—and then lost—the golden tablets and how he translated them into the *Book of Mormon*, his militarism and plans to decimate the US Army and set up a theocracy in America, his obsessive sexual exploits, masqueraded as divinely ordained polygamy to seduce young servant girls as well as the mature wives of his own friends, all these facts were not faith-promoting and therefore false. But when Brodie refused to denounce her own work, her trial ended in conviction, and she was excommunicated."

"How can they do it?" Ben flipped through the pages of footnotes at the end of the book. "How can they deny reality?"

"Tell that to Fawn Brodie and all the other Mormon historians who were excommunicated or intimidated into submission. In fact, in September of ninety-three, the LDS church excommunicated six scholars, who were also fired from their academic positions. The church followed up with a massive roundup of documents. Bishops were told to collect from their wards' members all the old family letters, personal journals, and anything else that could contradict the official version of Mormon history or reflect poorly on the early days and thus fail the Mormon test of truth. The LDS authorities locked up all these documents in an underground bunker near Salt Lake City, outside the reach of any scholar—Mormon or Gentile—where they remain today."

Ben pointed at the easel. "Do you think they're still baptizing Holocaust victims?"

"No question about it. You can look it up on the International Genealogical Index website. Now it's all on the Internet. Search for Jewish names and you'll find plenty. I've found relatives there, also Holocaust victims, who were baptized recently. I complain to my Mormon colleagues in Salt Lake City, and they are always friendly, earnest, and forthcoming as they deny the facts or claim some imaginative error." Ginsburg chuckled. "Incredible, isn't it?"

"It's incredible that you continue asking."

"Eventually we will prevail," Ginsburg said. "Maybe not in my lifetime, but some day, when Christians and Muslims realize that the Mormons are stealing their parents' souls. There will be a huge storm, and the LDS leaders will realize that baptisms of the dead aren't worth it. Their president-prophet will have a divine revelation, and they'll stop doing it. Same thing happened with the ban on admitting blacks into the Mormon priesthood. It became too costly for the Church, and in seventy-eight, God told the LDS leaders that He had changed his mind about it."

"What about Joe Morgan?"

"What about him?"

"Is his Mormon faith relevant to his candidacy?"

"It depends. Which party are you affiliated with?"

"I'm an Independent."

"That's a copout, if you don't mind me saying. A person should take a stand and stick to it."

"What about you?"

"I joined the Republican Party while studying constitutional law in my first year at Georgetown more than fifty years ago. It's the party of Abraham Lincoln, which was—and still is—good enough for me. And I've never failed to vote in presidential elections since JFK stole the elections from Richard Nixon, which was probably before you were born, yes?"

Ben nodded.

"As a first-generation American, I consider voting to be both an honor and a duty. But in a few weeks, for the first time in my life, I will not be voting." Ginsburg's voice shook with emotions. "Have I answered your question?"

CHAPTER 42

Still reeling from what he had learned, Ben returned to the GS in the visitors parking of Shulger Roberts & Ginsburg. The attendant held back pedestrians as Ben rode across the sidewalk and joined the slow traffic on K Street. Sitting high, his line of vision open over the roofs of the cars, he glimpsed a white motorcycle about four or five blocks ahead. Watching more intently, he saw it again. It was white, but he couldn't tell whether it was a Ducati or a different kind of motorcycle.

Twisting the throttle, he sent the GS roaring forward, cutting between lanes of traffic. The light turned red as he approached the Spy Museum. He turned right, then left at the next intersection, now going parallel to K Street. He passed a queue of cars and buses, flew through three intersections, and reached the front of the line at a red light. Glancing left, down the cross street, he saw it go fast up K Street. Now he was certain—a white Ducati, its rider in a matching suit and helmet!

The Ghost!

Ben took off, scaring off pedestrians and a cyclist, who shouted a curse. Back on K Street, he cut again between lines of stationary traffic. He followed it through several turns, but suddenly, it was gone. Slowing down, he scanned the road ahead. Had he lost it?

Way ahead, on the right, the Ducati emerged from between cars, cut through the opposite lane, and entered a parking garage next to Ford's Theater.

Ben raced ahead, avoided an oncoming bus, cut off a car attempting a left turn, and swung into the garage entrance.

Delayed by the barrier at the automated cashier, he pressed the oversized button and took a ticket. The barrier ascended, and he rode into the dark interior.

He let go of the throttle, and the GS quieted.

The Ducati's exhaust note was faint, somewhere ahead.

Moving again, Ben followed around the street-level floor, made a right turn, then another, and another onto the downward ramp. He followed around three more right turns and down another ramp, deeper underground. Each level was designated by *P-1, P-2, P-3*, etc. The lower levels were sparsely occupied with parked cars.

P-6.

This level was almost empty.

He stopped the GS and listened. The Ducati emitted a sharp rumble somewhere ahead, then silence. Ben sped ahead, turned right around the corner, and another.

A solid wall faced him. He hit the brakes, barely managing to stop.

No Ducati!

On the right was a glass door, propped open. Above the stainless steel doors of an elevator he could see the numbers on a red display as they changed in reverse order: *P-4, P-3, P-2...*

There was only one elevator, and he was not going to wait for it to come down. Unlike the little Ducati, the GS might be too big to fit into the elevator, which was a slow one anyhow.

He turned the GS around and raced back, making the left turns around the empty parking spaces of level P-6 and up the ramp to P-5, where about a quarter of the spaces were taken by cars. Left turn, then another, and another.

Near the foot of the upward ramp to P-4, a large vehicle was pulling out of a spot. Ben honked and aimed to pass in the narrowing space between the vehicle and a concrete column, but the driver didn't stop, continuing to reverse until the rear bumper reached within a hair of the concrete column. Ben stopped abruptly, and as the bike was leaning into a turn, he had to struggle to keep it from tipping over, which was the reason he didn't notice at first that the vehicle was a white Suburban.

The lack of reverse gear on the GS had never put him in a worse disadvantage than now. His way blocked by the white Suburban, cars parked on his left and right, all he could do was push backward with his boots and try to turn. But it was a slow process, much slower than the person who appeared from behind and shoved something against Ben's neck.

A horrible jolt hit him.

Taser!

Completely limp, he was fully conscious as a cloth hood was pulled down over his helmet, blocking the view through the face shield. In semi-darkness, he was pulled off the bike, dragged into the Suburban, and pushed facedown on the floor in front of the middle row of seats. The vehicle moved forward briefly, the rear doors were opened, and a heavy object was loaded into the trunk—probably his GS, which they must have lifted and shoved in on its side. Ben heard the rear doors slammed shut, several people got in, and more doors were shut. The Suburban sped up the ramp.

The whole operation took seconds. They were professionals, executing an ambush that left him no chance to resist. The initial shock of pain and paralysis was fading. He felt the vehicle make left turns, go up the ramps between floors, stop briefly at the automated cashier, go over the bump at the curb, and join the stop-and-go traffic. A few minutes later, they were on an open road, rattling over frequent potholes and lane markers.

Ben tried to rise, his muscles barely responding to his will.

One of them placed a boot on his back and pressed down. His arms were pulled backward and cuffs locked on his wrists.

Hands went through his pockets, pulling out his iPhone and wallet. He heard the ping of the iPhone being turned off. After that, there was nothing—no talking, no radio, no music, only the sounds of the engine, the wheels, and the howling air around the moving vehicle.

Lying in this position, with yesterday's bruises still fresh, became increasingly uncomfortable. It was hard to breathe inside the helmet and hood. Anger built up inside him—not only at his captors, but at himself for falling so easily into their trap. But the boot on his back sent a clear message that any further attempt to resist would be met with a harsh response. Getting another Taser jolt would not help his chances. He stayed down and slowly flexed his limbs in small increments to prevent cramping and maintain alertness. They had not killed him yet, but after the boot in the forehead at the overlook, he had no illusion about their intentions. Still, if they made a mistake, he must be ready to take advantage and try to save himself.

After at least an hour on a highway, they travelled on country roads that meandered through hills and valleys. He lost track of time. Eventually the Suburban turned onto an unpaved road. It was rough, and the hard floor bumped him mercilessly. A staccato of wood beams told him that they were crossing an old bridge.

One of his captors—a man—was overtaken by a coughing attack. Ben hoped the others would say something, provide a hint about their identities or intentions. If they pulled over to give the guy some fresh air, it could provide an opportunity to attempt an escape.

But no one said a word, and the man's coughing subsided.

The Suburban stopped, and one of them stepped out, leaving a door open. Rusty hinges screeched as a gate opened. The vehicle inched forward, more screeching sounded, followed by the bang of the gate closing.

They were moving again down the unpaved path.

A few minutes later, they stopped again.

Doors opened, everyone was getting out.

Someone grabbed his arm and pulled him.

As he was getting out of the Suburban, Ben angled his head in a way that rubbed against the back of the seats and the doorjamb, causing the hood to fall off.

The Taser appeared in front of the face shield.

Ben recoiled. "Don't!"

They shoved him forward.

With the helmet still on, Ben managed only a brief look at the surrounding farmland and a white Ducati near a rotting wooden bench. The hood was pulled back on.

They led him into a house with creaking wooden floors, made him sit in a chair, and used a second pair of handcuffs to lock his ankles to the legs of the chair. He tried to move, but the chair was bolted to the floor.

CHAPTER 43

At first, Keera was angry. She had a brief window of time between getting home from the hospital, changing and putting on makeup, and getting to the club on time. On the rare occasions that Ben was running late, he always called ahead of time to let her know. She would then take a cab and leave the Mustang at home so that he could switch vehicles and pick her up when the club closed. But tonight he wasn't at home when she arrived, didn't call, and when she tried his phone, it went straight to voice mail.

But by the time she had to leave, Keera's anger had changed into worry. She had waited too long and had no time to call a cab. Driving her Mustang, she tried Ben again, reaching his voice mail. She hung up and called Mrs. Teller.

Ben's mom picked up after four rings.

"I wanted to thank you," Keera said, "for a lovely dinner."

"My pleasure, sweetheart. And thank you for coming. How are you two doing?"

Keera sighed, her hopes dashed. Clearly Mrs. Teller didn't know Ben's whereabouts. "Everything is fine." Before the conversation could go any further, she said, "Next time you'll come to us."

"I would love that."

"Wonderful. Talk soon. Bye."

Next she called Ray, who didn't answer, but called back a moment later.

"Ben is missing," Keera said. "He's always at home to take me to the club, or he calls to let me know he's late. But he hasn't called, and his phone is off. Do you know anything?"

Ray hesitated. "When did you see him last?"

"This morning. He was still in bed when I left. He didn't look like he was up to going anywhere, considering how both he and the bike looked."

"Do you know what happened yesterday?"

"I assumed he slipped in the rain," Keera said. "We had argued about the motorcycle only a day earlier. All I want is for him to get rid of the damn thing and buy a car, so when I saw that he had an accident and didn't break any bones, I was almost—"

"Happy?"

"Right."

"It wasn't exactly an accident," Ray said. "It seemed like someone messed around with his brakes."

"I knew it!" Keera pulled in front of Wisteria's Secret and beckoned the bouncer, who came around to take the car. "I told him to drop the Mormon investigation!"

"Same here. It's not worth it. They tried to intimidate him, but you know how he is. Everything is like football to him."

Keera hurried to the door of the club, the phone pressed to her ear. "What are we going to do?"

"Ben is resourceful. He probably got delayed in a meeting with a source, or he's watching a target, waiting for the perfect photo opportunity. Give him a few hours. He'll show up."

CHAPTER 44

Ben heard hushed words in the other room, but otherwise nothing happened for an hour or two. He sat with his helmet and riding suit on, sweating and on the verge of peeing on himself.

Sounds of footsteps approached him, and the hood was pulled off. He saw a woman and two men. They were older than he expected—late fifties or sixties. The woman fiddled with the strap under his chin and removed his helmet.

He was in a room that belonged in an earlier century. The floor was rough-hewn planks, the low ceiling pitched with exposed beams, and the small windows covered with flowery drapes. The walls were whitewashed, now darker with age, except for a few squares of the original white where pictures must have hung until recently. The air was musty, with a smoky tang from an open fireplace, where embers still crackled.

Noise from the other room told Ben there was at least one more person to deal with.

A black gentleman with gold-rimmed glasses and a crisp manner reminiscent of Colin Powell checked the inside of Ben's helmet.

"I need a bathroom," Ben said.

"Go ahead, wet your pants." The woman aimed a gun at Ben. Her voice was thin but devoid of weakness. She looked like Meryl Streep, but with longer legs and straight, silver hair.

Powell removed the handcuffs and stepped back. "Strip down to your undergarments."

The word choice was odd. Did Mormons use the word "undergarments" for every kind of underwear? Ben said nothing as he stood up on wobbly legs.

"One false move," Streep said, "and your stomach will be digesting lead."

They watched him take off his riding boots, pants, and the two-layered jacket.

Standing in his boxer shorts and t-shirt, he shivered. "Can I go now?"

They watched him for a long moment.

Powell asked, "Where's your undergarments?"

"You don't like my boxer shorts?"

"It means nothing," Streep said. "He's undercover."

Ben pressed his knees together. "I need to go!"

Streep pointed at a door.

The bathroom window was too small for an escape, and the door remained open. He urinated and returned to the chair. He wanted to put his clothes back on, but Streep made him sit down and cuffed him. He was really cold now—and out of ideas. They had not made a single mistake yet, and time was running out. He had to provoke them further, but not far enough to make them hurt him.

How?

One of them, a man with gray hair and reading glasses, pulled a chair over and sat down, facing Ben. "What's your name?"

"What's yours?"

He smiled, showing tidy, small teeth. His blue eyes remained cold. "We can do it the easy way or the painful way."

"Richard Dreyfuss," Ben said. "That's who you remind me of. *Tin Men*. Great movie. Remember it?"

"No."

"How about *The Apprenticeship of Duddy Kravitz*?"

"Yes. I especially remember Virgil. Do you?"

"The loyal friend?"

"Too loyal, which is why he ended up a cripple. I bet he missed being able to pee standing up." Dreyfuss gestured toward the bathroom. "Do you want this one to have been your last?"

"Do you?"

"I don't really care," Dreyfuss said, removing his glasses. "But if you do care about living longer in a functioning body, then you must tell us everything."

"The way you talk," Ben said, "you sound like a professor, not a killer. Try to sprinkle a few grammatical errors. For authenticity, you know?"

Dreyfuss sighed, and Streep, still holding the gun, stepped forward and, with her free hand, slapped Ben across the face. She was going to slap him again on the return, but Ben turned his head to face the coming hand, opened his mouth while tilting his head just right, and caught the side of her hand between his teeth, clamping down.

She released a shrill scream, but he had already let go. She staggered back, pressing her injured hand to her chest, and the gun fell.

Dreyfuss picked it up and aimed at Ben.

"No!" Powell raised his hand. "Not yet!"

Streep ran out of the room.

"There's a locator on my motorcycle," Ben said. "Men with bigger guns are on their way. You better run off while you can."

"It's clean," a man yelled from the other room. "I scanned his bike for electronic signals. There's nothing."

Ben recognized the voice—Zachariah's riding buddy! What was he doing here?

Rex appeared in the door. He was wearing a light-colored riding suit—not quite white, but close—and was pushing a dolly loaded with a large black box. It had knobs, a couple of gauges, and colored wires. He emptied a bucket of water on Ben.

"Hey!" Ben shook off the water as much as he could without hurting his wrists and ankles. His wet hair fell onto his face and he twisted his head to get it away. "What the hell—"

"There we go." Rex attached a wire to Ben's left earlobe with a clamp, another to the right earlobe.

Ben tried to bite his hand. "Stay away from me!"

"Don't move too much," Rex said calmly, "or I'll shock you just for discipline."

"Tell us what you know," Dreyfuss said.

"I know," Ben said, "that your prophet, Joseph Smith, was a con artist and a pedophile, and you're no saints but scum."

They stared at him. He expected Rex to flip a switch and send searing current through his head, but instead he smiled and said, "Clever. Very clever."

Ben's teeth began to rattle while the icy water dripped to the floor around him. "Thanks for baptizing me, but don't you prefer doing it to dead people who can't tell you how ridiculous your *True Church* really is?"

"Enough with the show." Dreyfuss moved his chair farther back from Ben. "Last warning, wiseass."

"What do you want to know?"

"Who told you to go after Zachariah Hinckley?"

"Now you're being specific," Ben said.

"Start at the beginning."

"First time I ever saw Zachariah was on Sunday. He passed me during the Marine Corps Veterans' Ride."

Rex said, "You're lying."

"Am not."

"Why were you there? You're not a veteran."

"My dad served. And I'm a reporter. It seemed like a worthy event to report on."

"Who sent you there?" Rex put his hand on the electrical switch. "Who ordered you to eliminate Zachariah?"

"Eliminate Zachariah?" Ben looked at them. "Are you nuts? Watching him die was the first time I had ever seen his face."

Streep reappeared and pointed with her bandaged hand. "Give him a jolt so he knows the price of lying."

"Hold on," Dreyfuss said. "How did you even know his name in the first place?"

"After they brought up the body, I peeked at the medic's report. The victim's name was Zachariah Hinckley."

"You lie well." Rex held forward a photo. It was taken from a distance at the Camp David Scenic Overlook, showing Ben with Palmyra and the psychiatrist. "Can you explain this?"

"Zachariah's wife agreed to meet with me, but all I heard was how mentally ill he'd been. It made me ever more suspicious."

"Do you want us to believe that a grieving widow invited you to meet her at the very place her husband died?"

"She wanted to see the place and convince me—and maybe herself too—that he had committed suicide. I think that's why she brought Dr. Neibauer."

"Your boss?"

"I'm self-employed."

"You met them at the isolated site of the accident to gloat about your achievement and receive new instructions from your Mormon masters, correct?"

"My Mormon masters?" The conversation was making less and less sense. "Wait a minute, who the hell are you people?"

"Let me show you who we are!" Streep reached over and flipped the switch on the batteries.

Cringing in terror, Ben opened his mouth to shout at the coming explosion of pain between his ears.

After three hours of work, going through the dance motions mechanically while thinking of Ben, Keera was done for the night. Ben's phone was still off. She asked the bouncer to bring her Mustang to the front and drove home expecting—against reason—to see the GS in the garage. When she arrived, the garage was open, but the GS wasn't there. She parked and entered the house.

It wasn't messy. In fact, everything that had been removed from the shelves and cupboards was placed on the floors and counters in an orderly manner. Even the framed artwork, mostly cheap posters, was lined up nicely after it had been taken down from the walls and separated to check if anything was hidden under the backings.

She turned on all the lights and called Fran to tell her what happened.

"Hang up and call nine-one-one," Fran said. "I'm coming over."

"I can't report it," Keera said. "Ben will be very upset if I let anyone in here without his permission, even the police."

"You've just been burglarized!"

"It's his home too, and this has to do with his investigation."

"The dead Mormon?"

"Yes."

"How do you know? Could be a regular break-in. Happens all the time."

"If you saw the way they left the place, you'd know. This wasn't done by a druggy or a housebreaker. They didn't take any valuables or electronics, there's no damage whatsoever, and the place is more tidy than it had been before they broke in. Come and see for yourself!"

When Fran and Lilly arrived, Keera was ready with a suitcase. She gave them a tour of the two-story townhouse.

"Neat," Fran said. "Never seen anything like this."

"What has he gotten himself into?" Keera glanced at her iPhone. The screen saver was a photo of Ben, smiling while pointing back at her. "I wish he'd call already!"

"I called in," Fran said, "and had one of my officers run a data search through all the emergency services—cities, counties, hospitals. There's nothing with Ben's name and no accidents involving a BMW motorcycle."

"I guess that's good news," Keera said.

"It is. Meanwhile, come stay with us, just in case."

Keera left the lights on, locked up, and followed them in her Mustang. She kept the iPhone visible between the front seats, Ben looking back at her. "Where are you?" she asked out loud. "If you get hurt, I swear I'm going to kill you!"

CHAPTER 45

The first thing Ben felt was a twitch, or a sting, a prelude to the horrible jolt he knew was coming. But Rex was swift, tugging on the wires before the full blast of electric current passed through. The clamps slipped off of Ben's earlobes. The two ends touched each other, causing an eruption of fireworks. Rex flipped back the switch, ending the show, which left a cloud of smoke.

"Wimp," Streep said. "Why did you do that?"

Rex untangled the wires. "Because I think he's telling the truth."

"I am," Ben said. "There's four years of my reporting, right there on the Internet! Why don't you look me up? Ben Teller. Mostly on NewZonLine.com, but I've had stuff in the *Baltimore Sun* and the *Washington Post.*"

Rex got an iPad from the other room and spent a few minutes on the site. "When you approached me at the pier, I thought you were working for them." He pushed away the dolly with the car batteries.

"Based on what?"

"The fact that you were able to find me at North Point, the questions you asked me about Zachariah—you obviously knew a lot about his private life. And the location of your meeting with Dr. Neibauer implied secret cooperation. Your actions hardly fit the facade of an unemployed news reporter."

"Self-employed."

"Anyway, that's why we decided to pick you up and question you about their plans."

Dreyfuss opened a window. "Aren't you a Mormon?"

"I'm Jewish, though not very religious. Aren't you Mormons?"

"Ex-Mormons," Rex said.

"Axed-Mormons," Streep corrected him.

"We're apostates," Powell said, "tempted away by Satan."

"Idealists," Rex said, "is what we are. Our mission is to expose the ugly practices of the LDS Church. Zachariah had information we wanted. We tried to obtain his cooperation, but the Ghost got to him first."

"I don't understand," Ben said. "Aren't you the Ghost on the white Ducati?"

"Mine is a decoy." Rex untied him. "If you look closely, what I'm riding is a beat-up 749. The real Ghost is riding a brand new Ducati Monster 848. Check your photos."

"Weren't you at the overlook? Didn't you kick me in the face?"

"Not me, though I can sympathize with whoever found it irresistible to kick you real hard."

"Second that," Streep said.

"Get dressed before you freeze." Rex pointed at Ben's riding gear. "I drove by the overlook while following Dr. Neibauer and took the photo of the three of you, but had to keep going or you'd have noticed me."

"I did notice the pickup truck go by."

"That's why I drive a common model." Rex chuckled. "Okay. Tell us the whole story from the beginning."

Ben told them how he had noticed Porter remove a floppy disk from the body, about his own initial search that uncovered the iTouch and some debris from the Harley, including the gas tank cap. He described the main parts of the journal, Porter's denial of finding a floppy disk on Zachariah's body, Ironman Cycles and tracking down Rex, the piece of Radio Shack packaging he found on the cliff, and the kick in the forehead. He described the deer hit, the discovery of a second floppy disk inside the gas tank on Zachariah's destroyed Harley, and the information shared by the attorney, Ginsburg. "Then I chased your white Ducati into a trap."

They looked at each other and laughed.

"It's not funny," Ben said. "And by the way, why did you follow the psychiatrist?"

"Dr. Neibauer," Dreyfuss explained, "is the LDS point man for handling troublemakers. He's licensed to practice psychiatry in every state with a substantial Mormon population—Utah, Arizona, Nevada, California, Idaho, Colorado, Massachusetts, as well as Washington, DC, and the region—Maryland, Virginia, and West Virginia."

"And the military," Streep said. "He's authorized to treat members of the army, navy, air force, FBI, CIA, NSA, and congressional staff."

"Correct," Dreyfuss said. "For decades, young Mormons have been instructed by their bishops to pursue government careers in preparation for the day when, as Joseph Smith prophesied, *'the Constitution will hang by a thread'* and Mormons will take over the reins of the US government."

"He said that?" Ben pulled on his riding pants.

"Smith and every succeeding president of the LDS Church have been telling the saints that they are destined to take over the United States, then the whole world."

"I see why they need a psychiatrist."

"He doesn't treat the leadership," Dreyfuss said.

"Maybe he should." Ben pulled on his jacket. "Who does he treat?"

"Rank and file," Dreyfuss said. "When a saint defies the leadership, Neibauer is called in. Usually the problem is solved by convincing the man or the woman—most of them are women— that the problem is their mental health."

"Why women?"

"Mormon men are kings," Streep said. "As boys, they are elevated to priesthood, ordained into the Aaronic Priesthood, then the Melchizedek Priesthood. They're called *elders* before some of them even need to shave. The women, however, remain servants of the men. Their destiny is childbearing, cooking, cleaning, washing—everything to improve their chances of convincing their husbands to take them to the heavenly afterlife of the Celestial

Kingdom. A woman can only achieve eternal exaltation by the grace of her husband."

"Let me guess," Ben said. "Your husband decided he'd rather spend his eternal afterlife without you."

"My husband beat me almost to death because I sought help for our daughter after I found him in her bed one night. The ER doctor didn't call the police. He called our bishop, who came to the hospital to pray with me and tell me that it was my fault if my husband wasn't satisfied sexually. He instructed me to forgive my husband and serve him better so that he wouldn't have to seek other outlets for his natural urges. When I threw a fit, they called Dr. Neibauer."

"How did that go?" Ben zipped up his jacket, still shaking with cold.

"He committed me to the Emma Smith Sanatorium for Women while my husband—a prominent LDS leader and businessman—continued to force our eldest daughter to serve him until she ran away. He moved on to our second daughter, a thirteen-year-old. She ended up pregnant, and her older sister came back and took her to California for an abortion."

"I'm sorry," Ben said.

"Me too." She wiped tears. "They're both okay now, at least as okay as they can be after suffering multiple rapes by their daddy."

"Now I feel bad for biting you."

She waved in dismissal. "Do you know that, thanks to women, Utah holds the record among all other states in prescription anti-depressants?"

"I didn't know that." Ben glanced at the dark windows. "But it reminds me that my girlfriend must be going crazy with worry. Can I have my iPhone?"

CHAPTER 46

Curled up on the living room sofa at Fran and Lilly's apartment, Keera held her iPhone to her chest as she fell asleep. She dreamed she was on the back of Ben's motorcycle, which became airborne, flying high over Washington, DC, then coming in for a landing on top of the White House, where guards sprang out from hiding with machine guns that didn't shoot bullets but lightning strikes in string-like flashes of electrical currents that hit her chest with strange vibrations and woke her up. It was the iPhone, which she had put on vibrate to avoid waking up Fran and Lilly. Ben's smiling face appeared on the screen, filling her with a mix of relief and dread. Would she hear his voice when she answered or a police officer telling her about an accident—

"Keera?"

"It's you!" She ran to the bathroom and closed the door.

"I'm sorry," Ben said. "I couldn't call earlier."

"Are you all right?"

"Fine."

"Thank God! I'm going to kill you!"

"Join the club."

"Oh, no!"

"It's okay. I'm safe now. You know I would've called earlier if I could."

She choked up. "I'm still…angry."

"Listen to me. There's no time to explain, but the business with the Mormons could get ugly."

"Already has."

He paused. "What happened?"

"They broke into our place."

"Were you—"

"I was at work."

"Pack up and go to Fran's. Now!"

"I'm already there."

"Good. She'll keep it hushed. Last thing I need now is a police investigation. I'll be the only one they'll prosecute. No one will look into the Mormons' actions until I have hard evidence."

"You can explain—"

"Explain my tampering with the scene of an accident? Removing victim's belongings? Keeping evidence from law authorities?"

"Fran could help."

"Yes, with one thing. Tell her I asked that she check out Inspector Porter, look at his record, see if anything smells bad. But nothing else. I don't want her to risk her job."

"Why don't you tell her. Are you on your way here?"

"No. I can't. Not yet."

"When?"

"I'm not sure. It might be a few days before I can contact you again."

"If you stop investigating, wouldn't they leave us alone?"

"Maybe."

"Then drop it! Come home!"

"I can't."

"Why?"

He was silent for a long moment. "Please don't ask me that. Fran will keep you safe until it's over. I love you."

The line went dead.

When Keera got out of the bathroom, she found Fran waiting in the living room, wrapped in a blanket. "Was it Ben? Is he okay?"

Keera dropped on the sofa. "He's fine, so far."

"What did he say?"

"Actually, he asked that you check out Inspector Porter, look into his record, sniff around for any suspicious stuff."

"I can't do that," Fran said. "He's an officer in the state police. There's nothing suspicious about him. And I told Ben to leave the Mormons alone—this investigation stinks of religious persecution."

"He's not imagining," Keera said. "They did break into our house."

"They did? How do you know who did it? Ben's investigations have irritated a lot of people. Maybe it's someone else he's crossed? Could be totally unrelated to this investigation. Remember the death threats he received when he was chasing the bridge contractor?"

"Oh, yeah." Keera groaned. "He didn't give up, and he's not dropping this investigation either, no matter what I say. I feel so stuck!"

"You're not stuck," Fran said. "It's your choice."

"Easier said than done."

"You got the power. It's your life, isn't it?"

"You think? I was in college when we started going out, and look at me now, graduating med school in six months." Keera held forth her naked fingers. "Do you see a ring?"

"Set a deadline and tell him this is it—propose or get out."

"Why should I stoop to arm twisting?" Keera pulled the blanket over her legs. "I don't want to get a ring by ultimatum."

"Does it matter?"

"To me it does. I want him to propose because he wants to, not because he has to."

"He's a man. They don't know what they want or what's good for them. They need to be manipulated. Like children. Or dogs."

Keera laughed. "You're not objective."

"On the contrary." Fran grinned. "I've tried both. Have you?"

"Ha."

"I can introduce you to a lovely girl. You might fall in love."

"I'm already in love. And I know he loves me too."

"But not enough to marry you?"

"Enough. He really does love me to death. But he's got some kind of a block, like he's afraid of marriage."

"Afraid?" Fran raised her eyebrows. "Ben?"

"Yes. I think it's about his dad. They rarely talk about the man, Ben and his mom, but I can read between the lines, see their pain. It's like they've never gotten over the loss, both of them. Ben carries his dad's photo in his wallet, you know?"

Fran shook her head. "It's sad, but what's the relevancy? Your clock is ticking, not his."

"But that's why Ben is afraid—not of being married to me, not of commitment, but of becoming a father."

"Afraid of doing the same thing?"

"That's right. Of having a son and then—"

"Everybody's carrying some painful baggage. If you make Ben feel the pain of your absence, he'll fear losing you even more than he fears hurting his future kids."

"No. I'm not going to manipulate him. If I leave Ben, it will be without notice, and I'll never see him again—no pressure, no negotiations, no second chances."

"Just like that?"

"I'm too crazy about him. If I start down that road, I'll go back and forth like a yo-yo. No. I'd rather suffer once and be done."

"Then set a deadline for yourself."

"I already have." Keera's tears were flowing again. "But now he's out there, risking his life for a stupid news story, which readers will forget the next day."

"That's his choice," Fran said. "You should make yours."

"How can I leave him while he's gone?"

"Why not?"

Porter sat in his unmarked Ford in the back of the parking lot at a Lutheran church in Rockville. The clock was approaching midnight. He tilted the bottle of apple juice all the way up, but nothing came out. Radio communications crackled back and forth between dispatchers and cruisers all over northeast Maryland, mostly traffic stops exacerbated by alcohol or stupidity, domestic violence incidents in areas not covered by local police and, every hour or so, a prostitution bust along the state highways and rest stops. Not a single mention of a motorcycle, let alone a black-and-yellow BMW. Ben Teller had disappeared without a trace.

The bang on his window made Porter reach for his sidearm, but he relaxed when he saw the white figure seated on the white motorcycle. It appeared out of nowhere—the only entrance into the parking lot was straight ahead, and the lamps were off.

He lowered the window. "How did you get here?"

The Ghost turned off the Ducati motor and leaned closer until the helmet almost touched the top of the window, watching Porter through the dark face shield, saying nothing.

"You lost him?"

The Ghost nodded.

"I was told you're the best."

No response.

"Have you put a trace on the girlfriend's car at least?"

A nod.

"What about their place? Did you search it?"

Another nod.

"No floppy disk?"

Head shake.

"Did you find anything else?"

The white glove reached into the jacket, pulled out something, and handed it to Porter. It was a passport.

Porter opened it and saw Ben Teller's photo. "That's a relief. Now we only have to hunt down the prick within the continental United States. Congratulations."

The Ghost held out a hand.

"Right." Porter collected a bundle of cash and a texting pager from the passenger seat and handed them over. "The pager is a prepaid piece. I don't think it's traceable, but only turn it on to check for messages every hour or so."

The Ghost pocketed the money and the pager.

"The black bitch is the key. I have a plan. We'll double up in a pincer to squeeze her bad enough to draw Teller out of hiding.

Then you'll arrange an accident, but do it somewhere isolated, so you can remove and destroy his iPhone, camera, and anything else he carries that could hold data. If an accident is impractical, make it look like a robbery gone bad. And finish him off this time. I don't want Teller climbing out of a gorge again, okay?"

There was no response from the dark face shield.

"I'll send you a text message with instructions." Porter rolled up the window.

The Ducati motor came to life, and the Ghost eased away with the lights still off. Once on the main road, the Ducati raced away.

PART V:

The Apostates

CHAPTER 47

After a night of deep sleep, Ben woke up stiff and achy. The last three days had not been kind to his body, and the old shoulder injury was acting up again. He lingered in bed until late in the morning. When he came out of the tiny bedroom, there was no one in the house. Stepping outside, he noticed a mark on the doorjamb, about two-thirds of the way up from the floor with a little hole at each end. It looked like the discoloration left after removal of a mezuzah—the traditional Jewish ornament in the form of a tube containing a scribed scroll and attached to the doorjamb with two nails. Someone must have removed it recently, just like the family photos inside the house, leaving an off-color shadow in its stead.

Rex was tinkering with the Ducati. "How are you doing?"

"As good as could be expected." Ben approached the GS, which had been unloaded from the Suburban and parked under a tree. It seemed no worse than it had already been thanks to the Ghost and the deer. He started the motor, listened to its sound, and checked for leaks, finding none. The tires seemed to hold pressure, and all the lights were working. "What's the best way out of here?"

"Do you really want to leave?"

"I want to find the floppy disk and confront Morgan."

A car engine sounded, and the Suburban appeared down the dirt road. Streep was driving, with Powell in the passenger seat and Dreyfuss in the back. They got out carrying grocery bags.

Rex took the bag from Powell. "Our guest wants to continue Zachariah's treasure hunt. Should we help him?"

"Sure," Powell said.

Ben followed them back inside. "First you try to kill me, and now you want to help me?"

"Things changed." Streep carried a log to the fireplace. "We thought you were working with them."

"Working? On what?"

"On removing all barriers from Joe Morgan's path to the White House, including exposure of his role in various unsavory practices of the Mormon Church. They'll do whatever it takes to help him win."

"Why?"

"Are you an imbecile?" Streep shoved a burning piece of paper under the log. "The saints believe it is the destiny of the True Church to take over the whole world, which is why they have a hundred thousand missionaries roving the globe continuously. But putting a devout Mormon in the White House? A Mormon as Commander in Chief? A Mormon as the leader of the free world? In a single strike they'll become mainstream. Legitimate! Respectable! Do you think China will continue to ban Mormon missionaries when President Joe Morgan occupies the Oval Office?"

"Probably not."

"That's right! His election would put Mormon conversions on steroids!"

"There's a downside too," Ben said. "It would put Mormonism under everybody's magnifying glass. They must be worried about this, considering how Mormon history is filled with stories of persecution and suffering."

"I grew up on these stories," Streep said, "of bloody Gentile attacks on our innocent ancestors in Ohio, Missouri, Illinois—culminating with the lynching of our prophet. It's only after I left the Church that I started reading the banned books and discovered the real complexity of our history."

"Which is?"

"It's true that most Mormons were hardworking farmers who did nothing to stir the anti-Mormon hostilities that almost destroyed them. But as a group, we were hardly blameless. Joseph Smith was blessed with incredible intelligence, creativity, and charisma, but he used these gifts not only for good."

"I have to agree with that," Dreyfuss said. "It wasn't just his religious activities. There were other new churches and Christian sects popping up in America at that time, and nobody bothered them. But Smith's messianic theology transformed into a theocracy. His control over the saints as a voting block, his claims that God anointed him to be king over the county, the state, the nation, and eventually the world, scared non-Mormon politicians and citizens. His failed business ventures cost many investors their life savings. His plural marriages, which he claimed were divinely inspired, triggered revulsion and animosity. Put together, all those things instigated armed attacks on Mormons, who formed militias and fought back, and many innocent people died."

"Hey there," Powell yelled from the kitchen, "breakfast is ready."

Rex glanced at his watch. "More like lunch, judging by the time. I have to go. See you all tonight."

"Good luck," Dreyfuss said.

Keera arrived late, which meant she had to park all the way at the end. A thin, cold drizzle accompanied her across the parking lot and the circular driveway in front of the hospital. It fit her mood. Waking up on Fran's sofa, having none of the usual comforts of home, missing most of her favorite toiletries, and not being able to kiss Ben before heading out together made for a miserable morning. How long before he returned? Tomorrow was Friday, and then the weekend. There was no way she would spend a whole nail-biting weekend on Fran's sofa.

"Good morning!" The gray-haired security guard waved at Keera from behind the reception desk. "How are we doing today, Doctor?"

"Sam!" She shook her finger at him, but still, being greeted with the same joke again and again had its own charm. Clearly the elderly African American guard was proud of her success. "Five more months," she said. "Don't jinx me!"

"Haven't so far, have I?"

"No," she said, though inside her, dread was rising that life was taking a dangerous, downward slide. "See you later!"

"Go save them," he yelled, like always, while she ran to catch the elevator.

Streep filled a plate with eggs and potatoes and placed it before Ben. "Now you understand why they'll do anything to get Morgan elected president of the United States."

"They?" Ben stretched his arms sideways and up, twisting his face in pain. "Who exactly are they?"

Dreyfuss sat down with his own loaded plate. "Have you heard about the Danites?"

"Let me guess," Ben said. "The Danites are a secret group of Joe Morgan's supporters who don't shy away from violence to ensure his election. Kind of like Watergate, right?"

"A worse kind." Dreyfuss dug into his eggs with a fork. "We're not talking about Nixon's clumsy plumbers breaking into the Democratic Party's headquarters. The Danites are history's most deadly political hit men."

"Never heard of them."

"Because the Mormon Church," Dreyfuss said, "is the most effective suppressor of its own history."

"Thanks for cooking," Ben said to Powell. "It's good."

"You're welcome." Powell sat down, a mug of coffee between his large hands. "The Danites were named by Smith for the Israelite Dan, son of Jacob by Bilha, the maid of his beloved wife Rachel. In Genesis, when Jacob's sons came to his deathbed to receive his last blessings, he said: *Dan shall judge the nation; Dan shall be a snake on the road, an adder upon travelers, who strikes the horse's hooves, felling its rider.* Do you understand?"

"Dan will be both judge and executioner."

"Exactly!" Powell raised his mug in a toast. "A big role for the smallest tribe of Israel!"

"That reminds me of something." Ben reached into his backpack and took out the Canon. "The day Zachariah died, the Ducati ambushed him near the Camp David Scenic Overlook. I took some photos of the path where I think the Ghost waited." He browsed through the archive of photos on the rear panel of the camera. "Here it is." He showed them the photo of the depression left in the weeds by the kickstand. "It's a custom piece with a design welded to the bottom of the plate. I thought it was just a cute stylish twist, meant to add traction to the kickstand."

"It's a snake," Dreyfuss said. "The Danites' symbol. And waiting in ambush is also predestined, as Moses is quoted in the last chapter of the five books of Moses, giving each tribe a last blessing before he died at the border of the Promised Land. He said that Dan '*shall strike out of the Bashan.*' Joseph Smith loved to borrow and twist biblical symbols to inspire obedience."

Ben put down his camera. "Smith started the Danites?"

"A few years into his career as prophet, Smith was facing a rebellion among his initial cohorts. These men had become his business partners in the new church after providing testimonies to support his tales about golden tablets and angels. In exchange, they expected to become rich. But when Smith's land and banking speculations failed, they recanted their testimonies and rebelled against his authority. By that time, Smith had collected enough believers to defend his flourishing sect. He conveniently announced a divine revelation that the rebels should be destroyed—a sermon known among Mormons as the 'Rebel Rousing Discourse.' He preached that, unlike what Christians believe, Judas had not hung himself after betraying Jesus, but had been killed on God's orders by the Apostle Peter. Similarly, Smith claimed, God had ordered him to form the Danites who would destroy the opponents of the Mormon Church."

"Sounds extreme," Ben said. "Are we talking historic facts or anti-Mormon speculation?"

"Documented history." Dreyfuss unfolded a sheet of paper. "This is a copy of the original Danite Manifesto. Read it."

Ben pushed aside his food and looked at the paper. It was a photocopy of a document whose serrated margins testified to old age. At the bottom, several columns of signatures appeared, crowded together. The text itself occupied the top half of the page and was handwritten in neat, old English-style cursive:

> *We have solemnly warned you, and that in the most determined manner, that if you do not cease that course of wanton abuse of the citizens of this county, that vengeance would overtake you sooner or later, and that when it did come it would be as furious as the mountain torrent, and as terrible as the beating tempest; but you have affected to despise our warnings, and pass them off with a sneer, or a grin, or a threat, and pursued your former course; and vengeance sleepeth not, neither does it slumber; and unless you heed us this time, and attend to our request, it will overtake you at an hour when you do not expect, and at a day when you do not look for it; and for you there shall be no escape; for there is but one decree for you, which is depart, depart, or a more fatal calamity shall befall you.*

Dreyfuss took back the paper. "These signatures at the bottom are of eighty-three leading Mormons, including Joseph Smith's brother, Hyrum."

"Interesting," Ben said. "How did they contend with God's commandment not to kill?"

"Good question. To justify murder, Smith said that the Danites in fact were doing their victims a favor, spiritually speaking."

"A favor?"

"*Blood Atonement*," Powell said. "The sinner, or even the innocent bystander, is redeemed by being killed and wins entry to heaven as a martyr. It's the same theological doctrine invoked by the Inquisition to extract confessions by torture and burn people at the stake. Today's jihadists also use this concept to justify bombing their fellow Muslims—including collateral victims."

"Come on," Ben said. "How can you compare Mormons to jihadists?"

"Let me quote for you," Powell said, "Joseph Smith's exact words as written down by the Danites' commander, John D. Lee, at the time: '*We will establish our religion by the sword. We will trample down our enemies and make it one gore of blood from the Rocky Mountains to the Atlantic Ocean. I will be to this generation a second Mohammed, whose motto in treating for peace was: "The Al-Koran or the sword!" So shall it eventually be with us: Joseph Smith or the sword!"*

"Within a short time," Dreyfuss said, "Caldwell County in Missouri became a totalitarian theocracy, where disobedient Mormons were literally destroyed. By eighteen thirty-eight, the Danites numbered over a thousand, and they attacked not only Mormon opposition but non-Mormons, whom Smith called 'Gentiles.' Soon enough, when Smith attempted to take over the state government, Missouri was in civil war, which ended with the Mormons' exile to Illinois, where the same pattern repeated. Joseph Smith created a theocracy in a city-state called Nauvoo, built his Danites into a militia force of over five thousand armed zealots, and in 'forty-four declared himself candidate for president of the United States."

"Did he?" Ben laughed. "That's ridiculous!"

"Not if you command a militia that was almost as strong as the United States Army at the time, and much better trained and motivated. The Danites were fed and equipped by the tithing of tens of thousands of hardworking believers who expected Joseph Smith to become '*King to rule over Israel.*' Unfortunately, the rest of the country was less receptive to his aspirations, and everyone was repulsed by the polygamous lifestyle he practiced and preached. Two more wars ensued, and the bloodshed ended only after Joseph Smith was arrested and lynched. The Mormons migrated to the Salt Lake region, which was still part of Mexico."

"And the Danites?"

"They continued to serve, basically giving Smith's heir, Prophet Brigham Young, total control over the region, killing and robbing westward pioneers while stomping on internal opposition. But they overdid it with the Mountain Meadows massacre."

"That rings a bell," Ben said. "I thought Indians did that."

"The Mormons used the natives to attack the travelers." Dreyfuss sighed. "The Baker-Fancher wagon train, about a hundred and fifty men, women, and children on their way to California through the Utah territory with all their cattle, cash, and belongings—a promising loot. But they fought back, and there was a standoff. The Danites' commander, John D. Lee, tricked the wagon train leaders into surrendering their guns in exchange for safe passage, and then his men murdered everyone."

"I remember now," Ben said. "There was a PBS documentary about it."

"The Mountain Meadows massacre," Dreyfuss said, "was a tipping point. The whole nation was outraged, and the Mormons didn't help themselves by proclaiming that all other Christians were Gentiles whose churches were false and whose souls required blood atonement. President Buchanan sent the US Army to subdue the Mormon rebellion, and Brigham Young was faced with certain destruction. He made the only logical decision and dropped the vision of an independent Kingdom of Zion in the Salt Lake Basin. Utah became a state, and Young became its first governor. Finally, as a token of appeasement for the massacre, Lee was shot by a Mormon firing squad at Mountain Meadows."

"Was that," Ben asked, "the end of the Danites?"

"No," Dreyfuss said. "Brigham Young appointed Orrin Porter Rockwell to lead the Danites, and they took an oath of secrecy: '*In the name of Jesus Christ, the Son of God, I do solemnly obligate myself ever to conceal, and never to reveal the secret purpose of this society.*' Rockwell himself went on to murder over a hundred men while establishing the Danites as a lasting secret force. They've remained a deadly force, eliminating every threat and opposition to the leaders of the LDS Church."

"Even today?"

"You bet," Streep said. "How else would you explain why, a few years ago, the Mormons unveiled a life-size statue of Orrin Porter Rockwell in Lehi, Utah, in a dedicated park, investing a huge amount of money to commemorate a known murderer who actually died of natural causes in jail as he awaited trial for one of his murders? The reason is that they don't see the Danites as murderers but as avenging angels who exact blood atonement as prescribed by the prophet Joseph Smith and by his successors."

"Sounds like fiction," Ben said.

"Is this fiction?" Streep reached over and poked the bruise on his forehead. "Who tried to kill you?"

"We believe," Dreyfuss said, "that the Mormon leaders in Salt Lake City ordered the Danites to eliminate any threat to Joe Morgan's chances of winning the elections and becoming president. Obviously you showed up on their radar screen."

"But my editor says that the baptisms of dead Medal of Honor winners will not be such hot news, which means it won't damage Morgan's chances that much."

"True," Powell said. "But lying about it? Abusing Zachariah? It's a cover-up!"

"Like Nixon," Ben said.

"We must expose Morgan," Dreyfuss said. "He was directing the pressure on Zachariah, and we believe all this is chronicled in the files of the Strengthening Church Members Committee."

"What's that?"

"It's like the Mormon FBI."

"Never heard of it," Ben said. "Does it really exist?"

CHAPTER 48

The pathology lab was located on the basement level of the medical school, which Keera always felt was creepy, as if all of them—cadavers, students, and the pale professor—belonged six feet under. On the other hand, unlike rounding with the other professors on the hospital floors above, where live—or barely alive—patients and their families provided ample fuel for stress and self-doubts, here there was only a cool, quiet interaction with uncomplaining patients who were at no risk of getting any sicker.

Today's subject was critical care. As part of the training in that demanding, intense part of medical care, students were required to attend the post-mortem pathology of patients who had died under their team's care. It was traumatic in some cases and less so in others, depending on how much time she had spent with the patient in the CCU and what the patient's mental status had been. A frail Alzheimer's patient with no communication capacity was easier to confront in mortality, but a vivacious cancer patient, who had become a dear friend over weeks of care, would turn a postmortem into a devastating experience of peeling away layers of familiar skin and removing the brittle organs of a ravaged body in which, so recently, a precious life had been breathing.

Thankfully Keera's subject today was a ninety-six-year-old man who had spent only two days in the CCU, unconscious and hooked up to a ventilator. The initial focus was his feet, which had lost blood supply days before his death and looked quite gruesome. By virtue of cadavers having two feet each, the pairs of medical students were able to work simultaneously, unlike the dissection of a nose or a heart, where only one could work at any given time while the other watched.

Keera exposed the underlying structure of muscles and bones as the professor had instructed. She put down the scalpel and stepped back. He was still in the front of the room, examining another student's work. With at least ten minutes to kill, hunger struck her.

Taking the stairs to the main level, Keera hurried to the elevators and up to the cafeteria on the fourth floor. Buying a cup of coffee and a donut, she found a window table flooded with sunlight. The clouds had moved away, and the warmth of the sun was especially nice after the chill of death in pathology. She turned to face the window while sipping coffee.

Below her, the parking lot was vast, hundreds of cars lined up in rows, waiting out the day. She tried to orient herself and figure out where the Mustang was parked. Tracing her route from memory, she remembered where she had left it that morning—all the way to the side, near the fence that bordered the highway.

Keera was about to turn away and head back downstairs when something drew her attention: Two rows away from the Mustang, in the shade of a minivan, was a white motorcycle.

"I'm not surprised you've never heard of it," Dreyfuss said. "The Strengthening Church Members Committee is a department of the General Authorities of the LDS Church. The term 'Committee' sounds benign, but you should think of it in the context of, let's say, Senator McCarthy's House Un-American Activities Committee."

"I beg to disagree." Powell was scrubbing a pot in the sink. "It's more like the KGB during Stalin's days, enforcing the strict dictates of a rigid party hierarchy."

"But with love rather than torture cellars." Dreyfuss chuckled. "Working with similar zeal, though, and in total secrecy. The LDS Strengthening Church Members Committee's mission is to investigate and collect information on every Mormon who is suspected of opinions that deviate from the Mormon faith, contradict Mormon doctrines, or question the total authority of the Mormon leaders."

"They investigate people's opinions?" Ben was intrigued. "Everyone has occasional doubts about faith, even the most religious people."

"Not among Mormons. To maintain one's good standing, a Mormon must regularly offer testimony of his or her faith that Joseph Smith was a true prophet who received from God the only true gospel. Testimonies are given in front of the congregation at weekly ward meetings. Each local bishop must report to the stake president, and up to Salt Lake City, any saints who deviate in any way. The committee collects files of public statements, such as speeches, articles, or interviews, as well as private letters, and statements from spouses, colleagues, or fellow Mormons who might have overheard the inappropriate statements."

"It's true," Powell said. "I've seen it in my own trial. The Strengthening Church Members Committee's file was thick with every little detail of my life, especially my academic research, communications with colleagues, and the efforts of good Mormons at convincing me to drop the issue. The file was used by my accusers to chronicle my sinful attempts at substantive discussions of the LDS's racist theology. Based on those files the tribunal found me guilty, declared me an apostate, and excommunicated me."

"We know," Dreyfuss said, "that Zachariah stood trial at the DC temple. The committee had transferred his file electronically ahead of time to the chair of the tribunal—the president of the DC temple. We must access the computer in his office and copy the file. Then we'll have proof of Joe Morgan's direct involvement in the events leading to Zachariah's death."

"A long shot," Ben said. "Have you tried hacking?"

"No chance. The LDS Church has top-of-the line Internet security. It would be easier to hack into the FBI system. We need to physically enter the temple, sit at a computer terminal, and sign into the system with a valid password. We had hoped Zachariah would agree to do it, but—"

"There was something on the second floppy disk." Ben turned on the Canon and searched the memory for the photo he had taken of Ray's computer screen:

User ID: Zachiboy
Password: DCMTDBS
File: BFD111995

Dreyfuss looked at it. "The password is an acronym: *DC Mormon Temple Data Base System.* And once you sign into the system with the user name and password, you'll be able to search for the file name."

"Which is also literal," Ben said. "*Baptism For Dead Eleven Nineteen Ninety-Five.*"

"There's the answer," Dreyfuss said. "This file is on the system at the DC temple, which would also have files of Zachariah's trial and evidence."

"Have you tried to enter the temple?"

"No can do. Each one of us is a known apostate. Security will throw us out as soon as we show up."

"Have you tried a mole?"

"Twice," Streep said. "Cost us a pretty penny. The first one was young, single college grad with good computer skills. A nice boy. We trained him for a couple of weeks and sent him to approach Mormon missionaries at the University of Maryland campus at College Park. He pretended to fall in love with the *Book of Mormon* and agreed to be baptized into the Church."

"And?"

"We lost him. Tried again, another nice kid, but we lost him too."

Ben was shocked. "The Danites killed them?"

"Worse. The boys became true believers."

"I don't understand."

"What's not to understand?" Streep laughed bitterly. "Our well-paid moles drank the same Kool Aid given to three hundred thousand converts who embrace Mormonism every year. It's a magic potion made of love, community, divine answers to existential questions of why are we here and where are we going when we die. I mean, the promise of godhood, for God's sake! And don't forget male hegemony, lots of sex as a divine duty, and a great deal of happiness."

"Happiness?"

"That's another interesting statistic," Powell said. "Mormon men are happier than any other category of men, except perhaps the members of the Saudi royal family."

"What about Mormon women?"

"The opposite. High levels of anti-depressants usage, compared to other female demographics."

"Then why don't you recruit a female mole?"

"No use," Streep said. "Mormon girls aren't allowed in the temple until the day of their marriage to a fertile saint in good standing."

"Why?"

"Because the temple symbolizes the soul's progression to the heavenly Kingdom of God, and a woman can't get there without her husband's ushering. Marriage is a bit much to ask of a hired mole, you agree?"

"So you lost both of them?"

"Not only that," Dreyfuss said, "but we have to assume that they told the Mormons everything about our efforts. Now the saints are on to us. Our only chance is to move fast, get someone into the DC temple, and expose Joe Morgan and his Danite henchmen."

"How?"

Powell gripped Ben's arm. "That's where you come in!"

Keera wondered why a motorcycle should be parked among the cars. There was a dedicated covered parking area for motorcycles at the front entrance of the hospital. Ben parked there whenever he stopped by to have lunch with her or bring her a treat when she was on call overnight.

Keera walked across the cafeteria and out to the hallway, passing through several nurses' stations and down two hallways, until she reached the southern end of the floor, which was the closest point to where her car was parked. Entering a patient's room, Keera smiled at the woman in the bed, who had a tube in her nose, and went to the window.

Much closer now, she saw the motorcycle—a white sport bike—leaning on its kickstand. Scanning the area around it, she finally spotted the rider in the shade of a tree in the green area near the outer fence.

Even from her distant observation spot, Keera could tell he was skinny and tall, wearing a white riding suit and a matching helmet, which he kept on—presumably because of the cold breeze. He was leaning against the tree trunk in a leisurely posture of a guy waiting for his girlfriend to finish working. But Keera knew he wasn't waiting for his girlfriend, but for Ben Teller's girlfriend. *For her!*

Her first instinct was to call security. Or the police. But what would she say? Anything she told them would involve Ben, perhaps even risk his life! She tried to call Fran, reaching her voice mail instead.

The white helmet was facing the hospital building. Could he see her among the hundreds of windows? Impossible! The windows were mirrored! But still, she stepped back and left the room.

"Here, read this." Dreyfuss handed him a book. "Better memorize as much as you can. We'll test you later."

Ben looked at the cover. *Mormonism for Dummies.* "Are you kidding me?"

"It's a good start. I'll give you a few more books later."

"Give me all of them now, and I'll choose which to read."

"Trust me. My last job was at the Missionary Training Center in Utah. The secret to the LDS success is that most Mormons don't know the true history of the Church or the details of its theology. They're too busy being happy." He patted the book with the photo of a temple on the cover. "There's more here than anyone will expect you to know, if they ever question you."

Opening the book, Ben chuckled at a cartoon that made fun of the Mormon ban on cursing. "Is self-deprecation permitted?"

"Absolutely, as long as it's light and not directed at the leaders of the Church." Dreyfuss headed out of the kitchen. "Have fun. Be happy."

"Hold on," Ben said. "Why did they kick you out?"

Dreyfuss stopped at the door and turned. "They didn't. I left of my own accord."

"After teaching tens of thousands of boys how to convert Gentiles to the True Church?"

"I'm still a believer."

"Excuse me?"

He chuckled. "True faith is like true love. It makes no sense to others, but when a man falls hard for a woman, or a woman for a man, completely and fully bewitched, it never goes away. Have you ever tried to tell a friend that he's in love with the wrong woman, that she's not a good fit for him?"

"Wrong move."

"Exactly. When a guy's in love, even if his friends point out the girl's major flaws, it doesn't matter. For him, she's perfect, magical, heavenly. Right?"

Ben nodded.

"Same with faith. It doesn't need to pass the test of logic or factual accuracy. It's an emotional thing, a spiritual passion, a conviction that our souls are godly and eternal. It's the faith I grew up loving, the faith I served with all my heart, the faith I taught to countless students. In my heart, my faith is true. And it never goes away, you know? Even when she gets wrinkles, age spots, and silver hair, you still see her as she once was—the light source of your universe. It's the same with my faith. I see the warts, but my heart still pounds with awe when I read the *Book of Mormon*. Do you understand?"

"I'm beginning to."

"Are you going to quote me in your article?"

"Anonymously, unless you tell me your real name."

"I can't do that."

"If you still believe, why did you leave?"

"Faith is one thing. Church authorities and their heavy-handed tactics are another." Dreyfuss pulled out a photo of a boy, perhaps sixteen or seventeen, redhead and freckled, smiling into the camera. The resemblance was unmistakable.

"Your son?"

"David was a great kid. He hit all the milestones for the perfect Mormon youth—Aaronic Priesthood, Eagle Scout, Melchizedek Priesthood, sailed through high school with top grades, certified by our local bishop for the honor of a two-year mission. He was perfect in every way...but one." Dreyfuss pocketed the photo. "He had managed to hide it well. No one ever suspected. But the Mission Training Center is very intense, and a brotherly embrace turned into something more. The other boy reported it, and my colleagues were in an awkward position. But the rules were clear. David lost his mission assignment, his Temple Recommend Card was taken, and he was sent for treatment."

"Treatment?"

"Of course." Dreyfuss chuckled sadly. "Homosexuality is a curable mental disease."

"He didn't have to go, did he?"

"He was a good boy. He did what his father told him to do."

"You had him committed?"

"I trusted my Church. Dr. Neibauer ran a clinic in Utah. It was very effective, according to him. Unfortunately, my David wasn't part of that statistic." Dreyfus removed his glasses and wiped his eyes on the back of his hand. "He wrote me a letter, apologizing for being a sinner, for succumbing to Satan's temptations. He was determined not to ruin our family's prospects of spending eternity together in the Celestial Kingdom, to which he could not rise to join us unless, of course, he was purified through the ultimate ritual."

"*Blood atonement?*"

"Exactly."

"He killed himself?"

"Suicide wouldn't work." Dreyfuss turned away and held on to the door frame. "He made a fake gun from wood in the arts and crafts room, went into the office during dinnertime, and called the police, telling them there's a young man who's gone mad and was shooting at staff members and patients. When the police arrived, he ran at them, aiming the gun. They shot him thirty-seven times. My poor David…"

Back downstairs, the hours passed slowly. Keera barely managed to answer the professor's questions about her dissection methods. His expression was even more dour than usual. He marked something on his pad and moved to the next cadaver. They continued dissecting up the shin and around the knees. Each time the professor returned, she had to force her mind to focus, setting aside the thought of the white Ducati that was waiting for her outside. She kept thinking of ways to get her car and speed away before he could catch up, but every idea failed in the details. Like in a game of rock-paper-scissors, a sport bike always beat an old Mustang. But when the three-hour class was finally drawing to a close, Keera looked at the skinned foot and came up with an idea that might just work.

On the way out, she grabbed a bundle of white cotton dressing. Crouched in the stairwell, she took off her left shoe and bandaged her ankle.

Limping through the lobby, Keera approached the security desk.

Sam saw her and got up. "What happened to you?"

"I tripped on the stairs," Keera said. "Stupid me."

He came around the security desk. "Are you okay driving like this?"

"Driving isn't the problem. Walking is." She fished her car keys from her pocket. "My car is all the way at the end. A blue Mustang convertible. Would you—"

"You got it!" He signaled the other guard, who nodded.

Moments later, her car pulled up in front of the building. Keera limped out and thanked Sam, who held the door open for her. She could tell he was wondering how she planned to drive a manual transmission in her condition, but she had bigger things to worry about. A dot of light appeared in her rearview mirror—far back, near the end of the parking area, the single headlight of a motorcycle.

Through the afternoon hours, Ben had been reading *Mormonism for Dummies.* It was jovially written and interesting, and he found similarities to other religions in the various myths, rules, and rituals. Eventually, when the sun was setting, smells of cooking drew him to the kitchen.

Powell was stirring a steamy pot. "Ready for a test?"

"A testimony," Ben said, "is the correct term."

"Very good! So…what is the First Vision?"

"Joseph Smith was fourteen when he went into the forest in upstate New York to pray for guidance about which church to join. God came down with Jesus. They told Joseph that all the existing churches were false abominations and that he must restore the True Church, which is the Church of Jesus Christ of Latter-day Saints."

"Correct," Powell said. "Between us, though, Smith's letters and writings tell an evolving series of stories about that event, starting with a mere dream, then something about an angel, or a personhood, and finally, in the last version, published after his death, it became God and Christ in actual bodies. But you should answer simply if the temple workers test you. Now, how about the *Book of Mormon?*"

"It's the True Gospel," Ben said. "An angel named Moroni told Smith to dig up golden tablets that had been buried by the last survivor of an ancient civilization of Israelite immigrants to North America a millennium earlier. Smith also found Urim Vetumim, a device that turned him into a seer—a man capable of translating the tablets from Egyptian to English. The book tells the story of how the lost tribes of Israel came to America and how Jesus Christ ministered to them before they were destroyed by the dark-skinned descendants of Lucifer, who are the ancestors of today's Native Americans."

"You're generalizing." Dreyfuss entered the kitchen and sat down. "Also, your tone isn't very convincing."

"Wait till he explains godhood," Streep said as she joined them.

"I'm not mocking," Ben said. "Mormonism isn't less plausible than other religions. If you believe that Christ rose from the dead in Jerusalem, why couldn't he have risen in America too and ministered to the natives?"

"Mormon boy!" Streep pointed at him. "Are you a good Christian? Are you?"

"Yes," Ben said. "I am. We believe in Jesus Christ and his mission of salvation and redemption."

"So what's the difference between you and a Protestant, a Catholic, or a Lutheran?"

"We believe that the *Book of Mormon* is divine scripture, that Joseph Smith was a true prophet of God, and that every successive head of our church, including our current church president, is also a prophet, a seer, and a revelator of God's messages."

"Go on," she said.

"We believe that God, Jesus, and the Holy Ghost are separate physical beings, just like men of blood and flesh. They're elevated humans who look and walk like us. God, for example, lives on his own planet with his godly wives. And all the saints who have achieved exaltations have also become gods and live with their own godly wives on their own planets and procreate many godly children."

"Hallelujah!"

"We also believe," Ben continued, "that all souls were created by God in pre-mortality and that they are sent here to earth to be born with a chance to embrace the True Gospel and live righteously as members of the Church of Jesus Christ of Latter-day Saints, which is the only path to exaltation."

"Men or women?"

"Both, but they have different roles. The man is the saint, the master who holds the priesthood of God, rules over his family, and goes out in the world to make money and provide for his family. The woman's job is childbearing. Her duty is to raise the children, take care of the home, and submit to her husband in every way."

"And the reward?"

"We believe," Ben said, "that only those of us—saints who follow the True Gospel to the letter—shall pass on to the Celestial Kingdom and live on as gods with our own godly wives who will be pregnant and give birth repeatedly forever—which is why we are sealed for eternity with our wives in the Mormon Temple."

"Nice, but you didn't answer," Streep said. "Are you—the Latter-day Saints—really Christians?"

CHAPTER 49

Keera had to make a choice: Run for it or pretend not to notice? The neatness of the burglary had given her a weird sense of confidence that these people were not insane criminals, but carefully calculating professionals. In all likelihood, the Ghost was here to watch her in case Ben showed up. They must have learned where she spent her days, but hopefully they didn't know where she was spending her nights. She decided to play the role of the oblivious babe. She would drive around until the opportunity came to make a run for it and lose the tail. Then she would go to Fran's place.

The exit road spilled onto I-95, and she headed south toward Washington, her usual commute home. Traffic was heavy, but it was moving steadily. The Ducati stayed way back, its headlight popping in and out of her rearview mirror.

A few miles down the road, approaching the exit for Rt. 32 West, she stayed in the left lane as long as possible, then cut across to the exit ramp on the right. A moment later, as she sped up on the merging lane, the Ducati headlight returned to her rearview mirror.

Traffic was heavier here, with tens of thousands of employees leaving the massive compound of the National Security Agency—the NSA, whose acronym was otherwise known to stand for No Such Agency.

She could stay on Rt. 32, which eventually curved northward and connected with I-70, where she could swing back toward Fran's place west of Baltimore. But first Keera had to lose the Ducati while pretending to be driving home. Her advantage would come from many weekends of riding behind Ben on his GS through the back roads of Howard County. He was always insistent that they map the ride ahead together, with her choosing the nature destinations and coffee stops. It was his way of making sure that her passive role as backseat passenger wouldn't make her feel like a needless appendage.

A tentative plan formed in her mind.

The exit for Rt. 29 South was backed up, and Keera kept her eyes on the side mirrors while maintaining enough room behind the next car for a quick lane change, in case the Ducati suddenly opted for more aggressive moves.

Heading down Rt. 29 South toward Silver Spring, she maintained a steady speed. The signs for Rt. 216 appeared. It was a local road that led into densely wooded areas of gradually narrowing country roads, rich with twists and turns, and plenty of places to hide.

From the third lane on the left, she crossed over to the right and slowed down.

About seven or eight cars behind, the Ducati did the same.

She put on the turn signal, veered to the shoulder, and stopped.

Traffic continued to flow. As she expected, to avoid exposure the Ghost kept going, passing by her window, moving apace with traffic—a white Ducati, a white riding suit, and a white helmet that didn't turn to look at her.

Knowing that he would look at his side mirror in a second to figure out why she had stopped, Keera turned right and held up her iPhone so it was visible through the front windshield. She redialed Fran's number. Again it went straight to voice mail.

Farther ahead, the Ducati was passing the exit, staying on Rt. 29 South. Keera hit the gas, accelerating at full power, and took the exit onto Rt. 216 West. Catching a last glimpse of the Ducati, she said out loud, "Ciao, asshole!"

"Yes, we are Christians," Ben answered. "We're definitely Christians. In fact, we're the only Christians!"

Streep finally smiled. "That's what I was looking for. Explain!"

"Those who call themselves Christians—Catholics, Protestants, Lutherans, Evangelists, Pentecostals, Born-againers, and so on—they're all Gentiles who follow false religions, abominations against God and Jesus Christ. They're not Christians."

"How can they not be Christians if they worship Christ?"

"They're misguided. Their Christ is actually his brother, Lucifer. Only Mormons follow the true Christ."

"Bravo!" Streep clapped. "Spoken like a true saint!"

"Just in case they ask you," Dreyfuss said, "about the other churches, here is something to remember." He showed him a photocopy of a page from a book. "This is the original language of the *Book of Mormon*, published by Joseph Smith in eighteen-thirty. Look at this, quoting from One Nephi, fourteen, three: '... *that great and abominable church, which was founded by the devil and his children that he might lead away the souls of men down to hell...*' And continuing here," Dreyfuss pointed at the next page, "Nephi elaborates about the two choices—the Mormon Church, which is the Lamb of God, and greater Christianity, lumped together as one whore. Here, starting in verse nine."

Ben held the page and read quietly:

> *Behold, there is save it be two churches;*
> *the one is the church of the Lamb of God*
> *and the other is the church of the devil.*
> *Wherefore whoso belongeth not to the church of the Lamb of God*
> *Belongeth to that great church which is the mother of abominations,*
> *and she is the whore of the earth.*
> *And it came to pass that I looked and beheld the whore of the earth.*
> *And she sat upon many waters,*
> *and she had dominion over all the earth*
> *among all the nations, kindreds, tongues, and people.*
> *And it came to pass that I beheld the church of the Lamb of God;*
> *and its numbers were few*
> *because of the wickedness and abominations of the whore*
> *which sat upon many waters.*

Nevertheless I beheld that the church of the Lamb, which were the saints of God,
were also upon all the face of the earth...'

"You see?" Dreyfuss pointed at the page. "That's what Joseph Smith taught his followers through the *Book of Mormon.* All of Christianity was the devil's whore, but his new church, the Lamb of God, was the only true church. Still is. Those who belong to the Mormon Church are the *'Saints of God,'* and one day they will replace the rest of Christianity *'upon all the face of the earth.'* In other words, only Mormons are true Christians. Everyone else— Catholics, Protestants, Baptists—are not Christians but Gentiles and devil-worshipers."

"Pretty harsh," Ben said. "Do Mormons still believe that?"

"You betcha!" Streep showed him a cross she was wearing on a plain silver chain around her neck. "No crosses on Mormon temples, churches, or necks, right?"

"Their obsession with secrecy," Dreyfuss explained, "is not a coincidence. They know how upset all Christians would be if they knew that Mormons consider themselves the only true Christians while all others are Gentiles whose churches are false, abominable, whoring, satanic denominations. It would interfere with the LDS corporate and business activities and hinder the political aspirations of people like Joe Morgan."

"That's right!" Streep tucked her cross back under her shirt. "Would you vote for someone who believes you're a devil worshiper?"

"Not to mention," Dreyfuss added, "the interference with their massive missionary work. We trained young Mormon missionaries to start contact with Christian prospects with a mild, friendly sales pitch that the *Book of Mormon* is nothing more than another testimony of Christ."

"That's arguably true," Streep said. "But who cares about theology? All the kid needs to know is what happens in the temple so he can get through security."

"What was that?" Ben looked from one to the other. "Have I agreed to infiltrate the temple?"

"It's the only way," Powell said. "Don't you want to find out what really happened to Zachariah, how involved was Morgan, who sent the Danites to kill you?"

"I do," Ben said. "But I want to confront Morgan myself. That's my condition, and it's not negotiable."

"Why?" Streep looked at him with creased eyes. "It's going to be risky, even if you manage to get to him."

"I have my reasons," Ben said. "Do we have an agreement?"

"Yes," Powell said. "It's a deal. We'll train you and get you into the temple. You'll steal the files and give us the data. As far as we're concerned, you can try to confront Morgan face-to-face, though I hope you have a good reasons to take such a risk."

The road narrowed to two lanes, separated by a solid line. Traffic was heavy in both directions. She couldn't pass, but there was no doubt in her mind that the Ducati was already catching up fast. If she waited any longer, the game would be lost.

Taking advantage of a lull in oncoming traffic, Keera veered into the opposite lane and pushed the Mustang to go as fast as it could, passing a group of slow-moving cars. A truck appeared around a curve ahead, and Keera slipped back into her lane, winning an angry honk for the car she had cut off. Farther ahead, the light was green at Pindell School Road, but it turned yellow as she approached. With the pedal pressed to the floor, she flew through the intersection.

A minute or so later, she saw the cemetery on the left, which extended all the way to the intersection with Browns Bridge Road, where she would turn right and head north, disappearing into the countryside beyond the Ducati's reach.

But the light at the intersection ahead was red, a line of waiting cars blocked her way, and oncoming traffic deprived her of a passing lane. Without giving in to hesitation, Keera twisted the steering wheel and dropped to the dirt shoulder, passing the other cars on the right. The Mustang made hellish noises as rocks hit the undercarriage, the tires pounded on the uneven surface, and the steering wheel literally tried to twist out of her grip. Just before reaching the turn, she noticed that part of the shoulder was missing, washed away into the parallel ditch by a recent rain.

It was too late to stop. The right front wheel dropped into the hole, the hood tilted sharply before her eyes, followed by a huge bang as the wheel hit the other side of the hole and sent the right side of the car leaping into the air. And as it came down, the rear wheel dropped into the same hole. The Mustang was caught in a three-dimensional figure-eight, twisting left and right, up and down, and back and forth like a bucking horse determined to throw her off.

Keera gripped the steering wheel desperately to keep the Mustang on its forward velocity on the dirt shoulder toward the stoplights and the perpendicular traffic out of Browns Bridge Road. Suddenly, the latches holding the convertible top broke off and the whole canvas top popped up, filled with wind, and flew backward, tearing away with a sickening sound.

"If I'm going to enter the temple," Ben said, "I'll need to know what to expect." He patted *Mormonism for Dummies*. "There's very little about it here."

"Because temple rituals are secret," Dreyfuss explained. "Mormons are sworn on their lives never to reveal the rituals to Gentiles. Temple participation itself is restricted to Mormons in good standing—men who have attained priesthood, married in a temple, obey their bishop, and follow all the rules, such as to abstain from tobacco, caffeine, and alcohol. They also must be tithing in full, which means that one dollar in every ten they earn must go to Salt Lake City."

"You should know," Powell said, "that saints are often called back to the temple to serve as proxy for the dead. With hundreds of thousands of dead Gentile souls awaiting salvation, the LDS Church faces a challenge of efficiency, because posthumous conversions have two parts. The immersion in a baptismal bath can be done in any one of the hundreds of wards, but posthumous endowments can only be done at one of the forty or so temples.

Before leaving the Church, I spent many days serving as a proxy. It's a wonderful experience."

"Same here," Dreyfuss said. "Mormon temples are heavenly places for the faithful. As a member of the missionary training leadership, I was fortunate to live near a temple and serve often as proxy for the dead. Even now, when I think back on receiving the endowments and practicing the rituals, I wish for one more opportunity to participate."

"I feel the same," Powell said.

"Suit yourselves," Streep said. "The whole thing makes me want to puke."

Ben laughed. "I'm with you, but if entry criteria is so tightly supervised, how am I going to get in?"

"Don't worry." Powell chuckled. "We'll take care of that part."

"And then? Once I'm in, what happens then? I don't want to look like an idiot."

"Patience," Dreyfuss said. "The first thing you want to understand is that the Mormon temple is designed to resemble the phases of rising through salvation and exaltation to the ultimate godhood. In other words, you're in for a treat, Mr. Teller."

Shocked by the hurricane of cold air, dazed by the jerky, roller-coaster ride toward the stoplights and cross-traffic, Keera's next move was born out of survival instinct rather than skill. As soon as the front wheels reconnected with asphalt, she twisted the steering wheel to the right and held on while the Mustang screeched and groaned and attempted to stand on its left wheels.

Somehow, despite the forward momentum, the car made the turn onto Browns Bridge Road. The sudden change in direction cut down its speed, bringing the storm of wind and noise to an abrupt calmness.

But not for long.

A cacophony of car horns came from behind, amplified by the missing roof. Keera knew she should stop and find the soft top. As aged and cracked as it was, a new one would cost a small fortune.

But she was too shaken to do anything but continue north on Browns Bridge Road, away from the scene of her nearly calamitous crash. Besides, the Ducati must have scrambled to turn around and chase after her on Rt. 216, and its mosquito-like agility would allow it to pass through traffic much more rapidly than her Mustang.

She sped up.

Driving with an open top under the darkening sky would have been pretty if not for the frosty air that swirled around her, reducing the ambient temperature to arctic levels. She cranked up the heat to maximum and crouched as low as possible in the seat, peering above the steering wheel at the road ahead—a two-lane twister that Ben loved to tear through on his GS, with her grasping his skinny hips for dear life.

She planned ahead in her mind. Two more turns, a total of less than three miles, and she would reach Rt. 32 West. From there, it would be twenty minutes to Fran's place.

Keera pulled her sleeves down to cover her hands, gripping the steering wheel as tightly as she could. Her hair was flying around. She reached across to the glove compartment and found the wool cap that had been there since the fall, when she occasionally enjoyed open-top driving.

Approaching a stop sign at Guilford Road, she downshifted, slowed down, and after a quick glance to the right, made the left turn and accelerated. Another minute or two, and she would be in the thick of commuter traffic on 32 West-North, lost to her pursuer. She imagined telling Ben about this little adventure, watching his bemused expression turn to concern and alarm at how close she had come to—

"Blue Mustang! Stop on the side of the road!"

Keera sat up and looked over her shoulder.

"Stop now!" The man's voice on the loudspeaker was now accompanied by rolling lights—not on the roof, but on the dashboard inside the car, which was a large sedan of the type used by unmarked police. "Blue Mustang!"

She hesitated, asking out loud, "Who the hell are you?"

As if answering her question, the loudspeaker announced, "Maryland State Police. Please slow down, get off the road, and come to a full stop on the shoulder!"

She obeyed.

"Turn off the engine and keep your hands on the wheel!"

In her haste and cold, Keera released the clutch while still in gear, and the engine died. "Here," she said. "Happy now?"

Rex came in, wearing a dark suit and a tie. "Blessings unto you, Brothers and Sister!" He pulled a laminated card from his pocket and set it on the table. "Welcome aboard, Sampson Allard!"

"You got him a Temple Recommend Card?" Streep examined it. "The face is similar, but the hair is wrong." She clasped Ben's dark mane with her hand. "You're not too attached to this, are you?"

"My girlfriend is," Ben said. "Can we just color it?"

"Have you ever seen a Mormon with long hair?"

"Joseph Smith, Brigham Young—"

"Long hair," Streep said, "had gone out of fashion together with plural marriages and horse wagons."

"I stopped at CVS on the way." Rex put a shopping bag on the table and removed electric clippers and a box of washable hair coloring.

Ben held up the Temple Recommend Card. "How did you get this?"

"I spent hours," Rex said, "watching people leave the Mormon temple until I saw a guy about your size and age with similar facial features."

Dreyfuss looked at the card. "Nice resemblance. How did you steal it?"

"Steal? That would be a sin." Rex grinned as he took out his wallet and produced a business card. The ivory paper was thick, embossed with a golden Angel Moroni holding a trumpet. Below that familiar logo, the card said:

Josiah L. Luntsman, Jr – Investigator
The Church of JESUS CHRIST of Latter-day Saints
Strengthening Church Members Committee
50 E. N. Temple., Salt Lake City, UT 84150

"I trailed the guy," Rex said, "to a gas station in Virginia and approached him. He went a little pale at the sight of my business card and had to sit down when I told him that he was under investigation for certain mocking statements he had made. He was contrite, assuming I was after him for telling jokes. But he professed his faith—he'd driven all the way from West Virginia to serve as proxy in receiving endowments for the dead. I assured him that this was a confidential investigation, that he would hear from us within one week, and that most likely he would be restored after proper repentance. But in the meantime, he must hand over his Temple Recommend Card."

"And he just gave it to you?"

"Mormons are conditioned to obey, especially to an officious saint from the Strengthening Church Members Committee."

"What if he contacts his ward's bishop?"

"Not after I made him take an oath of secrecy—normal procedure, I assured him, intended to protect his good name in the likely event that the issues are resolved without further action."

"Your turn now," Powell said to Streep. "We have three days to transform scruffy boy here," he patted Ben's stubby cheek, "from an individualist photojournalist into a conformist fellow-religionist. Changing his appearance is the perfect starting point."

"Let's go." Streep led Ben to the bathroom and sat him down.

He draped a towel around his neck.

She plugged in the clippers, which started with quiet humming. "Say good-bye." She ruffled his hair.

Ben sighed. "Easy now. Keera is going to be upset."

The trooper approached from the rear on the right side of the car while traffic continued on the left. He held up an open wallet, showing her a Maryland State Police badge. "What's the rush, young lady?"

"I'm in a bit of a hurry," Keera said. "Really."

"Did you leave the stove on? Your husband's dinner's burning?

"I don't have a husband."

"No husband?" He clicked his tongue. "A pretty girl like you?"

"I have a boyfriend. He's a reporter."

"Tell him you almost made the news." He held out his hand. "License and registration, please."

She handed both to him.

"Thank you." He glanced at her driver's license. "Keera Torrens. Occupation?"

"Student."

"What do you study? Fashion design?"

"Medicine," she said. "Perhaps I'll see you one of these days, Officer, on a gurney at the trauma center."

"Maybe, but for a future doctor you're showing total disregard for other people's wellbeing."

"Excuse me?"

He gestured at the road behind. "Exceeding the speed limit. Passing on the right. Driving on the shoulder. Endangering fellow motorists. Leaving the scene of an accident."

"An accident? What accident?"

"This." He pointed at the remnants of the soft top, a few jarred pieces of black canvas still attached to the frame behind the rear seat.

"But I didn't hit another car!"

"An accident involving a single vehicle is still an accident under Maryland law, and the driver involved may not leave the scene until law enforcement has completed its site investigation or until all debris has been removed and the offending driver has verified that no other motorists require assistance or otherwise require police involvement."

Keera sighed. "I didn't know that."

"Ignorance of the law is not an excuse." He walked back to his car.

She waited, shaking from the cold.

A few minutes later, he returned. "Miss Torrens," he said, "seems like you are fond of speeding—this is your third offense in the past five years, which requires mandatory suspension of your license. This vehicle will be towed to the police pound."

"Oh, no! I need my car!"

"Why don't you call your reporter-boyfriend. He can meet you at the station and give you a ride home?"

"He's not available."

"Can you leave him a message? Surely he'll put aside everything else in order to help you."

"He's away. His phone is off."

"Where is he?" The trooper pulled out a small writing pad. "I can have our dispatcher contact—"

"I was being followed," Keera said.

"Excuse me?"

"That's why I was speeding and passing illegally. Someone was following me."

He looked at her doubtfully. "And you waited until now to tell me this?"

"I didn't think you'd believe me."

"Why would anyone follow you?"

She knew why, but couldn't tell him. "Maybe he needs a fashion designer."

The trooper laughed. "Fair enough. I apologize. But really, do you have any idea why?"

"Am I supposed to read every creep's mind? I'm telling you the truth. Some guy followed me from the hospital."

"How do you know he was following you and not just driving in the same direction?"

"He was behind me from the hospital parking lot, down ninety-five south, then thirty-two west, and on twenty-nine south. When I slowed down, he slowed down, when I went fast, he went fast, and when I changed lanes, he changed lanes. Okay?"

"A persistent guy." The trooper gestured at the road behind. "Why did he give up?"

"I tricked him. He passed me, and I took the exit to the two-sixteen west. But I was afraid he would catch up. It's much easier to go fast on a motorcycle."

"A motorcycle?" The trooper's eyes lit up. "What was he riding? Can you give me a description?"

"A white Ducati."

"Here." The trooper handed her the license and registration. "Observe the speed limit, okay?"

Keera put away her purse. "That's it?"

"I heard on the radio that a white Ducati was observed speeding on two-sixteen, heading west. Unfortunately, the officer gave up the pursuit due to dense traffic conditions."

"Shit!" Keera covered her mouth. "Sorry."

"You're safe now, Miss Torrens. Drive straight home. I'll be right behind you." He handed her a business card. "Keep this handy. Any time you see anything suspicious, call me."

"Thank you, Officer." She looked at the card, which carried the Maryland State Police emblem. The lettering was small, and in the poor lighting she had to look closely to see his name: *O. Porter – Inspector.*

In the bathroom mirror, Ben's cropped hair was bleached, as were his eyebrows and eyelashes. His face was clean shaven. He used the towel to brush off his shoulders and chest.

"Wait a minute!" Streep made him turn. "What's this?"

They congregated around him and peered at the tattoo on the back of his shoulder. It depicted a football helmet with a *Bud Light* logo on it.

"The real helmet cracked," Ben said. "It saved my head, but my mom threw it away with the rest of my football gear, which made me real angry when I came home from the hospital."

"A tattoo," Streep said, "is a great way to get back at your mom."

"Oh, yeah." He laughed. "She lost her voice from all the yelling. It was great."

Dreyfuss touched it with a finger. "It has to come off."

"*What?*"

"Mormons don't have tattoos."

"Why not?"

"What do you think? No coffee, no booze, no cigarettes, but self-mutilation would be okay? Advertising beer, no less? It'll blow your cover!"

"They won't see it."

"In the temple," Dreyfuss said, "you'll be taking off your clothes. They'll see everything."

"Then let's paint it over with a black Sharpie," Ben said. "It'll look like a birthmark."

"A black birthmark of this size," Powell said, "will freak them out. They'll think it's the mark of Lucifer. It'll draw more attention than if you had a third nipple. Security will be called, they'll contact Salt Lake City to check your personal file—or rather," he glanced at the stolen Temple Recommend Card, "the file of Sampson Allard—and find out there's no mention of either birthmark or a third nipple."

Ben rubbed his shoulder, feeling the skin over his tattoo. "Removing it will take too long. It's a complicated process. We don't have time for this."

"I have just the thing for it," Rex said. "It's going to hurt a bit, but you'll be fine."

Porter watched the blue Mustang drive away. On his iPad, he activated the tracer he had dropped into Keera's handbag. The blinking locator beacon moved down Guilford Road and turned right at Great Star toward Rt. 32. He switched screens and typed a text message to the Ghost:

Girlfriend doesn't know where he is.
Tracer is in her purse. She'll be home soon.
Watch her until he shows up.

Satisfied, Porter turned off the rolling lights and started after her, providing the escort he had promised.

Fifteen minutes later, the Mustang pulled into the garage. He waited outside until the lights came on inside the townhome. She waved at him from a window on the second floor. He waved back and drove away.

Rex and Powell held his arms, and Dreyfuss gripped his head, keeping it forward, facing him. "Take deep breaths," he said. "One. Two, three."

"It's just liquid nitrogen," Rex said. "We used it to freeze moles from cows' udders. It leaves a blister, that's all."

Ben heard a hissing noise behind him and twitched involuntarily.

"Breathe," Dreyfuss said. "Deep!"

The hissing noise changed as Streep adjusted the sprayer.

"Careful," Powell said. "Layer by layer, or you'll freeze his muscles."

"Hold him," she said.

Ben tried to look over his shoulder. He felt the three men tighten their grip.

"Okay," Streep said. "Don't move!"

It felt as if fire touched his shoulder. He struggled to get away. She continued to spray in short bursts, and the pain flared up, radiating throughout his body. He shouted, "Enough!"

"Almost done," Streep said. "Don't be a baby."

Keera watched the Ford sedan drive away. She felt as if a belt were tightening around her chest, making it hard to breathe. Until he gave her his card, it had not occurred to her for a moment that he was anything other than a state trooper on a routine stop of a reckless motorist.

But his name was on the card. *O. Porter – Inspector.* It was the same guy Ben had seen remove a floppy disk from the body of Zachariah Hinckley, which he later claimed was a porn DVD.

Porter's appearance tonight could not be a coincidence. He must have coordinated with the Ghost, trying to flush out Ben by having her call him for help.

And what about Fran? She's also a state trooper. Are they working together, some kind of an operation to protect the presidential candidate? The discussion last night, when Fran made a case for Keera to leave Ben, suddenly took an ominous light. Was Fran trying to cause a crisis so that Ben would be forced to show up? Keera felt helpless. Fran had gone to high school with Ben, and they had reconnected when Ben was investigating a case involving a rigged state police bidding process. At the time, Fran had tried to dissuade Ben from investigating it, but when he found the dirt, she had apologized. Was this another case of conflicting loyalties? Was she friend or foe?

Keera closed the curtains and sat on the bed. "Goddamn you, Ben!" She hugged his pillow. "What have you gotten yourself into?"

The phone rang—not her iPhone, but the land line. She checked the caller ID. *Johns Hopkins Medical Center.* She answered.

It was a classmate, Jerry, who was taking overnight call with the chief resident in the Critical Care Unit. He had a question about a patient they had seen together during morning rounds.

She answered his question, but then an idea occurred to her. "Are you tired?"

"Very funny. It's not just tonight. I'm looking at three nights in a row—payback time for all the calls I switched with others when the baby was coming. And the chief resident is overloaded, so I'm getting—"

"Then you're in luck. My boyfriend is away. I hate being alone at home. Do you want me to take over?"

There was silence on the other side. "Really?"

"Say yes before I change my mind."

"What's the catch?"

"No catch. I'll be there in thirty minutes."

"You're an angel!"

Next she called Fran and left a message. "I have to go back to the hospital, take over for a friend. He's on this weekend too, so I might be staying continuously through Monday. I'll let you know. Thanks for having me over last night."

After calling for a taxi, Keera packed an overnight bag. She left a bunch of lights on, as well as the radio in the kitchen.

PART VI:

The Mole

CHAPTER 50

When Ben woke up, he was lying on his belly. The pain from his singed tattoo was dull thanks to a dressing smeared with topical anesthetic, but a deeper throbbing reminded him of the long recovery from his football injury a decade earlier.

"Good morning!" Powell entered the room and pulled aside the curtains. It was dark outside. "Or rather, good night again."

"How long was I out?"

"Twenty-four hours, give or take a few bathroom breaks. How are you?"

"Terrible." Ben sat up and lowered his legs to the floor. "It's like someone took a torch to my back."

"It's the price of perfection."

Ben cleared his throat. "What's next?"

"Study. Study. Study." Powell handed him two books. "The more you know, the better prepared you are to pass for a real saint."

"Yes, General!" Ben saluted and looked at the books. *The Mormon Mirage,* by Latayne Scott, and *One Nation under Gods,* by Richard Abanes. "Do real saints read books like these?"

"No. Books that criticize the Church or contradict the official line are considered satanic and are banned. You'll have to be smart about how you answer questions when you're at the temple. '*Know thy enemy, and you shall prevail.*'"

"It takes a lot of anger and bitterness to lead this team of avenging ex-saints. What happened to you?"

"A great life happened to me." Powell coughed, but was able to stop. "Do you really want to know?"

Ben beckoned at a chair.

He sat down. "I was a graduate student at Nevada State. Part of my scholarship was for serving as a teaching assistant. I fell in love with a freshmen girl from Utah. Sarah Benson. The most beautiful thing you ever saw in your life. She was reluctant, but I was determined, and it helped that she was having difficulties with math and statistics, which are my strong areas. Finally she started going out with me. We went to her parents for Thanksgiving, and I asked for their blessing in marriage." Powell sighed. "Have you ever watched *Guess Who's Coming to Dinner?*"

"I saw the remake."

"They were horrified. But it was the eighties, and the Church had just changed its policy to allow blacks into the priesthood and was eager to show its new tolerance. Sarah's parents were instructed by their bishop to accept me, provided I embraced the True Gospel."

"Did you?"

"I had been raised Southern Baptist, but didn't care much—we all worship the same Jesus Christ, right? When I called my mama, she warned me that Mormons didn't like blacks. But the bishop explained that it was part of a bygone past, that in 'seventy-eight, the LDS President, Seer and Revelator had a divine revelation that all men were eligible for priesthood and full status as saints, even those with dark skin who had been banned from the priesthood until then. And, sure enough, I was baptized, received my Temple Recommend Card, had my endowments and ordinances, and our marriage was sealed for eternity in a strange but uplifting ceremony in the Mormon temple. Two years later, with a doctorate in mathematics, I got a teaching position at Brigham Young, we had two boys, and life was happy."

"Until?"

"Until my son came home from Cub Scouts crying because a friend had told him that his soul was evil. I phoned the troop leader, an ophthalmologist I knew well from the ward, and he explained that my son, at six years of age, should already know that his dark skin was evidence of his soul's sins against God in the pre-mortal life. When I explained the change of nineteen seventy-eight, which was ten years earlier, he laughed and told me that the race manifesto was issued to get the Gentiles off the Church's back with all that civil rights craziness. But all the underlying doctrines had remained in place."

"Which doctrines?"

"That dark skin was the mark of the brother-killer, Cain, and his seed. That dark skin was God's punishment of bad souls who had sinned in the pre-mortal life. That dark skin was hereditary of Lucifer's followers. That dark skin was a sign of debasement and filth. All this had been a cornerstone of Mormon theology since Joseph Smith wrote the *Book of Mormon*, which described the Lamanites—the perennial bad guys—as '*dark and loathsome and a filthy people, full of idleness and all manner of abominations.*' And later, the second Nephi book elaborates that God '*did cause a skin of blackness to come upon them*' in order '*that they shall be loathsome unto my people,*' as they are '*full of mischief.*'"

"You memorized it?"

"Every word is burned into my mind." Powell knuckled his forehead. "It's like giving testimony, but of the truth. For example, Smith's translation of the Egyptian papyrus, in the *Book of Abraham*, where he described how evil souls were punished by God with a black skin. And his successor, Brigham Young, warned about those with '*flat nose and black skin.*' He said that they are '*uncouth, uncomely, disagreeable, and low in their habits, wild, and seemingly deprived of nearly all the blessings of the intelligence that is generally bestowed upon mankind.*'"

Rex came into Ben's bedroom with a bowl of chicken soup. "I figured this would make you feel at home."

Ben held the bowl and inhaled the steam. "Ah! This is the Jewish Celestial Kingdom!"

They laughed.

He spooned the hot liquid and slurped. "Very good!"

"Haven't lost my touch." Rex rubbed his hands. "It's been a while."

Turning back to Powell, Ben asked, "What happened next?"

"As an assistant professor at Brigham Young University," Powell continued, "I had access to a lot of research sources. The incident with my son made me interested in the civil rights movement and the way it had impacted the Mormon Church. I discovered that the leadership had changed the policy to allow blacks, Latinos, and Asians into the priesthood after years of political and commercial pressure, under fear of lawsuits, and because Mormon missionaries were thrown out of foreign countries, in addition to several states, such as New York, which considered legislation to ban racist proselytizing. Mormon racism was becoming too inconvenient, so the open priesthood manifesto was issued. But the Church left untouched the underlying doctrinal and theological foundation of the correlation between dark skin and evil souls."

"But surely Mormons no longer think that way, do they?"

"They're very charitable people," Powell said. "The Mormon Church is incredibly generous in donating food and medicine to African and South American countries. They're first to help in natural disasters. For example, the people of New Orleans can tell you how LDS teams arrived after Hurricane Katrina, saving lives and feeding the hungry—blacks and whites—while the federal government was spinning its wheels uselessly. Yet at the same time, Mormons believe that everything Joseph Smith and his successor prophets said is true including Brigham Young's warning: '*If the white man... mixes his blood with the seed of Cain, the penalty under the law of God is death on the spot. This will always be so.*' The last sentence," Powell explained, "resonates with every Mormon even today."

"How do you know?"

"By applying statistical models to social science research, I conducted confidential, blind surveys in which subjects were asked a long series of questions, most of them irrelevant to the real focus of the research."

"A diversion?"

"Correct. Of the Mormons who indicated that they hold strong belief in their faith, eighty-nine percent said that interracial marriage was sinful and eighty-seven percent said that they would forbid or discourage their children from marrying a dark-skinned person. I published the results in the *National Journal of Social Science and Society,* including other statistics that demonstrated the lingering racial prejudice among members of the Mormon

Church. My conclusion was that Mormon racism would continue until God provided our current leader—the LDS president, seer, and revelator—with an explicit revelation that erased and disavowed all previous black-is-evil revelations, scriptures, decrees, and admonitions."

"What happened then?"

"The response was swift. My department head instructed me to withdraw the article from publication due to 'errors in methodology.' He suggested that I focus my research on my ethnic heritage. For example, the statistical data underlying the failure of traditional family structure among African Americans in urban areas or the high percentage of black male incarcerations. This was not only insulting, but also fundamentally against any notion of academic integrity, or integrity in general. I went over his head to the provost, who was also an apostle and member of the Quorum of Twelve, which is like the Mormon Church's board of directors. I pleaded with him to take my research and conclusions to heart and work toward changing the Mormon racial doctrines once and for all. I told him: We can't fool the Gentiles forever—it's going to catch up with us!"

"Big mistake," Rex said.

"He laid his hands on my head and blessed me! Can you believe it?" Powell chuckled. "How else could I have interpreted his blessing but as the ultimate expression of warm support? I practically danced my way back to my office, where a letter soon arrived by messenger, suspending me from all teaching and research responsibilities and banning me from the library. *The library!*"

Having raised his voice, Powell coughed hard, pressing on his chest.

"I begged my colleagues to support me, but they were afraid to lose their jobs. Our bishop took away my Temple Recommend Card for 'safekeeping' until I returned to my senses. When I wrote a letter to the *Salt Lake Tribune,* our bishop instructed my wife to threaten divorce unless I backed down, which I might have done if not for my boys. It was their future I was fighting for! And my wife still loved me! But the pressure on her was relentless—the bishop, stake president, general authorities, her parents—and we ended up in court."

"Guess who's coming to court," Ben said.

"A bunch of very friendly Mormons—the judge, the lawyers, the social workers, the witnesses, and even the psychiatrist—the honorable Dr. Neibauer, who reported on his diagnosis, based on input from family and friends, of my acute schizoid-paranoid affliction. And there I was, in a lovely, wood-paneled courtroom, surrounded by the nicest white people in the world, all working in happy harmony to save my wife and boys from a raving lunatic in Lucifer's dark skin." He pulled out a worn photo. "Here, do I look insane?"

Ben examined the photo of a much younger Powell, smiling, his arm around a pretty brunette, the boys dressed in their Sunday best, their skin color a smooth chocolate. "Good-looking kids," he said.

"Don't bullshit me." Powell took back the photo. "I know what your white mind is thinking. *Half-breeds. Ugly little mutts.*"

"You *are* paranoid," Ben said. "My white mind was thinking about my black girlfriend and how one day we'll have kids looking just like yours."

Powell burst out laughing. "You're dating a black sister? I'd never have guessed that about you, boy! What's her name?"

"Keera, and she's not happy right now."

PART VII:

The Descendent

CHAPTER 51

It had rained the rest of Friday and all of Saturday, which mattered little as Ben had remained in bed, propped up on pillows, reading the books. Powell and Rex took turns in the kitchen, but there was no sign of Streep or Dreyfuss.

Sunday morning brought back the sun. After a breakfast of eggs, toast, and a fresh salad, Rex changed the dressing on Ben's wound and suggested they go for a ride.

Stepping out of the house, Ben took in the open views of the surrounding landscape. The stone house was only one of several farm buildings clustered together against a hillside. The farm was old, but not in disrepair—two large barns, an equipment shed, an inactive chicken coop, and a green tractor of an old vintage under a carport made from galvanized steel. There were no neighbors in sight, and the rolling hills showed signs of past cultivation, probably corn fields and apple orchards, now repossessed by nature.

"I put the bikes out of the rain." Rex pulled open the doors of a storage shed. Ben's GS was inside, together with the white Ducati, a black Harley Davidson, and a dual-purpose Kawasaki KLR650. He rolled out the GS and the KLR.

Getting into the jacket was a little painful, but once Ben was sitting on the GS, everything else disappeared into the back recesses of his mind.

Rex took off on the light KLR. The unpaved road was packed with gravel, which provided solid traction, except for areas where it had been washed away by the rain, leaving rutted mud that required careful balancing, especially for the heavier GS.

They reached a gate, which was locked. Rex stopped, got off the bike, and unlocked the gate, holding it open for Ben. After pushing his KLR through, Rex locked the gate behind them. Moments later, they reached a paved country road.

The pace grew faster. Rex seemed to know the area well, leading the way through hills and valleys, passing by active and neglected farms, across a dam and down to a rushing river, where he stopped, signaling to Ben to do the same.

From a duffel bag that was strapped to the back of his KLR, Rex took out a bunch of sticks, which he assembled into a fishing rod. After fixing a bait on the hook, he cast far into the water and sat on a rock.

"Nice spot," Ben said, settling down on another rock.

"I used to come here with my grandfather." Rex tugged on the rod, reeled in a bit, and let it sit. "It reminded him of a similar river, back in Russia. We fished every Sunday and fried the catch back at the farm, together with fresh onion and cabbage."

"Now it's your farm?"

Rex nodded. "I put it into a trust to keep my name out of the records. Harder to track me down that way."

"Can't they find you at Best Buy, like I did?"

"Not anymore." He tugged on the rod, but it loosened again. "I'll go back after this operation is over."

They sat in silence for a while. Then the line went taught. Rex reeled in and paused, reeled in more and paused, until a healthy-sized fish emerged from the dark water.

Ben helped unhook it into a net, which Rex tied in the shallow water to keep the fish alive until they were ready to leave.

Rex cast again. "We are betting everything on you."

"Why are you involved in this? How did the Mormons hurt your family?"

"No family to hurt." Rex reeled back the line, which came empty, and put a new bait on the hook. "I left the saints many years ago, soon after I finished my service."

"Why?"

He cast the line far in. "You like asking questions."

"It's my job."

"Do you know the Marine Corps motto?"

"*Semper Fidelis.*"

"That's right. *Always Faithful.* But faithful to whom?"

Ben waited for him to answer his own question.

"My grandfather escaped from Russia with his young wife after the Cossacks killed everyone else in the pogroms. Try to watch *Fiddler on the Roof* without the sound, without the songs and dancing, and you'll have a good idea of how Jews lived in Russia a century ago. They came here after a distant cousin lent them money to buy cheap land and recreated the life they had lost. My grandfather remained faithful to his Jewish religion and the only way of life he knew. But my father, an only son, hated everything about the pitiable, grungy existence his immigrant parents had imported from Russia."

"It's not unusual," Ben said, "for immigrants' children to become alienated from their parents, or even ashamed."

"True." The line tightened, and Rex tugged on it, but it came out empty. He hooked another worm and cast the line into the water. "For Grandpa, western Pennsylvania was heaven, a place to rebuild the same way of life, but without the murdering Cossacks. For my father, the farm was a gulag to escape from. He aspired to become a real American, free and successful, which meant going to college. The only school that gave him a full scholarship was Brigham Young. He left his Judaism behind, on the farm, together with the Yiddish yakking and Eastern European drudgery. As a freshman, he took the mandatory classes about LDS history and scriptures, joined his classmates on Sundays, and discovered Mormonism to be a real American religion, filled with pioneering spirit, strong community, and a celebration of material success. The fact that a blond, blue-eyed stunner was madly in love with him, well, that didn't hurt either."

"Your mom?"

Rex nodded. "My sisters got her looks. I'm a poor mix."

Ben laughed.

"By the time my dad was a junior, he was married with a kid on the way. A decade later, he was an executive with IBM. My parents had just bought a new house when dad crashed his car during a snowstorm, dying at the scene."

"I'm sorry."

"Me too. It was terrible during the first few months. But our Mormon community provided everything we needed—cooked meals, childcare, mortgage payments, and later, a series of potential husbands for my mom, who settled for a lawyer, a father of five whose wife had died in childbirth. My mom was soon pregnant again, and again. We all worked hard to be helpful and happy, but it was kind of fake. I spent my summers here with my grandpa and grandma. I was Jewish on the farm and Mormon the rest of the time. It was interesting."

"I bet."

"After doing my Mormon mission in Alabama, I enlisted in the Marines and spent time in Japan and Germany. Both my grandparents died during my first year back, and I discovered that you can't be *Always Faithful* when you face two competing values."

The line tightened, and it wasn't a false alarm. Rex reeled in a hefty striper that fought to get away.

Once it was safely in the net, Rex started disassembling the rod. "These two will give us enough food for tonight."

Ben helped him tie the rod sections together. "What values were in conflict?"

"My last name is Levi. Do you know what it means?"

"Your family traces its roots to the tribe of Levi."

"That's right." Rex shook the net with the two fish until all the water drained off and slipped them into a plastic bag. "When I left the Marine Corps, I found a job in Baltimore as a computer tech. I attended services at the LDS ward and dated nice Mormon girls who wanted a good husband and a bunch of kids. During my annual interview with the bishop, he gave me a date to do the posthumous baptizing for my grandparents. I hesitated, explaining how the old man was a Jew through and through, how my grandma was the daughter of a rabbi and so proud of it. The bishop was very kind, spending time with me, discussing Grandpa's life and our family's history back in Russia. In the end, I accepted that it was my duty to invite their souls into the True Church. But then, things went weird. I was called to meet the president of the DC temple and was asked to sign a statement requesting posthumous baptisms for all my relatives, not just Grandpa. Turned out that the Church had been dealing with unhappy Jewish leaders, who were resentful of posthumous baptisms for Holocaust victims. The LDS Church agreed to sign a settlement agreement, which led to more problems and another agreement. Now, only dead relatives of Mormons could be baptized by proxy."

"And your relatives include all Jews."

"You got it." Rex tied the duffel bag back on the bike. "My last name—Levi—meant that our hereditary line had been carefully maintained under Jewish tradition for centuries. It was a proof that I was a direct descendent of Levi, son of Jacob, son of Isaac, son of Abraham—the ultimate Jewish patriarch. It meant that, according to the Jews' own rules, I was a direct relative of all Jews who ever lived. Therefore, even under the strict settlement the Mormon Church had signed with the Jewish leaders, I had the right to request posthumous baptisms for every one of my dead relatives, i.e. every dead Jew in history."

"But you felt it was devious?"

Rex nodded. "It was technically defensible according to the lawyer from Salt Lake City, who flew in to obtain my signature on the paper requesting posthumous baptisms for all my dead relatives. But it stunk of deceit and put me in a terrible bind. I had to choose whether to be faithful to my Mormon Church or to Grandpa's memory. Being a young man, fresh out of the Marine Corps, I decided that *Always Faithful* wasn't about obeying authorities—military or religious. It was about faithful adherence to principles: Tradition. Integrity. Honor."

The ride back followed a different route, which took them into a small town with a single gas station, a general store, and a cemetery. Rex stopped the KLR on the side of the road. Without getting off the bike, he pointed at a double stone, set slightly to the side from the other graves. It was carved with a Jewish star and the name *Levi.*

CHAPTER 52

Ben pushed aside his dinner plate, having eaten every last crumb of Rex's fried fish with onions and cabbage. "That was delicious!"

Streep, Powell, and Dreyfuss nodded, their mouths still full. Rex was at the sink, scrubbing the frying pan. "Practice makes perfect," he said.

"Which is why I don't feel ready for tomorrow," Ben said. "By the way, what if they ask about the nasty wound on the back of my shoulder?"

"Memorize this information." Dreyfuss gave him a piece of paper. "Dr. Glenda Monroe is your dermatologist. She operated on you in her office last Friday, outpatient procedure, to remove skin cancer from your upper left back. Her office is near Inova Hospital in Fairfax, Virginia. She just left on a cruise to the Greek Islands, but her nurse will answer the phone and confirm your story, if it ever comes to that. Her name is Eve, and she's a friend."

He read the information twice and gave the paper back to Dreyfuss. "Got it."

"Tell me."

Ben recited Dr. Monroe's address and phone number.

"Good. Now, considering that Sampson Allard was in the temple only a few days ago, someone might question what you're doing back at the temple so soon. Your response is simple: The pathology results are due in a day or two, and the wound has been bothering you, so where else would you go for comfort and hope but to the temple, where God's rituals—"

"Ordinances."

"Correct. Ordinances and endowments. You hope the cancer hasn't spread, but you feel the need to be in the best position, just in case. Serving as proxy in receiving endowments for the dead will bring you closer to exaltation and help you win entry to the Celestial Kingdom of God."

"The way I feel," Ben said, "I won't be lying."

"Get a good night sleep," Dreyfuss said. "Tomorrow is the big day."

"One way or another," Streep said as she collected the plates from the table. "Whatever happens at the temple, don't underestimate the saints."

A few minutes later, when Ben was already in bed, reading *Mormon America – The Power and the Promise*, by Richard and Joan Ostling, there was a knock on his door. When he opened it, Powell was there, his hand held forward, his large palm brown and creased and meaty, dwarfing a small box.

"Take it," Powell said.

Ben looked at him. "What's inside?"

Powell opened the box. Resting on a felt cushion was a ring. At first it looked like brass, but Ben realized it was gold. The setting was a crown that hoisted the diamond over a circle of blue gems. The band was crafted as a leafy branch, fixed with tiny rubies.

"I don't understand," Ben said. "What is it?"

"A piece of history," Powell said. "The man who owned my great-grandfather had it made in England as an engagement ring for his fiancée, the daughter of another plantation owner in Georgia. The leaves are tobacco, the rubies are drops of slaves' blood. Three decades later, the owner and his four sons died in the battle of Columbus. After the Confederates lost the war, the wife deeded the land in small parcels to the freed slaves who had worked on the plantation, gifted her jewelry to the house slaves, and drank a jar of lemonade laced with arsenic."

"A sad ending."

"And a happy beginning of freedom for our family. Four wonderful marriages started with this engagement ring—including mine, which turned sour only after Mormon racism poisoned it."

Powell held out his hand. "Take it. It belongs on the finger of a beautiful black woman."

The proper thing to do was to decline, but Ben sensed that this was a test—not a test of his good manners, but of his true feelings about race. Was Keera's black skin the real reason for his ambivalence about marriage? "Thank you," he said, taking the box. "It's an honor."

PART VIII:

The Candidate

CHAPTER 53

When Ben woke up, he found a set of white Mormon undergarments neatly folded on a chair. Hanging from a hook on the back of the door, still in plastic wraps from the dry cleaners, were his clothes for the day—a white shirt, a white dress-suit, and a white tie. Before getting dressed, he shaved and asked Rex to change the dressing on the back of his shoulder.

A thin layer of frost coated the seat of the GS, and Ben wiped it off with his hand. The four of them watched him pull on the riding pants and jacket on top of the white suit. Underneath, the Mormon undergarments felt like plastic against his skin, but he didn't mind. The three layers would keep him warm. "Okay," he said. "I'm ready."

No one said anything, and the way they were looking at him made Ben realize their feelings were more complex than he had thought.

"Do you miss it?" Ben looked at each one of them. "Do you miss the life among the saints? The shared faith in the True Church? The wholesome community of brothers and sisters on the path to exaltation?"

Dreyfuss took off his glasses and pretended to clean them.

Rex looked around at the quiet farm buildings. "Sometimes," he said.

"All the time," Powell said. "I miss it every day, all these years."

Streep shrugged. "How can you not miss it? There's so much damn love there, so much kindness and support and joy—if you're lucky not to fall into the hands of a shitty husband, that is."

"It's true," Dreyfuss said, his voice barely audible. "For the most part, there are no people as good as the Mormons."

"Now I'm really confused." Ben pulled on his riding gloves. "If this is how you feel, why are you trying to destroy the Church? Why ruin it for all those good Mormons?"

"We're not trying to destroy it!" Powell pressed a clenched fist to his chest. "As God is our witness, we do not wish to harm the Church. On the contrary! We wish to save it!"

"It's true," Streep said. "By exposing Joe Morgan's posthumous baptisms of Medal of Honor recipients, the harassment and death of Zachariah Hinckley, and the murderous Danites and their masters, we will shake up the faithful masses. Mormons will congregate in their wards and rise up in protest. They'll force the sclerotic leadership to let go of the reins of power and step aside."

"Change will come," Dreyfuss said. "The saints will rebel against the strict chain of command, destroy the hierarchical Church authorities that dictate everything down from Salt Lake City. And then, the Church of Jesus Christ of Latter-day Saints will cast aside its anachronistic doctrines and come into the modern era."

"Sounds good," Ben said. "But how likely is it to actually happen?"

"We know our fellow Mormons," Streep said. "All they need is a spark to ignite their core of righteousness, to set free their suppressed recognition that the Church must change. They will fight to end racism, to end women's abuse and subjugation, to end homophobia, to end the dictatorship from the top, and to end the shameful suppression of the Church's true history!"

"A revolution!" Powell raised his big fist. "Just like the Arab Spring, we will instigate a Mormon Spring!"

Powell, Dreyfuss, Streep, and Rex took turns to shake Ben's hand. He mounted the GS and released the kickstand. "Okay," he said. "I'm ready to start a revolution. No pressure."

"You'll do fine, boy," Powell said.

Streep winked. "Go get them!"

"I'll pray for you," Dreyfuss said.

"Three things to remember." Rex counted on his fingers. "First, ride straight to the Rockville Metro, leave the bike at the station, and take the train to the temple—no stops or phone calls. Don't ride this monster to the temple—they might expect you there." He put his hand on the handlebar. "It's a beauty, but subtle it's not."

Ben nodded.

"Second, when you enter the temple, remember that Mormons smile a lot and never cuss. Third, as soon as you trigger the fire alarm, go straight to the office and download the files." He handed Ben a memory flash drive on a key ring with a pinky-sized figure of Angel Moroni with his long trumpet.

The helmet felt cold and loose on his short hair. Ben turned the key one click. The gauges lit up, accompanied by the beeps and chirps of the self-diagnostics. He waited, watching the display, and when everything seemed in order, he started the engine. It coughed twice and settled into a familiar exhaust sound.

Rex climbed into the Suburban and headed down the gravel road. Ben followed.

They spent nearly two hours on narrow country roads, passing through farms, vineyards, and small towns. At one point, they crossed the border from Pennsylvania to Maryland. When the signs for I-70 finally appeared, Rex veered to the shoulder and rolled down the window. Ben stopped next to him and raised the face shield.

"Take the first right turn," Rex yelled over the engine noise, "toward Frederick. Go west until you see signs for Two-Seventy South."

Ben held a thumb up.

"Good luck!" Rex made a U-turn. A moment later, the Suburban was gone.

Ben passed by the right turn Rex had pointed out and continued across the overpass above the highway. He turned left, heading east toward Baltimore. Change of plans. It was obvious he didn't have what it took to be an obedient saint.

The first highway sign told him it was twenty-seven miles to the intersection with Rt. 29 South. He settled comfortably in the saddle, bowed his head slightly to reduce wind noise, and shifted up to sixth gear for a smooth cruising at eighty miles per hour.

CHAPTER 54

Pulling up in front of the hospital, Ben maneuvered the GS to jump the curb and parked it next to the glass front. The security guard inside the lobby saw him and raised both arms in an Easy Rider imitation. His name was Sam, and Ben knew him from past visits.

Taking off the helmet, he pulled a Ravens hat from the tank bag, put it on, and went inside.

Keera usually left her mobile phone in her purse, which was stashed in her locker while she cared for patients. Sam, a black man with silver hair and a hearty laugh, knew the routine. He pinged three times on the public announcement system and announced, "Miss Keera Torrens, please contact the front desk. Miss Keera Torrens. Front desk. Thank you."

She called a moment later.

Sam pressed the speaker button. "Happy Monday, Miss Torrens. You have a visitor."

"Who?"

"A member of the media."

"Does he have a name?"

"Lucky Dog is here, braving the winter."

"Ben? Really?"

"The man himself."

"Thank God!"

"You want him to go upstairs or should I just kick him out?"

"I'm coming down!" She hung up.

Two minutes later, Keera burst out of the elevator and ran into Ben's arms. It took them a moment before noticing that a handful of staff and guests were watching them, chuckling.

Keera dragged him into a glass-fronted conference room. "What happened? Where have you been?"

He caressed her face, which was almost ashen. Her eyes were bloodshot, and her hair was rebelling against the confines of a bow. "How long have you been here?"

"Too long. I'm afraid to leave."

"Why aren't you staying with Fran?"

"I feel safer here." She touched his bleached eyebrows. "What's this?"

He took off the Ravens hat.

"Jesus!" Keera covered her mouth. "All your hair is gone! And the color! What in hell have you done to yourself?"

"It'll grow back."

"Kind of cute." She touched his cropped hair. "Are you coming home?"

"Not yet."

"You're still pursing that Mormon story?"

He nodded.

"I don't understand." She stepped out of his embrace and leaned on the conference table. "How can you do this to me?"

"It's almost over." Ben unzipped his riding jacket.

"Why are you wearing a suit and tie?"

He shrugged.

"And it's all white! Are you trying to look like Michael Jackson?" She tightened the tie knot. "Who shopped for you?"

"They're borrowed."

"Are you going to a funeral?"

"Not exactly."

Keera touched his face. "I've never seen you dressed up. Some relationship we have."

There was a knock on the glass door. Sam came in, holding a small bouquet of indistinct flowers, which he handed to Ben. "As you requested, sir." He winked.

"Thank you." Ben handed it to Keera.

"Give me a break!" She dropped the bouquet on a chair. "You think a bunch of flowers will pacify me?"

"Oops." Sam retreated.

"I'm sick of it," Keera said. "I've been living here for days and nights, worrying sick about you— about us!—and all you're doing is running around, risking everything for...what? I don't even know! You're obsessed!" She pushed the chair, and the bouquet fell to the floor.

Ben picked up the flowers. "I didn't ask him to get these."

She rolled her eyes.

"It's going to be over today. I promise."

"I have to go." She went to the door. "They're waiting for me upstairs. We're in the middle of rounds."

"Keera—"

"Don't!" Her voice was breaking. "Go away! Investigate! Have fun!"

"It's not fun."

"I'm not having fun either! How do you think I feel—my home broken into, afraid to leave the hospital, not knowing who's really a friend and who's an enemy, and the guy who's supposed to love me more than anything else is out there chasing ghosts!"

"I'm here, am I not?"

"And why is that? Why did you come here? To check that I'm still hanging around like a dumb broad who can't see the writing on the wall?" She pulled at the strands of her loosening hair. "Look at me!"

"You're gorgeous."

"Liar! I look like shit! And smell like it too! Is that what you came here for?"

"I came for this." He pulled Powell's small box from his inside pocket.

"What's this?"

Ben opened the box, held it forth, and kneeled. "Will you marry me?"

Keera's jaw literally dropped.

"I know this is not the most romantic setup, but, still, will you?" He picked the ring out of the box and held it between a finger and a thumb. "Will you?"

"No!" She clenched her fists and looked up at the ceiling, shaking her head. "This is not happening!"

"Please forgive me—"

"Hell, no!"

"I've been a complete schmuck, taking so long to realize how lucky I am."

"I'm going to kill you!"

Ben hopped toward her, still on his knees, and looked up. "Keera Torrens, I love you."

"I hate you!" She couldn't help but look down at the ring. Her face softened. "What...what is this?"

"It's your engagement ring."

"Don't say that."

He held up the ring. "It comes from a long line of happy marriages."

"It's...beautiful."

"I promise to be a good husband—despite evidence to the contrary."

She groaned.

"Will you spend your life with me?"

She unclenched her left hand and stuck it downward. "I bet it doesn't fit."

All he could do was pray that Powell's wife possessed a finger of Keera's size. He held his breath and slipped the ring on. It resisted around the second knuckle, but he forced it all the way.

Keera couldn't take her eyes off the ring. She touched the diamond and the gems around the band, raised her hand against the light, and turned the ring from side to side.

Ben stood. "May I kiss the bride?"

"Yes." She sniffled. "You may."

Outside the glass wall of the conference room, a half-circle of spectators began clapping. The P.A. system crackled, and someone started whistling a vague rendition of *The Wedding March*.

Porter was in his office, scanning the last batch of reported traffic accidents and violations involving motorcycles in the past forty-eight hours, covering Maryland, Virginia, Pennsylvania, and the District of Columbia. Only four came up, and of those, none was listed as yellow or black.

His private pager beeped. He grabbed it and read the message:

Bikerboy @ hospital 2 C black chick.

Exhaling in relief, Porter contemplated the message for a moment. He brought up the tiny keyboard on the beeper's touch-screen and typed with the tip of his forefinger:

Follow @ distance; wait 4 opportunity 2 finish off; report when U R done.

CHAPTER 55

Having lost an hour or so, Ben decided to ride straight to the Mormon temple. He took Rt. 29 South and then the 495 beltway toward Rockville. Traffic was moving at a snail's pace, all five lanes filled with vehicles. Impatient, he sped up, cutting between the lanes of cars and trucks, threading the large motorcycle through tight spaces, avoiding side mirrors that jutted out at face-level. Urban riding was an art, built on years of experience of calculated risk-taking, and he was very good at it. Two or three miles later, the clump of dense traffic thinned out, and he was able to go really fast. The heated handgrips kept his fingers from freezing, but the space between his collar and the bottom of the helmet allowed some air to enter, and he felt his neck beginning to hurt. But as the road curved to the right, farther ahead, the familiar sight of the Mormon temple came into view.

Approaching an overpass, he noticed a line of graffiti above the highway:

We're not in Kansas anymore, Toto!

A moment later, the white castle appeared, dominating the skyline ahead. The DC Mormon Temple was enormous, its towers and spires rising high above the treetops, reaching for heaven.

As he took the exit, Ben hummed, "*We're off to see the wizard, the wizard, the wizard…*"

He followed the signs to the access road, which was perfectly landscaped with shrubs and flower beds that seemed to belong in spring, not in winter.

Advancing slowly down the access road, he veered right, across the shoulder and through the knee-high flower bed, into a wooded area thick enough to shelter the GS. He took off the riding gear, which he rolled up and tied with a bungee cord to the seat. After lacing up the white dress shoes and straightening up the suit, he shouldered the bag Streep had packed for him and walked the rest of the way.

Crossing though the parking lot, where most vehicles were vans and SUVs that could accommodate large families, Ben noticed the abundance of political bumper stickers. It was not unusual to see those around the heavily partisan Washington area, but here there was an odd unanimity to it. Without exception, all the bumper stickers supported Joe Morgan and the Republican Party. At the same time, there was not a single off-color one. Most of them were simple, blue-and-red stickers with a straightforward message from Morgan's campaign:

Restore America's Soul!

Boot the Food-stamp President!

Yes, We Believe!

Socialism ≠ American

God + Freedom = American Exceptionalism

Ben crossed the plaza, and his gaze was drawn up to the Angel Moroni, a golden statue that was perched atop the highest spire, blowing a long trumpet. In his pocket, Ben felt the tiny angel on the key ring with the memory flash drive.

The phone rang, and Porter saw '*HR – Cindy G*' on the caller ID display. She had taken a liking to him when he had first arrived from Colorado and was processed by Human Resources. He knew the type—middle-aged divorcée with one or two grown kids and a pudgy midriff that spoke of long evenings in front of the TV. Being privy to his personnel file, she knew he had no children and was not a heavy consumer of medical services. His family status—*Divorced*—told her he wasn't likely to be gay.

He exhaled and picked up. "Porter here."

"And Cindy is here too," she said. "I missed you at the cafeteria. Did you go out, like, for lunch?"

"No," he lied.

"Are you a hungry bear now? If you wait till five, I'll feed you, like, if you want?"

Her flirtations were clumsy, but he had kept her optimistic, accepting her invitation for a Saturday night dinner in Towson and, another time, for a Sunday brunch at the Inner Harbor. She wanted to "show him around town" and laughed out loud at his humorous teasing and his compliments, which were never explicit enough to ignite an open solicitation on her part. He was careful not to cross the line, keeping her at bay with occasional hints at a painful breakup with his fictional ex.

"Maybe another time. I just had a quick sandwich. My morning appointments ran overtime."

"Anything fun?"

"Hardly. Traffic planning sessions with local churches ahead of the Christmas season. You know, staggering services so we don't have to send troopers to multiple locations at the same time."

"Of course! That's so important! I remember last year, like, at the end of our Midnight Mass, the traffic on Old Baltimore Road was horrible and—"

"I'll be right there," he said toward his closed door and picked up the handset, taking her off speaker. "Sorry. Got to go to a meeting."

"Oh, sure, I understand. Call me later, okay?"

"Sure. Was there something you wanted to tell me?"

"Not really, except that someone was, like, asking about you."

"Yes?"

"It was odd." She lowered her voice conspiratorially. "Someone was asking about your record and your previous postings and, like, any disciplinary proceedings—"

"Really?"

"I made you look good, sweetie. Don't worry!" She laughed.

"You're the best." Porter hesitated. His file had nothing in it to cause alarm, but if someone wanted to dig deeper and started calling people, the record might not hold. "Now I'm curious." He chuckled. "Can you tell me who it was?"

"It's confidential!" Cindy giggled. "But you can try, like, guessing?"

"A man or a woman?"

"I knew you'd ask that!"

"A woman?"

"Yes, you could say it's a woman, like, kind of."

That was a giveaway. "The butch lieutenant from Hate Crimes?"

"I didn't tell you!" Cindy laughed. "But you still owe me, like, a dinner or something?"

"You got it." Porter hid the anger in his voice. "And don't pay any attention to Fran DeLacourt. She's just fishing around because I caught a friend of hers messing around with evidence at a fatal accident site."

"Figures. These people are, like, immoral, you know?"

"I agree. Did she say anything?"

"Not really. I mean, not much to discuss, with your past postings being classified." Cindy's voice was touched by awe. "I'd love to hear about it sometime. Will you tell me?"

"Sure, but then I'll have to kill you."

"Oh, my God!" She burst out laughing. "You are so funny!"

"Call you later," he said. "Thanks!"

Porter left his office and walked by Lt. Francine DeLacourt's office. She wasn't there. Was she going to meet Ben Teller somewhere? How much did she know?

He kept pacing the hallways until he saw her leaving the ladies room on the second floor. He smiled at her, she nodded curtly, and he stopped, about to engage her in conversation.

His private pager suddenly beeped.

She paused, probably intrigued by the sound, which was different than the standard-issue pagers some of the old-fashioned troopers still carried.

Before she had time to ask anything, Porter entered the men's room. Inside a stall, he checked the message. It was brief:

Lost BT. He's too fast.

Porter cursed, and someone in the next stall cleared his throat. Sitting down on the toilet, he typed a response:

Where?

The reply came instantly:

495 W @ Silver Spring

It took Porter a moment to realize where Ben Teller was heading, and then it all became clear. He typed quickly:

He's @ the temple! Stop him!

Entering the Mormon temple, Ben found himself in an entrance hall that was painted white and furnished with heavy sofas and armchairs. A long reception desk was attended by temple workers, all of them elderly, devout volunteers in white garb. A line of people waited to be admitted, many of them holding bags or small suitcases.

When his turn came, he handed over Sampson Allard's Temple Recommend Card, which was about the size of a credit card, with the name and photo of the bearer in the front under the heading: *The Church of JESUS CHRIST of Latter-day Saints.* On the back of the card were the signatures of the lay bishop and the stake president, who had both verified his good standing as a churchgoer who avoided alcohol and caffeine drinks, didn't smoke tobacco products, and avoided extramarital sex while remaining compliant with tithing obligations.

"Welcome! Welcome!" The elderly saint smiled.

"Thank you." Ben returned the smile with as much warmth as he could muster.

"How are you?" He held up the card and compared it to Ben's face.

Ben forced an even bigger smile. "Wonderful!"

"Hum." He keyed the information into a computer. "How was your drive, Brother—"

"Samson."

The man looked up.

"Sampson," Ben corrected himself. "Sampson Allard. Yes. The drive was okay, considering." He touched his shoulder. "And you?"

"Good. Good." He leaned closer to the screen. "Back so soon?"

"I'm not well."

"Oh?"

"Minor surgery, but…we'll see." Ben looked away. "The pathology report will tell. That's why…I felt the need for… coming."

"Of course! Of course!" The man's creased face filled with compassion. He held Ben's hand between his hands. "I will pray for you, Brother Sampson."

Touched with guilt, Ben nodded.

"We can always use additional volunteers in the endowments for the dead."

The comments didn't surprise Ben because Dreyfuss had explained that they might assume he had come to the temple to serve as a proxy in the second stage of salvation for the dead who had already had their baptism done earlier in one of the wards by a different proxy. "It's an honor," he said.

"Brother Pat will help you now."

Another temple worker came over. This one was even older, his arms bony and covered with age spots. But he walked with a military posture, and his eyes were bright and intelligent behind horn-framed glasses.

Just as Dreyfuss had described, Ben was given a plastic bag containing the outfit needed for the washing-and-anointing part of the ordinances, and Brother Pat led him to the changing room.

Ben scanned the walls for the fire alarm. Along the way from the main entrance, they passed two fire stations, but he couldn't trigger either of them in full view of so many saints, as well as Brother Pat, who seemed to take his sacred job with great seriousness.

The dressing area offered limited privacy with white curtains hanging to create small stalls, each with a locker for street clothes and personal possessions.

He took off the white shoes, suit, tie, and buttoned-down shirt, and got out of the holy undergarments, which were moist with his sweat. Everything went into the locker, together with Streep's bag.

CHAPTER 56

Keera was standing in the hallway near a nurses' station with the wife and son of a recently deceased patient. She had spent the whole night in the Intensive Care Unit assisting the resident physician. The patient's lung cancer had stopped responding to treatment and his oxygen levels refused to rise. He had made it through the night and morning, but shortly after she had come back upstairs with a ring on her finger, the patient's heart finally stopped. Resuscitation efforts were not successful, as was expected. The patient's middle-aged son had just arrived from California on the redeye and, as was often the case with uninvolved family members, his reaction was hostile and untrusting. Thankfully, one of the nurses summoned Patient Relations, and they took over.

It was in this hazy state of tiredness and defeat that she found a voice message on her iPhone from Fran DeLacourt.

"Hi, girl. How're you doing? We miss you." Fran paused. "Been wondering whether you're avoiding us. Are you? Anyway, I got your stuff with me in the car, just in case you need a change of clothes. And I've done some digging about Porter. Not much to go on, but anyway, call me."

Holding her iPhone, Keera debated whether or not to call Fran back. But the single shower stall at the medical residents' overnight room was available, the green scrubs she was wearing stunk, and she had no energy to speak to anyone, let alone a friend who might not be a friend.

In the plastic bag Ben found a folded white sheet, which he shook loose. It had a hole in the middle for his head. The sheet draped his naked body like an oversized Mexican poncho. The Mormons called it 'A Shield," but to him it felt thin and scant against his skin. The bandage on the back of his shoulder created an unsightly hump.

He put on the white slippers, which were a size too big.

Also in the plastic bag were a white hat and a green waistband that was cut in a way that formed a large fig leaf in the front, which he knew were for the later rites, only he had no intention of going that far. He stuffed the plastic bag in the locker together with the rest of his stuff. Having no place to carry the Angel Moroni key ring with the memory flash drive, he held it in his fist.

Now he had to get rid of Brother Pat, who was waiting for him with a pleasant smile, rocking back and forth expectantly, his fingers interwoven.

"I need to use the bathroom," Ben said.

"Of course." He pointed the way.

Ben walked over to a door marked with a male figure. Inside, two of the ten toilet stalls were occupied, and a young man was washing his hands at the row of sinks. On the wall was a glass-fronted fire box containing an ax, a rolled-up hose, and an alarm handle. A sign above the box read:

In the event of fire, kindly do the following:
1. *Open box and pull alarm handle.*
2. *Assist disabled brothers and sisters.*
3. *Proceed to the nearest emergency exit.*
4. *Gather outside for prayer.*
5. *Await further instructions.*

Ben entered one of the stalls, closed the door, and listened.

The water kept running for a minute or two. Finally it stopped, and the paper towel dispenser buzzed.

Throat-clearing in another stall.

In the crack between the door and the frame, Ben saw a figure pass toward the exit.

A toilet flushed.

Ben exited his stall and walked between the row of sinks and stalls to the opposite wall. He pried open the glass door and grabbed the handle of the fire alarm.

A stall door creaked behind him.

Gritting his teeth, Ben shut the box, swiveled to the last sink, and turned on the water, pretending to wash his hands. From the corner of his eye he saw a figure leaving a stall and stepping to another sink.

In the mirror, Ben hardly recognized himself—the short, bleached hair framed a pale face, except for his cheeks, which had a reddish hue from a close shave—something he usually did once a week, at most. The bleached eyebrows stood out even more because of his dark eyes. But the most appalling was the loose white poncho, which completed the hospital-like appearance of a sickly guy in desperate need of a beach vacation and free supply of red meat and beer. Or at least a cup of steaming coffee.

Waiting in his office at the state police headquarter in Pikesville, Porter kept glancing at the pager on his desk, willing it to beep with a new message from Ghost. Finally it did:

U R correct. Found his GS @ temple access rd.

This was it! Porter rubbed his hands, contemplated for a long moment, and typed a final set of instructions.

Send him 2 the Celestial Kingdom.
Search 4 disk/other devices & destroy.

The reply was exactly what Porter wanted:

OK. Consider it done.

Porter removed the battery from the pager, dropped it on the floor, and drew his service revolver, which he unloaded. He kneeled down, held the revolver by the short barrel, and used the butt to smash the pager repeatedly until no piece was larger than a penny. After reloading and holstering the revolver, he collected all the pieces of the pager in a paper tissue, went to the bathroom, and flushed it down the toilet.

Just as one saint was leaving the men's room, two others entered. A toilet flushed in one of the occupied stalls. Ben realized he had no hope of being left alone long enough to trigger the fire alarm. Giving himself a last glance in the mirror, he walked out. But just before turning the corner, he reached over his shoulder, peeled off part of the sticky tape that held the bandage to the singed tattoo, and reapplied it over the key ring and memory flash drive. It felt very big to him, and as he rearranged the white poncho over it, Ben hoped the bulge wouldn't stand out to the casual observer.

"Ah!" Brother Pat cheerfully greeted him. "Feeling better?"

"Thank God." Ben followed him, memorizing the way.

They made two turns down wide hallways, passed by several doors, and entered a large room. The space was divided by white curtains, similar to the changing room, creating cubicles with a limited measure of privacy. But here the activity was more intense, and as they walked across the room, Ben heard murmuring and splashing behind the partitions.

Pat held aside the curtain for Ben, and they entered a cubicle. The hushed male voices now came from all directions, pronouncing rapid incantations that merged with each other into an incoherent stream of words.

A stool held a container and a folded white towel.

After positioning Ben before him, Pat unhooked a small rubber hose, glanced at a piece of paper, and said, "Brother Sampson! By the authority of the True Church, I now wash you for and on behalf of Aryeh Leib Belinski, who is dead, and you take the endowments for him."

Squirting water from the hose on Ben's forehead, he continued, "I now wash your head so that your brain and intellect may be clear and accurate." Wetting each of Ben's ears, he said, "I wash your ears so that you hear the words of the Lord clearly." Continuing to Ben's eyes, he said, "I wash your eyes so that you see clearly and walk in the way of the Lord...I wash your nose so that you may smell...your lips...that you may never speak evil..."

Too shocked by this flow of water all over his head and face, Ben barely followed the words while Pat reached under the white poncho and washed his shoulders, spine, and chest—"that your shoulders be strong...your spine carry you...your heart be a receptacle for pure and righteous thoughts..."

His ribs, internal organs, and bowels received their due blessings for and on behalf of the dead Belinski, "that they perform their bodily functions," as did his arms and hands, "that they may be strong and do the work of the Lord..."

Pat lifted the bottom edge of Ben's white poncho and said, "I wash your loins so that you may multiply and replenish the earth and sow your seed for your posterity." The stream of cold water made Ben flinch, earning a disapproving glare from Pat, which instantly turned into a grandfatherly smile.

As soon as Pat completed the washing and blessing of Ben's legs and feet, another man materialized from behind the curtain

In a scripted ritual they must have repeated hundreds of times, both of them dipped their fingers in the container of oil, laid the dripping hands on Ben's head, and recited a blessing that repeatedly included the word "Sealing." They made him sit down and continued anointing him with "consecrated oil" that was turning Belinski—by proxy—into a member of the Church and elevating him to priesthood. They proceeded to oil Ben's body parts in a manner resembling the earlier washing part.

Having gone farther than he had expected, with the two old men smearing him with oil as they recited blessings that conferred priesthood on a long-deceased Jew while their busy hands descended toward Ben's private parts under the soaked poncho, Ben was overtaken by a terrible urge to laugh. To masquerade the eruption of giggles from his belly, he began coughing violently.

Rather than scare them off, the coughing only invigorated Pat and his partner, who raised their voices and used copious amounts of consecrated oil to finish off the lower part of Ben's body—for and on behalf of Aryeh Leib Belinski, who must have been rolling in his grave—if he had a grave.

Pat offered him a towel while the officiating partner unfolded a set of undergarments, which Ben realized were intended for him, or rather, for the dead Jew who had just become a proud Mormon saint.

Ben quickly toweled himself under the white poncho and let the two old men dress him in the sacred garments—heavier than normal underwear, made of material that felt almost like plastic. The undershirt had the same markings as on Zachariah's military-style Mormon undergarments. The underpants had an exaggerated slit with an over-flap at the genitals, creating a visual emphasis of the duty—and ease—of procreation at every opportunity.

While the two men declared the dead Jew to be endowed now, by proxy, with various godly powers as a priest of the True Church in the afterlife, Ben got his slippers back on, shook loose the wet shield over the undergarments, and with a muttered apology pushed aside the curtains and left the cubicle.

CHAPTER 57

There was no time to waste on plans that had clearly gone wrong. Triggering a fire alarm was not feasible, and he had to find another way. According to Dreyfuss, the temple offices were in a hallway off the main entrance. Ben headed that way as fast as he could without raising suspicion.

Taking the left turn into the hallway marked *Administration*, he glanced back at the reception hall. His eyes met no curious gazes, as those waiting at the processing counter had their backs to him. But among the group, Ben caught sight of a tall figure in a white motorcycle suit, white boots, and a white baseball cap.

The Ghost!

Ben kept walking, but his mind was swirling with questions. How had the Ghost found him? Was one of the ex-Mormons a traitor? Who? Powell? Streep? Dreyfuss? Or Rex? None of them had given Ben any reason for suspicion, but now he was under one roof with a killer!

He passed several open doors to busy offices. There were only men at the desks, some speaking on the phone, others typing at their computers. A large printer spewed papers, and in another office a TV set showed a bespectacled man giving a sermon.

At the end of the hallway he found a set of double doors. A sign said: *Temple President.*

Gently pressing the door handle, Ben peeked inside.

A man was standing at the other end of the office, feeding papers into a paper shredder, which made loud buzzing sounds as each bundle of documents was chewed up by the blades. It seems like a reception area, with a desk for the secretary, where the man's jacket was draped on the back of a chair, and two waiting chairs under a large painting of white angels with wings.

Ben hugged the wet poncho to his body to prevent it from rustling as he tiptoed behind the man, opened a door, and slipped into an inner office.

It was large, plush, and empty of human presence other than the life-size oil portraits on the walls. He circled a mahogany desk and sat in a large, leather-upholstered executive chair. The wheels allowed the chair to travel back and forth on a plastic mat for easy reach to the bookcases and filing cabinets around it.

In the top drawer he found personal letterhead and envelopes embossed with the Mormon official whose office it was:

Church of JESUS CHRIST of Latter-day Saints
James R. Benson, Temple President
Washington DC Temple

Ben took one of the envelopes and scribbled on it in his finest handwriting:

To Brother Joseph Morgan
Hand Deliver – Personal and Confidential

Pulling a blank letterhead from the pile, he wrote the following note:

Dear Brother Joseph,
Please meet in private with the bearer of this note, Sampson Allard, who has an important testimony to share with you.
Brother James Benson

He folded the note and sealed it in the envelope.

At first he saw no computer. But pushing aside the sliding doors on a side cabinet revealed a Dell desktop. He moved the mouse, and the screen came to life.

It was a plain *Welcome!* window with blank spaces for the user's ID and password. Drawing on his memory, Ben typed:

User ID: Zachiboy
Password: DCMTDBS

An hourglass appeared, and the computer made typical sounds of coming to life. But it was taking a long time, and in the outer office there were suddenly sounds of talking.

He tiptoed to the door and found that it had no key.

Back at the computer, Ben faced a blank screen. Had they removed Zachariah's access already? When was the last time he had access to this system? The fact that Zachariah had left this code as a clue in the virtual treasure hunt for the incriminating floppy disk meant that he believed it would remain in effect.

The computer finally beeped, and a Windows Vista logo appeared on the screen.

Sitting back in the oversized leather chair, Ben pulled up a search window and typed in, again from memory, the file name Zachariah had left:

File: BFD111995

A picture folder appeared, and when he clicked on it, a photo opened.

Staring at it, Ben reached over his shoulder and pulled the key ring from under the bandages. He held the miniature statue of the Angel Moroni next to the photo on the screen. They were identical.

Moving the mouse, Ben ran the curser over the photo, causing it to change focus. The view expanded, revealing that the statue was positioned in the corner of a large hall with white walls, luxurious furnishing, and crystal chandeliers. Judging by the size of the furniture, the statue was about the size of a child, perhaps ten or twelve years old, but the long trumpet made the statue taller, almost the size of an average adult.

Another move of the curser over the photo caused the Angel Moroni to turn on its side, resting flat on the marble floor, its base visible. Glued to the bottom was an object. Peering closely, Ben realized it was another floppy disk.

By moving the curser again across the photo, he made the Angel Moroni stand up.

Concentrating on the hall, Ben realized how beautiful it was in a cleansed, other-worldly way. Zachariah must have assumed that whoever followed his clues would be familiar with that room. But Ben wasn't, and he wanted to yell in frustration. Where the hell was this room?

Suddenly it hit him! The style of the walls, windows, furnishings, even the floor, was reminiscent of the room he was sitting in! Not identical—this large office had colors by virtue of the portraits, books, and cabinets. But the feel of the place was similar, which meant that the Angel Moroni statue in the photo must be somewhere in the temple!

Sticking the memory flash drive into a USB port, Ben saved the file. Returning to the search window, he typed:

Zachariah Hinckley

After a few seconds of searching the temple's database, to Ben's utter amazement a folder came up in the search results list:

SCMC/Zachariah Hinckley/Trial Evidence and Proceedings

It took him a moment to figure out that *SCMC* stood for *Strengthening Church Members Committee.*

It was a large data folder. When Ben placed the curser on it and right clicked to find the *send* order, a voice startled him.

"You're a hard man to find."

He looked up.

The Ghost was closing the door behind…*her!*

There was no mistaking the tall figure and white riding suit. It was the Ghost. But her Nordic face was almost beautiful, marred only by a red scar that divided the right cheek. Her blue eyes were cold, and her blond hair was tucked under the white baseball cap.

Ben forced his finger to move the mouse and click *save*. The tiny light on the memory flash drive blinked as a copy of the folder was saved on it. He turned to her and said, "How did you find me?"

She smiled—not a friendly Mormon smile, but a frosty one. "Your black bitch must've been happy to see you."

The rage flooded him, yet he realized the Ghost was trying to unsettle him, make him reckless, easier to handle. He took a deep breath. "It's love," he said. "But you wouldn't know about that, would you?"

"True. Hot niggers aren't my thing." The Ghost stepped toward the desk, but stopped when the door behind her opened.

The male secretary poked his head in. "Excuse me, but what's going on here?"

"Please," the Ghost said, "come in."

Foolishly, he obeyed.

She kicked the door shut, chopped him on the side of the neck, and ripped open his white buttoned-down shirt. She peeled it off his shoulders and used the sleeves to bind his wrists behind his back. It was all done rapidly, without hesitation, not one second wasted. Next the Ghost pulled a green belt from her pocket—similar to the one Ben had seen among the temple garb he had been given. She looped it around the stunned secretary's neck, tightened a knot, and fastened the other end to the door knob, causing him to sit up with his back to the door, immobilized and suffocating.

The computer beeped to signal completion of saving the folder to the memory flash drive.

The Ghost turned to him.

"A real living, breathing Danite!" Ben pulled the flash drive from the USB port. "Never expected to see one."

She approached the desk. "Feeling lucky?"

"Blood atonement isn't how I'd like to get to heaven."

The secretary made gagging sounds. He jerked, rattling the door, but it only tightened the noose around his neck.

The Ghost reached the desk.

"Killing is a sin," Ben said, rising to his feet. "Joseph Smith's last words."

"It's only business, kid." She flexed her hands and smiled. Up close, her teeth were yellowish. "Nothing personal."

"Business? What about God?"

"Who?" She circled the desk.

Ben nudged the executive chair, making it turn on its wheels, the backside blocking the Ghost. He clenched the Angel Moroni in his fist and felt the long trumpet sticking out between his fingers. With the other hand he pointed at his forehead. "Barely a bruise from your kick. I should have realized it was girly."

She paused, surprised that he had the capacity to joke when his life was about to end.

"Next time," he said, "try to give it your all, like this!" He placed his foot on the edge of the chair and pressed with everything he had. At first, the heavy chair hardly budged, but then its wheels gained momentum and its back hit the Ghost in the stomach, propelling her backward and throwing her against a bookcase.

Ben knew he had only a second or two before this female assassin recovered from the shock of being knocked back by an odd-looking, sickly reporter wearing a wet white poncho.

Leaping forward, he mounted the chair and brought his fist pounding at her face. He felt the Angel Moroni's trumpet penetrating through the flesh and facial bones next to her nose, below her left eye. He pulled it out just as she moaned, her hands rising to her punctured face. But she wasn't disabled yet, and he knew that her killer instincts would soon cause her to shift from defense to deadly attack. There was no choice for him but to attack again, which he did, still perched on the padded chair, throwing a hook punch to the side of her face, where Angel Moroni's trumpet speared her again through skin, flesh, and delicate bones.

Now she screamed—a long, agonized, primal scream.

As he jumped off the chair, the Ghost collapsed. Something fell out of her pocket—a pack of cigarettes with the logo of the

House of Prince and the Danish royal crest. And while she was still down, he grabbed the side of the bookcase and pulled hard, causing it to fall over on top of her.

Ben ran to the door. The secretary's face was blue, his tongue sticking out. There was no time for fiddling with the knot, which had likely tightened with the man's dying struggles. Instead, Ben forced the door open until there was enough room for him to squeeze through.

In the outer office, rummaging through the secretary's desk, he found scissors, which he used to cut the green belt at the secretary's neck. The man dropped to the floor, his first breath shrieking through constricted airways. His hands were still bound behind his back, but he was alive. Ben turned and ran.

CHAPTER 58

The white slippers had been lost in the struggle, and a barefooted Ben reached the end of the hallway only to see the reception hall as peaceful as it had been before. Word had not arrived yet of the violence that had bloodied the fanciest office in the temple. He wished it was possible for him to cross the reception hall and leave through the main doors with the memory flash drive in his hand. But walking out while dressed in the white poncho would draw as much attention as dragging the bleeding Ghost across the marble floor.

Instead, he turned right and headed to the locker room, only to run into Pat, whose creased face seemed more bewildered than angry. "Brother Sampson! Where have you been?"

"I got lost," Ben said breathlessly as he kept going. "It's a big place."

"The House of the Lord is commensurate with His greatness." Pat kept up with him. "You need to change now and come to the Creation Room for the communal part of the endowment ceremony."

"Sure," Ben said, entering locker room. "Creation Room next."

"I'll wait for you here."

"Thank you, Brother Pat. God bless."

As he pulled his stuff from the locker, Ben's hands trembled and his panting was rapid. There was blood on his arm and he wiped it off with the white poncho, which he tossed away. He got out of the sacred underpants and undershirt, which were oily and wet. He forced the white suit pants onto his sticky legs, buttoned down the dress shirt, and slipped the white tie back on, tightening it around his neck. There was a dull ache in his shoulder, either from the old injury or from the fresh wound that had replaced his beautiful tattoo.

He unhooked the memory flash drive from the bloody Angel Moroni key ring, which he washed in a sink, wiped thoroughly to remove any fingerprints, and dropped in a trash bin. The memory flash drive went in his pocket, together with the keys to the GS.

With the unlaced white shoes on his bare feet, Ben left the locker room. He ignored Pat and headed left toward the main exit, but as he looked up, through the flow of white-dressed men and women, all the way at the other end, he saw the tall figure of the Ghost. She had a towel pressed to her face, but her eyes were focused.

Ben turned and grabbed Pat's arm. "Where's the Creation Room?"

They went down the hallway and entered a large hall. It was decorated with beautiful murals of glorious nature vistas, roaming wild beasts, and glowing angels. Men and woman sat separately in rows of chairs on each side of the room, all wearing white clothes and shoes. All of them had ceremonial green belts and white hats draped over their arms, ready for the next part. Ben pulled his from the plastic bag and did the same. Some of the women were very young, dressed in modest wedding gowns with no trains. On a large screen up front, a movie was playing,

Pat made him sit among the men on the right side of the room.

Ben watched the door, trying not to be too conspicuous. Part of his mind absorbed the ongoing drama on the wall-sized screen. It was apparently the story of the creation of the world according to Mormonism. There was little similarity to what he remembered from bible study. To begin with, there were many gods. Elohim was the Father, and Jehovah, who was also called Jesus, was his physical son. The third god, Michael, later became Adam and roamed the Garden of Eden with Eve.

At this point, the men put on the green belt with the fig leaf dangling before their genital area, just like Adam did in the movie.

The chief god, Elohim, asked Eve—as well as all the Mormon women seated on the left side of the Creation Room—to make an absolute vow of obedience to their husbands. The women took the vow with loud voices, promising to abide by the Law of Obedience and serve their husbands unquestionably as the only way to achieve their own spiritual exaltation in this world and in the afterlife. The men then followed up with a vow to obey God's commands as communicated through the prophet, seer, and revelator in Salt Lake City and down the line through the Church leaders.

Next was a vow to sacrifice anything—even life itself, yours or someone else's—die or kill in the defense of the True Church. Ben was too shocked to recite the violent words. They seemed to belong in another era, or a different reality, not in the contemporary American world that existed just outside the temple walls.

Brother Pat leaned over and whispered, "*That which is wrong under one circumstance may be, and often is, right under another, as God said: "You shall not kill" and at another time He said: "Thou shall utterly destroy!"*" Remember who said that?"

It was an easy guess. Ben whispered back, "Joseph Smith, the true prophet of God."

Brother Pat smiled approvingly and helped him put on the ceremonial hat. Everyone else did too, covering their heads with the puffed-up caps resembling chefs' hats, yet equipped with a strap and a clip to secure it to the collar and prevent it from falling to the floor.

Continuing the story on the screen, many gods, who all appeared to be strapping white males like those surrounding Ben at the moment, ruled their own worlds while procreating incessantly with their plural wives. Souls in white or dark skin went up and down, and Lucifer played a major role opposite Jesus. But it was hard for Ben to concentrate as the Ghost entered the hall, swathed in a white robe over her lanky figure, a towel pressed to the side of her face, and took a seat on the women's side of the room.

Brother Pat turned to Ben and held out his hand. On the screen, Elohim instructed everyone to practice a special handshake—The First Token of the Aaronic Priesthood. It was an elaborate maneuver, and Ben struggled to do it with the confidence of a saint who had already done this before and was doing it today only as a charitable proxy for the soul of a dead Gentile. There were other signs and tokens, which were intended to be practiced as well so that, when the great day came, each saint could prove to the angels guarding the Celestial Kingdom that he had indeed achieved salvation through exaltation in the True Gospel of Joseph Smith.

The next oath was to keep all these handshakes and hand signs secret even at the price of life itself. When Ben glanced over to the rear of the women's section, the Ghost's eyes were waiting for him over the white towel she held to her cheek.

The men passed first into the next chamber: The Lone and Dreary World. The room was decorated to communicate a desolate, desert-like space, similar to the bleak world that awaited Adam upon his banishment from the Garden of Eden. The women followed, everyone now fully clothed in white robes, which temple workers passed around to those who had not brought their own. The robes were heavy, giving a sense of being laden down with weights. A second movie started playing.

Now it was Satan's time to play, and Ben absorbed little of the dramatic attempts at corruption occurring up on the screen while the Ghost's eyes drilled holes in his back. But he was probably safe until she found a way to attack him surreptitiously, and he managed to follow the story enough to understand that Satan was trying to corrupt gullible men by preaching to them the main tenets of mainstream Christianity—that God was one, that He was without a physical body or earthy passions, that He sat on a topless throne, that he was everywhere always but nowhere in particular, that He was big enough to fill the universe yet small enough to live in one's heart—all of the basic elements of faith held by Christians. But then came the message that Joseph Smith had received from Elohim the Father and Jesus the Jehovah in the First Vision, that all the Christian churches were false abominations perpetrated by Satan, that in truth there were many gods, that the first god—Elohim the Father—was a physical man living on his own planet with plural godly wives with whom he was having regular intercourse and begetting godly children—among them Jesus the Jehovah and Lucifer the Satan, and that He therefore was in one place, not everywhere, and of the same physical size as any saint in this room.

Soon Satan was shooed away by John, James, and Peter, the prophets sent by Elohim the Father, who was now looking like an elderly Mormon man. Upon departing, Satan declared about "these people," that "if they do not walk up to every covenant they make at these altars this day, they will be in my power!"

An audible sigh of fear sounded in the room, which made Ben cough to hide a burst of nervous laughter.

With this, the ancient prophets taught the mesmerized audience more hand signs. Ben practiced with Pat the Sign of the Nail by pressing his index fingers into one another's palms, and the Sure Sign of the Nail, which was more complicated, connecting intertwined fingers and pressing against one another's pulse. The pantomimed penalties were then dramatized, representing the death and mayhem that would come to those who betray the secrets of the True Church.

To facilitate moving to the next room, part of the movie screen disappeared, and as if by magic, a white, wall-sized curtain came down. It symbolized the separation between this world and the next—the exalted Celestial Kingdom awaiting the righteous Mormon saints and their wives too, but only if their husbands chose to bring them through.

The men began to pass via slits in the heavy curtain and then reached to hold their wives, who remained on the side of the Lone and Dreary World. Ben realized that the husbands, some of whom were grooms in the process of marrying these girls today, tested the women on all the signs, tokens, and oaths taken today before they brought them through the curtain into the symbolic Celestial Kingdom.

Bother Pat passed first and reached through the slit in the curtain for Ben, or rather, for the dead Jew for whom Ben was a proxy. There was more replaying of the hand signs, secret tokens, and whispering of secret names and incantations that Ben didn't quite follow. He was occupied with watching one of the temple workers go through the routine with the Ghost.

Finally Brother Pat declared, "Well done, thou good and faithful servant, enter you into the joy of the Lord!" He grasped Ben's arm in one of the secret handshake maneuvers and jerked him forward and through the slit in the curtain into a vast room that was breathtakingly beautiful—and very familiar!

The unnatural magnificence of the Celestial Kingdom hall had an almost bewitching effect on Ben, who struggled to remain focused on the reality of his situation. Craning his head, he was captivated by the ceiling, which was much higher than in the previous room. It was artfully divided into lit-up squares and lined with glistening chandeliers. Around him, the saints and their women, angelically white in their flowing robes, either sat in deep sofas around the walls or kneeled at a leather-padded alter in the middle of the room, engaging in hushed prayers. The walls were mostly windows, not clear but hazy white, which gave the whole space an extra-terrestrial, other-worldly feel.

The Ghost, though, seemed neither mesmerized nor prayerful. Perhaps she had been here before and was impervious to the imitation-Celestial Kingdom effect. It was obvious that all she cared about right now was cornering him for a silent kill. The question was how, and her plan became more apparent as she moved around the room, getting closer. Their eyes met, her gaze dropped to his neck, and he understood what was on her mind: *She was going to trip him and break his neck, pretending it was an accident!*

Ben kept away from her by pacing between kneeling Mormons and along the sofas. As he reached a corner of the hall, he saw the Angel Moroni standing on the marble floor and realized in an instant that he was looking at the same statue as the one in the photo he had seen on the temple president's computer screen— the last clue in Zachariah Hinckley's posthumous treasure hunt!

Angel Moroni was holding the golden tablets of the *Book of Mormon* in one hand and in the other, a long, straight trumpet, which he was blowing toward the gilded ceiling.

"It's a simple trumpet." Brother Pat was shadowing Ben, whispering in his ear. "One day, Angel Moroni will blow the horn to announce Christ's second coming!"

"Third coming," Ben said.

Brother Pat blinked rapidly. "Third?"

"Wasn't the Second Coming when Jesus ministered to the lost tribes of Israel in North America?" Ben peered closely at the statue.

"Well...that's not how...we count."

"Really?" Ben pretended to trip and accidently bump into the golden angel, knocking it to the floor with a loud crash. He fell over it, hiding the base of the statue with his body. Women screamed, and men were rushing over.

But Ben had already found what he was looking for—just as in the photo, a cardboard floppy disk case was taped to the bottom of the base. He tore it off and shoved it into his pocket.

Brother Pat was pulling at his arm, helping him up. Other saints picked up the Angel Moroni, who had lost part of his elbow as well as the top end of his trumpet. Without the flaring bell of the trumpet, the Angel Moroni was left blowing into a long metal rod with a pointy end.

In the commotion, the Ghost made her move, coming at Ben with long strides. He headed for the door, and she shifted direction to block his way. With many of the kneeling Mormons now beginning to leave, the two of them kept moving about the large room as if charged by opposite magnetic fields.

Meanwhile Brother Pat and two other temple workers lifted the Angel Moroni and carried it toward the door. The statue was heavy, and they took a break near the door, placing it carefully on its base, the bell-missing trumpet pointing upward in the direction of Ben, who was at the opposite side of the Celestial Room, having been maneuvered there by the Ghost, away from his only escape route.

Positioned between him and Angel Moroni, she lowered the towel from her face, revealing the left side, between her cheekbone and jaw—bloodied and swollen from his two strikes. The sight of her mutilated face, which she probably exposed to shock him into temporary paralysis, instead served as a clear message of her deadly intentions. The room was almost empty now, and he had to choose between dying and killing.

Brother Pat and another temple worker stood by the door, facing away. It was time to act. Ben leaned forward, inhaled deeply, and broke into a sprint as if a winning ball was cradled in the crook of his arm while this woman in white was the only opposite team player blocking his way to a game-winning touchdown.

Shocked by his sudden mad rush, the Ghost had no time to dodge before his injured shoulder rammed into her chest and propelled her backward. Her hands grasped the air as she fell onto the upturned rod of Angel Moroni's broken trumpet, which speared her back, pierced her heart, and came out of her chest.

Pain shot through Ben's shoulder. He grasped it and groaned.

The Ghost's dying eyes followed him as he left the Celestial Kingdom. Brother Pat said something, but Ben ignored him. In a moment, they would notice the dead woman slumped over Angle Moroni, and all hell would break loose.

To the right, the hallway reached a dead end. There was an emergency exit. He pushed the bar, and a buzzer sounded as he exited into the sun.

Outside the temple, Ben found himself in a vast garden that was groomed to the point of looking unreal. He stripped away the white robe, the green fig leaf belt, and the funny hat. Reaching into his pocket, he pulled out the thin cardboard case. It was the same brand of floppy disk as the one he had found at the Camp David Scenic Overlook. He examined it, hoping to find the incriminating handwritten note that Joe Morgan had sent to Zachariah Hinckley. But it wasn't there, which meant that this was not the real floppy disk but another clue on the way to finding it.

He put a finger into the slit along the side and felt for a floppy disk. Feeling nothing, he looked inside. It was empty. No floppy disk!

He turned the square cardboard case over, looking at it closely in the sun. Sure enough, there was a scribble on it—not with a pen or a pencil, but with yellow highlighter, which was only legible by holding the cardboard case at an angle against the light:

JM SS MD

That's it? Three pairs of letters? Was it an acronym?

The only connection he could make was the first pair of letters—the initials of Joe Morgan. But the whole thing involved Morgan! And what about the second and third pairs of letters?

The third could stand for *Maryland,* but what about the middle pair?

SS

Then it came to him: *SS MD* stood for *Silver Spring Maryland.*

The whole thing was very simple: *Joe Morgan Silver Spring Maryland.*

But what did it mean? Was Morgan in possession of the incriminating floppy disk? There was only one way to find out.

Ben paused to orient himself. He figured out where the GS was and headed in that direction. His left shoulder was in agony, and he could barely move his arm.

CHAPTER 59

Porter heard the words "Mormon Temple" on the radio in his unmarked cruiser and jacked up the volume. The dispatcher rebroadcast an automatic notice that an alarm had been triggered by the opening of an emergency door. There was no 911 call from the temple, and no smoke alarms had gone off yet.

He responded on the open channel, addressing the dispatcher while others could hear. "Inspector Porter here, Community Affairs. We handle non-violent incidents at religious institutions. Mormon temple procedure requires their permission to enter the premises. I'm in the vicinity and will handle the situation. I'll call in for help if needed."

He waited a moment to see if any other unit responded, which would be surprising. The Mormon temple was treated with wary respect, almost as if it were a Vatican-like territory with its own jurisdiction. Hearing nothing more, Porter turned on the police lights and headed to the temple.

Ben reached the GS through the bushes. Pulling his iPhone from the hard case, he turned it on and checked Morgan's website. Quote of the Day: *Throw Out the Socialist Bums!* The candidate's daily schedule for this Monday included a FOX News morning show, a speech at a Norfolk, Virginia, shipyard, a lunchtime fundraiser with technology executives in Tyson's Corner, and an NRA-sponsored town hall meeting at the Watergate Hotel. The evening slot was described as *Family Home Night*, alluding to the Mormon custom. Judging by the time, Ben guessed that Joe Morgan was already on his way home from the Watergate, having completed yet another successful whirlwind day of campaigning for the White House. Tonight's Family Home Night, though, might not be as successful as Morgan's earlier events, considering Ben's planned visit.

Pulling the GS out of the bushes and onto the road left him panting and in pain. But there was no time to waste. He put the helmet on, mounted the bike, and rode off.

Moments later, Ben merged into the heavy traffic on the 495 beltway, which carried him toward Silver Spring.

Just off the exit was a Walgreen's drugstore. He parked, went inside, and bought a bottle of water and a dose of Motrin.

There was no one at the photo development counter. The computer was on. He connected to the Internet, signed in to his g-mail account, and composed a new e-mail titled: *Marine Vet Zachariah Hinckley: A Victim of the Mormon Church or of the Morgan Campaign?* Fitting the memory flash drive into one of the USB slots, he attached to the e-mail a copy of the folder named *Zachariah Hinckley – Trial Evidence and Proceedings* and sent the message to himself. A moment later, it appeared in the mailbox on his iPhone. He signed off and pulled out the memory flash drive.

Locking himself in the men's room, he swallowed the two Motrin pills and washed the blond dye from his hair and eyebrows. In the mirror, he was still pale, and his hair—while back to its original dark color—was still too short, making him look fifteen. But he didn't look like Sampson Allard anymore, which was good because he wanted to look like himself—to be Ben Teller—when confronting Joe Morgan.

As Porter turned toward the Mormon temple, he saw that the opposite lane of the access road was lined with cars. The worshipers were departing the temple, which usually closed early on Monday afternoons in consideration of Family Home Night. But he was the first on the scene, no fire engine in sight, and that was good news.

A visibly distraught elderly temple worker was waiting. "I'm Brother Pat," he said.

Porter shook his hand. "We received an automatic message that an emergency door was opened. Did you have a burglary?"

"No. Someone opened it mistakenly after the accident."

"Accident?"

He held forth a pair of white slippers. "We just called it in. Let me show you."

Porter removed his shoes, put on the white slippers, and followed the elderly man

down the hallways to the very last set of doors, which led them into the hall representing the Celestial Kingdom.

Expecting to see the dead body of the pesky reporter, Porter balked at the sight of the Ghost. He gripped the doorway, taking in the gruesome scene, and held back a curse.

"How did this happen?"

"The statue broke." Brother Pat held up the bell end of the trumpet. "People were leaving the room, and no one noticed the poor sister. She must have tripped and fell on it. Perhaps she was dizzy from her earlier injury."

"She had been injured before?"

"We don't know how it happened. She had arrived at the temple after being injured elsewhere, though no one noticed." He pointed to a bloody towel. "She was covering that part of her face."

"Anything else?"

"In terms of the media…all this could be misinterpreted."

"How do you interpret it?"

"It's all pre-ordained, of course." Brother Pat closed his eyes and quoted. "'*But their garments should be made white through the blood of the Lamb.*' Alma, thirty-four, thirty-six."

"Very nice," Porter said. "Did you see, by any chance, a young man interacting with this woman?"

Brother Pat made as if he was trying to remember. "I'm not sure. Everyone was in great distress."

"Did you see who triggered the emergency door alarm?"

"No. I'm sorry. And about the media—"

"I'm here for the state police, not the news." Porter stepped closer and peered at the sharp rod that remained of Angle Moroni's trumpet. "The Lord giveth and the Lord taketh away."

"God bless you, Officer."

"I need a few minutes alone here."

"Of course. I'll be outside if you need me."

CHAPTER 60

Pulling up to the curb behind the state police cruiser, Ben was impressed by the massive brick mansion at the top of a circular driveway. Illuminated by the last rays of the setting sun, the lush shrubbery and flower beds bloomed with rainbow colors, reminiscent of the landscaping abundance at the Mormon temple. But the grandeur of Morgan's residence had none of the fairytale whimsy of the temple. Rather, it evoked a British manor house with its sheer size, straight lines, and a slate roof whose long watershed was punctuated by several stone chimneys. The place projected an image of great wealth and power.

Ben took off his helmet and put on a baseball cap.

A trooper emerged from the cruiser.

Following Dreyfuss's advice, Ben smiled broadly. "Good evening, Officer!"

The trooper nodded.

"Christ be with you." Ben unzipped his riding jacket and reached inside.

"Hey!" The trooper's hand rested on the butt of his sidearm. "Keep your hands where I can see them!"

"It's just a letter." He offered the envelope with a slight bow, as if handing over a business card.

"A letter?"

"From the holy temple of the Church of Jesus Christ of Latter-day Saints." Ben kept smiling. "I am here to deliver it to Governor Morgan personally."

The trooper examined it.

"Have you heard a testimony of Christ yet?"

"Yes, I have." He smiled back. "Can you show me some identification?"

Ben handed him Sampson Allard's stolen Temple Recommend Card. "May I share with you a marvelous story I recently learned about the prophet Joseph Smith's last sermon in Nauvoo?"

"Another time, buddy. Are you carrying?"

Ben shook his head.

"It's just routine." The trooper patted him down, then again over his back, under his arms, and between his legs. He found Ben's iPhone in a pocket and fiddled with it, making sure it was a working phone. "Okay," he said. "Follow me."

They marched up the driveway, passing by a black SUV with federal government plates and a few late-model luxury cars. Approaching the house, they reached a set of wrought-iron gates connected to a tall fence, which was covered with a thick layer of ivy that made it disarmingly decorative.

The trooper spoke into an intercom, and the gate clicked open. Walking up a paved footpath, they entered a vestibule, which welcomed guests to the main entrance under a domed ceiling and a brass chandelier. The front doors, made of heavy wood beams braced by metal joints, seemed to have formerly belonged to a cathedral in Europe.

The door opened. A man in a blue jacket appeared. He took the letter and the Temple Recommend Card from the trooper and went inside.

They waited.

A few minutes later, the Secret Service agent reappeared. He handed Ben the Temple Recommend Card and beckoned him inside. The trooper turned and headed back to the street.

"Wait here." The agent pointed to a pair of armchairs on one side of the spacious foyer.

Another agent, nearly a carbon copy of the first, peeked out of a side room, where they had likely set up camp after the candidate was given Secret Service protection.

Porter searched the Ghost. He found the pager, a wallet with cash, a fake driver's license, a fake Temple Recommend Card of the same name, and the keys to the Ducati. She carried nothing else.

He examined her hands, which were cold and large, the fingertips burnt off with acid to remove her prints. The wristwatch was a cheap drugstore piece, which he removed, just in case. He stood back and looked at her, the bloodied face frozen with a blank expression, turned up to the gilded ceiling. No one would be able to find out who she really was. A true professional.

Covering her face with the bloodied towel, Porter left the Celestial Kingdom hall. "Too bad," he told Brother Pat. "A tragic accident."

"Yes, tragic."

In the lobby they found a fireman, who was unable to find out where to go in the huge temple. His frustration was boiling. "What the heck is going on?"

Porter held up his badge. "I'm with Community Relations. One of the worshippers fell on a statue and got herself knocked off. A freak accident, but it's done."

"Let me see her." The fireman picked up a red first aid box. "Where—"

"Please!" Brother Pat held his hands up. "Temple sanctity requires removal of shoes and street clothes. This is the House of the Lord."

The fireman hesitated. "I just need to see—"

"He's got a point." Porter pointed to his own feet in white slippers.

"You want me to take off my gear?" The fireman's radio crackled, and a tinny voice reported a car crash on Rockville Boulevard.

"Listen," Porter said, "there's nothing for you to do. She's gone. And I'm gone too." He smiled. "You guys will take care of the accident report, right?"

"Sampson?" A woman in a business suit walked out of another door. "I'm Katie, one of the campaign coordinators."

"Hi." Ben got up. "Are we going to win?"

"Sure looks like it." She laughed. "Please follow me."

He tugged on the visor of his baseball cap. It covered most of his back-from-the-blond natural hair. They walked down a hallway decorated with framed family photos of skiing vacations, sailing trips, and weddings. A doorless entry led into a kitchen that could easily belong in a busy restaurant. A cook was busy at the stovetop, and a woman in a maid's uniform was scrubbing pots in a stainless steel tub.

A long table was set against a wall of windows overlooking a well-lit backyard swimming pool. Twenty or so family members of all ages were sitting at the table. At the head of the table was Joe Morgan, who stood up and extended his hand. "Welcome, Brother Sampson!"

Ben shook his hand, which was dry and firm. Up close, Morgan's handsome face and silver hair were as impeccable as they looked on TV. "It's an honor, Governor."

"Oh, please, call me Brother Joe."

"Thank you, Brother Joe." Ben looked at the others. "Hello, everyone."

They chorused, "Hello, Brother Sampson!"

Katie circled the table and whispered something in Morgan's ear. He grinned. "Great news! You're a wiz, girl!"

Beaming, she left the kitchen.

There was an awkward silence.

Mrs. Morgan, sitting at the opposite end of the table from her husband, cleared her throat.

"Please, have a seat," Morgan said to Ben. "Jeremy is teaching us from the *Book of Mormon*."

Morgan's son, about twenty and every bit as handsome as his father, held up the volume. "I'm sharing the prophesies about the fate of the Jewish people."

Ben almost said, "How appropriate," but held his tongue, instead nodding and smiling at Beanie Morgan, the candidate's youngest daughter, who sat next to him. She moved her copy of the book closer to him so that they could share. It was a heavy volume titled: *The Book of Mormon – The Earliest Text – Edited by Royal Skousen.*

Noticing Ben's interest in the cover, Morgan said, "We like to study the original text. The prophet Joseph Smith said that the first version of the *Book of Mormon* is the closest to the word of God as it was revealed to him."

"We read in One Nephi, twenty-five," Jeremy said, "the prophet's recounting of the events during the years before and after the destruction of the Jewish Temple, the ruination of Jerusalem, and the exodus of his family, led by his father Lehi, over the oceans to the new promised land of North America. Nephi explained why the Jews, who hardened their hearts and rejected the message of Christ when He first appeared and then crucified Him, were therefore destroyed and exiled by God the Father as punishment. Nephi prophesized that they would suffer for generations—"

"A true prophesy," Joe Morgan interjected, "as we now know."

Everyone nodded in agreement.

"But he also," Jeremy continued, "predicted that they would eventually be restored to Jerusalem—another true prophesy, as it turned out. Let me read to you the pertinent parts. First, in verse nine, Nephi prophesized: '*And as one generation hath been destroyed among the Jews because of inequity, even so have they been destroyed from generation to generation according to their inequity.*' And continuing in verse eleven, he added: '*And notwithstanding that they have been carried away, they shall return again and possess the land of Jerusalem. Wherefore they shall be restored again to the lands of their inheritance.*'"

"Which indeed happened after two thousand years," Mrs. Morgan said from her end of the table. "In nineteen forty-eight, many centuries after Nephi had spoken, and also over a century after Joseph Smith translated the golden tablets and published the *Book of Mormon*. The establishment of the modern state of Israel confirmed the trueness of Nephi's prophesy."

"Which proves," Beanie said, "that he was a true prophet, because he correctly predicted that the Jews would be restored to the land of Israel!"

"And so did Isaiah and Ezekiel," Jeremy said. "But Nephi further prophesized that modern Israel would suffer from wars, which indeed has happened continuously since its founding. And he also predicted what will happen to the Jews when Christ the Lord comes again."

Ben caught the eyes of Joe Morgan, who was watching him with a pleasant, almost fatherly expression, except that he blinked rapidly a few times. Was it nervousness or the dryness of the indoor heating?

"Nephi predicted," Jeremy continued, "the future of the modern state of Israel: *'But behold, they shall have wars and rumors of wars, and when the day cometh that the Only Begotten of the Father—yea, even the Father of heaven and of earth—shall manifest himself onto them in the flesh, behold, they will reject him because of their inequities and the hardness of their hearts and the stiffness of their necks. Behold, they will crucify him!'*"

"Again?" The question came from one of the younger kids, probably Morgan's grandson. "They'll do it again?"

"I'm afraid so," Morgan said.

"That's right," Jeremy said. "Nephi prophesied it: *'Wherefore the Jews shall be scattered among all the nations…and the Lord hath scourged them…until they shall be persuaded to believe in Christ the Son of God and the atonement…that they shall believe in Christ…with pure hearts and clean hands and look not forward any more for another Messiah…the Lord will set his hand again the second time to restore his people from their lost and fallen state.'* And then," Jeremy concluded, "after another crucifixion of Christ and another destruction and exile for many generations, only then will the Jews finally accept Christ the Lord and be restored back to Jerusalem for time and eternity."

"Amen!" Joe Morgan looked at Ben. "Would you like to give testimony before we adjourn?"

Shutting his eyes, Ben recited from memory the sentence he had first read in Zachariah Hinckley's diary. "Joseph Smith is the True Prophet. The Church of Jesus Christ of Latter-day Saints, which he established, is the only True Church, and all other churches are false abominations perpetrated by Satan and led by him to divert souls from the path of the True Gospel."

Everyone chorused, "Amen!"

Joe Morgan hugged and kissed his wife and each of his children and grandchildren. He picked up the letter, which had rested by his plate on the table, and beckoned Ben to follow him.

Outside the temple, Porter found the white Ducati and searched it, finding nothing but a certificate of registration and an insurance card. The owner was a corporation based in the Cayman Islands. He tore both papers into small pieces, which he threw into the wind. The VIN on the motorcycle, Porter knew, would lead nowhere as well.

Driving slowly down the access road, he searched both sides for the black-and-yellow GS, staring deep into the vegetation. But the motorcycle was no longer here.

He stopped on the side and contacted the dispatcher on the radio. "Can you put me through to the guys watching Governor Morgan's house?"

She did as he asked.

"Inspector Porter here," he introduced himself. "Community Affairs. Who am I speaking with?"

"Trooper Baker. State police."

"You're doing security at the Republican candidate's house, right?"

"Yup. What's happening?"

"Probably nothing, but I'm just out of the Mormon temple. They had a small disturbance here. Since Morgan is a member of the LDS Church, I'm checking in, that's all."

"Fair enough," Trooper Baker said. "All quiet here, but I think the saints are ahead of you. We just let in a messenger from the Mormon temple."

"Probably a coincidence," Porter said. "Can you describe him?"

"Some guy on a motorcycle—a nice one, BMW, black and yellow."

"Interesting." Porter forced out a fake chuckle. "It's probably nothing, but I'll stop by to check."

"Do you want us to pull the guy out?"

"No need." He kneeled, drew his revolver from its ankle holster, and verified that it was loaded. "We don't want to overreact and embarrass ourselves or the candidate, do we?"

"No, sir."

"Right on." Porter drove off. "See you in a few."

Keera was paged to call reception. Hoping that Ben was back safely, she ran straight downstairs. But it wasn't Ben. Rather, it was Fran DeLacourt in her blue uniform and cap. She was chatting with the security guards.

"Hey," Keera said.

Fran turned to her. "Here you are. What's happening?"

"Same old, same old." Keera noticed her bag at Fran's feet. "You brought my stuff. Thanks."

"If Mohammed doesn't come to the mountain…"

"I'm sorry." Keera picked up the bag. "I figured I'd use the time Ben is away to do all my overnights for the month."

"So it's not about our poor hospitality?"

"Listen, I got to go back to work." Keera pointed up.

"You're right to be upset." Fran walked with her toward the stairs. "Lilly is totally pissed off with me, and she's right too. It wasn't my place to interfere—"

"You didn't interfere. You told me I should leave Ben. That's way worse than interfering."

"I'm sorry. Taking the girl's side is my weakness. I love him like a brother, but he's got to do the right thing, you know?"

"I sure do." Keera raised her left hand, turning it to show the ring finger.

Fran's eyes widened and she covered her mouth. "It's beautiful! Gorgeous!"

CHAPTER 61

The library was just as Zachariah had described it in his journal. The carpet was thick, the walls were covered with books, and the furniture invited hours of pleasant study, especially the sofa set in front of the fireplace, where steady flames glowed with the blue hue of natural gas over fake logs.

Ben walked across the room to the section of the wall dedicated to photographs of men in uniform. Some of the photos were of poor quality, but all the men displayed the Medal of Honor—two for each—except for the photo of a Marine Corps captain with dark eyes that gazed straight into the camera. There was only a single Medal of Honor on his chest because, as Zachariah had written in his diary, the second medal was awarded after the captain's fiery death.

Keeping his body turned away from Morgan, Ben slipped a hand into his pocket and pulled out the iPhone. First he opened the e-mail he had sent himself with the attached folder of Zachariah's trial and evidence, clicked *forward*, and addressed it to Ray and to Dreyfuss with the words: *Publish Immediately!* He didn't press *send*, though, but instead minimized the draft e-mail for later sending. Then he turned on the voice-recording application and dropped the iPhone back in his pocket.

Morgan came over with a silver tray. It held a thermos and two glasses. "How about some hot cider?"

"Thank you."

Morgan placed it on a side table and poured.

There was a knock on the door, and Katie came in with a bundle of papers. "Here are the fundraising numbers for last week. The conference call with the bundlers is about to start."

"Start without me," Morgan said. "I'll join in a few minutes."

She hesitated. "They'll expect you—"

"They need me as much as I need them." Morgan rested his arm on her shoulders, leading her to the door. "Thank you, Katie."

When the door closed, Ben asked, "I take it she's not *Sister* Katie."

"Not yet." Morgan smiled. "She's still a Gentile, but we're working on it."

"Satan fights to keep every soul from the True Gospel."

"Exactly. By the way, are you related to *the* Sampson Allard?"

"Not really." Ben sipped, savoring the warm sweetness of the cider. "This is very good."

"Sampson Allard was a great man. Carrying such a powerful name carries the weight of history. It's the embodiment of our divine mission."

"My mission is not so lofty."

"Oh?"

"My true mission is the truth."

Morgan watched him over the rim of his glass, expecting an explanation.

Ben said nothing.

Taking a long gulp, Morgan said, "Brother James knows the truth."

"Who?"

Holding up the envelope with the emblem of the president of the temple, Morgan raised his eyebrows.

"Brother James! Of course!" Ben finished his drink and put down the glass. "Shall we discuss the truth Brother James knows about?"

"I don't understand. Don't you have a message for me from Brother James?"

"I have a message. Yes." Ben gazed back at the familiar face, oddly close and real after years of seeing it only on TV screens—debating other candidates, extolling his own virtues in campaign commercials, attacking political opponents without losing the joyous expression he always wore. "What do you think the message is?"

"Excuse me?"

"No, really, what do you think Brother James wanted to convey to you via a messenger? What message would be so confidential that it must not be written down?"

"Could be a number of things."

"For example?"

"I don't like guessing."

"Risk it." Ben pointed at the soldiers' photos. "They took risks, didn't they?"

"Young man, I appreciate humor, but people are waiting for me. We're in the middle of a campaign to restore America's soul—"

"Please." Ben held up his hand. "No political slogans."

Morgan took a step back, clearly shocked by Ben's tone. "You're not a real saint, are you?"

"Far from." Removing the Ravens cap, he shook his head. "My name is Ben Teller. I'm a reporter."

"A reporter? Really?" Morgan's demeanor didn't change, his face remaining friendly. "Can't say I remember your name. Which media outlet do you write for?"

"Freelance. My stuff usually appears on *NewZonLine.com.*"

"I'd love to chat, but my schedule is very tight." Morgan headed for the door. "But if you contact my spokesmen with a list of questions, we'll definitely provide a comprehensive—"

"I'm investigating the death of Zachariah Hinckley."

Morgan paused, turned, and glanced at the heroes' portraits.

"I believe he was murdered."

"From what I've heard, the police investigation ruled it an accident. Reckless driving, I believe."

"That's a nice spin, no pun intended. But you know the truth, right?"

"Listen, Teller, you're on shaky ground here." Morgan waved the letter in his face. "Forging documents, impersonating, lying to police and the Secret Service—I mean, all I need to do is call in those guys and you'll be in deep trouble!"

"I wouldn't do it if I were you."

"Why not?"

Ben took out his iPhone and showed him the e-mail. "All I need to do is press my thumb on the *send* icon. Do you see this attachment? It contains the whole LDS Church's file about Zachariah Hinckley, all the evidence against him, the trial records, and so on."

Morgan shrugged. "So what?"

"Your people harassed him, punished him, isolated him, and drove him to the top of the hill at the Camp David Scenic Overlook—all of it to shut him up. The public will not be kind to you after that."

"My people? I don't have people like that. I don't send thugs to hurt my opponents. I'm a businessman, a politician, and a candidate for president of the United States! I'm not Don Corleone!"

"The public will draw its own conclusion from the evidence." Ben held up the iPhone. "The whole LDS file is ready to go."

"Have you read it?"

It was a direct question, and Ben knew that his hesitation had already given the answer. "Not yet."

"When you do, you'll see that any mention of my name in that whole record is only in the role of a family friend and a former lay bishop. I was trying to help poor Zachariah and advocate leniency for him."

"But the whole case is about his insistence that you tell the American people about your role in the posthumous conversions of their heroes." Ben pointed to the portraits.

Rather than concern, Morgan's face showed amusement. "You must be confused about the facts, Mr. Teller. This case was about how best to deal with Zachariah's erratic and unstable behavior. He was a very ill man."

"I don't believe you." Ben shook his iPhone. "You pressured him to drop the demand that you confess—"

"That's not what the trial record says."

"Did you change it? Did you replace the truth with lies?"

"The truth is in the ear of the beholder." Pacing to the other side of the library, Morgan pulled out a thick volume. The cover had a photo of Winston Churchill, and tabs had been placed in different pages. He opened one. "Aspiring to become a great leader, one must learn from history's icons. Here's what Churchill said: '*History shall treat me kindly, for I intend to write it.*' Do you understand?"

"It's called *lying* in the real world."

"Grow up, Teller." Morgan re-shelved the volume. "You're not ready to play in this league. Not yet, anyway. Shall we call it a night?"

Examining the ring up close, Fran shook her head in amazement. "Look at this beauty! It's an antique—the real thing!"

"You think?"

"Duh! Sixteen years in the police force teaches you something about valuable jewelry." Fran hugged her. "I'm so happy for you!"

"For both of us?"

"Of course." Fran looked around as if expecting to find Ben standing there. "When did he give it to you?"

A group of physicians walked toward them. Keera took her aside. "Earlier today. He was really sweet, completely took me by surprise, but also made me worried sick about what he's involved in."

"Why?"

Keera hesitated.

Fran looked her straight in the eyes. "You can trust me."

"Can I?"

"You're right. Earlier on, I wasn't receptive. My job is to prevent hate crimes, and Ben's story smelled of anti-Mormon prejudice, which I couldn't condone."

"That's unfair. Ben is the most tolerant person. You should know!"

"I do, and he is, which is why I decided to sniff around a bit." Fran glanced over her shoulder to make sure no one could hear them. "Inspector Porter's personnel file is almost empty. He has no record of service—it's all classified, even his training. I called the Colorado State Police, which is where he had supposedly served before being loaned to Maryland, but they had nothing about him either."

"How could that be?"

"It's possible that he'd been undercover, maybe inside an organized crime organization or a drug cartel. Occasionally these guys have to be given new identities to protect them."

"Like the witness protection program?"

"Basically. But it's unusual, and I'm concerned."

"About Ben?" Keera gripped her hand. "You must help him. But he wouldn't tell me where he was going, and he looked so strange—"

"Strange? In what way?"

"He was dressed in a white suit and a white tie under his riding suit. He was clean shaven, his hair was cut real short, and what's left was bleached—"

"Bleached? Like in blond?"

"Yes. The eyebrows also. He looked weird. Everything white. But he wouldn't answer my questions—"

"I think I know where he went." Fran pulled her by the arm. "Let's go to my car!"

Keera followed her, jogging to the glass doors.

In the cruiser, Fran used the radio to contact the dispatcher. "Fran DeLacourt here."

"Yes, Lieutenant."

"Have you received any calls from the Mormon temple?"

"Let me look." There was a sound of rapid keyboarding. "There's one report of an emergency door alarm being activated. That's all."

"When?"

"Seventy-three minutes ago."

"Was a unit dispatched to the scene?"

More keyboard rattling. "We had an officer in the area, an inspector from the Community Relations Unit. He stopped by to check it out."

Keera sucked air in, covering her mouth.

"Who?"

"Inspector Porter."

"Did he report back?"

After a moment, the dispatcher said, "Yes. Twenty-seven minutes ago. He reported that it was a false alarm. People left through the emergency door after an accident in one of the chapels."

"What kind of an accident?"

"Trip and fall. No foul play or anything."

"Fatal?"

"Yes."

Fran glanced at Keera, who grabbed the dashboard, her face a mask of fear.

"Lieutenant DeLacourt? Anything else?"

"Do you have any information about the accident?"

"Not really. Tripped over a statue. Irreparable damage to vital organs. No CPR was performed on her."

"*Her? A woman?*"

"Correct."

Fran exhaled in relief. "Thank you."

"No problem. Have a nice evening."

Fran was about to sign off, but something occurred to her. "Wait a second. Do you have any other record mentioning Porter after that?"

"I don't think so. Hold on. I'm searching. Yes, O. Porter, eleven minutes ago. But it's nothing, just a patch-through to another team."

"Which team?"

"Let me see." The dispatcher hit more keys. "He wanted to be patched through to…the…here it is. The guys at the Morgan residence."

"Shit!" Fran dropped the radio, turned on the engine, and flipped the siren switch. "Buckle your seat belt!"

Ben was momentarily shaken by the realization that Morgan had foreseen the possible exposure of the LDS files and had altered the record to reflect positively on his role. But this was a setback he should have expected, considering who he was confronting.

"Zachariah Hinckley's journal," Ben said, "describes the whole story, including how you told him to steal personal information from the Department of Veterans Affairs, how you insisted on being the one serving as proxy in baptizing the servicemen who had won more than one Medal of Honor."

"Wild imagination of a sick man." Morgan came over and grabbed Ben's arm, staring into his face. "Listen to me, young man! You're chasing a wild goose, and it isn't going to roost!"

"The journal—"

"What proof do you have that Zachariah Hinckley actually wrote that journal? Anyone could have posted electronic text to his computer or any other device. The liberal elites will do anything to stop me!"

"Can you explain why Zachariah's last word was *posthumous*, of all things?"

"How do you know?"

"I have a series of photos that show him—"

"Really? Is that so?" Morgan laughed. "Let me summarize your plan. You're going to come out in public, weeks before the elections, and make accusations against me based on lip reading of a dying man in still photographs?"

Ben nodded.

"And not just lip reading of a dying man, but of a man who's lying at the bottom of a ravine because he had raced his motorcycle, risked others' lives, lost control, and flew over the cliff. Did I get it right?"

"What about the floppy disk?"

"I don't know what you're talking about."

"The one with your handwritten note on it, instructing Zachariah to steal veterans' personal data from the US government's computers."

Morgan's smile faded. "Never happened. It's a lie."

"According to his diary, that was the point of contention—it was the only hard evidence he had in order to force you to come clean with the public about the heroes' baptisms. That's why his house and office were searched, his religious status taken away, and his life ruined. He hid the floppy disk, and I've followed the clues he left."

"Have you found it?"

"Not yet."

"Because it doesn't exist!"

"It does," Ben said. "The last clue was to come here, to your house."

"Well?" Morgan gestured around the library. "Do you see it here?"

"No."

"And you never will!" He went to the door. "This has gone on long enough. You must leave now, or I'll have you removed by the police."

The realization came to Ben suddenly—like a recurring memory of Morgan leaving this same library while Zachariah was standing here, holding the incriminating floppy disk. But in the journal, there was another presence in this room—an old copy of the *Book of Mormon*, which Morgan had pulled from the shelf to convince Zachariah of his religious duty to obey.

Ben scanned the shelves, recalling Zachariah's description of his last visit to this beautiful home library. The collectible books were kept behind glass doors on the first two rows of shelves. Looking up, he read the titles on the leather spines until he reached the one that fit the description:

Book of Mormon
First Edition
New York
1830

Ben opened the glass door, reached up, and pulled the volume out. It was heavy, the leather binding rough, the pages thick and brown with age.

"What are you doing?" Morgan rushed over. "Give me that!"

"The first edition of Prophet Joseph Smith's work." Ben flipped through the pages, stopping at the one where the silk string was left as a marker. There, in the margins, was the handwritten jotting

Zachariah had recorded in his journal, starting with '*I presume the doctrine of baptism for the dead has ere this reached your ears, and may have raised some inquiries in your minds...*'

"You have no right to touch this holy book!" Morgan pulled the *Book of Mormon* from Ben's hands, and something fell to the floor.

Ben picked up the square, thin cardboard case, identical to the others he had found before. He could feel by the thickness that this case actually contained a floppy disk. He turned it over.

Written by hand in neat, tidy handwriting, was this note:

Brother Zachariah,
God sympathizes with your righteous dilemma and good intentions.
However, your heart knows this: Lies + Disobedience = Sin.
The list must include ALL Medal of Honor recipients.
Joseph S. Morgan, IV.

"Touch down," Ben said. "Game's over."

There was a knock on the door, and Katie poked her head in. "We're ready for you, Governor. The bundlers from Vegas, L.A., and Salt Lake are on video feed—"

"He's busy right now," Ben said.

She seemed shocked. "Governor?"

"Not now," Morgan said. "Continue without me."

The door closed.

The first thing Porter saw in the glow of lights by Morgan's mansion was the black-and-yellow BMW motorcycle, propped on its kickstand behind the state police cruiser. He parked at the curb and stepped out.

The evening had brought temperatures down, and Porter buttoned up his police jacket while approaching the cruiser.

One of the troopers came out. "Are you Porter? Let's walk you in."

Going up the long driveway, Porter glanced around at the artfully lit landscaping. Near the house, a gate clicked open.

A Secret Service agent stepped out of the house. "What's cooking, fellows?"

"I'm Inspector Porter, Community Relations Unit." He handed over a business card.

The agent examined it. "You need face time with the candidate?"

"A moment, just as a courtesy. There was a minor disturbance at the Mormon temple earlier. I think he'd want to know the details before it hits the media."

"Sure. Let me watch your gun for you."

Porter unbuckled his service belt and handed it over. "I understand he's already meeting with someone."

"Yeah, a guy came with a note from the president of the temple."

Gesturing at the street, Porter said, "The news pests will arrive soon. You might want to prepare."

"Will do!" The agent beckoned. "You go right in. They're in the library. Straight down the hallway, first left, past the kitchen, end of corridor, on the right."

"Thanks."

The agent turned to the trooper. "Let's set up a perimeter."

Following the agent's directions, Porter passed by the kitchen, where maids were cleaning up. He went down the hallway and found the door to the library. Glancing up and down the empty hallway, he pressed his ear to the door and listened.

Morgan's eyes went from the old book in his hands to the floppy disk in Ben's hands, back and forth. "In the Lord's name, it never occurred to me. So that's where Brother Zachariah hid it...right here in my house! And we've spent all this time—"

"Looking for it? Abusing Zachariah?"

"He was...an ill man."

"It's the moment of truth, Governor."

Morgan reached up to replace the *Book of Mormon* on the shelf. He sat down in one of the armchairs by the fireplace and rested his chin on interwoven fingers. "Look now, this is totally out of context. Posthumous baptizing is a charitable deed, but the Gentiles have a hard time understanding it. You're an intelligent young man, yes?"

"Go on." Ben pocketed the floppy disk but held the iPhone forward to get a good audio recording as well as to communicate a clear threat that he would send off the information unless truth was spoken. "I'm listening."

"We believe that the souls of those who have not accepted the True Gospel during their mortal lives are in deathly abeyance, in suffering, in something akin to hell. Therefore, it's the greatest service we can provide them—an opportunity to accept the only True Church. My intentions were pure!"

"Pure intentions don't lead to stealing souls."

"There's no stealing! They have a choice—every soul can decide to reject the message of the True Gospel according to Joseph Smith and remain a Gentile!"

"If posthumous baptizing rituals are just offers to those souls, which they can refuse, how come you list them all—millions of Jewish Holocaust victims, world leaders, and countless others—as full members in the LDS Church's membership rolls?"

"Because none of them has ever refused!"

"How do you know? Have you heard back from anyone you've posthumously baptized into the Mormon Church?"

Morgan shook his head.

"Has your prophet, seer, and revelator in Salt Lake City heard back from Anne Frank? From Daniel Pearl? From Simon Wiesenthal? Or from President Eisenhower?"

"No, because no Gentile soul would refuse the offer to accept the True Gospel, embrace the True Church, win exaltation in the afterlife, and be admitted to the Celestial Kingdom of God!"

"You're certain of that?"

"I am! There's no doubt that every soul accepts the offer extended through proxy baptizing and posthumous temple endowments! No doubt!"

"Your certainty is born of a twisted logic," Ben said. "But I'm not here for a theology debate. Not interested."

"That's my point!" Morgan smiled with renewed confidence. "You're not interested in dead souls. Most people aren't interested in them either. It's a unique virtue of our Mormon faith.

Unfortunately, because of this misunderstanding and prejudice, voters will hold it against me. Is that fair?"

"It's democracy. Voters are entitled to know the truth about every candidate so they can make an informed choice. And in your case, they have the right to know that you instructed Zachariah Hinckley to copy personal data, which you then used to baptize secretly in proxy some of the bravest American heroes in our nation's history. Voters deserve an informed choice."

"Even if it's a bad choice for America? A choice that will ruin the last chance to save America from socialist annihilation? To save the very soul of this country from the secular, liberal, European-style collectivism?"

"And you happen to be the savior?"

"Yes!"

"The prince on the white horse?"

"Clever play of words," Morgan said. "Don't you care about the dangerous policies of the current administration? The huge deficits? The apologetic foreign policy? The sapping of entrepreneurial spirit? The food stamps?"

Ben shrugged. "Not really."

"That's the problem with your generation! You're spoiled and you don't care about anything! This election is about the soul of America!"

"Spare me the demagoguery. You're not running for America's soul. You're running for personal gratification."

"Wrong! You think I need a bigger house?" He waved around him. "Or more money? No! I'm running for president on a mission—to save us from the ruinous decline engineered by the liberal elites! America is on the same downward path as ancient Greece and the Roman Empire! Our nation is inflicted with the same cancerous menace that brought down Spain and England, which turned their backs to the values that had made them great! Don't you see that there's much more at stake here than the religious affiliation of a few dead heroes?"

"Your actions are the issue here."

"Why? All I wanted to do was a righteous favor for the dead!"

"Violating their memory by posthumous conversion?"

"You're contradicting yourself." Morgan shook a finger. "What do you care about some dead soldiers? Or the Jews from the Holocaust? They're dead already!"

Ben went to the wall and removed the photo of the Marine captain. He took it to Morgan and placed it on the coffee table before him. "Do you remember this man?"

Morgan shrugged. "It's been many years."

"He was the last one, the only name that Zachariah Hinckley kept out of the list. This hero was the reason you sent the floppy disk back to Zachariah with the incriminating note." Ben patted his pocket with the thin cardboard case. "Rings a bell."

"So what?"

"This Marine captain received his second Medal of Honor posthumously for driving a burning fuel truck away from a group of American boys—including Zachariah." Ben pushed the framed photograph closer to Morgan. "Do you remember his name?"

"How can I remember a name after so long?" Morgan hit the armrest with his hand. "What's this got to do with anything?"

Ben pulled out his wallet and took out a small photo, creased and chafed from years of rubbing against bills and credit cards, yet still clear enough to show the serious face and dark eyes under the Marine Corps cap. He placed it on the coffee table next to the framed portrait from the wall.

"What is this?" Morgan looked closely. "It's the same person. Who is he?"

"Captain Abba Teller. My father."

Morgan sat back and exhaled.

"Do you remember him now?"

"So...you're not here about...Zachariah."

"No."

"This obsession...has been about your father."

"He was a proud Jewish Marine who died courageously for his country while saving the lives of Zachariah Hinckley and his fellow Marines. You stole my father's soul and defiled his memory."

"But...it was...so long ago."

"It's not long ago that Zachariah Hinckley died at the Camp David Scenic Overlook, destroying the same life that my father had died to save. An irony, isn't it?"

"Oh, no!" Keera pointed at the rolling lights. "Is this Morgan's house? Something bad happened! We're too late!"

Fran hit the brakes, making the tires screech. "Stay in the car!"

Keera ignored the order, jumped out, and followed Fran.

Two state troopers were busy setting up red flares and traffic cones in a wide circle around the entrance to Morgan's driveway. A man in khakis and a blue jacket was directing a dark SUV that was reversing away from the mansion until it blocked the driveway, its hazard lights flashing.

Fran approached the civilian. "What's going on?"

"That was quick," he said, signaling the driver to stop. "You guys are on the ball today—for a change. Why don't you take that side." He pointed to the left. "Make sure they park their vehicles without blocking any—"

"They?" Fran looked around. "Who's *they?*"

"The media."

"Hold on!" She raised her hand. "Did you let in another trooper—Inspector Porter?"

"Yeah. Community Relations or something like that."

"Shit!" She broke into a run, passing by the SUV.

Keera followed her.

Another civilian came out of the driver's side of the SUV and grabbed Keera's arm. "Secret Service! Stop!"

"My boyfriend's in there!" She pointed. "That Porter guy's going to kill him!"

"Keep her here," the Secret Service agent ordered one of the troopers and ran after Fran. His partner followed, and they caught up with her at a steel gate in front of the main entrance to the mansion.

"Please," Morgan said, "you must understand my position. My faith. Your father was a courageous man. Honorable. Baptism was a way to elevate him. I meant to show him respect by serving as a proxy—"

"Save it for the cameras." Ben pocketed his wallet. "My job here is not to argue about religion. I don't believe your bathtub submersion had any effect on my father's soul, or anyone else's soul, for that matter."

"Then what else do you want?"

"You must confess. That's what Zachariah wanted."

"And destroy my campaign? Lose everything I've worked so hard to achieve?"

"It will be a sacrifice worthy of my father's memory and that of his fellow Medal of Honor recipients. It's an opportunity for you to show similar courage by telling the American people what you've done to our heroes. You owe it to Zachariah, considering what you did to him."

"I did nothing!"

"White House residency isn't intended for murderers."

"How dare you?" Morgan stood up. "Brother Zachariah was a sick man who committed suicide—the worst sin! I spent an hour yesterday on the phone advocating for him with our General Authorities in Utah to convince them that his mental illness justifies forgiveness. They restored his status as a saint! His widow couldn't stop thanking me for taking time from my campaign to do this for her and the children's celestial future, which is sealed to his."

"How charitable of you, but Zachariah didn't commit suicide. He was pushed off the road by the same killer who later came for me. She's one of the Danites—I had to kill her today at the Mormon temple."

"My dear God!" Morgan stumbled and held on to the back of the chair. "I had no idea this was going on!"

"Aren't you a bigwig in the Mormon Church? Surely the Danites don't engage in blood atonement without explicit orders." Ben gestured at the envelope he'd brought with him. "Brother James must be part of the chain of command, no?"

"There are no Danites." Morgan dropped in the armchair, deflated. "It's an urban legend. They've been gone for decades."

"She fits the bill."

"No, no, no. Mormon women are wives, homemakers, not killers."

"This one's a Danite killer all right."

"It's a hoax. A diversion."

Ben touched the bruise on his forehead. "She was real and deadly, came after me again and again."

"What did you expect?" Morgan pointed to the elections button on the lapel of his jacket. "It's my face on the front, but behind me stand very powerful people who have bet billions of dollars on my victory—oilmen, defense contractors, casino moguls—they have fortunes at stake in the elections, huge interests in government contracts, infrastructure projects, energy production. They're betting on enormous profits, all riding on my election as president of the United States, all dependant on me taking over the administration and appointing thousands of sympathetic officials to countless powerful positions in the federal government. They're counting on me as the next commander in chief, protecting their global interests. Do you think such men would sit back and let a patsy like Zachariah Hinckley derail my candidacy and ruin their plans over some...*posthumous baptisms?*"

"Who are they?"

Morgan balked. "I can't tell you!"

Ben held his thumb over the iPhone screen. "I'll send off this e-mail!" He pulled the floppy disk from his pocket and showed Morgan his own handwritten note to Zachariah. "This note all by itself will destroy your election prospects! I'll blow the story right now, unless you tell me the whole truth!"

"I'm telling you the truth!"

"Names! Give me names! Or I'll press the—"

Porter drew his revolver from its ankle holster, threw the door open, and surveyed the room. Against a backdrop of wall-to-wall books, Ben Teller stood with his iPhone in one hand and the floppy disk in the other. Governor Morgan was sitting in an armchair by the fireplace, looking ashen.

"Drop the phone!" Porter aimed the gun at Ben. "And the disk!"

"Stop!" Governor Morgan leaped off the armchair. "Don't shoot!"

Ben glanced at the iPhone, his thumb hovering over the screen, seeking the right spot to hit *send*.

Behind him, Porter heard sudden commotion. One of the Secret Service agents yelled something, and then, of all things, Fran DeLacourt's voice, "Porter! It's over!"

There was no time left. Porter grabbed his revolver with two hands, bent his forward knee slightly, and slid his finger into the trigger slot. He shot at the reporter's iPhone, hitting it, and shifted his aim to the face, right between those irritating dark eyes—

"No!" Governor Morgan jumped sideways and collided with Ben just as Porter's finger pulled back the trigger. A shot sounded, Governor Morgan yelled, and his body twisted, turned like a screw, and fell over, taking Ben down too.

Porter followed, trying to get a fix on the reporter, when he heard two pops behind him and felt his own body rise in the air, propelled forward, out of the light and into darkness.

Lying in a heap on the floor with Governor Morgan, Ben's ears rang from all the shooting. The room smelled of gunpowder. Urgent voices yelled incoherent orders.

Morgan rose on an elbow, his face pale, but strangely humorous. He said something.

"What?" Ben's own voice sounded as if he spoke through a tunnel.

"Are...you...okay?"

Ben nodded. "I think so. You?"

"Never better." Morgan cringed as the two Secret Service agents turned him on his back. "Careful, boys!"

"Left arm," one of them said, tearing off Morgan's sleeve. "Small caliber. Shallow flesh wound. Get me the first aid kit."

The other agent ran from the room.

"It's nothing." Morgan sat up and held on to the agent. "Help me stand."

Fran turned Porter's body over and felt the crook of his neck. "He's a goner," she said. Lifting one of his hands, she examined his fingertips. "Prints were burned off. Who the hell is this guy?"

"Another Ghost," Ben said. "It's an infestation."

"And you're the bait." She grabbed his arm to help him stand. "What are you doing here?"

"Saving your ass." She checked him all over. "No bullet holes?"

"I'm wearing holy underwear." Ben held up his hand, turning it, finding no injury. Porter was a good shot, but Morgan's leap had thrown his second shot off target. Searching the floor, Ben found pieces of his iPhone. It was completely ruined.

"Looking for this?" Morgan held up the floppy disk in its cardboard case.

Ben's initial urge was to step forward and snatch it, but somehow the Secret Service agent sensed his intentions and gave him a hard look.

Morgan tossed the floppy disk into the fireplace, where it shriveled and melted before igniting in a small puff of smoke. "Win some, lose some."

"I'm not conceding," Ben said.

"I just saved your life. Doesn't it count for anything?"

"Why did you?"

"Had to." Morgan gestured at the photos on the wall, the decorated servicemen looking back solemnly. "Peer pressure."

Ben nodded.

"Captain Teller is very proud of you today, son."

"You think?" Ben glanced at the ceiling. "Can they see us from the Celestial Kingdom?"

"I believe they can," Morgan said. "One day we'll both find out. But while we're still in this world, what would it take—"

"I've already told you. A confession. You owe it to Zachariah Hinckley."

Katie ran into the library. "What happened here?" Her eyes landed on Morgan's bloody arm. "Oh my God!"

"I'm fine," he said. "Do me a favor. Show this young man a copy of our draft press release about the posthumous baptisms. If it's okay with him, send it out to our media list."

The request seemed to shock her even more than the sight of the injury. "Governor, the damage from such—"

"Do it!" Morgan pointed at the door. "Now!"

Ben followed her to an office off the foyer. She sat at a computer, did a quick search, and printed a one-page document on the campaign's letterhead, which she handed to him.

> *To: Media List*
> *For: Immediate Release*
> *In response to questions raised by veterans' families, GOP presidential candidate Joe Morgan confirmed today that, as part of his lifelong commitment to his faith, he has in the past served as proxy in posthumous baptisms. Governor Morgan further stated: "The practice of offering salvation to those who passed on has always been part of the charitable spirit of our Christian faith, inspired by the writings of Joseph Smith. As with every faithful member of any religion, one cannot pick and choose which tenet to obey and which to skip. Back in the nineties, when I served as lay leader of our Silver Spring Ward, we asked one of our members to assemble a list of names that included winners of the Medal of Honor. I personally served as proxy during the baptism ceremonies—an honor I still cherish. But even though my intentions were charitable, I now realize that, for some, the practice could be offensive. For that, and for any pain caused to relatives of the fallen heroes, my sincere apologies and heartfelt sympathies. We, as a nation, will only achieve a full restoration of our great American future by honoring those who made the ultimate sacrifice for our freedom." Candidate Morgan directed all further inquiries to the spokesman for the Church of Jesus Christ of Latter-day Saints in Salt Lake City, Utah.*

"Clever drafting," Ben said.

"Thank you. I'll send it out now." With rapid keystrokes she copied and pasted the press release onto an e-mail, addressed it to *Media List*, and hit *send*. "It's going to cost us a lot of votes."

"How come you had this press release drafted and ready to go?"

"We have many of them." She gestured at her computer. "We're prepared for every possible contingency. It's standard practice in political campaigns. Every candidate has skeletons in his or her closet. The trick is to respond instantly in the event a clever journalist such as yourself manages to dig up something."

"You want to control the narrative."

"Of course." She took the page from him. "We must set the tone, especially when damaging information comes out. We can minimize the negative reaction by dominating the news, presenting the candidate's version, gain voters' sympathy right away by emphasizing the—"

"Faith-promoting truth?"

"Excuse me?"

"You'll learn," Ben said, "when you become Sister Katie."

He found Fran waiting in the foyer. Down the hallway, family members and a few staffers congregated around Morgan, who reassured everyone that he was fine. Their eyes met, and Ben nodded. The candidate smiled and winked.

"Let's go." Fran held the door. "I need a beer."

As they passed through the gate, Keera ran up the driveway and fell into his arms with tears and kisses.

They held each other, pacing slowly down to the street while Fran went to get the car. Ben removed his camera backpack from the locked case on his motorcycle and asked one of the state troopers to keep an eye on the GS until the next morning.

At the edge of the lawn was a long line of campaign signs. Ben pulled one out.

Save America's Soul!
Morgan for President!

"I might as well keep this," Ben said, "considering I could have ruined it for him tonight. Still could, actually. Or maybe not."

"You don't make any sense," Keera said.

"Nothing makes sense anymore. The only physical evidence I had against him has just gone up in smoke."

"Is it over? Tell me it's over!"

"Almost. Can I borrow your iPhone?" Ben took it, got on the Internet, and signed into his g-mail account. Finding the e-mail he had sent to himself with the attached file of Zachariah Hinckley's trial and evidence, he forwarded it to Rex. "It's up to them now. I'm done."

"Good." Keera put her arm around his waist. "And I'm done being single. Got me a fiancé! I love saying it! *Fiancé. Fiancé. Fiancé.* God, isn't it a beautiful word?"

"Yes, my dear fiancée."

She laughed and rested her head on his shoulder.

"Ouch!"

"What's wrong?" She touched the back of his shoulder, feeling the bandage under his shirt. "You're injured!"

"Not exactly." Ben let Keera into Fran's back seat and got in next to her. "You know that football tattoo you loved so much..."

The End

ACKNOWLEDGEMENTS

As with my other novels, the historic details underlying the story required extensive research and verification. In achieving this level of authenticity, I have benefited invaluably from the works of many scholars and biographers.

Special mention is due to Richard Ostling and Joan Ostling, authors of *Mormon America – The Power and the Promise,* Richard Abanes, author of *One Nation Under Gods: A History of the Mormon Church,* Deborah Laake, author of *Secret Ceremonies,* Latayne Scott, author of *The Mormon Mirage,* Martha Beck, author of *Leaving the Saints,* Michael D. Quinn, author of *The Mormon Hierarchy— Extensions of Power,* and Jon Krakauer, author of *Under the Banner of Heaven.* (A comprehensive list of primary bibliographical sources appears next.)

From a genealogy point of interest, the LDS database at www. FamilySearch.org is a fascinating destination. It has amassed upward of 2.5 billion names through a global effort aimed at obtaining copies of every available source of population records. Unfortunately, the database currently allows only members of the Mormon Church to search individual names for information on posthumous baptisms.

I am grateful to editor Renee Johnson and the team at CreateSpace, as well as to my friends and family members, whose thoughtful input, critical comments, and enthusiastic encouragement have sustained me along the way and made this novel possible. Thank you!

Last but not least, to my readers, whose enjoyment is the purpose of my work. As always, your comments and thoughts are greatly appreciated. An e-mail contact is provided through the website at: www.AzrieliBooks.com

BIBLIOGRAPHY

Books:

Skousen, Royal, Ed. *The Book of Mormon – The Earliest Text.* New Haven and London: Yale University Press, 2009.
Ostling, Richard N. and Ostling, Joan K. *Mormon America – The Power and the Promise.* New York: HarperCollins - HarperOne, 2007.
Abanes, Richard. *One Nation Under Gods: A History of the Mormon Church.* New York: Four Walls Eight Windows, 2003.
Brodie, Fawn. *No Man Knows My History – The Life of Joseph Smith.* New York: Alfred Knopf, 1945 and First Vintage Books, 1995.
Bushman, Richard Lyman. *Joseph Smith: Rough Stone Rolling.* New York: Knopf, 2005.
Krakauer, Jon. *Under the Banner of Heaven.* New York: Doubleday, 2003.
Quinn, Michael D. *The Mormon Hierarchy—Extensions of Power.* Salt Lake City: Signature Books, 1997.
Anderson, Devery S., Ed. *The Development of LDS Temple Worship 1946-2000 – A Documentary History.* Salt Lake City: Signature Books, 2011.
Laake, Deborah. *Secret Ceremonies – A Mormon Woman's Intimate Diary of Marriage and Beyond.* New York: William Morrow and Company, 1993.
Scott, Latayne C. *The Mormon Mirage.* Grand Rapids: Zondervan, 2009.
Decker, Ed and Hunt, Dave. *The God Makers.* Eugene: Harvest House, 1997.

Beck, Martha. *Leaving the Saints: How I Lost the Mormons and Found My Faith.* New York: Crown, 2005.

Ahmanson, John and Archer, Gleason L., Tran. *Secrete History – An Eyewitness Account of the Rise of Mormonism.* Chicago: Moody Press – The Fieldstead Institute, 1984. (Originally published in Denmark in 1876 under the title *Vor Tids Muhamed* – "The Muhammad of Our Time.")

Articles and Essays:

Pyle, Richard. "Mormons, Jews Sign Agreement on Baptizing Holocaust Victims." *Associated Press Newswire,* May 5, 1995.

Eden, Ami. "Sister Golda, Brother Bashevis: Mormon Baptizers at it Again." *The Jewish Forward,* July 27, 2001.

McEntee, Peg. "LDS Church Reaffirms No Proxy Baptisms of Jews." *The Salt Lake Tribune,* December 11, 2002.

Walsh, Paton Nick. "Russians fume as Mormons buy souls." *The Guardian,* November 22, 2003.

Urbina, Ian. "Again, Jews Fault Mormons Over Posthumous Baptisms." *The New York Times,* December 21, 2003.

Makotoff, Gary. "Posthumous Baptism is a Terrible Insult to Jews." *Deseret Morning News,* January 11, 2004.

Thiessen, Mark. "Sen. Clinton Joins Effort to End Mormon Baptisms of Holocaust Victims." *The Associated Press,* April 20, 2004.

Radkey, Helen. "Proxy Baptism of Jews: The Splash Goes On." *Avotaynu – The Int'l Rev. of Jewish Genealogy,* February 7, 2006.

Young, Neil J. "Southern Baptists vs. the Mormons." *Slate,* December 19, 2007.

Heneghan, Tom. "Catholic-Mormon Tension over LDS Baptism of the Dead." *Reuters Blogs,* May 8, 2008.

Marshall, Kelly. "Mormons and Jews Reach [another] Agreement on Posthumous Proxy Baptism." *CNN,* September 2, 2010.

Burt, Brandon. "Rabble-Rouser Helen Radkey Keeping Tabs on Proxy LDS Baptisms." *Salt Lake City Weekly,* September 20, 2011.

Dreher, Rod. "Are Mormons Stealing Grandpa's Soul?" *The American Conservative,* October 19, 2011.

Slosson, Mary. "Mormon Church Apologizes for Posthumous Baptism." *Reuters*, February 14, 2012.

Editorial. "Mormon Posthumous Baptism, Again." *The Jewish Week*, February 14, 2012.

Sheffield, Carry. "A Mormon Church in Need of Reform." *The Washington Post*, January 29, 2012.

Keneally, Meghan. "Mormon Church shuts down whistle-blower's access to list of people posthumously baptized...but says it is to 'protect' Jews and Catholics not hid the names." *The Daily Mail (UK)*, March 8, 2012.

Kaylor, Brian. "Prominent African-American Southern Baptist Condemns Mormonism as Racist." *Ethics Daily*, June 15, 2012.

Mason, Prof. David V. "I'm a Mormon, Not a Christian." *The New York Times*, June 12, 2012.

Visual:

Whitney, Helen, Dir. *The Mormons*. New York: PBS – American Experience, 2007.

Roos, Bram. *The Mormon Rebellion*. New York: A&E – History Channel, 1997.

ALSO BY AVRAHAM AZRIELI

Fiction:

The Masada Complex – A Novel
The Jerusalem Inception – A Novel
The Jerusalem Assassin – A Novel
Christmas for Joshua – A Novel

Non-Fiction:

Your Lawyer on a Short Leash
One Step Ahead – A Mother of Seven Escaping Hitler

AUTHOR'S WEBSITE:

www.AzrieliBooks.com

Made in the USA
San Bernardino, CA
12 May 2018